# Praise for Dominic Smith and his unforgettable novels. . . .

*THE BEAUTIFUL MIS...*

"Fantastic . . . an utterly fresh loo... ...ow a child can grow beyond parental expectations and find the genius of being himself."

—*People*, 4 stars

"This unusual, gorgeously written novel is filled with pleasures . . . Best of all, though, is the book's invitation to wonder—about the imponderables of life and death, the nature of intelligence, and the ultimately inexplicable relationships of fathers and sons."

—*Booklist* (starred review)

"[Smith] conjures Nathan's colorful, mysterious new existence with vivid detail. The real story in this touching, gracefully wrought novel lies around the edges of the plot. It is really about the weight of family dreams and expectations . . ."

—*The Boston Globe*

"Wry and affecting."

—*Texas Monthly*

"A finely modulated second novel . . . the unerringly true dialogue is a delight . . . a luminous addition to novels about fathers and sons."

—*Kirkus Reviews*

**This title is also available as an eBook.**

"With an ear for language and a gift for lyrical prose, Smith has written a novel that investigates love and loss, success and failure, the nature of genius, and particle physics. It is ambitious."

—*Austin Chronicle*

"A thoughtful story that explores the nature of intelligence, the intangibles of life and death, and the connection between a father and a son."

—*Buffalo News*

"With an exquisite ear not just for language but for emotional truth as well, Dominic Smith has written an ambitious and strikingly unusual tale about what it's like to grow up in the shadow of a brilliant father."

—Julia Glass,
author of *Three Junes* and
*The Whole World Over*

"One of the most original coming-of-age stories I've read in a long time. It's about gawkiness, particle physics, bereavement, and memory, but it's also a dazzling inquiry into a universe that is at once breathtakingly elegant and irrevocably mundane."

—Anthony Doerr,
author of *The Shell Collector* and
*About Grace*

## THE MERCURY VISIONS OF LOUIS DAGUERRE

"Highly entertaining . . . fascinating . . . [Smith] has a talent for descriptive imagery."

—*The New York Times*

# the beautiful
# miscellaneous

## a novel

# Dominic Smith

WASHINGTON SQUARE PRESS

New York   London   Toronto   Sydney

Washington Square Press
A Division of Simon & Schuster, Inc.
1230 Avenue of the Americas
New York, NY 10020

First Washington Square Press trade paperback edition June 2008

WASHINGTON SQUARE PRESS and colophon are registered trade-
marks of Simon & Schuster, Inc.

For information about special discounts for bulk purchases,
please contact Simon & Schuster Special Sales at 1-800-456-6798
or business@simonandschuster.com.

Manufactured in the United States of America

10  9  8  7  6  5  4  3  2  1

ISBN-13: 978-0-7432-7123-3
ISBN-10:      0-7432-7123-8
ISBN-13: 978-0-7432-7125-7 (pbk)
ISBN-10:      0-7432-7125-4 (pbk)

FOR EMILY

# one

As far as near-death experiences go, mine was a disappointment. No bright whirring tunnel or silver-blue mist, just a wave of white noise, a low-set squall coming from an unknown source. I was gone for ninety seconds and spent the next two weeks in a coma. I sometimes imagine the moment when my miniature death ended and the coma began. I picture it like emerging from a bath in absolute darkness.

I woke in a hospital room during the last week of July 1987. I was seventeen and it was the middle of the night. A series of machines stood around my bed, emitting a pale, luminous green. I stared at a heart monitor, mesmerized by the scintilla of my pulse moving across the screen. Tiny drops of clear liquid hovered, then fell inside an IV bag. Voices— muffled and indistinguishable—carried in from a corridor. I felt unable to call out. I lay there quietly, looking up at the ceiling, and waited for someone to confirm that I was back among the living.

# two

My parents wanted a genius. My father had achieved a measure of fame in particle physics for his experiments with the quark, and my mother came from an old New England family of clergy and museum curators, men prone to loftiness. Together they waited out my early, unexceptional years, hoping for an epiphany.

When I was nine years old, in the winter of 1979, my father and I drove to Manitoba to watch a solar eclipse. He was hoping this would mark a whole new era for me. On the nighttime drive up from Wisconsin, we passed farms banked in snow and entire prairies of ice. My father talked about the great eclipses of the past, of the one in 1970 when he saw the yellow tail of a comet revealed as the Mid-Atlantic states were shot with half-light. His face was cast with the soft light of the dash and his tangled beard—a cross between a northern woodcutter's and a German philosopher's—appeared to be glowing. He talked in bursts and then fell quiet for fifteen-minute stretches. Each time, it felt like we were passing out of the ice flats and into enormous valleys of silence.

As we crossed into Canada from North Dakota, my father listed the benefits of a summer eclipse. "Birds stop singing and go to roost. Flower blossoms close. Honeybees stop flying." He'd been drinking coffee straight from the thermos and his breath smelled bitter. The word *honey* smelled the worst, and I pretended to look out my window to get away from it. "Nature thinks it's naptime, Nathan. What you might call an astral power nap," he said. In the dimness of the front seat, his small, neat teeth appeared from behind his beard and formed a tight smile. I thought he was going to laugh but then he deadpanned, "Duration will be two minutes and forty-nine seconds."

"That's not very long," I said.

He took his pale, thin hand from the stainless steel thermos and gestured through the dark interior with a flattened palm. "In physics *that's* an eternity." He positioned his hands on the steering wheel at exactly ten and three o'clock but continued to stare at me, waiting, I think, for me to agree that three minutes is really a massive spool of time. I started to nod, but he was already tapping the wheel in a caffeinated sort of way. He switched on the radio and found a hiss of static. "The truth is, Nathan, time is fluid. Do you hear that static?"

"Yeah."

"Ten percent of it is due to residual microwaves from the Big Bang. It's all still happening from that one singularity." Now he shook his head, a little incredulous. That my father didn't know how to speak to children was widely known in our Wisconsin hometown. I once found him on our front lawn, deep into a rant with the paperboy about parabolic motion.

Although my father was an atheist, this trip was a pilgrimage for him. We were driving through the night to see something that would last less than a Top 40 song. But I was also undergoing a test. My father believed that greatness began with a purifying moment—an awakening. He told me that Einstein, as a convalescing boy, was given a compass and this forever changed his view of the world. It made him want to know the hidden mechanics of the universe. My father had been searching for good omens and epiphanies for a while now—a cosmic champagne bottle to smash over the prow of my youth.

At eight o'clock in the morning, we parked the Oldsmobile on a plowed blacktop and waited for the spectacle. We waited for the moon to drift toward the rising sun. Vast snowfields, scattered with box elders and limestone boulders, extended before us. There were pockets of bluish shadow spread across the snow. A few brain-shaped clouds plodded north toward the arctic, but otherwise the day was clear. We stayed inside the car with the engine running, trying to keep warm. The heater breathed noisily through the dash, filling the air with a mechanical stutter.

My father pulled back his shirtsleeve and looked at his watch. I could see his spindly wrist and the bald patch he'd scratched on his arm. "Almost showtime," he said. What he meant by that was an hour of sitting in the cold car waiting for the moon to inch-crawl in front of the sun. We hadn't eaten since Minnesota, and I would have, in those sixty minutes, traded a total solar eclipse for as little as three Fig Newtons. Finally, the darkened outline of the moon arced into the solar halo and a small bite appeared at the western edge of the sun. My father retrieved our safety glasses from the glove compartment and we put them on. The light began to change—the deep blue shadows on the snowfields blurred and lightened; narrow bands of light shifted through the bare maple crowns. Everything dappled.

"The shifting light is caused by the sun shining across jagged lunar valleys," my father said.

"I wish we hadn't forgotten the hot chocolate," I said.

He reached for his door.

I said, "Can I stay in here and watch things? Because I think I can see better if the wind isn't in my eyes."

He looked at me, O-mouthed and appalled. With his oversize safety glasses he was a parody of a blind man. "*Watch things?* This isn't fireworks in somebody's backyard. This is celestial. This is very big. A big, celestial moment. Now exit the vehicle."

He turned and opened his car door, stepped out onto the road, and began wandering in the direction of the eclipse. I followed his tall, gangly figure and we began hauling across the fields, snow skirting his knees and my thighs. The air was damp and cut with pine sap. "It looks like incinerating glass," my father said as he slowed, his head craned upward. I had no idea what incinerating glass might look like, but I imagined it was very bright. Through the safety glasses everything seemed a little flat and brown. We stood perfectly still. A tiny sliver of light remained, a sunburst cresting from behind the dark disk of the moon. We watched it blink, then disappear. Darkness flooded everything. A row of pine trees became an inky, amorphous silhouette. I could hear the deep, slow metronome of my father's breathing. He had the stilled countenance of a man in prayer.

When the moon fully blocked the sun, the darkness seemed something between dusk and night. My hands were jammed into my pockets and my breath smoked in front of me. Some of the brighter stars had appeared and the great slow clouds had darkened. In that cindery pall, the facade of the moon cold and white, I could believe we were watching the end of the world.

After the eclipse, a ribbon of sunlight streamed into view, the sun's corona dimmed, and northern daylight blasted in all directions, as if someone had lifted a veil. My father took off his glasses and squinted his tea-brown eyes against the sudden brightness.

"That was it, Nathan," he said.

"What?" I whispered.

"Your epiphany and suchlike."

A long silence.

Finally, I figured things were completed out on the snowfield, so I turned for the car.

"It's a brand-new day," he said. "We'll drive into town and get some breakfast to celebrate."

"We didn't have dinner last night," I said. There was a hint of anger in my voice, and it was somehow amplified by the rising wind.

My father clapped me around the shoulders and attempted a sympathetic laugh. But then he looked off into the white distance and said slowly, "That was the world's shortest day. So, it's breakfast at dawn. Buttermilk pancakes for our young Copernicus."

He tromped toward the road and I followed. We got in the car and I cranked the heater. I was shivering and I tried to exaggerate it by chattering my teeth. It was a statement of protest: a call for food and shelter. Of course, my father didn't notice. We drove through a series of towns where they sold venison jerky and pork chops but no pancakes. Finally, we gave up and I bought a box of stale Ritz crackers from a general store and we drove on. The Oldsmobile Omega passed through the snowy backcountry, now cloaked in dusk, and my father rambled about the special properties of light, about how there is no such thing as emptiness, about how charged particles can manifest out of the voids of space. The idea of matter appearing in a vacuum seemed to hold certainty for him that we would someday find my gift.

We passed log cabins set back from the road, hunting shacks nestled in the woods; occasionally I'd see the buttery light from a window and wonder about these people's lives, about what they did up here in the dead of winter and what they might be speaking about during my father's scientific monologue. I tried to follow what he was saying but I found myself staring into the woods, looking for lighted windows and other signs of normal life.

# three

We were a single-child family living in a Victorian house in Wisconsin. It was my mother's childhood home, inherited from the dead aunt who raised her after my grandparents were killed in a train wreck in New Hampshire. Although my mother often indulged in nontraditional food and clothing—Indian curries, batik shawls, lapis lazuli earrings—she was, deep down, a New England girl and had filled the rooms with family heirlooms. Nantucket baskets, braided rugs, Amish quilts, Shaker sideboards. She believed in the beauty and simplicity of objects. In the summertime, she carefully arranged bowls of damson plums and Michigan peaches and was slightly crestfallen when my father or I removed a piece of fruit to eat it. In the bedroom she shared with my father, her side was lined with antique china dolls and old music boxes, keepsakes from the ten years with her parents. By contrast, my father's side of the bedroom held piles of yellow legal pads, home-brewing manuals, books on competitive chess, and aging copies of *Scientific American*. He was known to wake in the middle of the night, take a notepad into the bathroom, switch on the light, and rush something onto an empty page. My mother would find sheets of paper on the bathroom floor the next morning, scratchy vector diagrams and Greek-lettered equations.

Each day, when my father went to work at the college where he taught physics and I went to the Jesuit school for boys, my mother had the place to herself. After swimming laps at the YWCA pool each morning, she returned home and did housework for several hours while listening to NPR. She was a news junkie, keeping up with Australian elections and African civil wars. Sometimes she talked back to the radio—"You've got your head in the sand!" and "Leave it to the politicians!"—while mopping the hardwood floors or kneading bread in the kitchen. Occasionally she had friends over for lunch, and most afternoons she spent an hour reading English novels before trying a dinner recipe from a foreign cookbook and serving my father and me a strange but usually delicious meal at six thirty sharp. We arrived home to Ethiopian stews and Peruvian soups. After dinner, my father slinked off to his study—the one room my mother was not allowed to clean—and drank one of his home brews while listening to jazz albums and working on obscure physics problems. For several hours the banter of news radio was quelled and the house filled with the shuffling bass of Charles Mingus, the brassy drawl of Duke Ellington, the syncopated cool of Dave Brubeck, the riffing out-of-timeness of Thelonious Monk. I think that for my father jazz offered a kind of deliverance from ordinary time, the way it bent and warped individual notes and intervals; it was a craft that could be as esoteric and rigorous as quantum theory.

My mother and I heard his records from the kitchen, where I did my homework and she washed the dishes. We could tell how my father's night was going by what he played. If things sounded jumpy and off-kilter—Dizzy Gillespie's "A Night in Tunisia"—then he was getting frustrated. But if Ellington's *Uptown* album played, we knew he was forging ahead: "Take the 'A' Train" would bound down the hallway—"Listen to these rails a-humming"—making my mother sway and shimmy at the sink. One night, her hands submerged in dishwater, she said to me, "Your father has taught me to like jazz and I've taught him to put a napkin on his lap when he eats. Does that sound like a fair trade?" I looked up from my homework and said, "When you're not around he eats sardines straight from the can." My mother flicked some soapsuds at me and continued to move with the music. Perhaps she thought I was kidding.

After I went to bed my parents sat in the room my mother insisted on calling the parlor. It was really a normal, middle-class living room, except we did not own a television—a source of early estrangement for me at school. From the top of the stairs I would sometimes secretly peer down at them. As an only child I was always looking for signs of my parents' private world, waiting for the uncensored words they might say to each other after a glass of wine or a bottle of homemade porter. The two of them reclined in pools of lamplight. In winter, an oak fire burned in the fireplace. My mother sat with a novel splayed on her lap, sipping a glass of claret. Scented candles burned from the mantel while the low hum of Dixieland sifted in from the study, an occasional rattle of trumpets. My father read an academic journal, drained his beer, tapped along to the music in his stocking feet. They seemed content enough. Every now and then my mother would make a comment about her book, share a funny line or phrase. It would take my father a moment to be wrested from his article, but he would always make the effort to look up and grin or nod. I knew, and I'm sure my mother knew, that he was faking his responses. He hadn't read a novel since grade school and seemed incapable of investing himself in a narrative. Movies, fiction, even newspapers largely washed over him. He had fond boyhood memories of watching Groucho Marx, the Three Stooges, Laurel and Hardy, but precisely because each moment stood in its own right; they were comedies of distilled cause and effect. One night, after my mother read a lyrical passage aloud from *Tess of the d'Urbervilles*, my father chided, "They mention the weather a lot in that story you're reading." My mother stared at him, blew some air between her lips, and returned to her book.

ONCE A MONTH, SOMETIMES MORE, this homely existence came undone when my father had a migraine attack. He had the classic onset—an intuition of the coming pain, a tingling sensation in his fingers, flickering lights in his peripheral vision. My mother and I kept out of his way and for an entire day he fussed, trying to find refuge from sunlight and the noise of the furnace. He ran into things, recoiled, and headed in the other direction, like a wasp looking for strongholds.

My mother locked the doors to certain rooms for fear that my father, like some deranged sleepwalker, would ransack her sewing room or break the robust Shaker furniture apart. One time he did knock a bowl of Concord grapes onto the hardwood floor and mash them with his bare feet without noticing. And she never forgot it. But usually when the pain arrived, it was so literal and pure that my father physically shrank and retreated to his study. His shoulders hunched, his brow pinched, his eyes vacant. Surprisingly, in this state, my father would have some of his best insights about physics. He explained this once by saying that on a cloudy day you can get the worst sunburn because only the strongest solar radiation penetrates the clouds. "Insight cuts through the cloud cover of pain," he told me.

When it was over, usually the next morning, he would appear in the kitchen, blearing as if through a hangover. He drank a cup of black coffee in silence, tasting each sip. Then he would say things like, "The body thinks it's real. That's the problem of modern physics. How to convince our minds that they're not our own." My mother and I knew better than to respond. She made him bacon and eggs. I buttered his toast. We were more curious than scared. He was like a wild animal we'd brought in from the woods, a half-man waiting to be civilized. He tasted food as if for the first time and rationed his eye movements. After breakfast he would disappear to his study and spend most of the day there combing through the notes he'd made while dazed with pain. Months later, we would learn that in the midst of the migraine, he had conceived a groundbreaking theory about the nature of subatomic charm and spin.

# four

Being less than brilliant with a genius parent is like being the bum who stares, midwinter, through the restaurant window at the plump diners inside. There was my father, on the other side of that window, eating food so delicate and sumptuous it made my teeth ache. The seat opposite him was empty and expectant, but I never made it past the glass.

I was a mildly precocious child, but my parents mistook two traits as signs of early genius: an ability to pose cutting questions, and a slightly better-than-average memory. The first trait was a kind of reflection of the world. Questions made me seem smarter than I was; they mirrored the minds of people around me. I asked my father things that sounded like Zen koans: "Why does it snow?" "Does the sun become a star at night?" "Why am I the only person I know who's not afraid of Kodiak bears?" They seemed like signposts, telegrams from a vibrant, interior world. But, like most children, I had no sense of irony in my questions. The perfect answer to why it snows was "Because it gets cold." The second trait—memory—convinced my parents I was unnaturally gifted. My father posted the periodic table on my bedroom door, hoping I would internalize the names and atomic weights. I remembered ten elements, in no particular order, and no atomic weights. I drew arrows connecting the ones that began with the same letter. It was pattern recognition, savvy, but nothing like genius.

But my parents' hope outweighed the evidence. A piano appeared in the parlor. My mother's violin came down from the attic. She began leaving it in conspicuous places, casually at rest beside the fireplace, propped on a bookshelf, hoping that I would pick it up one day, take it back to my bedroom, and fill the house with heavenly stringed laments. But the violin sat in its case, marooned in the parlor, sinister as a baby's coffin. I felt it waiting for me—the burnt-orange velvet swaying inside, the strings slackening against the bow. I could never bring myself to open the lid.

By the time I was nine, I'd spent years at math competitions in high school gymnasiums, in chess tournaments at the scout hall, and in whiz-kid summer camps. The major events were filmed in sixteen-millimeter. My mother cooked my favorite food the night before a big event—lasagna with mashed potatoes. My father made me breakfasts of "brain food"—carrot juice and steak. It was a recipe that one of his colleagues from the physics department swore by. The taste of pan-fried steak and the juicy pulp of carrots signaled the start of so many days in which we tried to unearth my talents.

During this quest my father discussed school as if it were a trifling formality that a genius-in-training must endure. "Jump through their hoops," he said, "and I'll teach you about reality at night." "Reality" turned out to be basic algebra and the foundations of science. He taught me about gravity, motion, and light, about the conspiracies of molecules and atoms that held things in place. We looked at water drops and their animated worlds under a microscope. We collected pollen and watched ice crystals form. I imagined hydrogen and oxygen bonding, spinning toward each other, making water and ice some kind of chemical choreography. We talked about the sun burning helium and the moon governing tides; we coaxed electricity from a voltaic cell.

When he thought I was ready, my father inducted me into the quantum universe. It seemed to contradict all the science I had learned so far: nothing was really held in place. The essential stuff of the universe was nonmatter, pulses of energy and information, flickering in and out of existence. Everything was up for grabs. A table, a chair was a fluid arrangement of probabilities. Sometimes I expected the uncertainty principle to kick in and find strangers masquerading as my parents, or that our house had been razed by some great atomic upheaval. It was about this time I started sleeping with the light on.

MANY EVENINGS WERE DEVOTED TO math and science drills. We sat in the kitchen and my father wrote out simultaneous equations for me to solve. We plotted curves and functions on tablets of graph paper. My mother served us blueberry pie or crème brûlée or baklava. She sat in a wicker chair with a pencil and a *New York Times* crossword puzzle, whispering clues to herself. She was good at crosswords, knew a lot of arcane words garnered from a lifetime of reading, but sometimes, especially if she'd had a glass of wine, annoyance flushed her cheeks. "Good Lord, they expect a lot from a person." My father and I would look up from our equation or graph. She would rock back and forth in her chair, indignant, while her hazel-flecked eyes and patrician features narrowed. I knew how she felt; most of the time my father wrote out problems that I could not solve on my own. One night, as we looked at her, she wrapped her long brown hair into a bun, stuck a No. 2 pencil into it, drained her wineglass, folded and refolded the newspaper, and said, "These tyrants! Fine. They want war. I'll dig a trench and take aim. Go on with your numbers, boys." After a glass of wine and an infuriating crossword clue, my mother could pass for Charlotte Brontë.

Sometimes, when dessert was over, my father and I took a drive. We cruised the Oldsmobile through town and he drilled me on boiling points, formulas, and symbol names— scientific bric-a-brac. I sat up front on the crimson vinyl seat, my hands against the dash, imagining myself the copilot of specialized aircraft—Delta 10s, Apollo rockets, zeppelins— and I watched out the windshield as the headlights singled out trees and houses through a low fog or a summer haze. When I performed well, we circumnavigated the town only once—a slow, ten-mile loop bounded by the railroad, the subdivisions, and the college campus with its minarets and raised walkways. But if I did badly, erring on atomic numbers and evaporation temperatures, then we drove in endless concentric circles, narrowing in on downtown, the ground zero of failure. If I saw the stonework of the banks, the civic emblem on the town hall, I knew it was all over. Resigned, my father would turn for home and we would continue in silence, the car gliding along the empty streets with a maritime grace.

One night I remember heading toward home, exasperated, brain-numbed, as we came into our neighborhood. Out my window I could see a row of six or seven neat houses where the men were out in their coats shoveling snow. My father slowed down and we surveyed the scene: the gleaming slow arcs of the snow shovels, the men hunched over the curbstone, their breath like smoke. A few of them clenched cigars or pipes between their teeth. An elderly neighbor stamped up and down, salting the sidewalk from a bucket. The men, settled in an after-dinner chore, a moment's bracing contact with the elements, joked and called to one another as they worked. With their dun-and-ale-colored coats, peaked hats, and hooded faces, they appeared medieval— members of a fraternal guild plying their trade. And by comparison, I felt a strange sense of privilege and isolation from inside the car. My mother paid a man to clear our driveway of snow and ice. I'd never seen my father hold a shovel or a rake. I felt like the son of an industrialist, touring the proletariat, waltzing past the rowhouses and saltbox shacks of the poor. I didn't like this feeling, so I wound down my window and waved at the men. A few of them waved back with big-mittened hands. They were normal people—car salesmen and restaurant owners—and a complete mystery to me. My father nodded and said quietly, "The endless battle." I didn't know whether he meant against snow or against some invisible, more defiant enemy. Up ahead I could make out our house. The Victorian roofline floated above the bare rim of the orchard, the stand of apple trees that buffered us from the rest of the street.

# five

My parents sent me to St. John's, a Catholic school run by Jesuit priests, even though my father was an atheist and my mother had grown up Methodist and was now agnostic. They sent me here because my father claimed that the Jesuits were great scholars. "Celibate men with lots of time on their hands, it speaks for itself," he said. Father Clayton, the principal, had a PhD in chemistry, which won my father over instantly. As a condition of attending the school, I had to participate in its Catholic rituals—scripture classes, Wednesday mass, confession—and this made my father nervous. "Ignore the applied science in the Bible," he told me. "Combusting bushes, men living to nine hundred, ghosts impregnating virgins. Not even quantum physics can explain those things."

My mother liked the school because it fit with her sense of tradition, seemed part of a distant era of superior manners and grooming. In our parlor, an entire wall hung with sepia photographs: picnicking families on sunny lawns, suited uncles rowing wooden boats beneath their wide-brimmed hats, a picture of her parents—a bearded, stalwart minister with piercing eyes and a woman in a lace-trimmed dress with a kind, open face. That wall had the air of a family shrine, of paying homage to our ancestors who, in the days of rheumatic fever and typhoid, were the last of a happy generation.

My mother felt a longing for the past. Sometimes she sat on the landing above the stairs and told me about childhood summers in our house. Aunt Beulah—originally from Vermont, where an apple farmer betrayed her in love—scrubbed creosote from the fireplace, dug her own pantry cave with a pickax, and canned the world one fruit at a time. Beulah was from a generation of spinsters who whistled while plucking a hand-wrung chicken and took a glass of rum and seltzer every night before bed. Every day was set to a domestic rhythm—wash day, canning day, baking day—and all of them filled with Beulah's quips and jokes, muttered folk songs and country sayings. It was little wonder, then, that my mother had inherited some antiquated ways of speaking and kept house on a military schedule. Even when she deviated from Beulah's homespun rigors—putting up a Kashmiri tapestry or a Turkish prayer rug—she had merely supplanted one set of traditions for another. All her ethnic jewelry and artifacts tended to be antiques, lifted stories from the past. I suppose now that St. John's was just another relic and therefore a comfort to her.

In school I applied myself and went along with the search for my endowment. Because I had a good memory I did reasonably well. I worked hard and stayed patient, even though I got bored of the constant drills and quizzes and extracurricular trials. I believed the hand of greatness was above me, waiting to cup my skull in a benevolent embrace. Wednesday afternoons I attended the Young Chemists' Club, where eight other boys and I listened to Father Clayton talk about noble gases, about the formation of coal, about peat forming inside bedrock over millions of years. We made acids and alkaline solutions; we learned the names for chemicals and elements. During Friday lunchtimes I went to the geography brown-bag lunch. Over peanut butter sandwiches and celery sticks I watched as Father Dustoyov, a Russian émigré, pulled down maps of Eastern Europe and sub-Saharan Africa, revealing the swaths of pale pink and ink blue that stood for nation-states. He pointed to the amorphous blob of fuchsia that marked the Soviet Union, noting simply, "I am from this ocean of pink, right here." Every week he gave us a quiz on Eastern Bloc cities; I took some pride in knowing we were the only kids in America who knew that the Baltic Sea, like Michigan, resembles a raised hand.

Through all this I believed genius was a job you grew up to perform, no different, essentially, than becoming a fire-man, a doctor, or a jeweler. Geniuses were small-framed men, bespectacled and loping; they had bad taste in shoes, were prone to gravy stains and tweed. But these men—and they were always men—were also unpredictable: it was just as likely for their throat-creaking speculation to result in a tor-rential belch as it was in a new system of fuel combustion. A genius wasn't something you were or weren't, so much as something, with the right training and parentage, you could become.

FOR MY TENTH BIRTHDAY MY father took me on a sur-prise trip. He woke me early one morning, handed me the clothes my mother had laid out on the bed, and we drove for an hour in light snow before stopping for breakfast. Over oatmeal, my father said, "Happy birthday, Nathan. This is going to be a big surprise." His tone was secretive. My chest tightened. I pictured arctic tundra, some sky watch over an ice field.

"Where are we going?" I asked.

He smiled and said, "You won't believe it."

We drove to the Madison airport. I had never been on a plane before and had only been inside an airport a few times. A cold, white light hung at the windows while businessmen sat leafing through newspapers. A woman's voice droned departure warnings on the PA system. A platoon of nuns stood in their habits, drinking coffee from Styrofoam cups. There was something morbid about the grim men in suits, about the brightly clad families returning from Hawaii with suntans in the dead of winter. I could feel a hollow sensation in my stomach. I stood by the windows and watched jets land and take off, the de-icing of their wings, while my father settled at the end of a row of plastic seats and wrote in a notebook.

As we lined up to board our plane, I looked over at the ticket desk, where a uniformed man announced that our destination was San Francisco. I knew this was in California. I also knew Disneyland was in California, though I wasn't sure in which city. The likelihood of my father taking me to Disneyland seemed so remote that I didn't allow myself to get excited. But then, on the plane, amid the humming turbines and the metallic-smelling air, my father said things that suggested we would spend the day at a giant amusement park.

"This place is a tribute to physics," he said, rotating a bony finger in the air. I pictured octopus rides and Ferris wheels, odes to centrifugal motion.

"Speed, motion, light. Everything you could want in one place. Makes me feel like a boy again." He pointed with his fork at his in-flight meal, as if it were a scale model of where we were going. Gesturing to one end of his turkey sandwich, he said, "The mountains sit here, watching the whole show in silence." I allowed my muscles to relax. Someone had told my father to take me to Disneyland and he'd found a way to tie it in with my scientific education. I pushed my food tray aside and looked out the window. I stared at the streaming clouds, riveted now by the thought of traveling across the continent at four hundred miles an hour.

When we landed in San Francisco, we rented a car and traveled half an hour. California was sunny and bright. It was everything I needed it to be. We drove along the freeway, my father gunning the engine whenever he passed slower drivers. I saw the mountains and guessed we were getting close. My father slowed and pulled off onto the shoulder. We got out and stood on the edge of the freeway, long-distance trucks hauling past us to Seattle and Portland, commuters flashing by. We walked a little ways and stood on an overpass. Fifteen feet or so below us there was a two-mile-long structure that resembled the boxcars of an enormous freight train. It ran through a ravine, between stands of scrub oak and manzanita. I stared down at the tunnel.

"What do you think?" he asked, one hand combing his beard.

"What is it?"

"Particle accelerator."

I could feel my hands curl into fists. "A what?"

"The Stanford Linear Accelerator. It's an atom smasher." He leaned against the guardrail and pointed up toward the Santa Cruz Mountains. I hated him in that moment and could imagine pushing him over the side. I was suddenly very thirsty and had to keep swallowing. My father said, "The electrons start their dash up toward the base of the mountains. Just near the San Andreas Fault, which I think is fitting. Anyway, they're accelerated inside a long copper tube buried underground. The superstructure houses the klystrons that feed microwave power to the tube."

I said nothing.

He grinned. "A pulse of electrons rides the electromagnetic wave at close to the speed of light. A couple microseconds later each electron has gained upward of twenty billion volts." He paused, took out the small notebook he kept in his top pocket, feinted with his pen as if about to write a remarkable insight, then put it away again. Finally he stared back at the tunnel and said, "Twenty billion volts. You could light a few porches with that kind of energy." He abruptly stepped back toward the car and I followed. I was mad with myself for getting excited. We drove down to the accelerator campus and I couldn't look at my father.

But as we entered the compound, my mood changed. We checked in with a mustached security guard at the main gatehouse and were issued visitor badges. We pulled past the checkpoint and stopped in a parking lot outside an administrative building. As we walked toward the drab, squat building, a middle-aged man with a red tie and enormous sideburns came out to meet us. He greeted my father with an earnest handshake.

"Dr. Nelson, we're so delighted to have you back." The man placed his other hand over the handshake like a protective seal. I'd never seen this before, nor had I ever heard my father be called *Doctor*.

"This is my son, Nathan," my father said. "Nathan, this is the director of the accelerator, Dr. Benson." The man bowed forward a little and held his big, blotchy hand in front of me. "Delighted," he said. I shook his hand. It was warm and sweaty. "A little chip off the old block is what we have here," he said to my father. At ten, I already had my father's tall, lanky build and his dark, unruly hair. I suddenly realized, with some embarrassment, that my father and I were wearing identical powder-blue oxfords.

"It's Nathan's birthday," my father said.

Dr. Benson said, "Of course. I remember from our telephone conversation. Please, bring the birthday boy inside. We'll head down to the control room in just a little while." He stepped aside and delivered a small flourish with his hands. We entered a long white corridor broken here and there by office doors, notice boards, and wooden mailboxes. After about thirty feet or so we stepped inside an alcove and Dr. Benson, now rummaging through the pockets of his corduroy trousers, gestured to a vending machine. "Perhaps Nathan would care for a soda," he said.

My father looked at me and I shrugged. "By all means," my father said. "Sprite is the beverage of choice, I believe."

"Coke," I corrected.

Dr. Benson inserted a quarter and handed me a can of Coke. It was extremely cold and I pictured liquid nitrogen smoking inside the vending machine. I took a long sip and we continued down the corridor. We stopped by Dr. Benson's disheveled office, where he collected the car keys for a Department of Energy van from under a pile of papers.

We drove in a white government-issue van down to the main control room, where we would spend the day. I learned that this was where my father had started coming several times a year. He was working on some experiments aimed at finding what he called the ghost particle. A discovery that would extend the standard model of subatomic physics. He and some colleagues from a large international collaboration fired electron pulses at targets of hydrogen and waited to see if anything new was deflected. The collisions happened at close to the speed of light and might create, for a nanosecond, a particle that did not ordinarily exist in nature.

We moved about the control room, my father introducing me to physicists in short sleeves and jeans. I'd imagined lab coats. My father tried to explain the operation. The tunnel, I learned, was called the *beam switchyard*. The place where the subatomic particles roared into their targets was called the *cave*—a chamber where magnets and spectrometers lay waiting, where plastic tubes flashed blue every time the electrons made contact. Some graduate students were eating take-out Kung Pao chicken and monitoring the collision controls. Once the accelerator was warmed up, there were many collisions per second. I sat with my father at the front of the darkened room, though the only thing to observe was a small monitor that showed a series of display events— scatterings of lines in a cross section of tubing. The assistants huddled around, glowering at the phosphor screen. They held expressions of men watching violence—not physical violence like boxing or wrestling, nothing involving cheers and blood cries, but acts of defiance against matter: car accidents, bridges collapsing, buildings imploding. They stood waiting, arms folded, faces drawn, braced. The particle detectors, the lead apertures, all of it served this moment of collision. I stared at my father's face and watched him blink when the monitor showed a vector-spray of distributed matter. "Bump," he said, grinning. It was a pronouncement, delivered with a papal nod. The assistants laughed and loaded another event display.

I tried to be drawn into the violence as I imagined it. But each collision display was anticlimactic; the idea of particles colliding at the speed of light was better than the reality. I wanted to stand inside the concrete tube and hear the electrons streak by, to hear a subatomic explosion.

"Does it sound like a bomb going off?" I asked.

A man with reading glasses perched on the bridge of his nose stared at me.

My father said, "These collisions are beyond all of our senses. There's nothing to hear."

After a couple more collisions, they had a little birthday party for me. My father, in a rare act of thoughtfulness, had brought a brownie slice from the airport as a surrogate cake. They didn't have any candles so one of the men, a smoker, held his lighter on top and I blew it out. I ate the brownie and they went back to their readouts. Soon after, my father and I emerged into the sunny afternoon. The California sky was halogen-bright. We drove ten miles to our hotel, a place where the Particle Physicists of America had a group discount. My father and I ordered a pizza from room service and he let me watch television while he went over his notes from the accelerator. I flipped through the channels, trying to find something that would draw him in. Eventually, I found an old Three Stooges movie—*Have Rocket, Will Travel*—and my father sat on the bed beside me. The trio work as janitors at a space research center and accidentally travel to Venus, where they encounter a monster, a verbose unicorn, and a mad robot. My father grinned and chuckled as they escaped various misadventures. Although technically the movie had a plot, it was really a series of eye pokes, face slaps, and pratfalls. The Stooges return home as heroes and attend a black-tie reception. Despite their best efforts to be polite, Curly has a run-in with a couch spring. He ends up bouncing around the room with the spring attached to his rear end, bumping into famous scientists and dignitaries. My father gave out a full-throated guffaw, then wheezed into something silent and red-faced, as if this were the funniest thing he had ever seen in his life. I faked a laugh and he slapped me on the back. I'd never seen him like this. That a man who knew how to diagram an electron-positron scattering event found Curly with a spring in his butt endlessly amusing seemed like an eternal mystery. Was he, beneath it all, simply a fan of screwball physical comedy and fart jokes? Was everything else a veneer? I couldn't be sure, but I wanted him to keep laughing.

When the movie was over we got ready for bed. Two twin beds stood parallel to each other and I chose one and got under the covers. I watched my father strip down to his underwear. His white undershirt was tucked into his white boxers, and when he removed his tight black socks, there were grooves on his ankles from the elastic. I found myself staring at his feet. They were pale, hairy, and somehow silver. I looked up at the ceiling. In my mind, I kept seeing Dr. Benson shake my father's hand, a solemn grip with the protective left hand on top. Surely it was the way statesmen and diplomats and mayors shook hands. I listened to the sound of my father assessing a number of sleeping positions.

When he got comfortable he said, "Some movie, huh? Sometimes when I go to those faculty dinners I feel just like Curly. Like I could end up knocking the dean over by accident."

"That's why Mom goes with you," I said. "To stop you from killing somebody."

"I suppose so," he said. Then, after a pause, "Good night, son."

"Good night," I said, closing my eyes. In that moment, I consciously forgave my father for the likelihood that he didn't know Disneyland was also in California.

# six

For my mother's thirty-fifth birthday I suggested my father order her a surprise cake, which he did. We went across town to pick it up. I was eleven. It was a prewar bakery with glass-fronted display cases of gnarled farmers' loaves and plaited wedding bread. The baker was French, a man of talent and good taste, exiled no doubt by scandal or bad luck to our small town. He lived with his family and they didn't mix outside of their business dealings, but despite this he had a cheery disposition, and insisted on serving the counter himself. My father and I walked in there ten minutes before closing and the baker was drinking a demitasse of espresso next to the cash register. Behind him, in the back, amid the steel racks of baking trays, his teenage son was sweeping the floor.

"I'm here to pick up a cake," my father said.

"Ah, yes, Mr. Nelson. I thought about calling but I wondered if, perhaps, this was not some kind of surprise. Is this for your wife?"

"Yes, that's right. How much will it be?" My father moved closer to the cash register, his face down.

The baker wore an immaculate white apron. He had a big, square jaw but soft green eyes that made him look to me more like a painter than a baker. "Well, I didn't know whether you wanted . . . perhaps, some kind of message. I don't know . . . 'Happy Birthday.' You could choose and I'll have Michael pipe a message with some frosting."

My father looked down at the glass counter, contemplating the pastries. I stood beside him, touching the base of a cake tray.

"We could write her a message, Dad," I said.

"Yes," he said. "I'm aware of the possibilities, but here's the thing: your mother doesn't like a fuss. What if—?"

"Mr. Nelson, we could just simply write 'Happy Birthday.' Nothing else. And I kept the piping bag aside. It would be no problem."

Again my father stared down at the unsold pastries—blintzes, strudels, Danish, croissants—the United Nations of baked goods. Was he deciding about the cake message or counting forms, categorizing the pastries by nationality and geometric shape? I looked up at the clock. The shop was due to close in five minutes.

"I say we tell her happy birthday," I said.

"Yes, okay, that's what we'll do, then," my father said. He stared out the windows at the dying afternoon.

The baker smiled at me and called back to his son in French. In a moment the boy appeared with the layered chocolate cake and a piping bag. Tiny pearls of white icing clung to his hands.

"This is my son, Michael," the baker said. He pronounced it Mee-karl.

My father, roused from his private speculation, turned reluctantly and looked at the cake, but not at the boy.

"Hi," I said.

I watched the baker's son unfurl beautiful white letters from the bag—a tightly looped cursive that was both festive and elegant. The baker nodded and winked at his son, who was clearly proud of his skill.

"Michael here is going to own this place one day."

My father said, "Just the Happy Birthday for the message. You could include an exclamation point at the end—or—Nathan, is that a little much for your mother?"

I couldn't look at my father. I wanted him to ask the baker about his life, about his son and what kind of apprenticeship he had done. The baker, sensing my father's lack of curiosity, tried to draw out interest like a drunk telling a story. His eyes locked on my father, who was inspecting a troublesome fingernail.

"Michael has been baking for many years now. He started when he was six. He stood on a chair and measured cups of flour. Rye, wheat . . . it's in his blood. In France my great-grandfather was the first to make sourdough in the north. He carried some yeast all the way from Switzerland in a handkerchief."

"Wow," I said.

Michael looked up from the cake and flashed me a smile.

"I assume you put it in a box," my father said.

The baker stared at my father for a moment, then back down at his son's steady script. Without looking up, he said in a low voice, "Of course it comes in a box, what do you think, I let you carry my cake in your bare hands?" He was convinced my father was the man who pushes past you in elevators and splits small restaurant bills with a calculator.

My father nodded and bit his lip. The offense in the baker's voice was as foreign to him as the previous attempt at camaraderie. He paid for the cake and we went outside and got in the car.

"That was kind of rude," I said.

"Hmm?"

"He was trying to chat and you ignored him."

"I did?" He narrowed his eyes at a point in the distance.

"Yeah."

"Well, what did he say?" he said vacantly.

"You were there," I said.

"All the same. Some details?"

"He said his son had been baking a long time and that he was going to take over the shop someday."

"And what did I do?" He turned to look at me, suddenly interested.

"You acted like he hadn't said anything."

He put his hand on the steering wheel, tapped his fingers against it. "Should I go and apologize to him?"

"Maybe."

"I see." It was a slight tone of regret, more at being caught than for appearing rude.

"I mean, we come here all the time. Mom gets her tea cakes here."

"Fine, then. I'll say that I was thinking about something else."

I looked out the window; night was surrounding us. "What were you thinking about?"

He looked down the street, at the storefronts coming alight. "I have no idea."

"Maybe you'd better apologize."

He looked at me, nodded once obediently, then opened the door. I watched as he walked up the pavement, cake box in hand. He stood there in front of the windowed door. I wanted to follow him and hear his apology. A thin arm appeared and pulled down the old-fashioned blinds and twisted a sign that now read "closed." My father stood there a moment, one hand poised to knock, the other hand, flat as a plane, resting beneath the cake box at shoulder height. After a moment he knocked. The door opened and the baker, now apronless, stood there in the last minutes of daylight, staring out at my father on his stoop. Some nods and head tilts, my father looking at the cake several times, gesturing to it. After a moment the bakery door closed and my father walked back to the car. He turned the engine over and we pulled down the street.

"What did you say?" I asked.

"I said sorry and told him I had a reputation for this kind of thing."

"And he forgave you?"

"Geez, Nathan, it's not a crime. I didn't rob the register."

A silence lasted several blocks.

"I've never heard you say geez before."

"Well it's your mother's birthday. It's a special occasion."

He tapped the top of the cake box smugly—a man tapping a briefcase full of money. "Your mother is going to be super surprised."

"Super," I said, feigning excitement.

"You want to know what I got her as a present?"

"Sure."

"A Navajo Indian necklace. It's made from turquoise and silver. She likes that kind of thing."

"You thought of that?" I said, surprised.

My father looked down at the dashboard. "Well, a secretary who works in the physics department office suggested it. She knows your mother from a book club or something."

"Good thinking," I said.

"Yes, Mindy Monkhouse really saved my skin on that one." A moment later he added, "Because I was going to buy your mother a new raincoat."

We drove the rest of the way home in silence. I watched the town roll past. People were out walking their dogs or leaving work with newspapers under their arms. I wondered whether all geniuses were plagued by simple errands, if they were unhinged by domestic routine. In my father's mind finding the right birthday gift was more complicated than using trigonometry and the stars to measure latitude.

# seven

During the accident I sustained a gash in the right side of my head. From the size and shape of the injury it appeared to have been caused by a flying object. A few of the doctors believed I was brain injured. They noted in the charts my lack of speech and occasional dreaminess and wondered whether this was more than standard coma shock. Since the brain swims in fluid, it could have bounced against the rear of the cranium during impact, injuring the left anterior lobe—resulting in things like speech problems or social withdrawal. They waited for things to change, for signs that I was the same before and after the accident.

I stared out the window, watching the processions of high summer—the sun-dappled elms, the Day-Glo sheen of the cropped hospital lawn, birds flitting and wheeling above the telephone poles. My mind flooded with memories. A copper teakettle in a kitchen drenched with sunlight. My mother kneading bread, the windows chill with morning. The halting gait of my father on the stairs—a gangly bustle and a waft of talcum powder—as he descended for breakfast. My former life was a montage of images and smells.

My mother, who'd been staying in the area, was the first one to see me after I woke from the coma. I sat propped with pillows. When she came into the room, her face was pale and drawn; there were ashen half-moons beneath her eyes. I recognized her immediately, but she came to me as a collection of objects more than a living person: the thin nose, the slender hands, the long brown hair pulled into a barrette. She was wearing the Navajo necklace that my father had given her for her thirty-fifth birthday. I couldn't formulate any words. She set her purse down on a chair and gently placed her hand on my head wound—there had been nine stitches just above my right eyebrow. "Oh, God," she said. "My boy." Somehow, her voice was brown and seemed to stay in the air. She put her cheek to my face.

One of the doctors stood beside her. "He's still in coma shock. We don't know all the test results yet."

She grabbed my hand and I could feel her pulse against my wrist. "Yes, I see. Nathan, I'm right here." She pushed a strand of hair back from my forehead and I remember taking ahold of her necklace. I touched the edges of the silver pendant. "Is he all right?" she asked.

"Fragile. It will take time."

The doctor left the room and my mother pulled up the chair beside my bed. She looked at me, crossed her legs. "Your father is on his way with Whit. You remember Whit Shupak, don't you? Your father's colleague. They were both here but had to return to the college for a few days. How do you feel?" When I didn't respond she looked around the room. Her mouth pursed in the corners; she was on the verge of tears. "I'm afraid of what I'll find when we make it back to the house. Things need repair. I suspect the eaves are rotting on the north side and God knows your father doesn't know how to climb a ladder." Now that she was composed, she sat there and spoke to me like a neighbor: how rising damp was claiming the basement, how she had planned her fall garden, how she hadn't had any company in a long time. She folded her arms and stared at her feet and said, "You're alive and that's the main thing." Then she opened her purse, pulled out a pristine handkerchief, and dabbed at her eyes. "You've been asleep for a long time. You must be starving! What would you like to eat, Nathan? If you could have anything to eat in the world, what would it be?" I tried to think about food but her words got in the way—tan-colored waves that got in the way of my hunger.

# eight

*N**athan was a solitary youth*. That's how my mother sometimes describes my early and pubescent years, before the accident, when I was a cut above average at the Jesuit school for boys. She likes to word things in a particular way. In our house, it was never a *couch* or a *sofa,* it was a *davenport,* a *love seat,* a *divan*. My father's *study*—essentially a rummage of books and papers with a desk—was never called an office. My father wore *trousers* or *slacks,* never pants. My mother had been to Europe once, as a high school graduation present. This one trip, eighteen years prior, apparently gave her the right to refer to it as *the Continent*.

But if I was a loner at St. John's, it was because I was stultified by our quest for my hidden talents. I wanted to make friends, but I had adopted the stance of a kid who might someday have a college building named after him. Despite my lack of talent, I was hard to reach. And, in turn, the other boys were standoffish with me—for years they'd seen my father trundling me down to the physics lab at the college or whisking me off to a speed-reading seminar. They expected and feared great things from me. Then they grew suspicious when my mediocre annual test scores came out. A genius can be aloof. An unnaturally gifted athlete can set a new school trend. But the average and the mildly gifted—those flitting like tadpoles at the deepest place of the bell curve—are expected to be sociable and easy to get along with. I was neither of those things.

This state of affairs was even worse when it came to girls my age. Since there were no girls at St. John's, only the most confident and enterprising boys had girlfriends. They were part of an elite, a legion of daredevils who spoke to girls in movie-ticket lines and in bowling alleys. They made passes at the girls from Sacred Heart, the sister school of St. John's that was located three blocks away. Riding their BMX bikes into the outer suburbs, they would stand beneath girls' second-story bedroom windows. They made out in parking lots, under beds, in the backseats of cars, on stadium bleachers. The rest of us heard their stories of conquest and listened with awe, slack-jawed at the thought of a girl's tongue inside our mouths.

I might have stood a chance with the girls of Sacred Heart if I'd had the gumption to approach any of them. Every weekday afternoon I passed their school as they were lining up for the buses—standing in twos and threes, braiding one another's hair, animated with that day's scandal. But when I walked by, their banter slowed and I felt their eyes on me. I have my father's dark hair and brooding eyes but my mother's high cheekbones, fine nose, and pale skin. It is a face that's both troubled and refined. One day a girl was half pushed from the bus line and with her eyes on the sidewalk said, "Do you have a girlfriend?" Stupidly, I said, "What?" as if I were annoyed by this intrusion. The girl's cheeks fumed red and she darted back to her snickering friends. They never spoke to me again.

But back at St. John's, I tried to correct the image of my standoffishness by inviting two of my classmates home. Max Sutherland and Ben Thornberg were both from the nearby subdivision known as Maple Ridge. Their fathers were salesmen. This particular weekend my father was holed up in his study, listening to Count Basie, and had asked for no interruptions. So for most of the day we played outside in the orchard. Max, a shrewd boy with glasses who headed the junior debate team, and Ben, a quiet oaf of a boy, got hungry after swinging and jumping from trees all morning. We went inside and found my mother baking in the kitchen.

"We're completely starving," I said.

"Is that right?" she asked.

My mother opened the oven door and pulled out two loaves of bread.

Ben said, "I've never seen bread like that."

"Like what?" my mother asked, smiling.

"You know, in the oven," Ben said.

"My mother's a terrible cook," Max said. "Strictly beans in a can." He wiped his hands down his T-shirt.

My mother put the bread on the table and removed her hands from the oven mitts. A burst of old-time jazz came from my father's study. "Would you boys like some sandwiches?" she said.

Max, in an ingratiating tone, said, "We'd like that a great deal, Mrs. Nelson."

My mother looked at him oddly; there was something vaguely flirtatious in his tone—the sixth-grade debate captain trying to come off suave. She said, "Nathan, why don't you take some slices of bread and jam to your father in his study? He's been in there for three days and heaven knows what you'll find. Tell him to send me a postcard sometime." She arranged a plate of thick-cut bread, a dollop of jam, and a butter knife. I took the plate from her and began to leave the kitchen. Max and Ben were right behind me; they had only ever glimpsed my father from afar. I knocked with medium loudness on the study door, trying to be heard above the music. There was no answer, so I opened it. The room was draped in shadow except for a dusty slat of light that came from a high window and divided the room in two. Piles of books and jazz albums were everywhere. A row of unlabeled home-brew bottles were arranged in a perfect line on his desk. A small kerosene heater rattled from one corner. The Count Basie LP spun and crackled from an outmoded record player. My father sat with his back to us, in his undershirt and some loose-fitting slacks, his bare feet up on the windowsill. Taped to the wall in front of him was a sheet of white paper. It was completely blank except for a black squiggle, dead center.

"Dad?" I said.

He did a half-turn with his head. In the dimness I could see the whites of his eyes.

"Who is that?" he called.

"We have some bread for you," I said.

"It's hot and fresh out of the oven," said Ben, swallowing.

"Good," my father said, allowing us further entry.

The study had the musky bite of infrequent bathing and the hopsy scent of ale.

I set the plate down on the desk and planned my retreat.

My father stood and rubbed his bare arms. "What are you boys up to, then?" he asked, coming over to the desk.

"Commando raids in the orchard mostly," Max said, stepping forward, trying to get a better look at my dad.

"Fearless," said my father. It was the tone of a benediction. He picked up a piece of bread and looked underneath it. He broke off a piece, dipped it into the jam, and wedged it into his mouth. It disappeared behind his beard.

"What are you working on?" Max asked.

"Me? Oh, I'm scraping the mold off some old heat dissipation theorems."

"What's that mean, exactly?" Max asked, his hands behind his back.

"Come on," I said. "Let's go eat."

My father said, "Ah, that means I'm trying to reduce the molten core of the sun to a known numerical value. In terms of its potential heat dissipation." There was jam in the corners of his mouth.

"So, like, you're trying to tell when the sun is going to explode," Max said, leaning over the desk for emphasis.

My father squinted slightly at Max, then looked at me: a visual comparison. "That would be one way of putting it," my father said, staring out into the hallway.

"I'm really famished," Ben whispered to no one in particular.

My father inched back toward the window. He picked up a marker in his right hand and held it poised in the air. "If you boys have a few minutes . . . I can show you the theorem. See, I figure the differential between the sun's radiation and known—"

"Dad, we haven't eaten lunch," I said.

"Ah, then," my father said, registering slight disappointment. He swiveled his body and glowered at the paper on the wall. "Eat!" he boomed, one arm waving us off. "Yes, by all means, eat your mother's bread." There was a pause, then he said contritely, "Thank you boys for the visit."

"Good luck with the sun, Mr. Nelson," said Max.

We walked down the hallway toward my mother's fresh bread. Max quickened his pace and announced, "Your dad is definitely weirder than both our dads put together." His dad sold cars in a Buick dealership and Ben's father worked at a carpet store. I turned and saw my father's silhouette in the study doorway. We'd forgotten to close the door and I wondered if he'd heard Max's comment. I looked away, guilty that I'd invaded his sanctuary, that I'd brought the sons of petty commerce into his private kingdom and now he would be a school-yard mockery. We stepped into the kitchen, where my aproned mother held out a pyramid of cut sandwiches on a plate. I noticed that the sandwiches had been cut as if for preschoolers—into triangles and with the crust removed. There was a sprig of thyme on top. I felt a flush of embarrassment for everything in our house.

"Any sign of life in there?" my mother asked me.

"He says thanks for the bread," I lied. I took the plate of sandwiches from her and led Ben and Max outside and away from the house.

# nine

At the end of the seventh grade, there was a science fair inside the St. John's church hall. Apart from the student exhibits, there was going to be a quiz, in which I was entered. My father drilled me in the Oldsmobile as we drove across town. "What's the first element of the periodic table?" he asked, his eyes narrowing in the rearview mirror.

"Hydrogen," I said.

"Very nice," my mother said.

He was starting with easy questions: the molecular composition of water and glucose, the nature of photosynthesis.

"Was it Galileo or Copernicus who thought the center of the universe was the earth?"

"Copernicus."

"Correct," my father said. He smoothed a wrinkle in his shirt. "All right, let's get the machinery going. What's the difference between endothermic and exothermic reactions?"

I paused, looked out the window at a row of sparrows on a fence. I was a little nervous. "Something to do with heat."

My father placed one hand on the dash and said, "Be precise, for God's sake."

My mother registered a glance in his direction.

"Endothermic reactions absorb heat, exothermic put out heat," I said.

"Good," he said, exhaling. "According to Einstein, why can't anything travel faster than the speed of light?"

"Dad, they're not going to ask me about Einstein's general theory of relativity. It's the seventh grade."

"Well, then, let's talk about Newton. He's the right level for a seventh grader."

And so it went. By the time we arrived at St. John's I was harried. I got my display out of the back of the Oldsmobile— a papier-mâché volcano with a pump powered by a voltaic cell battery. It could spew magma and lava with the touch of a button. At the base of the volcano was a small model village that eventually became submerged in gelatinous imitation lava. The exhibit had been my idea; my father tolerated its simplicity because he was primarily concerned with the science quiz. We went inside the hall and I set up at a card table. The competition wasn't for another few hours, so I sat at my table and answered parent and student questions about volcanoes, demonstrated the lava pump. The hall filled with kids and their displays: dissected frogs in brine, popsicle-stick bridges that could withstand the weight of ten encyclopedias, battery-powered windmills, aquascapes, tarantulas and scorpions glazed inside box frames, chemical reactions involving dry ice. Darius Kaplansky, a suspected genius from my school, had a display involving rats inside a maze. His maze contained three white rats: one had been injected with parasites from birth, one was normal, and one was made to listen to Mozart for an hour each day. The Mozart fan, Darius told his admirers, won the dash through the maze every time.

After a demonstration, Darius explained to the onlookers, "We're interested in neural coherence as a result of the symmetry in the music." I sat with my jelly lava, suddenly humiliated by my display's banality. Of course, since each rat looked identical, it was impossible to know which rat won. It may have been a trick. Besides, I suspected that his father, a psychiatrist, had designed the experiment.

I spent the morning watching Darius eat powdered donuts and chatting with onlookers at his crowded booth. His face was slightly feminine—full red lips and long eyelashes. His hair was slick and parted, his shoes spit-shined. When we were called to the stage I looked at him and saw the undilated pupils of steely confidence. "Good luck," I said, hoping to get inside his head. He smiled a little warily. My parents sat in the front row. My father wore his new black polo shirt—a recent attempt of my mother's to spruce him up. The competitors took the stage: a girl from Sacred Heart who smiled behind the weight of braces, a curly-haired boy wearing a tie, a hefty-set boy with a Dodgers cap, and finally serene Darius. We sat behind a long table like contestants at a pie-eating competition.

Father Rajmani, my science teacher—an Indian man with round glasses and a thin mustache—was the quizmaster. He held pink index cards in front of him and launched himself onto the balls of his feet as he asked each question. Darius and I dominated. I was surprised by how much I knew. I looked at my father, who held a program up to his mouth and blew across its edge. My mother nodded and smiled every time I got a question right. I knew how hot lightning could get (70,000 degrees Fahrenheit), that dry ice is the solid state of carbon dioxide, that the world's first computer was switched on in 1946. Darius and I were evenly matched, but sometimes his hand shot up before mine. The girl with the crooked teeth put her face in her hands; she didn't answer a single question. The boy in the Dodgers cap picked at his chin and shot up his hand when Rajmani asked what *dinosaur* meant.

"I think maybe it means terrible lizard. Is that right?" he said.

"Correct," Father Rajmani said, relieved that another student had answered something.

I looked at Darius. He was staring at the back of the pink index cards, as though the answers were printed there in indelible ink. When Darius and I had twenty points each, Father Rajmani requested a round of applause, and the other children took their seats with their parents. Darius leaned so far forward in his chair that his head practically rested on the table. My father grinned. My mother's arm was linked through his. All those years of scientific cross-examination had paid off. Had I arrived? I sat back in my chair, confident, allowing the brain food and my DNA to do their work. Where Darius hesitated, I jumped in. I guessed the multiple choices when I didn't know the answer and kept getting them right. My question arm cramped and it felt good, like the tendons and muscles were pulling their weight.

"Next section: astronomy," Rajmani said.

The church hall was filled with late-afternoon light. The whistle of the overhead fans coated the room. The planets and stars spoke to me: Pluto takes 248 years to orbit the sun; iron gives Mars its reddish color; it takes eight and a half minutes for the sun's light to reach Earth. I was ahead by two points. Darius's father—the psychiatrist and secret designer of the rat experiment—sat a row behind my parents with his hands gripping his knees. My father's face revealed itself before me; his eyes were ablaze with hope. The final section was physics. I took a deep breath.

Father Rajmani had two blooms of sweat in the armpits of his starched cleric's shirt. He picked up a set of index cards from a table.

"Best of five questions. Darius, you need to get all five to win. Nathan, you need only answer one right to take the match."

My father tilted his head to one side, craning to listen.

"Who proposed the law of motion that for every action there is an equal and opposite reaction? A., Albert Einstein, B., Isaac New—"

Darius had his hand in the air. "B.—Isaac Newton."

"Correct. Does a strawberry look red because: A., it absorbs light, or B., it reflects light?"

Darius and I shot our hands into the air at the same instant, but Rajmani called on him.

"B.—it reflects light. Actually," Darius went on, "it absorbs every other color except red, which it reflects." He swallowed.

The Darius troops let out a loud whoop, causing my father to turn around abruptly and ask them to be quiet. I heard his voice and the word *concentrate*.

Rajmani nodded. "The distance between two consecutive crests or troughs on a wave is called the: A., wavelength, B., amplitude, or C., frequency?"

"Amplitude," I yelled.

"Incorrect. Darius?"

"That would be wavelength."

"That is the right answer," said Father Rajmani. I couldn't look at my parents. There were two questions left. I tried to imagine a vacuum as a way of relaxing, to conjure a velvety black void—a technique my father used before giving lectures at conferences. But Darius caught my attention; he was hunched over the table, his backside off the chair, finally nervous.

"Whispering creates sounds of about: A., five decibels, B., twenty decibels, C., seventy decibels?"

Darius rose with both hands in the air and said loudly, "Five!"

"Correct. Final question." Rajmani rocked onto the balls of his feet.

We were tied. The hall turned silent save for the mechanical whir of the fans. I looked around at the card tables loaded with flashing LEDs and chemical glassware. My volcano emitted wispy strands of smoke. My father was saying something to my mother and I wondered what those words could be. The priest's voice came to me like a television from an adjacent room—dull and filtered.

"Who devised the general theory of relativity? A., Copernicus, B., Einstein, C., Oppenheimer, or D., Newton?"

The question was so easy that I didn't even need to think. Einstein was evoked in our house as a guardian spirit, warding off the non-relative. Although general relativity evaded me in its subtleties, I knew who was responsible for it as surely as I knew our telephone number. I shot up my hand before Darius and stood, because I wanted the full effect of the hall audience exploding to life. I wanted to see Darius's father, the shrink, walk to the back of the hall and put his rats inside a shoe box; I wanted to see my mother kiss my father in public. I stared at the clock on the rear wall, the luminous face, the needle-like hands, and I caught a flash of the years that lay ahead of me—chemistry sets for every birthday, each one surpassing the last in its complexity; late-night drives with my father, talking about the half-spin of quarks, about the density of black holes; summer vacations to NASA and the Stanford Linear Accelerator instead of Disneyland; road trips that traversed points of scientific interest; he might even take me to Newfoundland so I could stand in the very spot where Marconi made his first transatlantic radio transmission.

My father hunched forward and my mother clutched his arm.

"Oppenheimer," I said.

The Darius crowd was out of their seats, waiting to rush the stage.

"Incorrect. Darius, for the match, do you know the answer?"

Darius looked at me for the first time during the quiz. We both knew that I knew the answer, and he hesitated, wondering. He looked down at his own father, who was already inching toward the stage. I believe in that moment Darius also saw what could lie ahead for him. Already he spent his summers at a science camp where smart boys in shorts fired Bunsen burners and filled beakers with boric acid and smoked their fathers' cigars out in the piney woods. Things would only get worse. If he was a genius, he was destined to be the worst kind—the slow and plodding, the salaried, the unrecognized. A prophecy that was already beginning to show in his body: he was the only seventh grader with stooped shoulders.

"Not only can I tell you the answer but I also can tell you about the general theory," Darius said.

"Just the name is fine, Darius," Rajmani said.

"Albert Einstein."

"Correct. Congratulations."

Rajmani shook our hands and gave Darius a trophy—a pair of bronzed petri dishes suspended like the scales of justice. Darius trotted down the steps into open embraces. Students began packing up their ant farms and crystal radio sets. Families loaded into station wagons and minivans. A janitor was already at work on the balloons and posters. I stayed in my seat. My parents walked onto the stage, unsure of how to approach me. My father placed his fingertips on the edge of the table where I sat. I looked up at him.

"You knew, right?" he asked. "Of course you knew."

I couldn't move.

"Well," he said, "not to worry. We'll dive a little deeper into this area over the summer . . . perhaps a camp or two. Now we better get the volcano home . . . before that lava congeals . . . " His voice trailed off as he started for the stairs. I could hear my mother breathing beside me; she was sitting in Darius's chair.

"No more science camps," I said. My mother took my hand and held it; she'd seen this coming. She no longer stayed up late, making my father and me hot chocolate and serving us pie as we pored over undulating sine waves or squat letter variables. She knew it wasn't a cathedral we were building; it was a chapel at best, maybe a shanty made of driftwood. My father stopped and turned on the stage stairs, but did not turn around completely. He spoke as if to someone in the wings. "Our minds are not our own, Nathan. They belong to the universe. No different than ozone or black holes."

My mother placed her hands flat on the table. "Oh, stop it, Samuel. Stop making him jump through all these hoops. Just let him be himself." I could feel a biting pain in the back of my neck. My father played with a button on his shirt, then raised his eyes briefly, like a man offering a somber good morning. He walked to the back of the hall, foisted my volcano, and left a trail of smoke as he carried it out to the car.

# ten

After the science fair, I stopped attending the whiz-kid camps and began to spend more time with Max and Ben. We roamed on bicycles, carved wooden figurines with pocketknives, chased tennis balls into storm drains. None of us, during early and midpuberty, were good with girls. Our exploits centered on a rock quarry and a swimming hole behind our property. Max was the leader, bespectacled, tan, and barefoot; Ben was the sidekick, squat and needle-voiced, the butt of many jokes; and I was the audience, the observer. My father may not have engendered a rigorously analytical mind in me, but he had given me some of his distance, occasional moments when I felt as if I'd been sent among the living to record their deeds.

"Attack the fort, Nate. We'll hurl these rocks at Ben over there!" Max roared at me one summery day at the rock quarry. I was staring down at the sandstone and quartz shards that crunched under our feet. His enthusiasm baffled me.

"Let's build things," I said. "A rock temple."

Max spread his lips in disgust. "We've got a man in there waiting to be captured." He charged toward the rock mound where Ben lay in wait. In a moment I heard Ben yowl, rushing from behind the mound, holding his head. For Max the rocks were simply weapons. I hated to admit it, but a part of me still wondered about what forces of nature, what ancient lava spills and eroded tablelands created these rocks. Max marched out from the rock cover, apologized to Ben, and huffed past me with the disdain he reserved for traitors and double agents. He'd needed an accomplice and I had let him down.

Around this time my mother—capitalizing on her interest in foreign culture and clothes—joined and soon headed the Levart (*travel* backward) Club, which met in members' living rooms and discussed world destinations. They cooked Indian, Thai, and Greek, collected foreign handicrafts, and planned group vacations. Some afternoons I would come home to a dimly lit house smelling of coriander and sweet basil, and a dozen housewives nursing glasses of wine in the parlor. I could picture these women sitting on far-flung beaches, reading racy novels in the sun. One night, during a Polynesian Island meeting, I heard my mother say, "Imagine wearing a skirt made from hibiscus flowers!" She sat on the couch in a tartan skirt and jade earrings, her legs crossed, her cheeks flushed with wine. The other ladies smiled and nodded and I could tell my mother enjoyed these interactions. She'd spent too many years holed up with her stoic husband and her faltering son. Now she was finding something for herself, even if it was sitting among middle-class housewives and being vaguely scandalized by her bare-chested, tribal cousins.

My father spent his evenings with Charles Mingus and obscure physics problems. In the mornings, he left for the college before I was awake. We ate dinner together and found it difficult to talk. For years we'd spoken of this contest and that math program over my mother's elaborate cooking. Now we struggled to find new ground. At the dinner table he often stared at his place mat or out the windows at the orchard. One night, after a sprawling silence, my mother said, "Samuel, could you make the slightest effort to live on this planet? Could you? Would it kill you to ask us about our days and chat about the weather or current affairs?"

My father looked up from his place setting and smiled meekly. "How is everybody?"

My mother said, "It's too late now. Learn your lines for next time." My mother gave me the dish of chicken cacciatore to hand to my father. "Give your father more, please, Nathan." He was being punished with food. I took hold of the glazed dish. It was painted a Moroccan blue, little islands of chicken floating off a sapphire shore. Without looking at my father, I heaped some chicken pieces and sauce onto his plate while he held his silverware plaintive and upright. He said, "You both treat me like a child." My mother, retreating to the kitchen with some dishes, said, "And why do you think that is?"

My father and I sat in silence and continued to eat.

MY PARENTS WERE MARRIED THREE months after they met. During and immediately after college in Madison, my mother had dated dentists, businessmen, and trial lawyers, older men who went trout fishing at their summer cabins and made alimony payments. I wonder now if these men were father figures, if they represented an orphan's misplaced affections. They had names like Brewster Macintosh and Jimmy Butterworth. I think she planned to marry well and have lots of children. She had dreams of living abroad, of joining the diplomatic corps. Then Aunt Beulah died and left her the house. My mother couldn't bear to sell it or rent it out, so she moved back to her hometown. Soon after, she met my father at a potluck being hosted by a college professor's wife. My father, fresh from graduate school at Stanford, was an assistant professor of physics at the college.

"He was standing all by himself with a plate of mashed potatoes," my mother had told me once. "Back then his beard was almost stylish. I think they called it a Van Dyck beard. He was all dressed in black and looked like a Basque poet. Anyway, he finally got up the gumption to walk across the room and talk to me. We were the only unmarried people there."

"Did he ask you if you'd like to solve some quadratic equations and order pizza sometime?" I asked.

"Believe it or not he asked me if I'd like to go hear some modern jazz. He was very shy but I liked that. He spoke softly and precisely, and when he listened I felt like I could have told him anything in the world."

My mother folded her arms and smiled when she told me that. I tried to picture my parents flirting in a room full of tweed. I imagined them in Madison, sitting in smoky basement clubs listening to difficult, off-tempo jazz. What did they *talk* about? Had my father once been capable of charm? Now, fifteen years and one mildly gifted son later, they had little to talk about. They were prone to epic silences and kept up their little hostilities like rubbed bronze.

IF MY FATHER WAS MORE distracted after the science fair, he also tried to make contact again in his own way. He made regular trips to the Stanford Linear Accelerator, where he was working on a collaboration project. Sometimes he re-

turned like a gambler walking away from a heavy
hands jammed in pockets, red-eyed and slumped. He spo
of endless data, the bumps that didn't quite pan out, the
physicists who were making bigger breakthroughs. On those
returns I sometimes saw my father stand in the adolescent
grunginess of my bedroom (my mother had mostly relin-
quished title to my room), watching me. I don't know how
often this occurred, but he stood there with his hands in his
pockets, maybe thinking about the blue-lit collisions of electrons, about copper wires that edged out of the San Andreas
Fault, and he stared at me while I pretended to be asleep. I
can't really say what he was thinking, but it's enough to
know that he came up there for comfort, to check on me in
some way, to assure himself after banging subatomic particles together that his son was still breathing under the aus-
pices of gravity and motion.

My father began to spend more time with Whit Shupak,
a colleague from the physics department who had been re-
cently divorced. Whit, a fellow home-brewing enthusiast,
was the originator of the brain-food recipe. He was also a retired air force major and onetime astronaut who'd spent two
months in a fixed orbit in space in the early seventies. The
rumor was he'd had some kind of a breakdown when he was
up there spinning and had never been the same since. My
parents seemed to have adopted him; he started hanging
around the house, staying for dinner, and, eventually, sleeping several nights a week in our guest room.

If by nothing else, my father was intrigued by the fact
that Whit had seen our small blue planet from a distance.
Also, he was someone who was comfortable with obscurity
and distance. For my mother, Whit was an admirer of her
cooking and an eternal fix-it man. Whit was happiest in the
throes of an obscure and long-overdue errand or repair—

chopping down dead trees in the orchard, removing wasp nests from the rafters, varnishing outdoor furniture. When I asked my mother why Whit was always around, she said, "Ever since space, Whit's been looking for a unit to join. He's one of those people who can't be alone."

Whit had bright red hair, a square-set jaw, and a wrestler's stride and swagger. He coasted on the tails of his one jaunt in space like a rock star who's had a single smash hit. At parties and potlucks and barbecues there was Whit buttonholing a Levart husband with stories of take-off g-forces and Earth vistas, reaching for a fork to illustrate the angle of ascent, talking of the space dust that finally sent him a little nuts.

"Never been the same since. Something in all that spinning . . . " He turned and whirled his hands through the air, like a slow-motion disco move.

When Whit walked in our orchard, he pulled apples straight from the trees to eat them. One day, staring at the red McIntosh in his hand, he muttered about his ex-wife, who'd left him, or so he said, for another astronaut—Chip Spates, an actual moon lander. "Good riddance to old luggage," he said.

Whit, my father, and I were walking toward the creek. Behind us, twenty Levarters gathered at wooden tables, eating yams and spit-roasted pork. The meal had a Hawaiian theme. It was dusk; clouds banked across the sky. My father and I were still standoffish with each other.

Whit said, "When I was in orbit they gave us these little squirt tubes of applesauce. I used to dream of the genuine article—a gigantic Granny Smith."

By now I'd heard every imaginable story of Whit's training and his six weeks in orbit: the stress-making machines, the large centrifuge called the wheel that flung Whit around at the navy's Acceleration Laboratory, the in-flight meals he called TV dinners, the gravity-free dreams, the death chill of the moon.

It was in this setting, in the silence of space orbit, Earth's continents adrift below him, that Whit first took up writing poetry. Unfortunately, a trait that afflicted his speech also damaged his verse: malapropism. Whit constantly used words and expressions incorrectly. *It's a doggy-dog world. That's just an old wise tale. It's a mute point.* After a good night's sleep he was known to comment that he'd slept like a house on fire. The only poem I ever read was entitled "Space Recipes" and began with the line "Up here in the dark, far from the poi-holloi . . . " It was a celestial lament for home cooking. My mother loved that poem.

The three of us walked through the trees, away from the party. Whit spoke from the side of his mouth at me. "Truth is, Nathan, space is a great teacher. All my best lessons were learned up there. Solitude. Stars for amigos. That's not every man's idea of a night out."

"I'm envious," said my father, putting his hands in his pockets.

"I'd like to go back up, personally. But NASA is becoming like Lloyd's of London—way too conservative. Risk is what got us to the moon in the first place, dang it." Whit generally allowed himself three ways to swear: *dang it, hiney,* and *cripes.*

"Did you take photos up there?" I asked.

"A few. But most of my photos are right here," he said, knocking against his temple.

The Levart people were playing hula music and a couple of them shimmied with glasses of rum-spiked tropical punch in their hands. Whit looked over at them. "Natives are getting rested," he said.

"Sometimes I think the Levart Club is just an excuse to get drunk," my father said matter-of-factly.

Whit said, "You're getting cynical, Samuel. These people crave exotic gods and zesty cooking. Anybody can see that."

We walked along the creek toward a hill that pitched abruptly. We climbed it and stood on a ridge, facing west. The banks of cloud had turned from pewter to bands of saffron and purple. We sat down on the grass, watching.

"Pretty sunset," I said.

My father and Whit looked at each other, then my father said, "We really can't use that kind of terminology anymore."

Whit sighed.

"What terminology?" I asked.

"*Sunset*. You see, when Whit was up there, dangling in space, watching our planet spin, he was reminded that, for the most part, we're the ones that are moving. The sun doesn't set or rise."

"I know that," I said.

"We prefer to call them *earth dips* and *earth rises*. Still not quite accurate, but much more sensible," Whit said.

I polished the apple I'd been carrying and went to take a bite. Whit took it from me. He held it up, tilted it on its axis, and began to turn it.

"Sometimes things move so gradual-like that you don't even notice. Out there, Earth's a big ol' bowling ball coming down the lane at you." A brief silence fell over us as the light crested, then receded.

"*Earth dip* sounds weird," I said.

"Things can be weird and true," my father said to the descending darkness.

Whit said, "You expect the sun out there to be kind of yellow. No, that would be incorrect. It's more of a bluish white, and perfectly round. Actually, it reminded me of the huge arc lights we used to have back at the Cape. It was so bright I had to use filters to look directly at it."

"So what does the earth dip look like from out there?" I asked.

"Good, see, he'll catch on," Whit said. He leaned forward, nodded at the horizon. "Well, I first witnessed it over the Indian Ocean. The sun seemed to flatten out a bit just as it *appeared* to sink, and a black shadow moved across the earth until all the part facing me was dark, except for this ring of light on the horizon. Earth kept spinning and the more it moved the more the sun band turned from white to orange. But there was red, purple, and light blue thrown in there. Made my blood freeze. A diamond sun-blast. I expected angels to appear."

"Can I have my apple back?" I asked.

"No problemo." Whit handed it back to me.

We sat on that ridge until it was dark and the North Star appeared above our heads. Whit spoke about families of fractionally charged particles. "They keep a low profile. Edge out of the muck when you least expect, hit a home run from an electron traveling at twenty clips." And my father saying, "Yes, somehow they snuck up on us. Fractionally charged— imagine growing half an apple." He said this and they both paused, considering that unlikely statistical probability. From the orchard we could see the Levart people lighting lanterns and hear the faint sound of exotic music lifting into the air.

# eleven

It was 1984. The year that two astronauts made the first untethered space walk and two physicists were awarded the Nobel Prize for their role in discovering new subatomic particles. Field particles W and Z. They sounded like courtroom exhibits, indictments against my father's line of work. "I know these fellows from conferences. A Dutchman and an Italian. I shared some collision data with them one time," he said blandly on the morning of the Nobel announcement. I thought at the time he might have been inflating his own work, but when I go back and read the scientific journals of that period I see that he was right: the name Samuel Nelson is mentioned in the same articles that trace the experiments that yielded the Nobel Prize.

It was also the year that my father destroyed the mystery and scandal of sex for me. It happened after my mother found a magazine called *Ribald* under my bed and demanded that my father have a talk with me. The magazine was open to a page in which a man and woman were engaged in what my mother called "mutual oral gratification." She called my father and me up to the bedroom, holding the magazine with two fingers.

She said, "He had this stashed under his bed, Samuel." I had been reduced to third person.

My father was holding a copy of *Scientific American* in one hand; she had roused him from his study. My mother handed *Ribald* to my father and he took it with some dismay, staring down at the fellatio tableau. She made a clicking noise with her tongue and said, "I think you should have a talk with him, Samuel. A man-to-son." She left the room and closed the door behind her. I expected my father to be panicked, but he calmly set his own magazine down on my dresser and crossed to my bed slowly, holding the porn magazine firmly with two hands, as if it weighed as much as a city phone book. I sat in a chair opposite him. He flipped through the pages, registering only curiosity at each turn.

"They seem to have a thing for biracial couples," he said.

"I guess," I said.

"Puberty is a wake-up call to the neurotransmitters. You know what Whit calls sex?"

"No."

"Wow-time. Never stops thinking about it."

"What do you call it?" I asked.

"I don't know. It never really—" He paused, turned the magazine on its side. "This kind of thing interests you?"

"A little."

He turned a picture toward me: a man with a ponytail having sex with a woman against a tree. "You have any questions?"

"Not really."

"Keep the magazines away from your mother. Try the garage. She never goes in there."

He got up from my bed, grabbed his own magazine, and plodded down the stairs, back toward his study to read about new developments in polystyrenes while listening to Coltrane's *Giant Steps*. Part of the mystique of sex was destroyed for me by his casualness. At least my mother's puritan discomfort on the topic had the hope of keeping pornography a going concern for my adolescent interest. For a while following, Ben, Max, and I huddled in our garage, amid defunct lawn mowers and appliances, home-brewing supplies, and discarded toilet seats, flipping through yellowed and dog-eared porn magazines. In the winter, with our condensate breath—dragon smoke, we called it—heavy and misting in front of us, we appraised every scenario in terms of viability, argued about whether a woman's leg could really endure that position, debated whether a penis could really be that large and angled. We sketched diagrams on the concrete floor, plotted, poised index fingers to underscore a crucial point. We conjectured and hypothesized about sex between various couples, between our parents, between family pets.

Then, shortly after, Ben and Max defected and both got girlfriends. To make matters worse, Whit Shupak—ever the congenial fix-it man—threatened to clean out the garage. The thought of our porn collection contributing to Whit's wow-time depressed me, so I burned the lot out behind the orchard. It felt like the end of an era.

# twelve

My father, when he arrived with Whit, didn't seem to know what went on in hospitals. He reeled at the sight of gurneys and bandaged head wounds. As he entered my room, pale and washed out under the white fluorescence, he went stone-faced. His eyes stammered between my bed and the illuminated machines.

"Hey, little Indian," Whit said, standing at the end of the bed. Somehow, his voice was bright, stippled, and orange.

My father touched my mother's shoulder briefly and came to stand beside me, glancing at the IV bag suspiciously. I stared at the cross weave of his beard, the gray and black threads leading to his mouth. "Hello, son," he said. "Cynthia, what are all these machines for? Is he getting enough oxygen?"

"Be positive," my mother said. "Keep the conversation . . . *general*."

"Very well," my father said, berated. "A general sort of talk. Nathan, you might be interested to know that the Stanford Linear Accelerator—can he hear me? What is that coming out of the bag, Cynthia?"

"Glucose and something else. They say he might understand but is in some kind of shock," she said.

Whit said to me, "Hey, I got you a present." He placed a small box on the bed tray and slid it closer to me. I studied the gold paper, the neatly folded corners. "Open it," Whit said.

"I don't think he can," my father said.

"Nonsense," my mother said. She took my hands and placed them on the gold box. "Nathan, would you like to rip this paper up and see what's inside?"

I nodded once. They smiled and my mother put her hand to her throat, moved. It was the first sign. My mother slid my hands over the box, along the edges, and rippled the paper. A tear appeared and I stuck my fingers inside it, pulling it toward me. My fingers and hands were clumsy; my skin felt loose over the joints. I grappled with the cardboard box— about the size of a shoe box—and removed the lid. Inside was a long plastic needle, attached to some kind of engine.

"I made it from a model," said Whit. "It's just like the spaceship I went up in."

"Very sweet," said my mother.

"Boosters still attached, configured as if it's just left Earth," Whit added.

"A rocket ship. Good," my father said.

Everyone, including me, had forgotten that I was seventeen.

Whit took the spaceship from me, launched it, and began to fly it around my bed with his hands—up toward the ceiling, sweeping across my pillow, then coming to land, vertically, on the terrain of my stomach. I shot out a laugh, surprised. My father suddenly said, "Nathan, do you know who we are?"

"Don't rush things," my mother warned.

"Two feet on the ground," Whit said.

"I just want to know," my father said. He leaned close to my face, his breath bitter and warm, and tried to make eye contact. I was staring out the window at a squirrel scurrying and leaping in the treetops.

"Nathan, look at me a minute. Do you know who I am? I am your father and I taught you algebra and geometry in our kitchen when you were seven. Do you remember how to graph a parabola? Just nod if you do," he said.

"Stop it, Samuel," my mother said.

My father grabbed the bedrail with both hands. I pointed at the window; I wanted them to see what I saw.

Whit said, "There's a squirrel out there. Hi, little guy! He's a fat little booger."

"We're strangers to him," my father said. "You raise a son, you teach him things—"

"He can hear you," my mother said.

"And in the end it's all for nothing because time steals everything. My son is alive but most probably damaged in some way. This is the argument against a moral God. Right here in this room. I won't—I will not understand it."

"You will not say another word," my mother said.

"Samuel, come with me and we'll get you some coffee," Whit said.

"I'm sorry," my father said. "I don't know why I said those things. Nathan, I don't know. I promised myself I would talk about positive things like picnics and an article I read on people who take warm baths and how it makes them live longer. I'll get coffee and come back and I'll say some general, chitchatty things." He stood and walked out of the room with Whit. From the corridor I heard him say, "This was not supposed to happen."

# thirteen

**B**ut it did happen. Earlier that summer, my mother went on a tour of the Greek Islands with her Levart group and my father, Whit, and I went to stay with my grandfather, Pop Nelson, in the Upper Peninsula of Michigan. We drove my mother to the airport before heading north. Whit drove because he liked to play pilot, his aviator sunglasses capturing the day's glare. My father sat up front, reading a journal, and my mother sat in back with me. "I'll call when I get into Athens," she said.

"Do they even have phones in Greece?" Whit asked.

"Very funny," she said. "The Greeks invented democracy and medicine."

Whit said, "I don't see them sending any rockets to the moon." He rolled down his window and considered the passing traffic.

"Everything will be fine," my father said, putting away his journal. "We'll be with Pop for three weeks. We'll be back in time to pick you up from the airport."

"I'm nervous," said my mother.

"Chew gum on the plane," Whit offered.

"You heard the man," my father said, turning to touch her knee.

We pulled beside the curb at the airport. My father got my mother's bags from the trunk and stood holding them in each hand. My parents stood together on the sidewalk, saying good-bye, and I saw my mother brush some dandruff from my father's shoulder. I had to look away. I could hear them speaking.

"You could have come," she said.

"What would I do in Greece?"

"Relax on the beach."

"A physicist with a tan could never be taken seriously."

I turned back to see my mother smiling.

"Make sure Nathan eats properly. God only knows what your father has in his cupboards," she said.

"Good-bye, Cynthia." He touched the sleeve of her cardigan.

"I'll call."

"Yes, call us, good, you'll telephone." He handed her the bags.

They kissed mildly on the lips and my father squeezed her shoulders. Whit gunned the engine, stuck his arm out the window, and patted the exterior of the door as if it were a horse's flank. I noticed a group of fifteen men and women from the Levart group were gathered by the curbside check-in, waiting with sun hats fastened and sleeves rolled up. My mother opened my door and leaned inside.

"Be good," she said.

"What trouble can I find in Michigan? Helping Pop build a model warship isn't going to get me arrested."

"Don't let your father quarrel with your grandfather."

"I'll do my best. Plus Whit will put anyone who steps out of line in a headlock."

Whit smiled and nodded from the front seat.

She kissed me on the forehead and closed the car door. She waved at Whit—who honked once—before joining her travel companions. A nervous, chatty woman I recognized from the meetings held at our house was dispensing complimentary document pouches with the Levart seal: a palm tree silhouetted against a pale blue sky.

POP NELSON WAS A WIDOWER, living in an old brick house near the shores of Lake Michigan. He was a small-town man with strong opinions, and when he walked down a busy sidewalk he was never the one to yield to an opposing pedestrian. He walked square-shouldered, like a soldier. Twice a week he ate a counter lunch at the local drugstore with the town's fire chief. When he came home in the afternoons, he emptied the coins from his pockets and dropped them into a mason jar on the top of the television. Clink. *Another day spent.*

That my father was this man's son puzzled me. My father stood a bony six feet tall. Pop Nelson was short with cropped hair, a drinker's flush in his cheeks, and a belly that sat snug behind jeans and suspenders. Pop Nelson drank Miller High Life and Budweiser while my father brewed his own porters and amber ales. Pop Nelson was religious—well, at least he believed in the fury of God—and my father was an atheist. Nothing of the father echoed in the son. I wondered how my father had become the awkward, socially withdrawn scientist as the son of an ex–naval officer who could talk to gas station attendants and pretty girls in department stores. My father had three brothers, all of them older. They had all moved to California and New Jersey, and the few times I met them at reunions and weddings I remembered them as lumbering men with wisecracks and firm handshakes and buxom wives. A stockbroker, a pilot, a policeman. They called my father Sammy. Perhaps the bravado of the older brothers and Pop Nelson had forced my father inward. He was an introverted kid with asthma. When my grandmother died—a churchly woman with an active, generous mind—my father was still in grade school and suddenly there was nothing feminine and thoughtful in the house. I pictured him as a rangy kid in his room with a chemistry set and a box of magnifying glasses, trapped in a house filled with fly-fishing poles and cross-country skis.

It was much more conceivable that Whit was Pop's son and, predictably, Pop took to Whit. They were both ex-military, keen fishermen, suspicious of big government. One evening Pop took Whit down to his basement workshop, where he was building a 1:350 scale model of the USS *Massachusetts*. He had a collection of modern and vintage warships down there. I saw them from the top of the stairs: two men gazing at gun turrets and miniature rivets, putting their fingers inside access hatches, crouching behind to-scale gun sights. Their voices, softened by laughter and cigar smoke, uncoiled through the house.

I passed my father in the hallway. He stopped and looked at me as a burst of camaraderie came from the basement. He said, "Would you like to play a game of chess?" There was a slight edge to his voice. I wondered if he was jealous and wished he'd been invited to see the warships.

"Sure," I said, though I really wanted to watch television.

"Good. I'll get us some ice cream while you set up the board."

I walked toward the living room while he lingered for a moment, listening at the top of the basement stairs.

THE FOUR OF US SPENT the days fishing in a small lake behind Pop Nelson's property. Oddly, he never fished in

Lake Michigan. "Too much like the ocean," he said. Pop had been in the navy for twenty years. He owned two small dinghies and we paired up in different combinations to fish. The first day I went with Pop Nelson, just after sunrise. Pop didn't speak until the sun was high enough to make him squint. He rested his feet on the tackle box and watched for ripples.

"Your father doesn't believe in God. I suppose you know that," he said.

Pop had given up discussing religion directly with my father; now he was going through me. Once, during a heated argument, my father called the Pope a phony and Pop Nelson threw a soupspoon at him.

"Yeah," I said. "He believes in the unified field." According to my father, the unified field was the plane of reality where all forces merged, where all matter and energy pulsed into being. Gravity, electricity, even radiation were mere waves in this undulating, unified ocean.

"The what?" Pop growled.

"Where everything is made of the same stuff."

"Call it what you like. It amounts to the same thing . . . atheism . . . godlessness." He took a can of beer out of his cooler and popped it open. He took a long sip. "And what do you believe in?" Pop asked.

A little unsteadily, I said, "I'm still making up my mind."

Pop blew a cloud of smoke over the lake and said, "Can't sit on the fence your whole life, kiddo."

I FISHED WITH MY FATHER at dusk, just as the moon was coming up. Whit was in the other boat with Pop, drifting about thirty feet from us. I could see fireflies on the shore, flashing among the evergreens, and they made me think of the Fourth of July and the fact that I had spent it, lamely, setting off a few Roman Candles on Pop's back acreage. I heard Whit say to Pop, "It's my consensus, Pop, that there hasn't been a good American president since Roosevelt." Then Pop said, "Truman wasn't bad for your nickel."

I turned to my father. "Pop asked me if I believed in God."

"Let the Godspeak begin. I wondered when he'd start in on you."

"He asks me that every time we come."

"What do you say?" my father asked.

"That I'm still trying to decide for myself."

"Good answer."

I dipped my hand into the lake.

My father said, "Pop thinks God's an old guy with a beard and an ulcer and a scoreboard."

I said, "Maybe God does keep score."

"If He existed, why would He bother?"

Whit and Pop drifted closer.

"Are you two fishing or clap-trapping?" Pop asked.

"We're talking about God the Almighty, actually," my father said. The tone was snide and pompous and I could see Pop sneer, even in the half-light.

"Good, because I was thinking that maybe Nathan could come to church with me sometime while you're here."

"Up to him," my father said, looking away. "He's old enough to decide for himself."

"Well, you've obviously brainwashed the boy so much that he thinks going to church is crossing to the other side. Never understood your stubbornness."

"He goes to a Jesuit school," my father offered.

"Yes, and you contradict everything the Bible says."

"I've made a few corrections, that's right," my father said.

My father took one hand from his rod and touched his beard.

"Well, how about church on Sunday, Nathan? We can go out to eat afterward," Pop said.

"That's cool with me," I said. Pop had told me his church was frequented by Catholic schoolgirls.

"If Nathan wants to go along and hear some old priest mutter in Latin, a language, I might add, that conquered and pillaged half the world, then he's welcome to," my father said.

Pop Nelson's neck went taut. "They don't speak Latin anymore. The odd phrase, that's all."

Whit said, "Look at that crescent moon. We're crossing into the shadow."

"You never respected anything. A fine example for your son," Pop said.

"Don't start with me," my father warned.

Their boat drifted closer. I realized that Pop Nelson was drunk. He stood in the back, wobbled a moment, then threw a piece of fish bait at my father. It landed in his beard—a dripping, smelly morsel. My father removed it calmly and dropped it over the side. Pop was no more than six feet from my father, still standing, arms gripped by his side. He had a small tattoo on his right forearm—an eel the size of a post-age stamp—and in the waning light it looked to me as if it were preparing to swim up his arm. Suddenly my father picked up his oar and whacked Pop across the back of the legs. It wasn't a brutally hard strike, but enough to send Pop, in his inebriated state, over the side.

"Fucker!" Pop yelled.

"Man down!" Whit bellowed. He reached out to Pop with his oar but Pop didn't take it. Somehow, Pop still had a beer can in one hand. Whit and my father both jumped into the water at the same time. Pop didn't look like he could drown; his chin broke the surface and he was swearing enough that he must have been getting air. "Ignorant son of a bitch!" "Godless skinny punk!" Whit and my father grabbed an arm each and pulled Pop to the side of the other boat. Whit got into the boat and helped Pop scramble aboard.

Pop began wringing his wet clothes, saying nothing. He reached for both oars and rowed toward the shore. Whit waved to us as he was pulled into the shallows.

"I don't think that was a wise thing to do," I told my father.

"He's the most irrational man that ever lived," he said, spitting water.

Pop Nelson and my father didn't speak to each other for the next two days.

THE FOLLOWING EVENING WHIT AND I fished alone. Pop had gone to have dinner with a lady friend who owned a feed store in town, and my father was reading inside the house and listening to *The Benny Goodman Story*—the only jazz album he could find in Pop's country-and-western-dominated collection. Whit and I fished for some time without catching anything before Whit reeled in a large catfish. He unhooked it and threw it back in the lake. When he recast his rod, I asked him what he thought about my father and Pop Nelson's behavior.

"Hotheads," he said.

"Mom always sits them at different ends of the table at Thanksgiving."

"Samuel is a great thinker. I've never seen him get so hot under the turban." Whit swayed his fishing rod in the breeze. "The question of God is an interesting one. When I was up there I saw this thing, it was like a cloud of jellyfish. I radioed to the Cape and they didn't know what it was. Glow-things, jellyfish, floating in space. Luminescent, I guess. They were so tiny that they didn't make any noise when they hit my ship . . . "

"What's that got to do with God?"

"Oh, that's a good one. 'What's that got to do with God?' Perfect." He reeled in a yard of line. "I saw four earth dips and rises in twenty-four hours. They were about the shortest days I've run into. You don't need to believe in gravity to take a ride in an airplane."

I nodded but I had no idea what he meant. Now he was talking about Cape Canaveral and the room where astronauts waited before a mission.

"We had this nurse, Delores, and she decorated the room where I spent those last few minutes on Earth. Room S205, inside the hangar. She thought the colors should be relaxing and restful—robin's-egg blue on the walls and champagne-colored drapes and beige nylon couches. TV, radio, a clock. But you know what I did in there for forty-five minutes?"

"What?"

"Three things: I shaved one last time. I took an epic dump. And I prayed as if my life depended on it. Time stops and God listens in that room."

Whit caught another catfish. I imagined for a moment that it was the same one he had caught just moments earlier. You couldn't help being drawn into the dimly lit theater of Whit's mind; even fish found themselves listening. It was getting dark. The lake was fringed with trees and their shadows lengthened across the sandy shore. Whit put the fish back. I was seventeen and, in a sense, paralyzed about the question of God. I didn't want to decide whether flashing data-bytes and streaming photons were part of a divine plan, threads in a conspiracy of meaning, or just part of a random cosmos studded with variety.

TO CHURCH POP NELSON WORE his Sunday best: a gray suit worn thin in the elbows and a tie with the U.S. Navy insignia on it. I wore a pair of jeans and a polo shirt. We drove in his red Ford pickup through countryside of pine ridges and old copper mines. Already at ten in the morning it was hot and cloudless. He smoked a thin cigar on the way, and I noticed a stash of beer cans in a cooler behind the front seat. I wondered if he drank beer for breakfast and whether my father realized that he drank in his car. In the last few years, Pop's drinking had taken a turn. We drove with the windows down, without talking. Pop's face was bleak in the morning light, a man about to deliver a dreaded apology.

When we got into town we parked behind the St. Ignatius Catholic Church. It was a sandstone building with tall windows and a small bell tower. We were among the first to arrive. Inside, it seemed familiar: the smell of frankincense and candles, the stained-glass depictions of downtrodden saints and rising angels, and, in the corner, an organ ruminating at the hands of a woman in her eighties. As we entered, we dipped our hands in holy water and made the sign of the cross. I noticed Pop looking back at me as I performed the holy gesture. He led me to a pew near the front of the church.

"This is a traditional Catholic church," he said. "Not like some around here."

I picked up the hymnbook in front of me; it smelled of old newspapers. I flipped through some pages and recognized the same songs, the same phrases that I'd heard caroled at St. John's—*Glory to the heavens, prevailing peace, Almighty God*. The church was half full when the robed priest came out to the altar, but sadly all the Catholic girls must have been away at camp or the 4-H club. The congregation was a clutter of retirees and young families with whiny children. The priest was a tall man with a pointed nose and a perfectly trimmed mustache. He spoke mostly in English, but occasionally intoned in Latin. It was possible that I understood more of the Latin than Pop Nelson, since I'd been forced to learn some basics at school. *A Deo lux nostra*—Our light comes from God. *Ad majorem Dei glorium*—To the greater glory of God, the Jesuit motto. Pop's face was focused; he sat straight-backed, eyes set in concentration. He watched the priest handle the communion bread and wine carefully, unblinking, the way he looked at miniature turrets and patches of sailcloth, the ballasted ship hulls in his basement.

When it came time to kneel and pray he let out an arthritic sigh and lowered himself onto his knees. I knew from Pop's navy stories that he had a bung knee—not from active duty, but from a first officer named Tripper who launched a baseball into Pop's right kneecap during an on-leave game. Pop squeezed his eyes shut and tightened his lips. The priest prayed aloud. Sweat appeared on Pop's forehead. Now I knew why he came: punishment. For what I couldn't be sure, but I realized that the times that I'd been to confession, I'd failed to take my penance seriously. Twelve Hail Marys and two Our Fathers didn't seem so much like punishment, more like trivial tasks, shopping errands for a lapsed conscience. For Pop, I could tell it was different. He was convinced that God was taking payoffs.

When church was over, Pop's mood seemed to lighten. He greeted a few of the other parishioners and became jovial. He joked with an old couple that their new Cadillac was too stylish for them. He led me by the shoulder and introduced me around. People seemed to genuinely like him. They laughed at his quips, waited eagerly for his deadpan jibes.

After church, Pop Nelson took me to lunch at Maxwell's drugstore—a combined pharmacy and sandwich counter. We sat on tall stools with chrome legs, ordered hot pastrami sandwiches and chocolate malts. The waitress wore a pink blouse with a name tag: Rosalie. She and Pop Nelson made small talk back and forth—about a new restaurant in town and how good their food was. I sat and listened to him describe to Rosalie a steak he'd eaten in a London pub twenty years earlier, on a rainy Sunday afternoon, a steak perfectly seared, so rare that it was a delicate shade of blue in the middle. She giggled, then swallowed. "You're making me hungry. Stop it!" If only this one gene, the courtesy and small-talk gene, had been passed on to my father, I thought. I left them talking and wandered around the adjacent drugstore. On a high shelf were antique pharmacy items—a mortar and pestle, a rustic beaker, some glass bottles labeled with archaic drug names. The pharmacist was a grim-faced man. This town seemed to be full of them—the sour-faced sons of copper miners. He sat behind a rectangular window on a raised platform, looking like a judge at the bench.

Greeting cards spilled sympathy and consolation in one corner of the store, right next to the foot creams and Band-Aids. When I got bored and Pop Nelson had finished his coffee, we went outside and climbed into his pickup. He rolled his window down and lit a cigar. He insisted that I put my seat belt on, but failed to do the same. He took a beer can from behind his seat and popped it open.

"Churchgoing ain't so bad, is it?" he said.

"It was all right," I said.

"Want a beer?" he asked.

"Sure," I said, with sudden bravado. This was a complicated transaction; I knew it even then. I took the beer and drank from it. He patted my shoulder, confident that I could learn to believe, learn to fear. That he was in a care-free mood after grimacing on his knees made me wonder whether he was onto something—a kind of weekly re-demption that made him a man of light spirits; a man who, after meeting the gaze of the crucified Jesus for an hour, could flirt with waitresses twenty-five years his junior.

The Ford passed through the copper country at a steady clip. We drove with the radio on, drinking beer. Hank Williams's "My Bucket's Got a Hole in It" filled the cabin. I became aware of details. The world moved slowly, as if through a pane of ice. People mowing their lawns, the air thick with grassy fumes. A red bicycle, seemingly unattended, resting upside down on its seat and handlebars by the side of the road, wheels spinning. A dog—a German shepherd—making eye contact as we dashed the bright roadway. The windows open, driving swiftly, wind funneling all around us, the springy warm sound of Hank Williams rising faintly above the roar. It was the hottest day of that summer. Pop Nelson was telling me about the navy.

" . . . in the belly of a boat, you sleep different." He took a long sip from his can and wiped his mouth with the back of his wrist. The grain of skin, the stiff white hairs.

"When I retired I couldn't sleep in a regular bed. Your grandmother bought a tape of ocean noises and played it in the bedroom. I slept on the floor . . . "

A truck hazed toward us, caught up, floating through the sheen of the road. Limbless tree trunks were strapped to the trailer bed.

"I took a lot of baths. Like a kid—"

The radio crooned: *I seen the crabs and the fishes—Doin' the be-bop-bee*

Then the grind and shriek of an engine.

The truck's grill bore down on us with a placard that read: FREEDOM FIGHTER.

I remember my grandfather saying, "What now, for Pete's sake?" as if he were talking directly to God, accusation rising in his voice.

I keep going back to those next few seconds, trying to slow down the mind reel. The details flicker, then rise through the murk of memory. There are disembodied sounds, amorphous and looming, like moans from a shipwreck. The explosion of the radiator, the keening wail of steam, the metallic wrench of the pickup chassis. The granular sound of a million shards of glass as Pop Nelson takes flight like an ejected fighter pilot and launches through the windshield. Liquids—human blood, beer, scalding fluid from the exploded radiator—rain down everywhere. The dash, the drink holders, even the levers and dials are covered. I don't remember the object hitting me in the head. But I remember putting my head slowly to my chest and feeling something cold on the back of my neck. Was I leaning toward my brief death yet? A bracing plunge in the underground river. If so, where was the sense of time compressing into a single moment? Fifteen years later, I sit here in a darkened room of my apartment, watching a family splash around in the motel swimming pool across the street. The kids shriek and dive-bomb and I wonder if we all carry our deaths packaged inside us—the time, the date, the manner—bundled and inert. Maybe what I carried all those years until the accident was not shrewd intelligence or the strange light of genius but the glimmer of my own death. Maybe that was what my parents were really looking at when they stared into my eyes and sensed something extraordinary.

# fourteen

In the aftermath of the coma, I saw spoken words and certain sounds as airborne colored shapes. I didn't tell anyone about this for a while, even when my speech started to return a week after waking up. I spoke a few words at first, then phrases that faltered in the middle, and then complete sentences. My father took this as a cue that I was really back from the dead and decided to tell me that Pop Nelson was no longer with us. We were due to drive back to Wisconsin, where I was booked into a children's hospital for additional testing and observation. In light of the coma and the head injury, the neurologists were taking extra precautions.

My father took me for my first walk outside before we got on the road. It was still summer, but it felt like fall—an unseasonably cool day. The hospital stood surrounded by woods. The air smelled of smoke; some men in overalls were clearing several acres of scrub and brambles nearby. We walked out past the incinerator, where the walkway became a gravel footpath. I was overwhelmed by the sensations around me—woodlarks calling, the sharpness of wood smoke, the descending cool.

My father said, "We can't measure things precisely. If we could, Nathan, we could predict the future based on exact knowledge of the present. We're more interested now in possible outcomes than definite results. Everything is gray."

His voice trailed behind him as a bright yellow line.

"No," I said. "It's not gray."

He looked at me for a second, then extended a hand toward the woods and the sky, a gesture designed to encompass everything, from chlorophyll to ozone. "The world blurs everything together."

"Okay," I said. I'd taken up the habit of saying this whenever a response was expected of me. It became my answer to anything I found confusing.

"Pop is not with us anymore. A lot of different things could have happened during the accident, but what did happen was he died. We buried him at the back of his property near the lake. That's what he wanted. Everybody dies sooner or later."

I nodded at my father slowly, giving him permission to go on.

"I thought you should know. He was my father and your grandfather." He shrugged and folded his arms. "Your mother says I don't feel my emotions. Women say these sorts of things from time to time. Technically, that's not true. I loved him in my own way and I'll miss him."

"I'll miss him, too," I said softly. Something about me, the unaccusing stare, loosened him.

"He was basically a decent man. Drank too much, didn't forgive easily. I always felt like he was standing on the opposite side of a bridge from me. He never understood what I did. As a boy, he bought me model airplanes—World War Two bombers. I made them, assembling each piece at a time, using Q-Tips to spread the glue." He pulled his hands from his pockets, held them poised in front. "Then I would take them in the backyard and drop house bricks on them. I was always more interested in what would happen when they smashed. The sheer force of gravity and acceleration. I wanted to understand why things broke apart the way they did."

He slowed because I was getting out of breath, and we turned back toward the hospital.

"He always thought that it was disrespectful. Later, even when I had a PhD in physics, he thought I was a godless hoodlum with a high IQ."

I remembered Pop on his knees in that small-town church, that when he ate out he ordered a bowl of vanilla ice cream at the same time as dinner. But I couldn't picture him beside me in the car. I could remember eating hot sandwiches and staring at antique pharmacy wares but couldn't picture his face just before he died. It saddened me not to see his face in my mind. He was my link to the ordinary branch of our family and now he was gone.

We neared the hospital doors where Whit and my mother stood in the wan light of the afternoon. My mother held my red suitcase while Whit gripped the shoe box that housed the spaceship. One of the doctors came out and shook my hand. I waved back at the doctor as we made our way to the parking lot. We reached the Oldsmobile and I heard the metal door handle as my father lifted it. My mother placed the red suitcase in the trunk. My father helped me into my seat and buckled me in back, next to Whit. The car doors closed. Metal on metal. The sound of air being drawn inside. My father turning the key in the ignition.

"I don't like this," I said. Heat rose in my stomach and throat, a scalded feeling. I could feel the engine rumble to life, the spin and tension of the fan belt as the instrument panel illuminated a sickly yellow. The small dials, the white needle of the speedometer. I needed out of that car. My father's hands clung to the steering wheel, the rubber grabbing at his palms. I tried to unfasten my seat belt but my fingers slipped off the buckle. I pulled at the metal latch.

"We'll be back in Wisconsin before you know it," my mother said cheerily.

I was burning up. I kicked the back of my father's seat and threw my head against the headrest.

"What *exactly* is happening?" my father asked.

There was a strange taste in my mouth. Whit put his hand on my shoulders, then grabbed my chin like he was trying to prevent an epileptic from swallowing his tongue.

"Get him out!" my mother said.

"Right," said Whit. "Come here, chief." He unbuckled my seat belt and pulled me across the seat toward him, then out the door. As soon as I was clear of the car I took off running for the woods, looking for safety. The air was crisp and bracing. My body came alive. Images flashbulbed through my head—a bright roadway, an old man's wrist. I leaped over brambles and fallen trees, my chest heaving. I could hear someone behind me, chasing, but I didn't want to turn around. I scanned the undergrowth and thickets for strongholds and hiding places. The leaves were dry underfoot, cracking like broken glass. The taste of blood was in my mouth and I realized I'd bitten my tongue. I spat a stream of scarlet on the ground. I could see the men in overalls clearing the stands of scrub up ahead, their fires low-set and bluish through the cross-hatching of tree limbs. Then, a hand at the back of my neck; it was light but definitive, the confident grip of a man who's seen our planet from outer space. I fell to the ground, winded.

"Easy does it, now," Whit said softly. "Breathe easy. Come on, now."

He stood over me. My face was flush against the ground. I could smell the dirt, the composting leaves. The grainy montage of the accident roared with new images—Pop Nelson taking his last sip of beer, the truck already upon us, Pop's broad hand wrapped around the can. My mother and father arrived, their faces aghast. My mother took off her sweater and put it around me. She told my father to go get the doctor. I sat up and looked around. My father set off running toward the building. He fell into a loping jog through the woods—his brown corduroy jacket disappearing now and then in moments of perfect camouflage. Had I ever seen him run before? He returned with a doctor and everyone crouched around me. A light probe shone in my eyes.

"Nathan, can you hear me?" the doctor asked.

"Something about the car," my father said, short of breath.

Pop Nelson let go of the wheel as his body lifted off the seat. I was looking straight at him. His arms swung out wide, then went behind his back. The truck hit us at an angle, severing the rear of the pickup. I watched him take flight, his arms drawn behind him like a felon in handcuffs. The glass windshield didn't shatter so much as explode into a million splinters of light. This was the last image before I died, the last memory of that old life: a blinding radiance before it jump-cuts to black.

# fifteen

In the end they gave me tranquilizers to get me back to Wisconsin. I woke up in the children's hospital with three other boys sleeping in my room. St. Michael's was twenty miles from my house and my parents had gone home to bed. It was the middle of the night. I heard sick children breathing in the small hours, the sound of bodies on the mend, air sifting through the ceiling vents. Out in the corridor there were flickering lights and the faint sound of a television. In the last few weeks I'd spent hours in front of *The Price Is Right, CHiPs,* and *The Love Boat.* After so many years without television in our house, I was mesmerized by anything. I could get lost not only in the words, but in the grain of the screen, the neon pixels. Even though my father hated television ("Random photons swimming in a vacuum tube . . . "), he allowed me to watch all I wanted in the hospital. The sick and the resurrected were apparently entitled to all the mind-numbing programming they could handle.

I stood in the corridor, my legs stiff from sedation. I was in pajamas again; somebody had changed me while I'd been on Valium. The children's hospital was cheerier than the Michigan hospital. There were framed prints of alpine lakes, misty coastlines, and northern cabins dusted in snow. Instead of white, everything was painted sky blue. The nurse stations had Mickey Mouse night-lights. The smells were less intense: lemon instead of ammonia, lavender soap instead of surgical issue.

I walked past a nurse station where a young woman dozed at her desk. The TV lounge was a narrow alcove off the main corridor. Two rows of vinyl chairs faced a color television on a stand. I sat down and pulled my legs beneath me. On-screen, a man stood in front of the state of Wisconsin, pointing at it with his index finger. A mass of cloud swarmed east across the screen, red arrows flashing. *Gusty winds are likely all of tomorrow morning ... afternoon showers, keep the umbrella in the trunk ...* The word *gusty* was white and dull, like a ball of wax. I watched the weatherman's lips move as he spoke, thought I could detect the slightest delay between his mouth moving and the sound.

As the days passed, I soon realized that the nurse at the nearest station fell asleep every night. Lights went out at ten and I waited an hour before stealing down the corridor. Some nights I watched the news and weather, others it was an old Western or sitcom—whatever happened to be on. The theme music from *Jeopardy!* was a parade of cyan discs; Alex on *Family Ties* spoke in platinum waves; Bill Cosby's voice projected a series of royal-blue spheres. The colored shapes and sounds blended together as I flipped channels. Documentaries intercut with infomercials and cowboy adventures, detective shows juxtaposed with cooking classes and gangster movies. Like particle physics and jazz, channel surfing warped time. In the stop-frame dash from one channel to the next, one show bled into another. The voices of

small-time racketeers in fedoras smeared across trivia con-
tests; they were trying to swindle cash prizes and Bermuda
island cruises. TV was the dream of a coma patient—
disjointed, surreal, animated in a kind of chemical way. It
wasn't hard to believe that the sensory assault was coming
from an old man on a gurney somewhere, anesthetized and
drip-fed, the seep of his mind spilling across the screen.

During daylight, I underwent various tests and read a lot
of *Time* magazine. I noticed now that reading, like remembering and hearing, was also different. Words and individual
letters had a distinct form; they had lives of their own: *burn*
resembled an upright man with a mustache; *spare* was flat
and rectangular, a gray floating window; *safe* was something
substantial, a stone house. Every word was married to a
mental image. I had to keep my attention on the string of
words, instead of each one, so I could decode the barrage
and take in meaning. Sometimes I wondered if I was halluci-
nating. I had a recurring fear that before long I would find
myself talking to a colored blob hovering above my bed.

I SPENT SEVERAL WEEKS IN the children's hospital and
consequently missed the beginning of my senior year of high
school. My mother came each lunchtime with pies and strudels and stayed for the afternoon. My father came by after
lectures. The day after my high school went back, he arrived
carrying the senior math book he'd obtained from my
teacher.

"I thought you might want this," he said, setting it gingerly on the bedside table. "The kids and your math teacher
send their wishes."

"Thanks," I said. "I probably won't open it until after I
get out of here."

"No rush," my mother said.

My father said, "Mathematics is no different than the piano. You practice until the structure becomes invisible."

"Maybe if you want to be a concert pianist or a mathematician, that's true," my mother said.

My father shrugged and turned to me. "Have you applied to your colleges yet for next year?"

"Not yet," I said. Earlier in the summer I had been looking into a half dozen schools, from Dartmouth and MIT to the University of Wisconsin in Madison.

My mother said, "Samuel, he's been in a coma."

"I know that, Cynthia. I'm aware."

Not long after, my father brought one of his old slide rules and left it beside my bed, as if, magically, I would pick it up and topple an engineering problem. It reminded me of the way my mother had left her violin in the parlor all those years before, hoping for music. The thought of almost losing me had done something to my father. It resurrected a languishing hope that my mind was just like his.

My mother took me for walks, partly to keep my father from lecturing me on the benefits of knowing thermodynamics before college. The leaves had turned early—sorrell and gold, strewn across the browning lawn of the hospital. There was a fountain and a sundial at the end of a wheelchair path. There was a river lined with limestone boulders behind the main building. She wore Indian paisley scarves and woolen mittens months before winter came. My mother has always felt the cold; her fingers and joints ache when the weather turns. One day, as we walked, she held my hand—something she hadn't done since before I was ten.

"Nathan, I've noticed your father's moods. He's plotting something. The slide rule is not a good sign. Ignore it."

"It's his way of dealing with this," I said.

"Your father doesn't deal with things. That's the whole point. He lives in a universe made for one."

Something about this comment stayed with me. That night in bed I saw my father everywhere on television. He was the outsider—the sackcloth recluse; the pious mendicant; the Confucian kung fu master; the bunkered anarchist; the hillbilly mountain prophet sermonizing from an Appalachian cave; the gold prospecting seer of an old Western; the blind penitent out in the desert; the Crusoe castaway on a lost island, waiting for a ship to pass. In all these personas he walked alone, haltingly, like a man in leg irons. He had a face shaped by solitude—his dead stare and wary mouth, the unlined forehead of a loner. I knew exactly what my mother meant. On some level, my father didn't believe that other people existed.

LATE NIGHTS WITH THE TELEVISION continued. The doctors and nurses knew I left my room after lights out, but they didn't seem to mind. I began reciting dialogue to other patients. The three boys in my room—Woody, brain damaged from a horse accident; Andrew, a football neck injury; and Mitch, who had cerebral palsy and was recovering from surgery on his legs—listened as I spoke from the side of my mouth, imitating gangsters, or talked with the brio of a game-show host. I saw their words flash before me, sometimes with taste and smell. *He was a guy on the lam. He was about to meet with a headache, you understand me?* They would pretend to change channels and I would instantly dissolve into another genre. *The deputy is the man to watch. Watch his hands, I tell you . . .* Click. *The barometer is steady. Temperatures are falling. If it feels uncomfortable, you're not imagining things.* Click. *Fry without oil. Steam is your friend.* Click. *What is Tegulcigulpa?* I continued for hours, the other boys urging me on. I captured the accents and tone of delivery. Words swept across my mind no different than clouds spiraling across America on the Weather Channel.

One night, at the end of fall, they discovered my new talent. Dr. Cleaves, a chain-smoking intern, had watched television with me a few times before. By now I was known as the midnight man. We sat in the vinyl chairs, our feet resting on a coffee table piled with Christian youth magazines. A late-night movie came on—*The Body Snatcher,* with Boris Karloff. Dr. Cleaves went to change the channel, but I held on to the remote control.

"I watched this yesterday," I said. "They must be replaying it."

"Do you want to watch something else?" he asked.

"No, leave it for a minute."

He left the TV on that channel and I leaned in.

I was surprised by how much I remembered as the titles dissolved onto a picture of Edinburgh Castle. I felt I was watching something I'd created in my own head—the bony white horse coming down the lonely street; the young medical student sitting in the abandoned graveyard. Just as Dr. Cleaves was about to change the channel, I began reciting the dialogue, saying each line a moment before the actors. I had their accents and timing down perfectly. I spoke the dialogue between Mrs. McBride and Donald Fettes as they stood by the grave of her newly departed son, a small terrier standing guard.

*He'll not leave the grave—not since Wednesday last when we buried the lad.*

Dr. Cleaves took his feet off the magazines. Sometimes I spoke at exactly the same time as the actors—Mary Gordon and Russell Wade. My voice lilted like hers, contained traces of a working-class Scottish upbringing. His voice, as I mimicked it, was less broad, more earnest: a poor boy making a go of it in the city, becoming a doctor.

"What are you doing?" Jason asked.

I could hear his voice, faintly, and smell the nicotine on his fingertips. He got up from the couch and disappeared for several minutes. When he returned, the sleepy nurse was with him. They sat down beside me, alternately looking at me and the television.

*I'm studying under Dr. MacFarlane—that is, I've been studying until today . . .*

We continued like this for close to an hour. My dialogue echoed theirs, sometimes overlapped. I stared at the screen, transfixed by the filtered light, the gloomy examination rooms where Dr. MacFarlane probed his patients, the gleaming marble tables in the anatomy room. If someone had asked me what the movie was about, I don't know that I could have given an answer. It was like staring too closely at a smudge on a pane of glass, oblivious to the view on the other side. A few other nurses and another intern stood by the wall, watching. Nobody spoke. By the time someone realized it was one in the morning the movie was half over.

*It's because you were afraid to face it—and you're still afraid . . .*

Dr. Cleaves switched off the television, but I continued to recite.

*No, I'm not afraid. Tell! Shout it from the housetops . . .*

"Nathan, it's time to go to bed."

I stared at the blank screen. I could hear the TV's diodes cooling. I clearly saw the Scottish pub where MacFarlane and Gray were having their drunken argument about experiments on the dead. Dr. Cleaves touched my arm and helped me to my feet. The other nurses and the doctor went back to their stations. We walked slowly down the corridor to my room, where the other boys were fast asleep. Their shoes and slippers were placed neatly beside their beds. I got under the sheets and put my hands behind my head.

"Get some rest," Dr. Cleaves said.

He sat there a moment longer, made sure that I was going to fall asleep.

"At the end of the movie you know what happens?" I said.

"No."

"The white horse and carriage go over a cliff," I said.

"It's just a movie."

"I know," I said.

"Get some sleep," he said, walking out into the corridor.

I closed my eyes. The white horse whinnied as the carriage fell toward the sea.

# sixteen

After my TV recital I underwent a battery of memory tests. A neuropsychologist, Dr. Lansky, was brought in from a nearby hospital—a man with a graying goatee and a bald head. He gave me things to memorize: pages from the phone book, restaurant menus, baseball scores. Each time, I recited the information exactly; it didn't matter whether the words came to me through reading or by hearing. He double-checked my X-rays and CAT scans and confirmed that there was no visible change to the brain from the accident. Yet I could now remember thirty pages of a phone book, with names, numbers, and addresses. Initially, I needed somebody to guide me to the information—the first line of a movie, the first name on the phone-book page—then the cascade of images took over.

One day, Dr. Lansky had a cold and as he recited a table of numbers to me, his voice cracked and thickened. Previously, I had been able to recite a series of random numbers, nonsense syllables or meaningful words in any order, forward and backward, so long as I had a few seconds in between each word during the initial memorization. It was simply a matter of laying each word or sound image on a pathway—the street where our house stood—and naming them as I walked along the street in my mind. I laid objects and people on doorsteps, on rooftops, and in swimming pools. Numbers were the easiest to remember because they were all people with a definite gender: *1* a stoic, tall man; *4* a waif of a woman with her arm in a sling; *9* a skinny man with a large head. . . . For some reason on this occasion, Lansky's voice was changing the images, sending splotches across my number-people's faces. I couldn't remember past the first three numbers in the series.

"Having an off day?" he asked.

"Your voice," I said. "Normally it's silver and smooth. Today it's scuffed and brown. It's getting in the way of the words."

He looked at me, jutted his bottom lip slightly. "What do you mean?"

"I can't see the numbers because of your voice."

He rushed a note onto a piece of paper and told me I was free to go watch television.

My father insisted on seeing all the results of the tests and looked at them as if they contained the same kind of data as his electron collision readouts. He devised memory drills of his own, showing up with *Merriam-Webster's Collegiate Dictionary*. There was something about it he didn't trust. He watched my eyes scan the dictionary words and definitions. After several pages he took the book and placed it beside my bed.

"Tell me what you remember," he said.

"All of it?"

"Say them," he said, his eyes slightly closed.

I started with *aardvark,* calling it a burrowing insectivorous mammal, then *aardwolf,* a hyena-like mammal, making my way to *acclimate*—to accustom or become accustomed to new surroundings or circumstances. He touched his face delicately and stared at the dictionary. He looked up at me.

"Where are you getting this from?" he asked.

"The words remember themselves. They follow me around."

"You've changed the frequency of your brain. It's like you're eavesdropping on the unified field." He looked out the window. "This is an anomaly, Nathan. Anomalies only occur when something's brewing."

"What do we do?" I asked.

"We test this. We ask the right questions." He puckered his mouth, tasting the possibilities.

"All right," I said.

"Yes. All right, then. Let's ask the questions," he said.

During my next visit with Dr. Lansky, he gave me a series of tests involving sound tones. He produced certain pitch frequencies using something resembling a tuning fork with thin, red wires attached to a readout device. After each tone, he asked me what I experienced. They all produced different images in my mind: bronzed circles, silver strips, glistened steel, earth-colored ribbons with tongue-like edges. Many of the images also had tastes and smells. For example, one sound came as a contrail of neon pink that made my tongue taste watermelon. He repeated these tests over the next week, and every time the same variables produced the same sensory experiences.

My parents and Whit watched me undergo these tests, half scared, half proud. When Dr. Lansky called us into a conference room, my father was prepared for anything. He had a notebook in his lap. I sat between him and my mother.

"How's the gray matter holding up?" he asked the doctor.

My mother shot him a look. I fidgeted with my hands.

"This is a remarkable thing," Dr. Lansky said. He sucked on a cough drop. I could smell eucalyptus filling the room.

"What do we have here?" my father asked, drawing a margin of black ink down a fresh notebook page.

Lansky said, "It seems that Nathan has developed synesthesia."

"I'm not familiar," my father said.

"It's a condition in which the boundaries between the senses become fuzzy. We sometimes call it cross-modal association. The most common form is colored hearing, when sounds elicit specific visual effects. But Nathan has a mixture of joined sensations. For example, when he hears or sees the word *bell* he sees a series of undulating purple lines, but he also tastes something bitter on his tongue. Some words also give him a feeling of a certain texture, like sand or cement, let's say. Sometimes there are smells, too. It's the exact same sensation for the same word or sound every time."

"Is it brain damage?" my father asked, looking at his empty page.

"No. It may be that people with synesthesia simply pick up perceptions caused by words and sounds at a more primitive level. The rest of us have learned to block out these sensations. Some theories say that newborns up to four months blend the senses together—they hear colors and taste shapes—but later the brain differentiates at a higher level. Nobody really knows."

"Sometimes I get goose bumps when I smell gasoline. Is that kind of the same thing?" Whit asked.

"Not really," said Dr. Lansky. "A synesthete's associations are more abstract. For example, you or I might imagine a certain kind of landscape or scene while listening to Bach, but what synesthetes experience is less elaborated—they see colored blobs, spirals, and lattice shapes; they feel smooth or rough textures, and they might taste agreeable or disagreeable tastes such as salty, sweet, metallic. All of it is quite involuntary."

"And this is well documented?" my father asked.

"Yes, although knowledge is limited. There have been some well-known historical cases. Nabokov had it, so did the composer Scriabin. It's possible Kandinsky had it and his art tried to represent the synesthetic experience."

My mother crossed her legs and smoothed her pleated skirt. "How does that relate to Nathan's new memory ability?" she asked.

"Words and sounds create a kind of visual storyboard in Nathan's head. They're so vivid that he can't forget them. We haven't been able to determine any real limit to what he can remember."

"I can't remember words not having colors and tastes," I said.

"Now your mind forgets that words are just symbols," my father said.

"There's a classic book in memory studies called *The Mind of a Mnemonist* in which it's revealed how a subject named S has synesthesia and develops a prodigious memory as a result," Dr. Lansky said.

"This is very weird," Whit said.

"Predictions are that about one in twenty-five thousand Americans have synesthesia, though most of these people will never learn what their condition is called. These people always do extremely well on the Wechsler Memory Scale because of their vivid sensory associations with words and numbers. In a way, Nathan has a psychedelic experience when he hears sounds or reads words. It's not really all that different from the synesthesia that is produced with LSD or sensory deprivation."

My father wrote something in his leather notebook.

"Is Nathan ready to come home?" my mother asked.

"That's up to his doctor, but from my end he's rehabilitated. Back to normal, but with a twist," Dr. Lansky said. The word *rehabilitated* swept across the room—it was a streak of mercury-colored lightning, but it had no taste.

# seventeen

The cold came early that year; the hospital windows took on a chill. Everything was muted and white. The only colors were the words inside my head, sans serif font emblazoned across a colorless sky. My feats of memorization continued: mechanic's manuals, old magazines, Bible verses, stock market figures. I discovered new things about my gift. If I read the menu when my parents took me to a restaurant near the hospital, the words got in the way of eating. If the menu was badly written or printed, I was convinced that the food was inedible. If the waitress said the words *ice cream* nasally or flattoned, then the whole experience was ruined—I saw the ice cream as a pile of ash. If I ate while I was reading, the taste of the food got in the way of the words, drowning out their sense. One day, as I sat with Whit and my father over a restaurant meal, I said, "You know why they have music in restaurants?"

"Tell us," Whit said, thinking maybe it was a joke.

"Because it changes the taste of everything. The water here tastes salty in these glasses," I said, holding up an aqua-blue tumbler.

Whit stopped midchew. My father sipped his water and held a swallow in his mouth, then said, "You've reinvented your mind. Music changes the taste of things. It's quite wonderful." He smiled, allowing his own words to charm him a second time. "I wonder what listening to Thelonious Monk would do to the taste of water."

A FEW DAYS BEFORE I was released from the hospital, my father and Whit took an unexpected trip. After telephoning various research centers and university psychology departments, they visited a psychologist at the University of Iowa who had done extensive work on memory and limited work on synesthesia. Dr. Terrence Gillman also directed a program called the Brook-Mills Institute for Talent Development, located about an hour from Iowa City. My father and Whit had visited the institute and brought me back a pamphlet. The front of it read: *"The mission of the institute is to recognize, support, and research those with profound intelligence or prodigious skills, and to help them apply their talents at an optimum level."* Below this inscription there was a bucolic scene of some Iowa farmland, an old Victorian house, and two teenagers and an old man gathered on a sunny lawn. One of the teenagers, a boy about my age, sat reading while the old man and a girl were posed in what appeared to be a debate. Inside, there was a photo of hundreds of eggs, all of them lit from above, and a lone blue-tinted egg in the middle. Below, it said that one in ten thousand people were in the range of profoundly intelligent, and one in a hundred thousand people had some highly developed gift or skill that was not easily explained. These were the institute's target populations and accordingly it attracted gifts of every stripe—child geniuses, phenomenally talented artists, daring inventors, but also people with extraordinary psychic or intuitive abilities.

The institute believed that all these talents could be nurtured and studied for the betterment of society. Individual researchers, mostly educators and neuropsychologists, came from all over the world to study these esoteric talents.

My parents and Whit stood around my hospital bed.

Whit said, "It's a big brain camp down there."

My father said, "We heard about a mechanical genius who makes perfect scale model buildings from a photograph and some twin boys who are devising a new mathematical model for ethanol combustion. There's even a girl they call a medical intuitive who can diagnose diseases just from talking to a patient on the phone."

My mother seemed wary of the whole thing.

Whit said, "They don't seem to care how weird the talent is. They study it all. We had a psychic in the air force. We used to call him Déjà vu."

My father said, "But it's serious science and education they're interested in. How the brain manufactures these skills and how to make the best use of these talents. Those are the two questions before them. We told Dr. Gillman about you and he seemed very interested to have you stay for a while. He's known some cases where synesthesia develops after some kind of brain injury or traumatic event. One boy he mentioned developed it after encephalitis."

"We said why not, let's take a look under the hood," Whit added. He lifted his Yankees cap and groomed his flattened red hair with one hand.

"What about his senior year of high school?" my mother asked, crossing to the window. She was happy for me to come home, to bundle me as an invalid and fill the house with soup steam.

"They have regular academic classes as well," my father said. "They have teachers and tutors who work there."

"What if I don't like it?" I asked.

My mother came back to the bed and touched my arm. "Then you can come home. If you want to think about it you can. Whit and your father wish they were going there themselves."

"Yes," Whit confessed. "I love Iowa. All that open prairie . . . makes me want to eat large breakfasts at dawn."

"It does sound good," my father said. "Let's find out how deep this thing goes."

"Do they have television?" I asked.

Whit and my father looked at each other, trying to remember if they had seen one.

"I'm sure it could be arranged," my father said. "Especially in your case."

"I'll go," I said. "As long as there is a color television."

My father nodded, satisfied. He'd lost a father and nearly a son, but maybe he had another chance at a child prodigy. If he were ever likely to believe in God, it was probably right then—in that hopeful-blue room, the windows spilling wintry light, his hands resting calmly in his lap, thinking about me naming a thousand words and definitions from *Merriam-Webster's Collegiate Dictionary*.

# eighteen

The Brook-Mills Institute for Talent Development stood on an old corn and soybean farm in the middle of Iowa prairie. It was five miles from Selby, a small college town with a drugstore and public library. The original farm-house—a humble green box with a basement—stood toward the back of the farm, near the fields, and was now used as a workshop. The main building was a large Victorian house that had been built after the farmer made his fortune leasing easements to railway companies. It stood high-windowed and shuttered, shingled on the roof and overhangs. The house had a walk-up porch and a spire at the western end that gave it an elevated feel, as if the old farmer-turned-real-estate-tycoon had wanted more distance from the soil when he built his new home. The house and the farm had been do-nated to the institute when the farmer's savant daughter—a musical prodigy—died at an early age and the man quit Iowa for the Florida Keys.

Whit and my father dropped me off late one Sunday while my mother stayed in Wisconsin to oversee repairs to our leaking basement. I suspect, also, that at first she didn't want to be drawn into my father and Whit's scheme; she had been at peace with my normality for some years now. It was arranged that I would stay for an initial period of six weeks. During this time they would study my memory and synesthesia before recommending how I best develop and apply them. It had been a long drive. I was over my fear of being in cars by now, could hear the engine turn and not think of shattered glass. We pulled into the parking lot beside the old farmhouse and walked up a gravel path toward the house. The light was gray. Harvested corn stalks stood like crosses in the open fields. A rim of bare trees separated the fields from the acre of kept lawn.

My father carried my suitcase in front of him, with both hands. We climbed the stairs to the front door and Whit pressed the bell. A middle-aged woman appeared.

"We've come to drop off my son," my father said.

"Nathan Nelson," Whit offered.

"Please come in," the woman said. "I'm Verna Billings. I look after guest accommodations." I liked the wheat-colored word *guest* much more than the canary-yellow *patient* or slate-gray *subject*. She turned to me and reached for my coat, "You must be Nathan." She was pale and thin, her lips a deep red. "How do you do?" she asked. "You're all just in time for dinner." She led us inside and down the hallway.

Persian rugs lay on the floor and old portraits of farm life and trains hung on the walls. Steam engines billowing smoke as they came out of mountainside tunnels, weathered men standing beside John Deere tractors. Everything belonged to a different age. I thought of my mother. Here was a house where *living room* would never apply—muscat-colored drapes, glass-fronted cabinets, floor-to-ceiling bookshelves, a slightly disheveled and dank feel to the corners. A house of nooks.

We followed the long hallway and entered a dining room where five people were seated at a table in high-backed chairs. The table was laid with linen napkins, silverware, and a vase of carnations. Their conversation—hushed and stilted—came to a sudden stop. They all looked at us.

"Everyone," said Verna, "I'd like you to meet Nathan Nelson, his father, and—"

"Whit Shupak, retired astronaut," Whit volunteered, taking off his baseball cap.

Verna said, "And let me introduce our current guests. Roger is here from Vermont and he specializes in mechanical reproductions."

Roger, an old man with a five-day growth, nodded at me.

"And Dick and Cal Saunders are from just up the road in Iowa City and are both studying mathematical models for better ethanol combustion." The identical twins had sandy-blond hair and wore plaid shirts. They looked about fifteen.

"Nice to know you," one of them said.

"And Toby is our musical wonder of the moment," Verna said.

A boy with dark, hooded eyes grinned in our direction and said, "A pleasure. By way of introduction, I'm blind," Toby said. "The lack of eye contact has nothing to do with my self-esteem." Toby smiled to himself and tapped at his silverware.

Verna said, "And Teresa is a medical intuitive. She helps diagnose disease in the early stages."

"And not so early," Teresa added. She was a pretty girl, my age, with black hair and a cryptic smile.

"Owen is not eating with us tonight. He's a calendar calculator," Verna said.

I had no idea what that meant but I smiled and nodded.

Verna said, "And there are others that you will meet, but they only come when a researcher flies them out here for a study."

Verna seated us at one end of the table and sat nearby. Cal Saunders was staring at me, probably trying to guess my talent. A mind for trivia and rote memorization sounded hollow next to redesigning ethanol combustion. My father took a sip of his water, his eyes scanning the room above the glass rim.

"Dr. Gillman should be here any second. He just got in from Iowa City and will be staying a few days," Verna said.

"Excellent," my father said.

A moment of uncomfortable silence took hold of the table. Roger, the old man who made replica basilicas and skyscrapers, had one eye cocked at me as if through a gun sight. I affected a smile at Teresa but realized she was probably looking at the row of windows that overlooked the fields behind me.

Finally, Dr. Gillman arrived. He was in his sixties, with dark, thinning hair and salt-and-pepper sideburns. Dressed in a worsted blazer, he had an air of tired academia about him.

"Good to see you, gentlemen. Quarks, right?" he said to my father at the table. His face was pale and papery, his eyes a washed-out and nostalgic blue.

My father and Whit stood to shake his hand.

"Astronaut," he said to a beaming Whit. He sat down and whisked a linen napkin onto his lap in one fluid motion. "And you must be Nathan. Very nice to meet you."

I said hello and he passed the breadbasket around. He picked up a corked wine bottle and poured red wine for himself and then for Whit and my father without asking. "Another day," he said brightly. "I assume Verna has introduced you gentlemen around."

"Yes, thank you," my father said.

Gillman tore off a piece of bread and popped it into his mouth.

A woman in an apron began to bring out meals from the kitchen. There was a gap of several seats between the other guests and us. Whit leaned close to Dr. Gillman and said, "So they're all geniuses?"

My father was sipping his wine gingerly. His eyes locked on Gillman at the word *geniuses*.

"That depends on your definition," Gillman said. "Geniuses have the ability to learn in great intuitive leaps. They trust their ideas, however strange their source. Einstein used to compose theorems in . . . " He ate another mouthful of bread. I would learn later that he was infamous for his mid-sentence pause. " . . . in his dreams and when he walked his dog. Those ideas revolutionized our worldview. That's genius." He carefully layered butter onto another piece of bread. Cal Saunders looked at our end of the table, trying to make out the thread of conversation.

"Einstein had the bases loaded," Whit said, staring into his wineglass. "He was the full deck."

"You're saying that relativity came to Einstein in a dream?" my father asked Gillman.

"The experience of time can change with motion. That sounds dreamy to me," Gillman said, setting his bread roll on his plate.

My father angled his chin cautiously. "Do you know about physics?"

"In the beginning Newton created heaven and Earth and . . . " A sip of wine. " . . . falling objects and then Einstein said let us understand light. Light and movement. Modern physics is a bit of a smoke-and-mirrors show, don't you think?" Gillman was enjoying his own conversation; he chuckled—there was no other word for it—and angled his wineglass toward his mouth. My father, who essentially had no ear for irony, squinted at Gillman, trying to comprehend a hidden layer of antagonism or meaning.

Whit laughed and looked eagerly at my father. "A smoke-and-mirrors show. A horse-and-pony show. I think this guy does know physics." Only Whit could ever call a man who brought to mind Arthur Rubenstein a *guy*. My father, falsely affronted, shifted his eyes between the table ornaments and the high windows, between substance and reflection. Gillman sensed my father's displeasure and turned toward me.

"I'm very interested to find out more about your synesthesia. How's the memory?"

"Fine, I think," I said.

"We had a young man here not so long ago who memorized the entire set of *Encyclopedia Britannica*."

"What happened to him?" my father asked, casually but still miffed.

"He works on a game show. Helping with the questions." My father visibly deflated. There was no chance I had been resurrected to work on a television game show. Gillman swilled the wine in his glass, held it up to the light. Somebody placed a plate of beef Stroganoff in front of him and he whistled with delight.

"Ah, Doctor," my father said. "There is one thing I wanted to discuss."

"Certainly."

"Nathan has quite an attachment to television. He's concerned about watching plenty of it during his stay. Myself, I don't see the point, really. Scattered photons in a tube . . . "

"I love television. *Cheers* and *Night Court*," Whit attested.

"Television is just information. Info-bytes masquerading

as entertainment. Nathan can watch whatever he wants," Gillman said, almost dismissively.

"See," Whit said to me. "Nothing to worry about. What a life!"

My father nodded and turned his attention to his plate. I ate several bites of my beef Stroganoff. Beef tasted exactly the way the word suggested—dense, bovine, salty.

I overheard Cal talking to his brother. "No, listen, stupid, $K$ is the set of all statements of a language $L$ on one hand, and $M$ is the set of all models definable in a class $N$ consisting of a definite set of objects and of definite sets of relations of order . . . "

Dick Saunders, a little heavier, elbows on the table, cut him off: "Let's cut to the chase. Do you know what that means, jerk-off?"

My father didn't hear the brotherly exchange. He squeezed my shoulder and leaned close. "Isn't this place something?"

I tried to make eye contact with Teresa, the medical intuitive, but again she avoided my gaze.

AFTER DINNER I WALKED OUTSIDE to say good-bye to my father and Whit. As we walked along the gravel walkway to the Oldsmobile, my father jangled some loose change in his pockets and looked up at the house.

"Your mother will like this place when she comes to visit," he said. "It's her kind of house."

We arrived at the car and Whit got in to warm the engine.

"Wish I was staying. That meal was wonderful," Whit said out the open window.

My father took his hands from his pockets and handed me a brass compass. It was mountaineering style, with a lid and an eye gauge. He said, "I got you a coming-out-of-hospital present." He stared for a moment at his feet. "The thing of it is, Nathan, we're going to find something here to nail to the masthead. We're going to find that thing you'll hang the rest of your life on. This is the place for that. We comb the data, ask the questions, do you see that?"

"Let's see what happens," I said.

"Ready to board," Whit said.

My father started for the passenger side, then suddenly came back. He opened his arms and shouldered toward me for an awkward embrace. I looked at the ground and hugged him. I hadn't hugged my father since grade school. He rested his hands delicately between my shoulder blades. I felt his twill coat against my face; he was still a good foot taller than I was. He smelled of vintage suitcases, of musty leather and medicated shampoo. I suddenly felt as if I were being left behind with strangers. In fact, I was.

"If I don't like it here . . . " I began, but he was already gone, sitting on the other side of the windshield. Whit got out and gave me a bearish hug, lifting me several inches from the ground. "We've got ringside seats, little guy. We're here for the prizefight and we're proud as punch. Drunk with pride we are." Whit climbed back into the car and honked the horn several times as he rounded the gravel drive. He delivered a maniacal wave from behind the steering wheel. As they pulled out toward the street, I saw my father open a book and switch on his travel reading light—a meek cone of white light from inside the dark and swaggering Oldsmobile. Already he'd moved on, already this place had vanished.

# nineteen

That first night I found it hard to sleep. The coma had left me with the occasional fear that if I fell asleep I wouldn't be able to wake. Fatigue throbbed in my limbs and hands, but my mind was racing. I mentally recited average rainfall statistics to help me relax. I shared a room with Toby, the blind musical prodigy, and Owen, the autistic calendar calculator. Owen could tell you what day Christmas would fall on in 3026 but needed help tying his shoelaces. Tonight Owen had gone to bed early and snored extravagantly while holding the bedsheets between two tightened fists. Toby reclined on his bed with a set of headphones on. Bursts of opera came from his ears. I switched off the light and got into my bed. When the music stopped, Toby sat up and turned his face toward me. In the low-cast glow from the hallway, I could make out his broad nose and high forehead. His eyes stuttered through the dimness, shifting across my side of the room as though he were watching a landscape from a speeding train. He cracked his neck to the side. "So you've got some kind of special memory?"

"Yeah," I said.

"Is that what you're in for?"

"I suppose so. Words and sounds stay in my head. How long have you been here?"

"Three months."

"Do you like it?"

"The piano sucks. A fucking church-hall upright."

"Is Owen retarded?" I asked, looking over at his bed.

"Mental case, dumb-ass, lowball . . . that gist of meaning."

"Oh."

"But Christ he knows the calendar. By the way, he stole a pair of my shoes, so watch your footwear."

"I'll do that."

I looked out the window at the silhouette of the old barn and the corn-stalk horizon. I thought of my father and Whit on the road, somewhere near Dubuque, perhaps stopping for coffee and donuts at a diner. What was I going to do here for six weeks?

Toby put his headphones back on and slumped against his mattress. The sound of trumpets and drums rose through the dimness.

THE NEXT MORNING I WOKE early to find Toby gone, his headphones lying across his perfectly made bed. Owen was still asleep and I saw, in better light, his flat, moonlike face with its perennially wet mouth. I dressed and stepped out into the hallway, where I could hear the faint sound of piano music. I followed the music, drifting toward the west wing, where a music practice room and a classroom were located. I stopped short of the music room, listening to Toby play. Much of the piece took place on the right side of the keyboard, a sound like syncopated church bells. I stood watching from the door frame and saw Toby hunched over the keys, his face just inches from the white veneered edges. The faster the notes came, the more he leaned forward. His right foot pumped the brass foot pedal and I could hear his humming, forced through a falsetto, as he ravaged the piano. White, white, black, white, white. I saw the notes flash into the air; a series of high C's came as a quivering manganese blue line. He descended into a slower sequence, allowing his back to straighten before he jumped an octave and landed an enormous chord onto a set of bass sharps.

When he finished he breathed slowly and ran his fingers along the lip of the piano. His eyes fluttered. "Who's there?" he whispered.

"It's me," I said. "Nathan."

"Did you listen?"

"Yeah. I've never heard anything like that."

"A Russian composer nobody's ever heard of. He's a flamethrower, don't you think?"

"He's very blue," I said.

Toby shrugged.

I asked, "How long have you been playing?"

"Since I was five. Perfect pitch and I can play any piece of music after one hearing." He came toward me, his eyes roving all over the place, and moved out into the hallway. "Let's go have breakfast."

Toby ran one hand against the wall as we walked. We passed several bedroom doors before he stopped in front of one. "This is Teresa's room."

"She's the medical psychic?" I asked.

"Medical intuitive. Sees gallstones and aneurisms and shit like that just from talking to sick people."

"Weird," I said.

"This place is the Taj Mahal of weird."

The door was decorated with magazine cutouts and photographs—black-and-whites of men diving from cliffs, trapeze acts, a cannonball rolling down a hill. At the bottom of the door stood ransom-note lettering that read: KNOCK IF YOU'RE NORMAL. We stood for a moment in silence.

"What's her door look like these days? She's only been here a month and they say she changes her door decorations every few days," Toby said.

I told Toby what I saw.

"I bet all she wants is a quarterback with nice teeth. Maybe a farm boy. She's bored by the gifted," Toby said.

"You think?"

Toby touched the artwork on the door, then suddenly looked up. "Shit," he said.

"What?"

"You don't smell that? They've burned the fucking toast again for breakfast. You'd think at a school for the gifted they would know how to operate a toaster."

Toby took off down the hallway, his hand running along the wall.

# twenty

There was something depressing about the Institute. During my first few weeks, the other guests and I lived in relative harmony, but a kind of loneliness floated through the high-ceilinged rooms. The cold, windy days came and went behind wine-hued drapes. The rooms were netted in shadow. There was little conversation at dinner and in the hallways. The smell of old carpet was everywhere.

I kept to myself mostly. Initially, I underwent extensive testing. Dr. Gillman and a few associates from the University of Iowa orchestrated massive memory drills in a clinical room at the back of the house. I repeated manuals and catalogs, word for word and over several days. They tested my range and on-demand recall. They connected me to various measurement apparatuses during my recitations—tracking my pulse, my brain waves and metabolism, and the electromagnetic activity in my skin. They told me synesthesia was generated in the left hemisphere of the brain and came with a sudden drop in cortical metabolism. This meant that blood flow in the cortex decreased as compared to the normal increase during mental activity. They believed that my synesthesia was coming from the limbic brain, the old mammalian part, rather than the cortex, where logic and reason reside. Dr. Gillman told my father that my brain, based on all the physical indicators, found synesthesia very relaxing, that my brain-wave coherence increased. My father replied, "He dips a little deeper into the quantum soup."

After these testing sessions I watched television until dinnertime. The television room was on the first floor and, like the rest of the house, had the feeling of a grandparent's den—doilies and tobacco-colored couches, lamps with enormous, yellowing light shades. The TV set was a 1981 Zenith console with a color screen that curved at the sides. It was housed inside a massive wooden cabinet that seemingly doubled as a side table, a place to set cocktails. If the TV ever had a remote control, it had been lost long ago. I was forced to sit close enough to reach out and change channels. But at least it had cable, and I mouthed along with the flashing river of voices. Pixilated streams flared and receded. Sometimes I would put the TV on mute to stop the noisy tirade. I would turn to the Weather Channel and watch a cloud front barrel across the continent. It gave me a strange sense of peace, seeing the jet stream hurl weather at the Midwest. For hours at a time I felt as if I didn't exist.

My head was still filled with television as I walked down the hallway to dinner. Our communal meals were stilted and filled with strange moments of eye contact. Dr. Gillman rarely made it to dinner unless new researchers were visiting. The math twins largely ignored the rest of us. Dick and Cal were members of the Culture Club of the Very Smart. They wore chinos with white socks, refused to speak on the telephone, and generally ignored anything that placed a blot on their mental landscape. They were like two halves of the same brain: finishing each other's sentences about fuel spray trajectories and prompting each other with rhetorical questions. Roger, who spent his days making models out in an old farm workshop, had no mental prowess that I could determine and didn't speak unless asked a direct question. Toby was the perennial cynic and wisecrack and Teresa was a willing audience, engaging him on occasion with her own banter. But there was also something withheld about Teresa, as if she cut conversations short for fear of her own impending boredom.

I'd been raised in a household where my father ignored me unless he was holding up an intellectual hoop for me to jump through, and where my mother's dream of family solidarity was all of us sitting in the kitchen eating pad thai while playing gin rummy. But even with this training in solitude and disconnection, I felt adrift. Part of me felt abandoned by my parents, whereas I think most of the other young guests felt it was the other way around: they'd escaped the domestic tedium, the docility and dotage of their too-proud parents. I still held a distant vision of my father overcome with pride as he welcomed me into his private club. I would find "something to nail to the masthead," and everything would be different; we'd eat steak dinners together and wear matching blazers, and because now I was bona fide, christened in the holy waters of greatness, he'd be free to loosen up and talk to me about everyday things— his dreams, his boyhood, the attractive female students in his class—and I would teach him about baseball and we'd take camping trips together. We'd sleep in a tent under a dome of named stars and he'd tell me about the first time he'd kissed a girl. He'd tell me where to keep my condoms and how to handle standoffish fathers.

That none of this fantasy could ever happen, no matter what the application for my gift, meant it stayed buried and lively, burned into my dreams. And during those first weeks I would wake, a hollow feeling in my chest as I rose from a dream in a darkened room, bedded in unfamiliar sheets. I knew I dreamed of my father but, as in real life, his presence evaded me—there were flashes of his beard, the sound of his voice calling across a lake, a tall shadow on a sunny stone walkway.

# twenty-one

Most weekends, my parents and Whit came to visit. My mother, by now, seemed supportive of my time at the institute. They took me ice-skating in Des Moines and to Pella, where we stayed in a period-style bed-and-breakfast. We drove through rural towns and my father tested my memory. He brought new material for me to memorize—*Gray's Anatomy* and the *Handbook of Applied Meteorology*. Apart from TV shows, I had memorized the 1986 *World Almanac* and *Guinness Book of World Records*. Each morning I scanned the *Des Moines Register,* capturing the obituaries and the personal ads. My mind was bound up in meteorological data, the bones of the hand, the sexual preferences of divorced stockbrokers. Every word and fact had its own secret, vibrant life. Sometimes the associated sounds and images were lovely to watch, as delicate as nets of smoke. The world was miscellaneous and random, but sometimes beautifully so—a yard sale of fine, unpaired shoes.

On our driving tours of Iowa, my mother or Whit drove because my father frequently had headaches or eyestrain. My father sat in the backseat with me as we hushed along the autumnal roads of Iowa towns—Marshalltown, Grinnell, Dubuque—trying to pin down exactly what it was that made my gift possible.

*latitude longitude and altitude of north american cities | abilene tex 32 27 05 99 43 51 1710 | akron oh 41 05 00 81 30 44 874 | albany ny 42 39 01 73 45 01 20 . . .*

"You see the words and numbers?" my father asked, looking out at the fields.

"It's an overall sense."

"What do you mean exactly?" He swiveled his body to face me.

"Some words have a taste and weight. Some have smell and movement. They're objects."

"Objects are particles and bundles of potential, really," he said.

"I don't know."

My mother turned back to us and interrupted his inquiry. "How about we stop and get some pie?" She made a point of never leaving me alone with my father, shuttled us between diners and historic points of interest, made light conversation in general stores.

When we returned from these outings, my father and Gillman drank brandy in the dining room before my parents and Whit drove back to Wisconsin. That they respected each other was obvious—both men of science, both chasing the invisible, whether it was the source of a black hole's density or the source of genius. They sat with long silences like Quakers waiting to be moved to speech. For brief moments their voices filled the dining room.

"Some are born with phenomenal talent; it waits to come out," Gillman said. "The rest of us are born with hope."

"The gifts find their way to us. A radio signal sent across

the void," my father said. I think he came close to finding the camaraderie he'd seen between Whit and his own father—but instead of model warships and a distrust for governmental authority binding them, it was the possibility that intelligence could be manufactured in the brain, that genius could descend.

# twenty-two

Dr. Gillman invited me to finish out the school year at the institute and participate in a decisive study on memory conditions. I would join a small class for regular high school instruction and apply to colleges for the following year. My father was delighted with this plan and I agreed to extend my stay at the institute. I settled into a routine of testing sessions, school, and long hours of television.

In the months that followed, other guests came and went—people with apparent genius and people with a single, unusual skill. There were inventors of data compression algorithms and computer programs, discoverers of growth factor antibodies, but there was also a middle-aged man named Arlen who was a known psychic. He came every two weeks as part of the same paranormal study that Teresa was participating in. Arlen appeared to be a drunk, showing up to meals with malt whisky on his breath. Supposedly the FBI sent him the swimsuits and toothbrushes of missing children and he helped to locate them. Roger became a part-time resident but retained his workshop full of scale models. Dick and Cal both attended a conference in Nevada where they presented their new model for fuel consumption. They returned wearing matching polo shirts from a Vegas casino.

I spent my afternoons sitting a few feet from the Zenith console—the altar of memory. I closed the drapes and let the chromium light of daytime television wash over me. The game-show hosts all had similar voices—a jaunty, smoky bravura. They seemed like somebody's gin-and-tonic uncle who, off camera, dispensed advice about time-shares and horse races. These men in Brooks Brothers suits cracked the audience up with their scripted innuendos, and were secretly delighted when the putz from Indianapolis—the gym teacher or mutual funds manager—faltered on a question and won a vacuum cleaner instead of a cruise to the Bahamas. I sat mesmerized by the promise of a big win. But also by the certainty of one's own fate. *Not him, not today.*

After dinner Toby and I retired to our room and talked on into the night. He asked me about what people looked like, because he was opposed to touching people's faces. "I don't want to know how big their noses are or whether they have acne scars. Tell me what color their eyes are, whether Verna has cleavage." So I told him about the way Gillman looked three feet to your left, how Verna didn't wear a wedding ring.

"Breast size?" he said, peaking his eyebrows.

"You're a pervert."

"Nonetheless."

"Average. But she's old enough to be your grandmother."

"See, that's where I have one advantage. Looks and age are less important to me. Life is simpler when you can't see. My biggest nightmare? Bad breath and sweaty hands."

He stopped talking when a melody seized him, plunging him into an intermezzo. He rendered concertos and arias in a low-toned, gold-and-russet hum. Measured silences and beats. Perfect inflection. His breathing had the intake of a bassoon player. One decibel above a whisper. I leaned back on my pillow and watched the colors unfurl.

We also spoke about our families. I mentioned my parents' desperate search for my talents, that my father knew jazz but was incapable of talking coherently about baseball or any movie that wasn't a screwball comedy. He told me about growing up in New York City, where his parents were both involved in music. His father was a conductor and his mother an oboe player.

"I grew up on the Upper West Side, you know, one of those big condos with views of the river." We lay in our beds, facing the windows.

"I've never been to New York," I said.

"My parents home-schooled me. They thought regular school was dull. They bought me records and had music scores turned into Braille. A guy in Chicago converts treble clefs into bumps." He turned on his side, held his head in one hand. "When I was a kid they'd take me into Central Park and let me play with dogs. We'd have picnics and my dad would bring this little transistor radio. There was always music playing, even in the shower."

"You were born into it, then."

"Yeah," Toby said. "One time my father took me to a concert he was conducting at Carnegie Hall. He sat me up onstage, next to the violins. I was probably six at the time, already playing Mozart—the easy stuff, he used to call it. Without ever seeing him, I knew how he conducted. I could tell from the music. He kept his elbows at his side, like he was tied up. His wrists did all the work."

"Did you ever play piano for big audiences?"

"Nah. Stage fright. I go to pieces if more than three people are watching me."

"How can you tell how many people there are?"

"I can tell, man. Little sneezes and coughs, the way people breathe. I know they're waiting for something and I go to pieces." Toby conducted the air while humming a burst of operatic scale.

Owen stirred in the corner and spoke in his sleep. " . . . it's a Tuesday . . . "

Toby said, "Everyone has a trick. The calendar kids memorize patterns and cycles and codes. Right now Owen is dreaming about formulas. Any normal kid his age is having wet dreams. He gets a boner thinking about leap years."

"What's your trick?" I asked.

"To memorize a piece of music, I hear the root note and imagine it as a straight line; every other note is either above or below it and I visualize the dots."

"That makes sense."

"Also my trick is I don't try too hard. That's the real secret." Toby inhaled heavily, as if he were about to sing, then said, "Who the hell knows why we do it?"

I JOINED THE HIGH SCHOOL class and sat in a musty room with Teresa, Toby, Cal, and Dick. Owen had his own special ed instructor who came to the institute several times a week. We followed the Iowa curriculum. During math the Saunders twins—who were younger than the rest of us— went off on their own, while Teresa, Toby, and I struggled with senior algebra and geometry. I stared at Teresa the whole time and Toby leaned in her direction. Each night we replayed and deciphered her every word and gesture, ran it through a process of speculation. Sixteen and a late bloomer,

Teresa was a mystery to both of us. For Toby she was a soft bustle of cherry-smelling gum and herbal shampoo, a throaty, ironic voice cutting toward him. Meanwhile, I watched as a girl who was all elbows and wrists was felled by womanhood. It seemed to happen in a single day. Her hip-slung jeans tightened. Her T-shirt swelled beneath an army surplus jacket. Walking under an elm, striding down the corridor, Teresa would suddenly become aware of her burgeoning body and fold her spindly arms across her chest. It was a warding-off stance, the icy pose on a sarcophagus.

She triggered something in Toby and me. We smuggled a copy of *Chick Fest* into our room. Once Owen went to sleep I flipped through the pictures with a flashlight, narrating the poses. I remembered my pornography phase with some fondness, when Max, Ben, and I had whiled away our early adolescence gawking at busty women in poorly composed photographs—shoddy light, loose focus, indistinguishable objects looming in the background. We were aficionados back then, untouched by real-life experience. Max and Ben were now high school seniors in Wisconsin and, I felt sure, no longer virgins.

Rote passages from *Gray's Anatomy* came to me.

*the external organs of generation in the female are the mons veneris the labia majora and minora the clitoris the meatus urinarius and the orifice of the vagina*

" . . . okay, in this one the blonde woman—"

"Which blonde? The leg-spread?" Toby asked.

"No, the other one . . . "

"Okay."

"She's got her legs up on this old-fashioned bed, but she's like lying on the floor on this rug . . . "

"What kind of a rug? Are we talking Persian, Turkish? Details are everything."

"I don't know. Persian, I suppose," I said.

"Of course, Persian. Does she have clothes on?"

"Sort of."

"What?"

"This little lacy thing. Underpants."

"Panties," Toby said gravely.

"What?"

"They're called panties."

" . . . and her tits are kind of pushed together."

"She's holding them?"

"Yeah."

Toby sighed. "I'm never going to be able to see a center-fold," he said. "I've felt breasts, though."

"Whatever," I said.

"One of my nannies. One time I asked her if I could feel her breasts, just like that. Like I was asking for a sleeping pill."

"You're pathological."

"I told her that I'd never be able to see a woman's breasts. She offered, actually. She asked me if I wanted to see what they felt like."

"And?"

"She leaned over my bed and I put my hand inside her shirt. At first I felt them the way blind people feel faces, then I started squeezing them and she got embarrassed, I think . . ."

"You horny bastard," I said, a little incredulous.

"I'm going to get chicks out of sympathy. I have it all planned out."

A short silence.

"I don't think my parents have sex anymore," I said. "I think my mother finds sex a little disgusting."

"Nah. They all do it."

"Not everybody."

"I can smell Teresa when she has a shower. Rosehips is what I smell."

"You couldn't smell your own shit."

"I'm telling you, it's shampoo with rosehips."

I got up and turned out the light.

NOT LONG AFTER THAT CONVERSATION, we found ourselves spying on the diagnostic session Teresa and Dr. Gillman had every Friday afternoon. We had tracked their schedule and movements for a week and now, ten minutes before they were due to meet, quietly entered Gillman's office on the second floor. There was a mahogany desk piled with folders and books that smelled like old churches. Like my father's study, it showed no signs of an orderly mind. We huddled inside a large coat closet, a hiding place I'd noticed during one of my meetings with Gillman, and waited in the dark, amid old raincoats and jackets. Eventually Teresa and Dr. Gillman came into the office and sat down. Somebody picked up the telephone and dialed a number: 308 long distance—I knew touch-tones by their sound-colors.

"Dr. Shavim, please," Gillman said. Several seconds of silence, then, "Good morning, Sean. Hope all is well. Now then, what do you have for us this morning?"

I could hear Teresa shifting in the leather chair. Gillman said "I see" a couple times and after a moment said, "Teresa, we're going to have you speak to a Mrs. Charnetsky. She's eighty years old and has been complaining of a sore throat. Lately she's found it hard to speak. No tests have been done yet."

"Let me talk to her," Teresa said. I heard Gillman walk around to the front of his desk. "Hello. How are you, ma'am?" A pause. Teresa probably covered the phone's mouthpiece because she said to Gillman, "She's just breathing. Is she going to speak?"

"She might be nervous," Gillman offered. "Do you get anything on her throat?"

"Mrs. Charnetsky? Hello? Yes. What? Me? I'm a teenager . . . No . . . I don't go to school exactly." Teresa sighed. "I'm sure he was a nice dog. No, that's okay. No. My grandmother is in a nursing home in Nebraska. We write letters sometimes."

Teresa continued to speak for a few minutes, about her grandmother's beagle named Scout and how cold the winter could get in her hometown of Chicago. Then she handed the phone back to Gillman, who told the doctor that he would call back shortly.

"Teresa, are you okay? Did you get anything?" Gillman said. "Usually you ask how they're feeling."

"No need," Teresa said. "It's in her throat and mouth. Looks like a water stain, all up behind her tongue."

"What is it?" Gillman asked slowly.

"Throat cancer."

I could feel Toby beside me, trying hard not to breathe heavily. We stood pressed against Gillman's overcoats and corduroy jackets, listening as several other phone calls were made. A Dr. Winthrop, a man named Rodney. Gillman asked about weather and wives in Philadelphia and Texas, then the phone was turned over to Teresa. She spoke to the patients without expression, asked them about their aching limbs and fear of sleep, listened to their complaints. Then she would say to Gillman things like "She has a lump in her head" or "I see a black cloud in his lung." Gillman would call the doctor back and translate the information into medical advice: "Do a CAT scan" or "Look for risk of pneumonia and X-ray the lungs immediately." I pictured Teresa spending time here, listening to cancerous men long-distance, tumor-riddled bones and disease-riddled kidneys coming in over the wire. How was this a gift? It seemed like a curse. She saw fatty tissues and clogged arteries wherever she turned.

The hour passed and finally Gillman and Teresa left. I opened the closet door and we edged out into the office. We went downstairs and took up our afternoon routines—Toby to the music room to play Bartok and me to the TV room. Out in the hallway, I heard Gillman strolling along, humming "Fly Me to the Moon."

# twenty-three

For a while Gillman allowed my memory to drift in the shallows, among the islands of daytime television, reference books, and the small ads. I found it hard to forget a detail, no matter how insignificant. I was dogged by the irrelevant. Even my dreams were full of trivia. In the middle of a strange dream—riding a bicycle inside a linear accelerator, kissing a girl in my parents' bed—I'd see fuchsia trapezoids and remember the words to the Treaty of Nations, or the chemical reaction resulting in sulfuric acid. If numbers banged at the windows for Dick and Cal Saunders, then random words broke through my bedroom door, determined as assassins. Gillman said it was time to develop *context* and *interpretation*.

"Sometimes I just want to hear the silence," I said to Dr. Gillman. We were sitting in his office.

"What silence, *exactly*, is that?" he asked, cocking his head to one side.

"The sound of not remembering."

"You mean forgetting?" he asked.

"I don't know. What's the difference?"

"Forgetting is when things slip. Not remembering is when you filter things out."

"Oh."

"I think it's time we made your gift relevant. It needs an application."

He told me a story about the Genius of Earlswood Asylum—one of the first documented savants. He was an Englishman who had rare talents in drawing and building models. He once built a scale model of the ship the *Great Eastern,* complete with miniature brass pulleys, copper paddles, and a million wooden pins that attached the planks to the ship's ribs. It made me think of Pop Nelson.

As Gillman told the story he moved his eyes between the windows and the bookshelves in his office. " . . . so old Pullen fell in love with this woman. Someone he met by chance at one of his exhibits. An admirer. Savants all have one weakness: vanity. If you don't praise them they dry up. Anyway, he wanted to leave Earlswood and marry this woman. Who knows what her intentions were. He was a genius, but I doubt he could order a meal in a restaurant. He demanded to be let out and refused to do any work until his demand was met. So the head doctor came up with a plan. He obtained an admiral's naval uniform, with the gold trim and the white gloves, the whole bit. The release committee brought Pullen before them and told him he was free to go. Then they said how sorry they were he was going, that his services would be missed, and that if he stayed they would give him a commission in the navy."

"They lied to him," I said.

"They made him an honorary admiral and he stayed. But they probably saved his life. His marriage might have lasted a month, then he would have turned catatonic. He wore that admiral's uniform every day until he died."

I leaned back in the leather chair, ran my hands up and down the armrests. "What's this got to do with my memory?"

He nodded slowly. "The gift demands loyalty. It also demands relevance." He swiveled in his chair. "*The Brady Bunch, Gilligan's Island* . . . they're hardly worth memorizing. And even when you memorize reference material, you don't have any context for it. What's the point of knowing the bones of the human skeleton unless you do something with that knowledge?"

"Why does information have to be useful?" I said. "Does music need to be useful?"

"I don't think that's the point. Your father and I thought you might take a break from watching television for a while and focus on learning information with a purpose."

*all-time top television programs | mash special | dallas | roots part viii | super bowl xvi |*

Outside the office window a cardinal sat on a ledge, pecking at some seeds Gillman had placed there. I looked out onto the trimmed lawn where the Saunders twins were playing Frisbee; Cal was running like a man resurrected, his arms flung wide, a half skip in his step. I was paralyzed by the thought of life without television. It had been my thread back into the waking world and was sometimes more real to me than my own thoughts.

*americas favorite television programs | bill cosby show | a different world | roseanne | 60 minutes | cheers | murder she wrote | golden—*

"But you said—" I began.

"It's time to learn how to use what you do."

"What if there is no use?"

"Everything has a use, Nathan. Your synesthesia allows your brain to be coded for retrieval. The miracle of recall."

He leaned forward and handed me a large textbook entitled *The History of the World.* "For tomorrow, I'd like you to memorize the chapter on agriculture."

I held the book in my hands, the size and weight of the Bible.

"You can memorize the entire book. Imagine that. You will have at your disposal the main facts of history. Now, that's an achievement." He smiled, indicating the end of our meeting.

I carried the book from his office and descended the stairs. Back in my room, I slumped on my bed and pulled a pillow across my stomach. I threw the book on the floor and it hit the carpet with a dull thud. I stared at it. I knew, eventually, I would give in and open it. I couldn't resist the seduction of information, the indelible colors and shapes trapped like watermarks in each and every page.

MAN AS HUNTER, MONARCHIES AND irrigation; the invention of money was treated under a heading called "Early Dealings Between Peoples." The book traveled from prehistory and the emergence of speech to the Cold War and beyond in seven hundred pages. The arrogance of trying to capture the entirety of recorded history in a single volume escaped me at the time. It seemed like a catalog, an inventory of dates and names, and to begin with I read it exactly the same way I would read a printout of stock prices. Every now and then my gaze slowed enough to wonder at the stylistic choices of the author: "Robust historians of the past deigned to speak of an agricultural revolution," and, "History is a fickle science left mainly to those who wish to enshrine the past."

Mornings, I read in bed, the book propped by pillows. In the hands of the author, history and prehistory were melodramatic—full-bellied narratives alive with hairpin turns and unlikely resolutions: ice bridges connecting continents, flint tools leading to fire and migration, coffee and tea transforming Europe, keeping the itinerant workers awake in the factories of nineteenth-century England. Occasionally I burst through the net of words, into the sweep of voyages and monuments: men peering out of oaken wheelhouses at desolate shores, claiming spice routes and jade territories; the keelhauling of pirates; the mead-drinking Vikings; the places of the holy and the poor, the buttressed cathedrals, the minaret-and-dome mosques; the broadloom cotton mills; the squat, thatch-roof houses smelling of mulled wine; the fields of barley and ryegrass; the pagan stone artifacts; the assemblages of the God-fearing. But much of the time history was a psychedelic parade of sketchy neon lines, of rusty iron tastes and ammonia smells.

I studied the author's portrait on the back cover: Thomson Weavill, sitting in a library, a wig of gray hair, eyebrows like archer's bows, a scholarly frown as if the roil of history had unsettled him. Now I realize that his tome was less about interpreted facts of world history and more about his views on nationhood and progress. It was, in fact, his story. How some nations conquered others, the rise of the intellect over brute impulses, all of it according to some cosmic plan, a guiding hand that favored white people over lesser breeds. Surely that was part of Gillman's plan—to teach me not to accept words on paper as irrefutable fact—but he never said anything to this effect. At our meetings, he asked how Mr. Weavill was doing, blandly, as if Thomson were an institute guest with a propensity for dates.

# twenty-four

Teresa kept to herself much of the time. She took walks out into the soybean fields and went horseback riding at a neighboring farm. Every Friday she listened to people with illnesses via long-distance. Some spring afternoons she swam in the creek at the back of the property. Afterward she sat wrapped in a towel, her hair still wet, and smoked a Marlboro under a stand of sycamores. I watched her from the lawn, the history of the world splayed on my lap.

One day I followed her partway down to the creek and she spoke to me on her way back to the main house. I knew the weather was going to turn and that rain would ruin her swims, so I'd watched her without my usual reserve. She breezed by, barefoot, arms folded, then turned back to face me.

"Are you following me?" she asked.

"Define following," I said.

"If you're stalking me I'll tell Dr. Gillman."

"No. Not stalking. Watching, maybe."

She adjusted the towel around her waist. A drop of creek water fell from her hair onto her forearm.

"You need to start smoking," she said. "You're always fidgeting with your hands."

"Oh."

"I smoke in the barn after dinner if you want to learn." She walked back to the house through the formation of Cal, Dick, Owen, and Arlen playing Frisbee. They ignored her. I wondered if their gifts blinded them to beauty. Did they look at a Rembrandt, a Monet, and fail to see the wan light, the Tuscan hills blued by distance? Outside of Toby's imaginings, nobody else at Gillman's seemed to suspect that Teresa was gorgeous. Perhaps they saw the skinny arms and legs but didn't notice the way her eyes held flecks of brown and green, the way she tucked her coal-black hair behind her ears to reveal her long, pale neck, or the fact that her mouth was brimming and red, as if she had just come in from a snowy walk.

Later that day, at dusk, I had my first smoking lesson in the split-level barn. It was a hundred years old with enormous rough-hewn timbers spliced together with dovetail joints. A resident cat kept watch from the hayloft. It was dark inside except for Teresa's flashlight. She waited for me in the entrance, a pack of Marlboros stashed in her back pocket. As we entered, it smelled of alfalfa and drying corn. She led me to an enclosure she'd made out of straw bales, igloo-like, where she sat and smoked each evening while the rest of us ate peach cobbler in the dining room, while Dick and Cal challenged each other with equations and kept score with Roman numerals. She sat Indian-style and gestured for me to squeeze into her bale-house cubby.

"No one would ever look for me here," she said. She took out her cigarettes as I climbed inside. The walls were three bales high and the roof was half open. I heard the cat rustling above us.

"You could burn this whole barn down," I said.

She removed a disheveled cigarette and lit it. She took off her shoes. I stared for a moment at her thin-boned feet.

*the skeleton of the foot consists of three parts the tarsus metatarsus and phalanges the bones of the tarsus are seven in number—*

"There are worse things than burning to death," she said, inhaling.

"Like what?"

"Drowning. Bowel cancer. Strangulation . . . "

She ashed her cigarette onto a patch of dirt floor, then handed it to me. I put the cigarette to the edge of my mouth and drew breath. The smoke didn't burn as much as I'd feared. I felt it in my stomach, then let out a single, truncated cough.

Teresa said, "Picture your lungs as balloons. Let the smoke fill them slowly. You might get a head spin the first few times. First time, I threw up."

"I'll look forward to it."

"Do you want a drink?" she asked.

"Sure."

"My older brother smuggles it to me when he comes to visit with the folks."

She produced a small metallic flask from inside her shirt. It was chrome-colored and resembled a TV gambler's hip flask. She unscrewed the cap, took a swig, and then passed it to me. We exchanged the cigarette for the flask. I took a sip. It was bitter-tasting, colorless—gin. She leaned back with the cigarette in her mouth, her chin pointing at the hayloft.

"You like me, don't you?" she said.

*some notable shipwrecks since 1850 | 1854 march city of glasgow | british steamer missing in north atlantic lives lost 480 | 1854 september arctic us steamer sunk—*

I couldn't speak. The cigarette glowed and smoldered

from the hill of her chin and mouth. Someone had sucked all the air from the barn—everything was smoke. My lungs felt constricted, asthmatic.

"It's okay," she said. "Boys like me. I don't care."

The word *boys* was oxide red. She handed me the cigarette. I attempted a gesture of composure, held the cigarette between my thumb and first finger like a drifter from a Depression-era movie. I let the smoke rise up into my face. My eyes watered. She laughed suddenly, touched the toes of her bare feet together.

"Why do boys like you?" I asked.

"You tell me," she said.

"I don't know."

"Is it my tits?" she asked, locking on my eyes. "Because they're sore and tender right now from my period and I wish I didn't have any."

*hurricanes typhoons blizzards other storms | 1888 march 11 to 14 blizzard eastern us lives lost 400 | 1900 aug to sept hurricane galveston tx lives lost 6000 . . .*

An impossible heat spread up my back, neck, and face. I was thankful for the descending darkness. I thought about Toby's nanny, the woman who allowed him to fondle her breasts, a woman more of kindness and charity, I now realized, than lust. I had pictured her with bright red hair and lipstick, but now in my mind she wore a hairnet or a bonnet, a woman waiting to be a grandmother. She didn't have *tits*; she had a *bosom*. Only women without mystery offered themselves so openly.

"I think it's your hair," I said.

"Spare me."

"What?"

"You've watched way too many movies. Guys only care about one thing."

"Two things: hair and eyes."

"No one's that naive," she said.

"And what do you care about?" The nicotine and the gin filtered into my speech. I felt a burst of chemical happiness. I wanted to kiss the long, pale path of her neck.

"Nothing."

"You must care about something. What about your patients?" I said.

"They're not patients until they're diagnosed. I make them patients because of what I see. Gillman says I have the eyes of God."

"Gillman says a lot of things," I said.

"He's jealous," she said.

"Of what?"

"All of us. That's why we're here. He wants to surround himself with talent."

"He's a smart man," I said. Suddenly I heard my father in that inflection, heard the lifeless rejoinder for which he was renowned. I looked at her, through the gossamer Marlboro air, and said, "He's going to make us all famous." I was drunk.

"Yeah, I'm going to join the circus. Men with gallstones and saggy balls will pay me five bucks to tell them what's wrong with them. That'll make me famous."

"You have an impressive gift," I said. I sounded like National Public Radio.

She took a long sip from the flask, followed it up with several drags on the cigarette. We passed the flask and cigarette back and forth. I understood now why people did this, why a perfectly somber man at one of my mother's Levart gatherings would dance a jig after three glasses of wine.

As we walked back to the main building, the fall of night felt heavy and liquid. A final sunburst ignited the western sky—an arsonist's dream above the cornfields. I stopped for a moment to watch. I heard a sigh and thought it was Teresa's. I leaned in to make a comment but the sigh turned out to be my own; Teresa had disappeared into the house.

I went back to my room and got under the covers.

Toby called out from his bed, "Where have you been, honey?"

"The barn with Teresa."

"As soon as you make contact with her nipples I want to know about it."

"I think I'm drunk," I said.

Toby thought about this for a moment, turned on his side, and said, "What's it like?"

I put my hands behind my head. "Like you're not afraid to say what you're thinking."

"Could be dangerous," he said.

FOR A MONTH TERESA AND I smoked cigarettes and drank gin in the barn. Sometimes we sat in the hayloft and coaxed the cat down from the rafters. Teresa took to bringing milk in an old Coke bottle from the dining room and letting the gray cat drink from her hand. I named the cat Albert, after Einstein. I made jokes my father would have laughed at: how Albert could catch any mouse in the universe, how he saw his rodent prey as collections of energy and information. Drunk, I had my father's sensibilities; I was prone to introspection and weak humor. Teresa occasionally laughed, but mostly she watched me learn how to smoke without coughing, drink without slurring.

We spoke about our parents and our gifts. She grew up in Chicago, the daughter of a cop and a housewife who practiced daredevil charity—a woman who sponsored cake drives

out in the ganglands and once walked through a city riot
without realizing what was happening.

"She was the first person whose body I could see
inside."

"What happened?" I asked.

"I saw my younger sister in her womb. She was making
pancakes. My mother was. And I just saw my sister—this
little walnut curled up inside of her."

"Did you tell her?"

"Yeah."

"And?" I said.

"I said, Mom, what's that thing inside your stomach? I
was five. She didn't even know herself."

"When I was five my parents expected me to be a prodigy," I said.

"But you weren't?"

"No. I was slightly smarter than average."

"And what about now?"

"I'm here because my brain changed after a car accident."

"So now Gillman plugs you into a light socket and you
can remember stuff?"

"You're not very nice sometimes. I suppose you know
that," I said.

"You try seeing the body's dirty laundry all day and stay
chipper."

"Point taken."

She made three perfect smoke rings that eddied around
us for a moment.

I said, "What do you see when you talk to people? Do
you see their organs?"

"It's not like X-ray vision. But every now and then I get a
glimpse. The stomach looks like an old football. I see the
part of the body that's giving them trouble."

"Can you see my stomach? Is there anything wrong with it?" I asked.

She nodded. "Indigestion. You probably need to fart but I appreciate that you're not."

Through the gin I could feel my embarrassment—a telegram from the world of sobriety. Every time I thought about kissing her she said something mildly disgusting or referred to my sweaty hands or my developing smoker's cough. Each night I returned to my room and answered no to Toby's hopeful inquiries.

# twenty-five

One night Teresa and I walked out toward the fields behind the main house. I carried the Marlboros in my rolled shirtsleeve, like a small-town hoodlum. I shone a flashlight on the ground between us. Teresa took my hand and led me to the workshop where Roger kept his models. The building had been the original farmhouse and despite some recent paint it looked neglected: the window frames were warped and bloated with a century of rain and snow, the weatherboards had separated here and there, spiders were suspended from the eaves, mildew blotted one wall. We stood on the front stoop, wiped our feet on the welcome mat. Teresa opened the door and took the flashlight from my hand.

"If we turn on the lights they'll see us," she said.

She walked into the dark interior, moved the flashlight beam across worktables and door frames. I closed the door behind me and followed. It was moonless outside and the windows were faintly set against the darkly painted walls. As the yellow beam traced our path, I saw how the house had been remodeled to accommodate artists like Roger. The rooms were painted black, spotlights hung from the cross-beams, a wall had been knocked down to create an open area; there were workbenches with vises mounted to the edge.

Teresa took the cigarettes from my shirtsleeve and lit one as we walked around. The place smelled of glue and saw-dust, and the floorboards were splattered with paint. I lit a cigarette for myself. We no longer shared the same one. I had discovered my own smoking rhythm was incompatible with Teresa's: she sucked the first half, barely stopping for conversation, while I took small, pensive puffs, considered the smoke in my mouth and throat.

We walked toward the back of the space. There was a narrow hallway that divided the rooms and we crossed into what had once been the farmhouse kitchen, now a studio. Teresa placed the flashlight on a counter. The cupboard doors had been taken off and the shelves held bottles of glue and small tubes of paint. On the old kitchen table were eight blocks of Roger's scale model buildings. It was an imaginary city—a basilica catty-corner from the Empire State Building, a baseball field adjacent to a Venetian chapel. It was part Gothic, part Art Deco, part modern.

"Jesus," I said quietly.

I pointed the flashlight at the city. The domes of the basilica were cut from copper and tin, the metals welded or glued together seamlessly. The windows had wooden frames the width of matchsticks and the cornices were crowned with mythical figurines—chimeras, griffins, and half-men. There were buildings with window glass the size of postage stamps, skylights that resembled tiny cubes of ice. There were traffic lights and stop signs and streetlamps. Wrought-iron balconies, water tanks. A city of brass and masonry. A miniature elevator could be seen inside a needle-topped skyscraper. A park bench and a bus stop, a penthouse apartment with a rooftop garden. Roger had made tiny potted plants from dried flowers and clay. A stone angel with unfurled wings sat in an alcove above the city. This could've been God's square mile.

"This is what Roger sees in his head," Teresa said.

She crouched to stare down the main street at eye-level. She set her chin on the curb that abruptly ended at the edge of the table. It was like the city had been built next to an abyss.

"Watch this," she said. She blew smoke through the window of a New York brownstone. It disappeared for a second before streaming through the cracks and rising out through the chimney. She ran her hand through the smoke cloud, ominous and Godzilla-like, above the fragile rooflines. I walked around to stand beside her, crouched to see the street-level view. Even the street signs were exact. Names like River and Opal Street, the letters perfectly set against the wafered metal. Roger had hand-cut the miniature bricks that stacked to form a city power station. She crouched down beside me, her elbow on mine. I was about to say something smart about a burning city, about a towering inferno, people stuck on rooftops and leaping from windows, when she reached over my elbow with her face and kissed me. The warm cup of her mouth on mine. Her hand behind my head. We kneeled, facing each other, kissed again. I placed my hand in the small of her back. I wanted to kiss her cheekbones, her wrists—these were movie gestures, the stolen poise of an experienced lover—but they came to me effortlessly. I could hear a rush of blood in my ears.

*the blood is an opaque rather viscid fluid of a bright red or scarlet color when it flows from the arteries*

After a moment she stopped kissing me and sat on the

floor. She took off her shoes and because this gesture seemed, in that moment, like an impossibly confident move, I realized she had kissed boys before. She sat cross-legged, barefoot.

"Sit here," she said.

I was afraid to look at her, in case a stare would doom what might happen, in case I began memorizing the imperfections of her face—the constellation of freckles, the asymmetry of her mouth. I looked over at the baseball stadium with its to-scale concession stands and bleachers. The scoreboard read Yankees 9, Cubs 7.

*the temperature of blood is typically about 100 degrees f*

I sat close to her on the floor, our knees touching. She took my hand and placed it on the top of her stomach; my wrist brushed her bra support, a plastic rib that later I would tell Toby was the "edge of the known world." For a moment I was lost, dislocated. Oddly I thought about my father and Whit, about men. Why had no one mentioned this? Surely they had experienced this one moment of confined bliss, been forced into a submissive silence—sinners now in church. Whit spinning in space, my father peering into an electron microscope the way an astronomer stares at distant planets and hydrous stars, men continuing their lives but surely living for this unbridled moment. I thought about the math twins and Toby. They couldn't afford to let this happen. A genius or prodigy in love or lust laid himself bare, like a castle in ruins. "Nobody told me about this," I said. Teresa told me to be quiet and switched off the flashlight.

# twenty-six

The workshop became our new escape. Sometimes we had to wait for Roger to finish his model making for the night. He would come into the main house in a flannel shirt, dazed and smelling of wood glue, and we would take off across the lawn. Inside the workshop we'd stretch out on a bolt of canvas together, talking and kissing beside Roger's holy city—the zip code where you could buy a World Series hot dog, then cross the street and kneel inside a vaulted cathedral. One night, after allowing my hand inside her shirt, Teresa said, "I'm going to die before I'm forty."

"What kind of thing is that to say?"

"An observation. A premonition. Ask me why."

"Why?" I asked.

"*Why?*"

"Yeah."

"Because I don't have enough hobbies for old age."

"You've got time. Besides, forty's not old," I said.

"The midpoint," she said. It was a declaration, punctuated with a raised index finger.

"Actually, the average age now for women is seventy-six," I said.

"Of course you know this," she said.

"What are your parents' hobbies?" I asked, then instantly regretted it. I was still finding my romantic groove.

"None."

"None?" I asked.

"Unless you call arguing for two days about the same subject a hobby. One time—we were on vacation—and they argued about gas mileage in a rental car for forty-eight hours. Hotels, airports, driving, it never stopped. If that marriage dies it will be because somebody forgets to keep a receipt."

"They've got stamina," I said. I drew on my cigarette.

"What are your parents' hobbies?" she asked.

"My mother cooks ethnic food and cleans house and plans exotic trips."

"How middle class."

"She belongs to a travel club where they talk about Europe and Africa as if they're paintings. My dad is a college professor and physicist. He makes his own beer and stares at his fingernails a lot."

We looked up at the windows.

She said, "I don't want to die in my sleep. That's my only hope. I mean, where's the point in that?" she said. "How do you want to go?"

She knew about the accident but not my clinical death. For some reason I guarded that information; it seemed like an admission of something.

She said, "Skydiving?"

I shook my head.

"Plane crash?"

"Nope."

She angled and rotated her cigarette, urging me to get on with it.

"In the accident I died. You know, briefly."

Her cigarette stopped moving. There was a silence. I looked at the little metropolis, the pedestrians waiting at the curbstone.

"I was dead for barely any time at all," I said.

"That's pretty fucking cool," she said, rocking forward.

"*Clinically* dead," I said, slightly boastful now.

"All the same."

"I don't remember much of it."

She looked down at the canvas for a moment. "A feeling?"

"What do you mean?"

"Was there a feeling? I've spoken to patients who claim to have died and come back and they say it's like—"

"Like what?" I said.

"One woman said it was like peeling off a wet swimsuit inside a golden tunnel."

"No."

"What, then?" She inhaled and on the out-breath said, "Tell me, if you want."

"I heard a sound like radio static. And I felt like I was rising out of warm water. That's about it," I said.

She raised her eyebrows. "You got gypped."

"I know. But now when I remember the death I get a weird taste in my mouth, like an old penny."

"How do you know what an old penny tastes like? Were you one of those neurotic kids who shoved crap in their mouths?"

"Somehow I just know. Sometimes when I remember things I get weird tastes in my mouth. The word *biscuit* tastes like raw potato."

"You taste things the rest of us don't."

"I guess."

"What do I taste like?" she said.

She sat away from me, an acre of canvas between us.

"I don't remember. Remind me," I said.

"A taste test," she said, scooting forward.

"Exactly."

We leaned forward at the same moment, two halves of a drawbridge coming back down. We kissed kneeling, slightly off balance.

"Like bread and oranges," I said.

She sat down. "Well, I eat a sandwich and an orange every day for lunch like a good little Mennonite girl." She paused. "You know what I taste?" she asked.

"What?"

"Spit."

"Thanks," I said.

"How can we find another person's spit bearable? That's one of life's great mysteries."

"I don't know."

She said, "The body is a river of fluids."

"You would know."

"The math boys have dry mouths," she said. "If you kissed Cal Saunders it would be as dry as chalk."

"I'll take your word for it."

We sat for a moment. A bell sounded for lights-out inside the main house.

# twenty-seven

Every March the Brook-Mills Institute held an open house featuring a talent show put on by the current guests. Parents, scientists, and a few local media attended. The intention was probably to demonstrate the benefits of the program, but the result was weeks of anxiety for the current residents. Toby spent long hours practicing the piano and would come into our room at night, exhausted, dizzied by musical phrases. Dick and Cal were going to hold a question-and-answer session on their patent-pending process, but mostly they argued and played backgammon in the lead-up to the talent show. Roger was coming back to exhibit some of his scale models. Gillman had asked me to recite some history from the new book he'd given me. Teresa boycotted the event, calling it a circus.

As the open house drew near, Gillman began to notice my tolerance for history was waning.

"I miss television," I said.

"It'll pass. You're not yet in command of what you remember. There's no selectivity. Your problem is that you are unable to forget." He turned in his chair and leaned forward slightly. "Your parents and Whit received"—he brought his hands together—"an invitation to the open house. It would be great for them to see a new side of your memory. Tomorrow, I'd like you to tell me the major poets of the Romantic period and recite some of the verse."

I pictured my parents at the talent show and immediately thought of the seventh-grade science fair. My dry-ice volcano, the look of betrayal on my father's face when I gave the final physics question to Darius Kaplansky. Did I want him staring up at me, his eyes brimmed with hope, as I named battles of the First World War or recited the love sonnets of the Romantics?

A WEEK BEFORE THE OPEN house, my father drove through the night with Whit to visit me at the institute. My mother called to warn me about his intentions.

"He wants to tell you about a physics experiment. He thinks it explains your memory."

"It's the middle of the night," I said.

"Tell that to your father. He doesn't sleep anymore. He tells me Michelangelo took three power naps every day while he painted the Sistine Chapel. Sleep is for the dead. He actually said that. Your father."

There was a hint of a rant in her voice. Without me in their house, my parents gave in to their excesses. My father stayed late at the college reading journals of psychiatry and physics while eating leftover pizza for dinner. My mother brooded in the house, read travel essays about Indonesian tree houses and Thai silkworms.

"I'll be on the lookout," I said.

"Nathan?" she said.

"Yeah."

"You can come home anytime. I've spoken to your father about it. He needs some convincing still."

Although I occasionally missed my parents, I felt mostly relieved to be out of their household. I looked down the hallway. Teresa's door caught my eye—the collage of imminent disasters. I didn't speak for some time. "I have to go to bed now, Mom. Thanks for the heads-up." I slowly hung up the phone.

Before breakfast my father and Whit drove up in the Oldsmobile. Whit sat behind the wheel; my father was reading in the passenger seat. Whit got out and stretched his arms and legs. I walked down the steps to greet them. I didn't want my father and Whit to eat breakfast in the dining room. I could see it in my father's eyes: he was crazy with an idea.

"Hello, son," he said.

"Hey there, Mozart," Whit said, grabbing me around the shoulders. "Did we make it for chow time?"

"Let's go for a walk," I said. "Then I want to go out for pancakes."

"Yes, a walk would be nice," my father said. "I have something I want to discuss."

I walked between them and led them out through the fields, toward the seasonal creek.

"Cows makes me nervous," Whit said. "They're like asteroids."

"They're nothing like asteroids," I said. I was annoyed that they were here. Whit had become my father's lackey.

Whit said, "If you've ever seen a lump of molten star-fuel spinning for you in orbit, you'd know what I mean."

"Whit may have a point," my father said. "He may have a very good point." Whit and my father now had the air of a long-married couple. My father needed a coach, somebody to coax him to the world of the living, while Whit needed an esoteric mind, somebody who would allow him to orbit.

Whit pulled at cornstalks as we walked in single file through the furrows. When we came to the creek, we sat on the gravel bed. My father picked up a handful of pebbles, weighed them in his hands, and said, "All my best ideas seem to come with the headaches these days."

"I know. Mom called me. She says you don't sleep anymore."

"Lots of brain food and twenty-minute naps," Whit said in the tone of a personal trainer.

"So what's your new theory?" I asked my father.

He cleared his throat and picked up a small piece of quartz.

"There's this experiment in physics. Bell's theorem. Very famous. It reminds us how our minds are not separate—they're waves in the infinite field. I don't know why it didn't occur to me before. You have this titanium box and you create a vacuum inside. There's a small hole at one end, big enough for a probe. Once the vacuum is created you weigh the box . . . "

"Now, the box is special," Whit said. "The sides are calibrated to detect the smallest change in mass inside the box . . . " He pointed at the creek, as if a titanium box were floating downstream.

"So you know that the vacuum state is present because the weight is almost zero. The closest thing to nothingness that there is. Do you follow so far?" my father said.

"Yeah," I said.

My father stared at the piece of quartz in his hand. "So the experimenter places an electron probe into the vacuum and takes a measurement. The only thing it can detect is the presence of an electron. When the probe is placed inside, the mass inside the box changes."

"Of course it changes," I said. "The probe weighs something."

"No. You deduct the weight of the probe and still there is a change in mass. What is it that gets inside the box?" he asked. His eyes were trained on the creek. It flowed brown with field runoff.

"Pass," I said.

"An electron, of course," he said.

"So what?" I countered.

"Where did it come from? One instant there is nothing. Then you stick in a probe and an electron is manifested out of the vacuum."

"And you know what else?" Whit said.

"What?" I said.

"If you stick in a proton probe, the vacuum creates a proton."

"What's this got to do with my memory and synesthesia?"

"Here's the thing," my father said, slightly out of breath. "The unified field creates a particle inside the titanium box based on the experimenter's intention. His question is illustrated by the kind of probe he sticks in there. The probe is the question. It's like your memory. The information is manifested at the time you try to remember it. You pluck it from thin air." He spread his hands apart, dropping the quartz back onto the creek bed.

I had no patience for my father's breathy earnestness, for the way he expected me to be wowed by his insights. I said, "You drove here to tell me this? I remember things because words and sounds are like fireworks. I don't pluck them out of thin air—they explode in the air."

"That description is not incompatible with my theory," my father said.

Whit looked apologetic. He understood the experiment but was hazy on its implications for why I could recite a metropolitan phone book. "We also came for the drive," he ventured.

"I'm going to tell Gillman about my idea. What if synesthesia is like the probe inside the vacuum? He might find it interesting," my father said.

"Dad, it's not interesting," I said, standing. "He'll think it's ridiculous." But I pictured my father pitching his theory to Gillman, a brandy balloon in one hand, the two men alone in the dining room. Speculation, hypothesis, proof—the capstones of science could hide the obvious and the bogus. They'd discuss the whole thing matter-of-factly, my brain like a crankcase, and Gillman would listen and nod, bound by the methodology, the scientific pact, occasionally throwing a piece of his own conjecture onto the pile. I started back for the house, hurried down a corn row. Someone was behind me. I could tell it was Whit by his footfall.

"I think you hurt your father's feelings. He's got a bee under the hood about your memory. It'll work itself out," he said.

"He spends his whole life thinking about things that don't exist or that nobody can see."

"That's the best thing about him," Whit said. I turned around. My father was still sitting on the creek bed, his hands sifting through stones. I continued walking. "You know what's amazing?"

I looked at him.

Whit said, "I've never in ten years heard your father gossip. He doesn't even notice what other people do with their lives."

"He notices what I do with mine, believe me," I said. "You don't understand, Whit. My whole life I've never had a normal conversation with him. He never asks me about my friends. He's never talked to me about girls."

"That's not his frequency." He hesitated, then said, "I can tell you about girls if you want to know. I'm a little out of practice but I still bat for the right team."

"It's too late. I had to learn on my own."

"Anybody here you're fond of?"

We came out of the corn and stepped onto the lawn in front of the barn. I couldn't look at the faded red planks of the barn without thinking of Teresa.

"Yeah. There's somebody," I said.

"I'd like to meet her. Why don't you invite her out for pancakes?"

I thought about it for a moment. "Does *he* have to come?" I asked. It sounded cruel and Whit visibly cringed. "Fine," I said, "but don't let him bore her to death. Your job is to stop him from mentioning quarks."

"That and a stack of buckwheats." He patted his flank, then gave me a gentle shove and turned back toward the cornfield. "I'll go get the general," he said. "Meet you back at the genius school."

I walked across the lawn to the main house. It was still early; breakfast was just getting started in the dining room. I decided to invite both Toby and Teresa. I tapped Toby on the shoulder.

"Pancakes," I said. "Want to come?"

"Who's paying?" he said, his face turned up.

"My dad. Teresa's coming as well."

"Never mind, then. You don't need me."

"Just come, you moron."

He stood, pushed his chair in, and took my elbow. We walked over to Teresa, who was hunched in her army surplus jacket, reading a book about witchcraft.

"My dad's here and he wants to take us out for pancakes. Do you want to come?" I asked.

"Can I smoke cigarettes?" she said.

"Sure you can," Toby said. "You can even smoke pot if you want. I hear Nathan's dad gets stoned all the time. Jesus. Are you crazy or just insane? You don't smoke in front of somebody's dad."

"He probably won't even notice if you smoke," I said.

We walked out of the dining room and down the hallway to where Whit and my father stood. My father, upon meeting Toby, extended his hand to him.

"He can't see," I said. "Remember?"

"Not at the moment anyway," Toby said. "But we're working on it."

"This is great," Whit said, ushering us outside toward the Oldsmobile. "We're going to have the most talented car in the Middle West."

My father looked at Teresa for the first time. I think it dawned on him that I had passed through puberty without him noticing. "How do you do?" he said.

"All right," she said, limply shaking his hand.

We drove into Selby and ate at Flo's Pancake House. The locals had come in for Saturday brunch—hog farmers in denim overalls and T-shirts advertising pesticides, families with neatly dressed children. We sat at a booth near the front window. Whit and my father sat on one side, facing us. A waitress brought us menus. My father smiled and looked out into the street for some distraction. I could tell Whit had spoken with him.

"What looks good?" my father asked the table.

"I'm a bacon-and-eggs man," Toby said. "Canadian if they have it."

"After my own heart," Whit said. "But I'm thinking about a tall stack of pancakes. A tower of syrup."

"What would you like, Teresa?" my father asked.

"Just coffee," she said.

My father nodded. She could have said bourbon and still he would have tried to appear unfazed. His casual mouth and approving head nods seemed rehearsed. The waitress appeared again and took our orders. When she left, my father began playing with his silverware, lifting the angle of his knife so that the edge of his side plate formed a fulcrum beneath it.

"How's the music?" Whit asked Toby. He'd obviously seen a physics application looming in the glint of my father's fork and decided to steer us for safer waters.

"Fine," Toby said.

"Never made it past the little lamb myself," Whit said.

"You've been up in space, right?" Toby asked. I wondered how he pictured space. Didn't he live in the same perpetual void?

"Sixty-two days. The big slow spin," Whit said with some nostalgia.

"Can you explain what it is you do, Teresa?" Here was my father guiding the conversation away from Whit's galactic adventure, a subject he and I knew would end in the closest thing to melancholy that Whit knew—a lament for the estranged wife who chose a "moon-lander" over him. My father and Whit had made a pact, I realized. No physics and no space stories.

Teresa was deep in thought, staring at the swill of coffee in her mug. "Sometimes I see things. Bodies. What's wrong with them," she said.

"It never ceases to amaze me," Whit said. "The world's talents. The guy who sacks your groceries is building a robot in his basement."

"I'm not a prodigy," Teresa said. She looked him square in the eye.

"I see," Whit said.

"It's not like being talented at the piano or being able to memorize a page from a book. I'm being used as a channel." There was something breezy in her voice.

"This is precisely what I'm talking about," my father said.

"Interesting," Whit said.

There was an awkward silence for a moment and we all looked out the window. An old man was walking his dog. A family with four kids drifted out of a toy store.

"Now," my father said, "do you see the body as matter or do you see it as energy? Do you see bones, for instance?"

The word *bones* was gray and brittle and textured like old cement.

Fortunately, the waitress arrived with our food and said: "This ought to stick to your ribs." I felt a gentle nudge under the table. I looked down and saw Teresa's foot beside mine, waving at me. *Yes, that's my father,* I thought. The waitress placed a six-stack of pancakes in front of Whit. He licked his lips like a cartoon fox. Whit could tuck a napkin into his shirtfront and get away with it, have people find it endearing. My father turned his plate around several times, waiting for his omelet to be in an agreeable position. I poured syrup onto my buttermilk pancakes. Teresa said to my father, "I see blood and bone. The organs all look different. The heart looks like a swollen hand." It struck me that she didn't like my father, that she wanted to pick a fight.

My father considered her statement, glanced out the window while he chewed, then said, "It's a little bit like seeing through a high-powered microscope. Skin, of course, is merely molecules—atoms stitched together. And atoms are full of empty space. We should probably all be able to see through it. If only we knew how."

"But you don't know how," Teresa said.

"No," said my father.

"I don't see through it exactly," Teresa said. She drained her mug and looked around for the waitress. "I daydream of what's inside. I close my eyes and this picture comes to me."

"I get it," Whit said. "It's like their bodies send you a little letter. Dear Teresa, I'm sick . . . "

Teresa's mouth opened, either in the after-bite of coffee or in sudden disgust at the reduction of her gift. "Sort of," she said. "Mr. Nelson, do you believe in God?" My father stopped mid-bite; Pop Nelson had sent an emissary from the other side. He stroked his beard with three fingers, a little nervous.

"What makes you ask that?" he said.

"Because if you do, then you probably think that God is sending me those daydreams."

"He doesn't believe in God," I said.

"I have moments where I think a creative consciousness must be out there," my father said.

"For my money, there's got to be someone making the sandwiches for the picnic," Whit said.

"I don't believe in God, either," Teresa said. She took out her cigarettes and placed them on the table. My father looked at the cigarettes, then at me. Everyone finished eating and Teresa asked the waitress for an ashtray. The waitress was nonchalant. Teresa looked older than she was and this was a woman who, from the pallor of her skin and the breathiness of her speech, had probably started smoking before she'd turned twelve—a career smoker. My father watched, mesmerized, as Teresa lit the cigarette and sent a stream of smoke up the front window. The smoking, the reference to God—Pop Nelson was determined to linger for my father. We sat there awhile longer. Toby had barely spoken since we arrived. I saw his lips moving slightly; he was humming his own private music, ignoring all of us.

My father and Whit stayed the rest of the day and left after dinner. Gillman and my father sipped cognac after dessert, discussing Bell's theorem and its application for memory and genius. Whit wrestled with Dick and Cal Saunders out on the lawn. I didn't smoke in the barn with Teresa. She had gone horseback riding by herself. I could tell she needed time alone. The price of medical intuition was a threshold with people, a nausea that rose when she couldn't stand to be next to another human being for a moment longer. The dark river of blood, the shanks of diseased bone—these deprived her of endurance for friendship, for sustained contact; they gave her a bent for solitude, like a medieval saint who saves the sick and the lame, then wanders for weeks in the desert, attempting to be rid of their gratitude.

# twenty-eight

My parents and Whit came the following weekend for the open house. On the Saturday, visitors arrived from all over the country to see the results of the institute's program. People were awestruck as Roger gave a tour of his miniature city. Researchers and educators had a roundtable discussion with Gillman on socialization and education of the gifted. There was a luncheon with the current guests. Then, in the evening, there was the talent show.

We all dressed up for the gathering except Teresa, who dressed in protest: ripped jeans and an old sweatshirt that warned PAIN IS NOT ENOUGH. She and I walked into the dining room, where the talent show was being held. I was wearing a dull and ill-fitting black suit my mother had found in my closet back in Wisconsin. We stood with my parents and Whit. My mother was dressed in a bottle-green frock with a Kashmiri shawl over her shoulders. She reached over and brushed some lint off my lapel. "Hey, little buddy," Whit whispered to me. My father nodded at me bleakly. He looked pale and his eyes appeared sunken. "Migraine," Whit said to me. My father shrugged, but irritation crept into his face.

Teresa and I continued around the room, meeting people's families. I looked for echoes between parent and child, relative and prodigy. Most of the time there was some physical resemblance—an inherited widow's peak, a distinctive jawline—but they were faces developed in different worlds. The parents and family members were weighed down by what their lives demanded, by errands and mortgages. The gifted had wrinkle-free foreheads, supple skin, eyes that were clear and luminous. They'd been given a place to hide.

Teresa introduced me to her parents. I was surprised they had come even though she wasn't performing. "We like to get out of the house for these kinds of events," Mr. Fenmore said. "I'm impressed by nature. That's why we came." He looked at me guardedly, shook my hand a little too tightly.

"Teresa tells me you've got a killer memory," he said, eyebrows raised. "I've got a good head for numbers." Teresa had told me his biggest flaw was competitiveness. Once, he arm-wrestled a sick uncle at Thanksgiving after the man accused him of being a slouch.

His wife straightened his tie. A woman who shopped in thrift stores and bought Christmas presents in August. She had a small gap between her front teeth, and as I watched her smile I thought this made her seem vulnerable. I don't know why exactly, but it made me like Teresa more. Mr. Fenmore asked me where I was from.

"Wisconsin," I said.

"Cheese." He stared at the space in front of him.

"Mosquitoes," I said.

"Heavens," Mrs. Fenmore said. "If there's one thing I dislike, it's creepy-crawlies." She gave a stage shudder.

"My mother sprays insecticides under our beds. She poisons us," Teresa said.

The daughter and the parents looked at each other for a moment. There was a history of arguments, perhaps violent ones, in that pause. Teresa said that we had to go so I could prepare for my performance. I shook hands again with Mr. Fenmore and we left. Gillman smiled at us as he mingled with the guests. He was dressed in a woolen tuxedo and wore a name tag. He stood among a group of academics at the back of the dining hall, where some of Roger's models had been assembled.

When it was time for our performances, we all sat and Gillman addressed the audience. My parents were in the front and Whit stood with his arms folded at the back of the room. I was nervous at the thought of my father watching my recital. He sat waiting with his hands in his lap. Gillman gave a brief update on progress at the institute before introducing Toby. My roommate stood up from his chair and made his way to the upright piano without a cane. He'd counted the number of steps between his seat and the piano.

He sat motionless, his tails draped over the piano bench, hands resting an inch above the keys. When he started playing, his fingers sprung open like startled spiders but he remained stone-faced, eyes closed, mouth tight, his foot tapping the pedal methodically. He punctuated each note precisely and the silences were notes played but not heard; he moved his fingers above the keyboard to measure the pauses, as if he were playing an octave outside our hearing. An inscrutable smile appeared during a change in pace. For a month he'd practiced with a tape of audience noises—muffled coughs, breathing, human whispers from concert halls. He'd ordered a tape from a company who sold these noises as sound effects to movie studios. Auditoriums full of nervous systems, irrepressible urges that came out under reverence and boredom. He'd tamed his stage fright, I thought. The polyrhythmic riffs, the delicate trills and hammered sixteenth notes came as a cascade of blue-white sparks.

When the crowd applauded he stood and bowed three times, a hand resting at the piano. He came toward me, smiling.

"Nice job," I said.

"That wasn't me," he said, "that was the Russian back from the dead." He walked past me and held out a weary hand for someone to take.

Next, Cal and Dick sat on bar stools and fielded questions about their ethanol combustion model, which no one seemed to understand except a mathematician from MIT who was nursing a sherry at the back of the room. After he'd asked a few esoteric questions, Dick and Cal said they'd answer any questions about math that people wanted to know. Mr. Fenmore raised his hand and asked them what zero multiplied by 1.6 billion was, to which Dick replied, "Congratulations, you have just asked the dumbest question in the history of decimalized mathematics. Zero is as zero does." From the side of the room Gillman folded his arms disapprovingly.

Next, my father raised his hand, blearing through his migraine, and asked, "Tell me, what is the square root of pi?" Cal and Dick looked at each other, then back at my father.

"Sir, to how many decimal places?" Dick asked.

"Twenty-five should do it," my father said.

In unison Dick and Cal said, "1.7724531023414977791 280875."

My father produced a small pocket calculator, punched a few numbers, and said, "Very nice."

After several more questions the twins took their seats.

Owen came out and was asked various calendar questions—what day of the week for distant Thanksgivings,

Christmases, and New Year's Days. Gillman sat with a perpetual calendar and confirmed his answers. Some of the occasional guests also made an appearance—a nine-year-old violin virtuoso, a man who gave a brief talk on his artificial intelligence system, a woman who spoke thirty languages fluently and translated between them for the crowd. I was the last to go up, and I believed on some level this was no coincidence.

"Our next resident is Nathan Nelson," Gillman said. "He's very unusual because his phenomenal memory developed after a near-fatal car accident. In fact, Nathan left the living for a very brief time. When he returned, his brain developed synesthesia, a condition in which the senses blend together. This has allowed him to memorize large amounts of information. Lately, he's turned his talents to history and poetry. Please give him a round of applause."

The audience clapped while I stood at the front. I looked at my parents and recalled the day of the seventh-grade science fair: Darius Kaplansky staring at the back of the index cards, my parents with proprietary smiles. They believed they were responsible for both my potential genius and mediocrity—it was their genealogy on the line. Now all that had changed. Something else was responsible for my gift. My father watched me intently. A probe inside a vacuum, the propagation of light in space, the relationship between energy, mass, and velocity—all these could be reduced to an equation, a formula. But this unknown radio frequency bothered him. Kept him awake at night.

I stood with my hands by my side, my ill-fitting suit inching up my back, and looked out into the dining room, making eye contact with the faces. My mind went still, then blank. I mentally reached for sonnets and an outline of British colonialism, but there wasn't a speck of information—

not a colored line or bitter-tasting spiral. I stood there for an eternity. A murmur passed through the crowd. Doctor Gillman smiled politely and cleared his throat. I couldn't look at my parents.

Then, I found myself saying, "Well, Mr. Smart, this is the famous Hawaiian detective now serving with the San Francisco police force. Inspector Harry Hoo." The words from a season-one episode of *Get Smart* came unbidden. Max has followed a KAOS agent to San Francisco and the agent has been murdered. Harry Hoo and Max discover the dead body and Max searches the corpse for clues.

My father lifted his chin. I stood motionless. Nothing moved except my mouth as I described the action and recited the dialogue. "Max leans over, reappearing each time holding up an item. Max says, 'Wallet . . . handkerchief . . . comb . . . keys to my apartment . . . ' Then Harry Hoo says, 'One moment, Mr. Smart, victim had keys to your apartment in his pocket?' "

I exhaled, losing the momentum of the approaching punch line. " 'Oh, you wanted me to search *his* pockets.' "

I looked out into the audience. A volley of small laughter came from Owen's family—barrel racers and antique dealers from Blue, Wyoming. This continued for about ten minutes until Gillman interrupted me and thanked everyone for coming. I didn't get the chance to recite any of the closing credits: Joey Forman as Harry Hoo, or Leonard Strong as the Craw, a Chinese man with a magnet for a left hand. The Wyoming folks gave an encouraging cheer as Gillman ushered me back to my seat. Quietly, he said, "Very disappointing." I tried not to look at him. My father sat on the other side of the room with his eyes on the floor. There was no point telling either of them that my brain had seized up onstage, that *Get Smart* came out on its own—the nervous scratch of a mnemonic mind. My father got up and came toward me, his walk slightly off balance.

"What was that?" he asked.

"A television show."

"This is the proof? Your time here amounts to this?" he said. One hand was at his temple. People walked away to stand in small groups. "You're wasting everybody's time."

He touched my head as if it were a tabletop, and I knocked his hand away. He glared at me.

He said, "That mind wants structure, routine, do you understand me? I'm fed up. We brought you here to find your calling, Nathan."

I took a step back. "I was hit in the head. I died and came back different. That was my calling."

"This is your ticket, your invitation . . . You see things differently than other people. Like me. I know you do."

I said, "When I look up at the stars I don't think about gases and molecules. Half the time I don't even look up."

He grabbed my shoulders tightly and yelled into my face. "Stop squandering what you have! Do you hear me? Take your place!" The whole room turned and looked at us, stunned silent. Dr. Gillman guided some researchers out into the hallway. It was the first time I had ever heard my father yell. He recoiled and stammered, "I need to sit. I can feel my pulse in my thumbs." He ambled back toward my mother, who appeared to be crying into an embroidered handkerchief.

I turned and headed for the back of the room. Some people had stayed for a small reception. The Saunders twins and their parents held court by a bowl of punch. The mother said to a stout man in a blazer, "Cal was late to toilet train and I think that's significant." Cal blinked at her and said, "Mother, drop dead, please." Toby was talking to an elderly lady who kept clasping her hands and saying, "Inspirational playing!" I walked behind him and leaned to his ear. "She's a hundred and eight, but she might give you a squeeze." He shot out a laugh and the lady said, "Now, boys." I was determined that my father's outburst wouldn't ruin my night.

Whit looked over at me and I got his attention. He withdrew from a circle of parents and walked over to me, beer in hand.

"Agent Eighty-six," he said.

"Can you get me a drink?"

"You don't mean apple juice, do you?"

"One of those," I said, pointing to his bottle.

"Your mother will string me up. You've upset her."

"Please," I said.

He disappeared behind a row of people and returned with a beer bottle wrapped in a napkin. "Be discreet," he said, leaving.

From across the room my father looked my way but, because he was squinting with pain, I couldn't tell if he'd noticed the beer bottle in my hand. He contemplated his Dixie cup of fruit punch.

I continued through the crowd and found Teresa by the doorway, taking a slug from her hip flask.

"Your dad might see," I said.

"He's used to it. My mother's a drunk."

"No way."

"Bottle of booze behind the fireplace logs. Her charity is an excuse to get bottles of cheap wine as tokens of appreciation."

"You want to go to the workshop?" I asked. She nodded, put her flask inside her sweatshirt, and we went out into the night. We stopped in front of the workshop. Teresa reached for the flashlight that was kept under a loose stone by the front door. As she leaned down, I stared at her back and shoulders. I asked myself, *Is she my girlfriend?* and thought, oddly, about the small gap between her mother's teeth. Looking at Teresa, knowing that I was about to press against her, I felt as if I were stealing something from her parents. Taking something from the gum-chewing cop and the charity worker—why was that exciting? They were sipping punch while I was about to get breathless with their firstborn. I kissed the back of her neck.

We walked through the dark house, quietly, touching the worktables and supply cupboards with the arc of the flashlight. I took out a cigarette, lit it, and took several sips from my beer. Teresa walked to the other side of the cityscape and pulled something from one of the cupboards—a small white candle in a brass holder. She took the matches and lit it. There was something elaborate and planned in that gesture of lighting the candle and it made me nervous. She stood behind St. Peter's Basilica, the domes shadowing her stomach like clouds. I took a roll of canvas and unfurled part of it under the table.

The candle stood on the edge of the main street, where the city abruptly dropped into dead space, and lightened the facades of the buildings, giving the illusion of the sun shifting through leaves. I watched as Teresa removed her sweatshirt. She stood in a tank top, something like defiance in her face. I was aware that I still had a boy's body—slender arms, a flat chest, barely a shadow of stubble on my chin.

"That has to be the ugliest suit in the world," she said.

"I know."

She kissed me, taking off my jacket and shirt. She tasted of grape punch.

We leaned against the model city and it shook momentarily. I placed my hands on her shoulders and pulled her beneath the table. She took off her shirt and lay back on it. She drew my face down to her and kissed me again. We liked to make out in places of confinement—the straw-bale cubby, the cramped workshop, under her bed—burrowed in, our limbs enfolded. Hiding gave our kisses urgency. Even in my daydreams, when I saw us inhabiting some prosperous future together, living in some immensely lit mansion, our naked clambering took place in the closets and underneath the stairs.

But tonight, even pressed beneath the table, I felt distracted. I pictured my father skulking inside the house, stupefied by his headache and his ungrateful son. Teresa whispered something through a sigh as I traced my fingers across the rise of her chest. She stared out the triple-hung windows, her head angled back. I followed her gaze out into the beryl-dark night. From the institute I could hear the low commotion of people standing, chairs sliding. The end of something. Prodigies going off to bed. In that house music and combustion had been reduced to algorithms, missing children had been dreamed back into reach, but it all seemed remote compared to the narcotic rush of a girl's kiss. If only tonight I could feel that oblivion.

Then Teresa's voice split the darkness like the winking edge of a knife.

"I need to tell you something," she said.

I stopped moving my hand across her body. "Go ahead."

She wouldn't look at me and her breath was all around us. She said, "It's in your father's head. The size of a plum. They don't know it's there."

My father had not been to a doctor since childhood. Mechanics, he called them.

She said, "I wasn't sure the first time I met him when he

dropped you off. But then I saw another flash when we went for pancakes. And then tonight, I'm sure. I see it clearly."

I felt the air go out of me.

She said, "I could be wrong. But I doubt it."

I managed to say, "A *plum*?"

"Yes," she said.

I sat up slowly and reached for my shirt. Voices lifted from outside. Then the sound of car tires on the gravel drive.

"I'm really sorry," she said.

I crawled out from under the table and stood up slowly. I felt faint and leaned against the table. I said, "Maybe you've made a mistake."

She got up and looked at me and neither of us spoke for a long time. It was dark and all I could see were the whites of her eyes. She said, "I don't think so."

I buttoned my shirt and went outside. Teresa followed. We walked in silence to the main house. Inside, the crowd had thinned to a clutch of tipsy parents and aunts. We went and stood by our parents and Whit. They sat in folding chairs, chatting about curbside recycling programs, whether cardboard needed to be bound in twine. Whit and Mr. Fenmore consulted their watches; it was getting late. My father stared down at his shoes. I knew in my gut that Teresa was right and now I couldn't look at anything except the back of his head. Buried inside was a blush of rampant cells, a bedlam of neurons. *The ghost particle,* I thought. *It's been waiting here all along.*

# twenty-nine

The weight of the news tortured me for a week before I told my father in early April 1988. Several times, after the talent show, I called home and almost told my mother. I knew she had a right to know. But each time I heard her recount the domestic dramas of life with my father—his hallway wanderings in the small hours, the surges of discordant jazz from his study, the way he drank milk straight from the carton—I knew this had to be done in person. And I felt like I owed it to my father to be the one to tell him.

Just before Easter my parents and Whit took Teresa and me to Des Moines to a new planetarium that had just opened. We drove an hour to sit under a domed ceiling and watch planets and stars angle across our universe. Whit called it "a chapel beneath the stars," as he chauffeured us along I-80. The outing had been his idea. I sat up front with him while my parents sat with Teresa between them in back. I heard them exchange comments about vacation plans and the unseasonably cold weather. Teresa was flying to Chicago that night to be with her family.

We arrived midafternoon in downtown Des Moines. The sky was cloud-capped, an expanse of bleached gray. We drove past storefronts decorated for Easter—an appliance store with baskets lining the window, a Mexican restaurant with festive lights blinking. Some families were out window-shopping in front of a department store. Whit honked and waved at them as we waited at a stoplight. One of the fathers waved back heartily. We drove in circles trying to find the planetarium. Whit assured us that he'd called ahead, that it was definitely a going concern.

Eventually we parked in front of a Methodist church. Catty-corner stood the planetarium. It was housed in an old brick theater whose roof had been replaced with an aluminum dome. A metal bubble set between 1920s office buildings made for a strange sight. We bought our tickets at an old-fashioned booth and were ushered inside. It was moderately busy, mostly families with younger kids. There was a concession stand with popcorn. Teresa and I stared at each other. It was the perfect outing for seven-year-olds. Whit stood in line and bought two buckets of popcorn. When he returned he handed a bucket to Teresa and said, "I hear they show the Big Bang. That's got to be a popcorn occasion, don't you think?" He went and stood with my father. Teresa came toward me, out of earshot of my parents. "Your parents were putting me to sleep in the car," she said. Normally I would have found this comment funny, might have offered a rejoinder about Whit's conversational habits, but today I found it callous. I suspected that people didn't exist for Teresa once she had named their maladies; they were reduced to damp lungs and spackled organs in Tulsa and Jersey City. I took a handful of popcorn and turned away.

Inside, we sat in a small auditorium with movie-style seats. There were two banks of them, mounted on raised platforms, facing each other. The seats were reclined so as to leverage their view of the domed ceiling. The small crowd divided itself somewhat evenly as ethereal music piped in from somewhere. I sat by my father; I didn't know exactly when it would strike me, but I wanted to be sure he was right there. He rested his head on the back of the seat, fatigued. I tried to make conversation with him and for a moment I sensed what it was like to inhabit his mind. I really just wanted to stare up at the white dome, to wait for constellations to appear, but instead I made myself communicate. Was this the weight he carried? Was it a resistance to reaching out, or simply that the view inside his head was so much better?

"How's college?" I asked.

He lifted his head from the back of the seat, turned a little toward me. "Fine. I'm teaching an independent studies course on quantum mechanics. The students are quite bright." His manner changed, as if he was caught off guard by my taking the lead in the parent-child dynamic. He sat up, crossed his legs. "Everything's coming along for you?"

"It's fine," I said.

"Last year of school. Then it will be college."

"I should be hearing from the schools soon," I said.

"They take their sweet time."

A silence.

He said, "I'm sorry about what I said at the talent show. It's your memory. You can do with it what you want." These were not his words, but paraphrases of things my mother had said.

"I didn't really mean to recite a TV show. It just came to me. It's like comfort food for my brain," I said.

At that moment the music swelled and the lights dimmed. With each increment of darkness a small speck of light appeared in the dome. A swarm of dots became the Milky Way as the entire image of the cosmos rotated above us. A deep, ministerial voice commanded the air. *This is your universe today. But it was not always so . . .* An asteroid spun toward us. Meteorites arced earthward. Cloud swirls drifted beneath Earth's opalescent atmosphere. Then everything faded until a single speck remained. *The moment before the Big Bang . . .* My father craned his neck and said, "The first hydrogen bomb." The narrator spoke of the universe's first explosion in a tone better suited for a particularly bloody battle of World War II—*opposing forces give rise to a cataclysmic event . . .* A white-orange flare, then a blue afterburn, as matter rushes into the void. *Compressed gases . . . nitrogen . . . carbon . . . life emerges on a piece of cooled aftermath . . .* The music changed suddenly to harps and lutes, birds calling through a synthesized chord. I saw Whit, mouth ajar, unblinking, his hand limp in the popcorn bucket.

There were numerous opportunities for me to divulge the cancerous growth that loomed inside my father's head. There was even a kind of poetry that I could appreciate by doing it under the starlit dome, perhaps as the supernova was reducing itself to cosmic dust. But I said nothing and we watched intently as the story of our universe unfolded. Then, as we were leaving, my mother and Teresa went to the restroom and Whit and I waited with my father. I glanced at Whit and he saw, I think, that I was on the verge of something. He excused himself and went out into the parking lot. My father stood in front of a poster that read COMING ATTRACTION: LIFE ON EARTH.

"What did you think?" I asked him.

He shrugged. "Very bright and loud. Mostly misguided facts. Entertaining enough."

"I kind of liked it. It almost made me appreciate why you like physics so much."

"That was Hollywood physics," he said.

*Average number of neurons in the brain: 100 billion*

We drifted for the empty concession stand.

"I've been meaning to have a talk with you, son," he said.

"You have?"

"I know I haven't always taken an active interest in all parts of your life."

"What do you mean?" Had the spinning celestial bodies loosened something in him?

"I don't always notice the right things . . . "

"It's okay. I know your mind doesn't—"

He put his hand on my shoulder and said, "I like Teresa very much. You make a good team." It was Whit-esque—the word *team*. But the sentiment was his. He leaned against the concession stand. A giant bag of unsold popcorn lay on the counter next to the open and empty register. He looked at it for a moment, puzzled.

"Look," he said, "somebody takes the popcorn home when it doesn't sell." It was the same look he gave in hospitals and in supermarkets—baffled by the props from other lives and economies; the neon sprawl of the cereal aisle, the neat bandage on a wound. People got sick and required treatment, popcorn was salvaged from movie theaters; for my father these were insoluble mysteries, infinitely more arcane than the warping of time.

"She likes you, too," I said.

"Good."

"Yeah."

He rubbed his head and said, "The headaches are getting worse. The other day I would have taken a lobotomy in lieu of breakfast."

I looked away, down the corridor, where I saw my

mother and Teresa emerge from the ladies' room and move slowly toward us. They both looked at us.

"Teresa has seen something inside your head," I said. "Which explains your headaches."

My father stood still, turned his back to my approaching mother. "I see." He closed his eyes for a moment. "Is her gift, how should I say—empirical?"

"She's diagnosed dozens of people."

"I know there's something in there. That's the thing. Nathan, I hate to admit it, but I can feel it. Someone is sticking a finger through the back of my head. That's not a scientific explanation. That's the patient's interpretation. Am I already a patient?"

Something in him knew.

"It's a tumor," I said.

He puckered his mouth and nodded almost imperceptibly. "*Wow,*" he said. "This is what Whit calls out of left field."

Quietly, I said, "It's big. The size of a plum."

He scratched the back of his head, then put his hands into his pockets. He pulled out a key chain and several quarters and looked at them, absorbing their dimensions. "A quarter seems manageable to me. Not so sure about a plum. That seems very large."

His lips thinned and his jaw tightened. I felt like my chest was about to cave in.

"This is definitely not good," he said. He slowly placed his coins and key chain back in his pockets as my mother and Teresa stood beside us. My father looked at the ground, then at my mother's face. I took Teresa by the hand and moved for the exit. We opened the glass doors and stepped outside. It was getting dark. The window-shoppers had quit the street. I turned back to face the concession stand and saw my parents through the glass doors. My father leaned back against the counter, steadying himself, his arms by his side. My mother, her back to me, pulled a cardigan around her shoulders, seemingly braced. The pink neon popcorn sign burned a halo effect around the scene. My father fidgeted with the change in his pockets, trying to find the words. Finally he lifted his eyes from the carpet. Then my mother took a small step backward and I knew he'd told her. It registered in her whole body; her shoulders, her hands, everything tightened, then uncoiled. People filed past them, oblivious. Strangers coming out into the dusk, bundling into coats and holding hands and reaching for car keys, but moving slowly, still a little dazed by the pinwheel of stars.

# thirty

The decline was rapid. The tumor had burrowed deep and slow, fissured the stem and cortex—the root cellar of the brain. Clustered cells, aggregating slowly, an inch a decade. But once discovered, it grew rapaciously. The brain-scan images blotted and rippled; the tumor was a nebulous cloud, a darkening whorl. It was buried too deep in the brain to operate. My father complained of blind spots, numbness in his fingers.

For a while after the diagnosis he retained his burning questions, was able to continue teaching. Then, just as winter can arrive in a single afternoon, the light was driven from him. His pensive air, the abiding speculation about the nature of reality, his jotting down of Greek-letter equations that tracked the permutations of force and momentum, all disappeared.

As the tumor grew, my father became a mockery of himself. In place of passivity and long silences, he was quick-witted and sarcastic. He contradicted himself within the same sentence, laughed at misfortune and cruelty. My mother banned him from newspapers and NPR news because she tired of his rejoinders to armed robberies and plane crashes. "Nobody asked you to get on that plane, did they? No. That was a contract you signed with the super-symmetric." Before full-blown cancer, the quirks and anomalies of the Newtonian and quantum worlds were ineffable but benign, now they were indictments, the pranks of some cosmic and acerbic wit.

All of it happened within a month. After the planetarium he returned home and underwent a battery of tests. My mother called not long after and asked me to come home. She said, "We need to start saying good-bye."

I arrived by bus into my hometown a little after midnight. It was raining and windy. My parents sat parked in front of the station with the hazard lights on. I could see the outline of my sleeping father in the passenger seat. He had a blanket around him. My mother opened her door and helped me put my bags in the trunk.

"You should have gone home. The bus is an hour late," I said.

"Your father insisted. He fell asleep just a little while ago."

She closed the trunk and embraced me, then we got in the car. The stuffy interior smelled of my father's talcum powder; I wanted to roll the window down but didn't. The radio murmured with classical music. Suddenly I wanted Whit to be there, longed for his chipper demeanor. We rode home fifteen miles under the speed limit—not because it was rainy and slick but because, I think, this was my mother's way of shielding us, this one act of extreme caution. Slow-driving was her way of saying there was enough risk in our lives, that even driving six miles or toasting bread or stepping out of the shower would now require caution. Life was coming undone.

We arrived home and I woke my father inside the garage. He jerked and reeled at me.

"You frightened me," he said loudly.

"We're home," I said.

I took his blanket, but he brushed me aside when I held out my hand. We made our way to the kitchen. Our house immediately felt familiar—the waxy smell of old furniture, the coralline hues of book spines. We sat in the kitchen and my mother made us tea. My father sat in a wooden rocker and rubbed his bare feet.

"Bones ache like teeth," he said.

"How are you feeling?" I asked.

"Like a fucking prince," he said.

My mother at the stove. "Language."

"Oops. I don't like swearing but it comes out. Before I know it. Actually, I do like swearing. Never really did it much before. I can see the appeal. You see the appeal, son?"

"Sometimes," I said. "But it's strange hearing you swear."

"The doctors say some of it is from the drugs," my mother said, lifting the kettle.

My father paused, considered, and then turned to me. "You want to do some trig?"

"I'm kind of tired," I said. "Maybe in the morning."

"Calculus?"

"Nah. I need to get to bed."

He sighed. "This house is a morgue. I'm bored out of my skull. And that's saying something, because there's a lot going on inside my skull."

"Maybe tomorrow we can use the telescope," I said.

*the least luminous star known is rg 0050 2722 in sculptor*

"Stars are history," he said.

My mother placed our tea on the table.

"I'm going upstairs," she said. "You boys lock up." I felt suddenly deserted. I didn't know what to say, what he might do. He stared down at his aching feet.

"How's the institute?" he asked.

"Fine."

*the size of a black hole will depend upon the mass of the collapsed star*

"Good. Next year is college. The big time." I nodded and he looked around the kitchen, carefully, like a man inspecting real estate. Then he said, "You know how some brains only have two speeds—sleep and insight? That's quite good. Anyway, Isaac Newton was obsessed with equations. One night he gave a dinner party and left the guests while he ventured down to his wine cellar. They found him there an hour later etching formulas into the dust on the casks. I've wondered lately if maybe he wasn't a half-savant. He died a virgin. I must tell my theory to Gillman. How is he?"

"He told me to send his best wishes."

"It'll take more than good wishes to crack this one. How's Mother Teresa?"

I hesitated. "She's good. Why did you call her that?"

"What?"

"Mother Teresa?"

"She saves people, doesn't she? Look, she saved me. Called a spade a spade. Told you I had a little apple cooking in the broiler. And here we are."

"Didn't you want to know?"

He shifted in his chair. "Maybe I did, but I don't think your mother did. She would have preferred a couple months of my swearing and then for me to drop off at breakfast one morning without warning. She's good in adversity, but after the fact."

I looked out the darkened windows and made out the suggestion of the orchard.

"Sorry, sorry. I say things. Go to bed. I can't sleep now," he said, waving a hand in the air.

"What will you do down here?"

"Don't worry," he said. "I don't play with matches. It's not like Alzheimer's. I'll do some trig on some graph paper, just like old times. I'll get bored with my inability to concentrate and come upstairs in a few minutes. Good night. I'm glad you're home and don't mess with the thermostat. You could roast a turkey in here but my bones need the warmth. Whit will come by in the morning. We'll make him an astronaut's breakfast. Little pancake moons."

I stood up from my chair. I wanted to hug my father, to shield him from his own firing neurons, but he never looked up from his tea. He wanted me to go away. I went upstairs to my bedroom. My mother had made my bed with my boyhood Superman sheets. There were posters of dinosaurs and ice-age chronology, a chemistry set, a mobile of the solar system—artifacts from the era of hope.

I turned off the light and lay in the darkness, listening to the sounds of our house. The furnace rattled in the basement. I could hear the wind under the eaves and the windows resisting the weather outside. I closed my eyes and heard my father in the kitchen. I pictured the tumor, marbled and knotted. Sometimes I saw corresponding images that went along with the ailments that Teresa diagnosed, the lumps and contusions, the ulcers and the pinched blood vessels. *Throat cancer* was an old man in a trench coat, his tongue gray, like a parrot's; *aneurysm* was a neurotic, middle-aged woman, secretive, like a pickpocket. What was *brain tumor*? I let the words eddy and still in my mind: it was somebody greedy and unapologetic—a fat man at a buffet, a look of doomed pride sweeping across his face as he makes a dozen trips through the food line.

BEFORE WHIT ARRIVED FOR BREAKFAST the next morning, I spoke to Teresa on the phone. After a brief stay in Chicago she was back at the institute.

"Everyone says hi," she said.

"No, they don't. Cal and Dick don't say hi even when I'm there."

"Okay, you're right. I'm trying to be nice. How's your dad feeling?"

"He's not acting like himself. Last night he said *fuck*."

"People change near the end."

There was a long silence. All I could hear was her breathing.

"Who says he's going to die?"

She said, "I just mean people change when they're sick."

"My mother thinks the medications make him act weird."

"I'm sure," she said. "The shadow side comes out. When are you going to come back to the institute? I've got no one to drink with."

There was something trite in her voice. I said, "I don't know."

Neither of us said anything for a while. I was at a loss for words and she waited out the silence, perhaps afraid of saying the wrong thing. The institute seemed like another world away.

"I'll call you again," I said.

"Yeah," she said quietly. "Keep in touch."

Whit arrived for breakfast and filled our house with his presence. He was our mascot now, our shrine against morbid wallowing. We each clung to him: my mother doting on him with chocolate chip pancakes; my father asking his advice about financial matters, about lawyers and wills; and me privately engaging him in conversation about women he'd slept with. After my halfhearted conversation with Teresa, I needed the distraction.

"During wow-time I like to play the numbers, cover the bases," he said.

"What about talking during sex?" I asked.

"You mean the odd remark or sustained discourse?"

"A remark or two."

"Sure. I like to say 'hi' to the crowd."

Whit talked about sex the way he spoke about sports and space, with the reverent vibrato of a fan, a believer. These subjects, in Whit's mind, were all related; they implied one another. Sex could not be discussed without reference and simile to baseball, and nobody could invoke space without conjuring sex, the wash of the unknown. As he talked I wondered how long it would be before I experienced sex. Virginity seemed like yet another form of mediocrity, even if Isaac Newton had died with his intact.

After breakfast my mother did the dishes and Whit, my father, and I took a walk. My mother bundled my father in a wool cap and a coat. We walked out into the orchard. A storm had dusted the branches of the apple trees with some out-of-season snow. As we came over the small hill at the edge of our property, Whit spoke to my father about his lawyer's credentials. "Joe's a good man. Looked after me in that divorce business. She got house, car. I got stocks, bonds, and space money."

"Space money?" I asked.

"NASA pension."

"I'll call him," my father said.

My father cinched his coat tighter and pulled up his

collar. "I'm going to die of cold out here. Whose idea was this? Son, was this your idea of a joke?"

"We can head back," I said.

"I can give you a piggyback," Whit said to my father.

"I am not getting on your back for all the Darjeeling in my wife's pantry."

We headed back to the orchard and I watched my father as we walked. His face looked on the verge of nausea. He told me the medicine he took tasted the way he imagined mercury would. Now he stopped and leaned against a gnarled apple tree, jammed his hands into the pockets of his coat. He looked around him, nodding, agreeing with the ruined appearance of the orchard, and then looked at me. I felt, for a moment, he was going to talk openly and clearly to me, to tell me what he was thinking, what he feared, to galvanize that single moment that would somehow allow his passage from the living. Instead he looked off into the distance and said, "I've had the strongest craving for fried chicken. Your mother refuses to make it. I have a tumor the size of a grapefruit and she won't deep-fry chicken wings. She feels it's uncivilized . . . " His words trailed off.

"We can smuggle you some," Whit offered.

"Oh no, she'd smell it. She knows if a mouse farts in that house."

I laughed in spite of myself. "We can take you out for fried chicken," I said. "There's a place on the edge of town."

"It needs to be spicy. What I'm saying at this point is that the last supper takes place at a wing joint."

WHAT MY FATHER IMPLIED ABOUT my mother's cooking was true: she refused to make anything she considered pedestrian or gratuitous. She would make meat loaf but not hamburgers, roasted chicken but not fried chicken. As my father's illness got worse, she spent little time with Levart and her cooking turned from exotic to early American. It was New England comfort food: boiled meats, bread puddings, chowders, baked cod, casseroles. These were the puritan meals of a people who didn't want to offend God with anything lavish or decadent. Every meal came with white linen napkins and a dried-flower arrangement in the middle of the table. The formality taxed my father. I think, at times, he pictured himself in a dusty one-room apartment with John Coltrane playing and a row of soup cans on the windowsill. Perhaps in that vision he felt like he was preparing for death more earnestly, more honestly. There was denial and atonement in my mother's cooking, as if she were trying to cook her way back to a simpler time.

One day, at the risk of causing a rift with my mother, Whit and I smuggled my father out of the house for fried chicken. We planned to be back in time for a homecoming dinner my mother had planned for me. We drove across town at lunchtime, Whit at the wheel. It was a neighborhood none of us knew: a working-class area wedged between the old northern highway and the railroad that once carried freight from Duluth. Convenience stores and small taverns lined the sidewalks; an enclave of taxidermists stood surrounded by vacant lots. An old warehouse lay in ruins, its windows boarded and its walls covered in graffiti.

"We're going to get food poisoning," my father said excitedly. By now I had become accustomed to his bluntness and occasional acrimony.

Whit said, "There's an inverse relationship between how good fried chicken is and the appearance of the place that serves it."

My father smiled. "Ah, yes, Newton's least-known physical law."

The diner was a weatherboard box painted bright orange. It had a broken neon sign that read BB'S CHICKEN AND RIBS AND BAR. I directed Whit to pull over and we parked beside a host of white Chevy and Ford pickups. We went inside and waited to be seated. The place was packed: construction workers and the grounds crew from the college, local factory workers and taxi drivers. Adjacent to the dining room was a bar with a narrow stretch of counter and wooden stools, a pool table, a jukebox, and a stuffed bass mounted on the wall. I asked my father where he wanted to sit. He pointed to the smoke-filled bar and said, "Where the action is."

We walked into the bar. I certainly didn't look twenty-one, but no one seemed to mind. The bartender, a blunt-faced man, shot us a glance as we took a table by the jukebox.

We looked at our menus.

"No need to ask what Samuel is getting," Whit said. "I think I'll get wings, too. How about you, Nathan?"

"Sounds good," I said.

The bartender wiped our table then, as if it were an afterthought, took our orders. As he walked away my father called out.

"And, sir, bring us three beers."

The man paused, looked at me, and then looked at my father. "Is he twenty-one?"

"As of today," my father said. "It's his birthday." I'd never known my father to lie or think quickly on his feet.

The man looked at me again, and then turned to my father. "Bud or Miller?"

My father looked at Whit. These were men who ordered home-brewing catalogs and spent months perfecting amber ales in the basement.

Whit, grimacing, said, "Make it Bud."

When the food and beer arrived we ate and drank in silence for some time. My father ordered a second round and it occurred to me that he wanted to get us drunk. His cheeks glowed and he scowled at the jukebox. A heavy-metal song rushed at us. *You were just a small-town girl with a head on fire . . . swallow me whole, baby . . .*

My father winced at the electric guitar solo. "You like this kind of music, Nathan? Is this the, what, the music of the moment? The anthem of the times?" His mouth was wet in the corners.

"Not really."

"What do they call this?" Whit asked.

"Heavy metal," I said.

"Lead, gold, that kind of thing," my father said, laughing. "Are we listening to the cutting edge? What would quantum theory be if you set it to music?"

"Opera," said Whit.

"Rap," I said.

"Both wrong. The sound track to quantum theory is a kazoo out in a forest."

"You're drunk," I said, surprised.

My father craned his head to the jukebox, waiting for the note that would crown the distorted guitar solo. He raised his index finger. "There it is. The ejaculation," he said. His hand shot to his mouth, then touched the top of his head.

"Hold steady," Whit said.

"Son, who's the Thelonious Monk of heavy metal?"

I drank from my beer. "I don't think they have a Monk."

"I see," he said, dipping a wing bone into some barbecue sauce. He brought it to his mouth, leaving a trail of sauce across his chest. "I'm hit," my father said, clutching the red stain.

The room came alive with our laughter. I could hear the pool table. The solid, wooden *plink,* the balls conspiring with the pockets.

"From all vantage points it seems I'm drunk," my father said. He raised his beer in the air. "A home brewer should have better tolerance than this."

Whit began the prelaunch sequence for a Budweiser bottle, his hands resting against the brown glass. "T minus five, four, three, two, one, ignition and liftoff . . . " He arced the bottle toward us. "Little things you don't even think about become important up there. The perfect parabola of peeing outside, that's something you give up. When I was still with Nancy I used to sneak out and pee in her antique rosebushes. Not out of malevolence, you understand, but—"

"Man's great desire to piss outside," my father said, cutting him off and turning to me. "Whit, here, is a Neanderthal in a space suit. Tell me, Whit, did you masturbate a lot up there?" My father let out a sharp, raspy laugh. Who knew what was going on in his brain? Some kind of chemical reaction involving his medication and beer hops? It could probably be written out and graphed, no different than photosynthesis. A paper trail that would explain his behavior. To see him suddenly have a bawdy sense of humor, to engage in banter, made me miss the father I'd never had. Sitting across from me was the man who might have taught me how to throw a baseball, made lewd comments about pretty girls crossing the street, defended me against my mother's puritan ways—*For crying out loud, Cynthia, give the kid some elbow room.*

Whit pushed a chicken bone around in some dipping sauce and smiled. It seemed important to him not to get caught out by my father. "There's a certain physics involved—what with the absence of gravity and so on—but suffice to say the lunar emptiness can make a man lonesome," Whit said.

My father's face became drawn; he looked down at the place mat in front of him, which depicted a chicken running from a wielded meat cleaver.

"I need another drink," my father said. He gestured to the bartender with a complicated hand flourish. The man hauled over to us with three more Budweisers and placed them on the table.

"Tell me," my father said to the bartender, "do you offer discounts for the terminally ill?" The word *ill* was steel-colored.

The blunt-faced man wiped the table, nonplussed. "Only senior discounts. Anybody over sixty-five?"

My father blew air between his lips. "I understand." The man took our plates and returned to watching a football game on the wall-mounted television.

"Maybe you've had sufficient," Whit said to my father.

My father took a sip from his beer bottle. "There's one thing I want to do before I die. Nobody owes me anything, so this would be a favor."

"Shoot," said Whit.

*number of cortical layers in the brain: 6*

"What is it?" I asked. Again I fell into the trap of imagining my father a normal man, that his terminal wish would involve the Concord or scuba diving on the Barrier Reef. He leaned forward and said: "Stanford Linear Accelerator. I want to see the switchyard one more time. Maybe even try to find the ghost particle. A new bump. This thing is waiting for me, I know it."

"Would they let you?" Whit asked. "You're not a member of the collaboration project anymore."

"We'll pull some strings. People will understand. A road trip to California, just the three of us. I'm picturing moderately priced hotels . . . "

"Continental breakfasts," Whit said, warming to the theme. Whit would captain the Oldsmobile and I would take shifts driving; my father would sleep in back as we traversed the Midwest. There was no possibility that my mother would agree to it, but I saw the earnestness in my father's face. Unknown particles were the closest thing he could imagine to the hand of God.

We sat and finished our beers and then Whit insisted on paying the bill. My father stumbled several times as he got up from his chair. He went over to the bartender and delivered a high-performance thank-you. He shook the man's hand. I had known my father to stand agape at a man's extended hand, as if he were a tribesman who found this gesture shameful, but here he was pumping the bartender's hand, saying, "A nice little business you have. Excuse my state. I'm not long for the road, you understand. My name is Samuel Nelson."

Out in the parking lot, Whit helped my father into the backseat, guiding his head to make sure he wouldn't hit it— the way a cop helps a felon into a squad car. I decided to ride in back as well. "Where to, kids?" Whit said.

"Home," my father said. "Where my wife is going to smell my breath for traces of alcohol and meals prepared off premises." My father wound down his window and let the air blow in his face as we drove back toward our neighborhood.

"You're plastered," I told him.

He said, "A slight tingling sensation permeating the central nervous system."

"Plastered as Paris," Whit said.

We arrived home and came in through the kitchen door, hoping to avoid my mother. It was getting dark outside and I realized we had lost track of time. The house smelled of baking meat and it immediately brought me to my senses. The kitchen was strewn with pans and dishes. We all stood—stunned—as she called from the parlor.

"About time. I've just set the table." She came into the kitchen and stood in the doorway, bristling. Whit was supporting my father, his eyes large and wavering, his grin maniacal. He could have been a tramp we'd rescued from across town. My mother formed a Gothic arch with her mouth—the facial architecture she reserved for disgust. She stood in a Celtic skirt with a turtleneck sweater, an amber necklace around her neck—a middle-aged matriarch, a woman who knew a cup of flour by feel but measured it anyway, who believed tradition and making things from scratch were life's great pleasures. She glared at all three of us: a trinity of blame. "What is that unholy smell?" she asked.

"Multiple choice," my father said. "A., domestic beer, B., fried chicken, C., the smell of the dying." My father winced with self-disgust. "I'm sorry. I'm drunk. I asked these two to take me out for some spicy chicken wings."

"I picked mint from the greenhouse to go with the lamb."

"We're sorry," Whit said.

"This is disgusting. I've spent the whole afternoon cooking. Forget it, just forget it, you bloody fools!" Anger blushed her cheeks. I thought of the Brontë sisters.

"I'll eat some mutton," my father said. He moved uncertainly through the kitchen. "On second thoughts, the capacity of the human stomach is finite."

My mother, on the verge of sobbing, left the room saying,

"From this day forward you can cook your own damn meals."

*the longest recorded hunger strike was 385 days in wakefield prison, yorkshire . . .*

We all looked at one another. What would we eat if my mother stopped cooking? The kitchen could not close. It was the engine of the house. It was bread steam that made that old house yield to earthly concerns, square meals that kept my father from floating completely beyond our grasp.

"That doesn't sound good," Whit said. "That definitely sounds like a woman at the end of her string."

"Rope," my father said.

"Yes, rope is the thing," Whit said.

"She would say *tether*," I said.

Whit said, "My God that was good chicken."

"I need a nap," my father said, suddenly exhausted.

Whit and I helped him into the guest room, where he slept these days. He claimed my mother's movements and her compulsive need for tucked sheets kept him awake. I helped him onto the bed and removed his shoes. His laces were badly frayed at the ends and I pictured him wandering campus, shoes untied, a slovenly pacing of gravel walks. Whit said good night and went outside to his car. I went to find my mother. I knew that it was me who had to apologize, to make amends. My father was dying and Whit was not a blood relative. It could start out as a ban on cooking, but soon the resentment could spread and deepen, ravage and poison the entire household. I went outside and found her in the greenhouse on the southern side of the house. Here she kept her flower and herb garden. We were the only family in Wisconsin who ate our own fresh basil in winter. She had sunlamps and heating ducts, a misting nozzle suspended from the ceiling. I watched her from the outside for a moment. It was dark except for a new moon low over the orchard and the warm glow of the heat lamps inside the greenhouse. She stood there weeding with a tiny trowel, her figure slightly warped and distorted by the mottle of the glass. I opened the door and felt a rush of warm, humid air.

"Quickly, inside," she said.

I closed the door behind me. The rectangular boxes were labeled: sorrel, tarragon, nasturtiums.

"Doing some gardening?" I asked.

"I swear the weeds come up overnight." Her tears were gone.

"We put Dad to bed."

"He'll feel wretched tomorrow. I suppose you considered that?" She brushed the leaves between her fingers.

"It was his idea."

"Yes, and if he decides to inject himself with drain cleaner we should let him."

She pulled a weed from among some violets, held it like a mouse.

I said, "I'm sorry."

She looked up, put the trowel to the side. "I've weeded these plants five times today."

I came and stood beside her. I was a foot taller than she.

After a silence she said, "Your great-aunt Beulah used to dry lime blossoms in here."

"What for?" I asked.

"It's a natural sleeping pill. She'd make tea out of it and drink it before bed. I think she was addicted."

"When you were a kid?"

"Yes."

She picked up a spray bottle and misted some violet leaves.

"You must have been lonely here just with her, after the train accident."

"Sometimes," she said. "But we were always so busy."

"I wish I could have known your mom and dad."

"That would have been nice," she said.

She lifted a bag of potting mix and leveled out a few cups into a pot.

"Are you really going to stop cooking?"

"Maybe."

"As punishment?"

"Retribution." She steadied her lips, considering a smile.

"We're going to starve," I said. "Dad doesn't know how to boil water."

"There's enough food in the deep freeze to last a year. Besides, I don't think learning how to operate the oven will kill you boys."

A gust of wind whistled through some cracks in the glass.

"Nathan?"

"What?"

She looked at her plants, as if she were talking to them. "Your father will be gone soon and we need to start preparing for that." She looked down at an herb plant, deciding which leaves to target. Then she dropped her pruning scissors and suddenly embraced me. The tears were back. I could feel the tension in her shoulders, the strength she'd developed from so many years of breast stroke at the YWCA. We stood there for a long time. Over her shoulder I looked out through the greenhouse walls. Night was everywhere now.

# thirty-one

My father shaved his beard off later that week. Thinking of this now, I realize it was the day he accepted he was going to die. He emerged from a marathon shower, his face full of razor nicks, and stood in the doorway while my mother and I ate oatmeal in the kitchen. Her ban on cooking hadn't even lasted a day. My father was born to wear a beard and had done so since the age of twenty. Some men may have appeared remade, retooled, without facial hair, but my father appeared stunted, baby-faced, like a man who could not tolerate sunlight. A face so naked it was hard to look at. His beard had, in fact, helped to conceal his death sentence, hidden the chromatic certainty that lives in the skin of cancer patients. My mother put her hand to her mouth and I stopped chewing. My father smiled this wide, hooligan smile, and it occurred to me that he was preparing us. He wasn't going to allow his terminal days to be awash in quiet resolve and unspoken anguish.

"This is what my face looks like," he said.

"Where is all that hair?" my mother asked.

"Composted out back," he said, still smiling. He put a hand to his jaw and rubbed it like a wound on the mend. "Is it acceptable?" he asked.

"Different," I said. "Definitely a perceptible change."

"You sound like me," he said. He came into the kitchen and sat down at the table.

I was still staring at his face, the rawness of it.

My father said, "Dear, there's something I want to discuss."

"You're not going," she said.

My father looked at me, suspecting I had betrayed him. My mother paused and then said, "Dr. Benson called from the Stanford Linear Accelerator to confirm your arrival."

"I've been having this dream and in it I see the ghost particle as clearly as Polaris. I'm going to check which Greek letters are unused and name it. Brush its little cheek with a stream of electrons. A goddamn river of electrons, you understand."

*longest dream measured by duration of rem is 2 hours 23 min*

"You're not well enough to go. The doctors say you may need to be hospitalized at any time."

I looked down at my bowl, wanting to leave the room but compelled to stay.

He said, "I don't think you understand what I'm saying. I have months, weeks."

"So you'd rather go out to California looking for something that may not even exist than spend the remaining days with your wife and son."

"I've invited Nathan and Whit to come along."

"I see," she said, nodding.

"You're more than welcome to come," my father said. "I assumed you'd rather stay here. I won't fly out there because of cabin pressure and its effect on the tumor, so we'll make a road trip out of it."

"What if something happens while you're out there looking for this ridiculous piece of dust?"

My father stared down at the tablecloth. For all I knew he was counting the shapes, tracing a hidden geometry, but then he spoke with such tenderness and tranquility that he sounded like a man roused from prayer. "I've been a bad husband, I know. I've ignored you. But I've always felt you here. The smell of bread . . . the wooden bowls of strange fruit. You've taken care of us. But I have to do this. My whole life comes to this, or it comes to nothing, Cynthia. Please give me this."

There were ten seconds of silence.

Then I said, "I'll look after him."

My mother stared at us, then collected some breakfast plates and carried them to the sink. She turned on the hot water and rinsed them, sending steam toward the windows. Without turning, she said, "If you die out there, I will never forgive you."

THE DAY OF DEPARTURE, WHIT sported around our house in a tracksuit and baseball cap, readying the Oldsmobile, checking tire pressure and radiator fluid with military precision. He prepared an emergency kit that would live in the trunk: a thermal space blanket, flares, a spare map, compass, flashlight, matches, reflective vests. I thought it possible that we were going mountaineering instead of driving to California on interstate highways. Whit was uncomfortable with my father's naked face and avoided looking at it directly.

I hugged my mother good-bye, uncertain whether I was in good standing with her.

"You're in charge of his medication. I've written it all out," she said, handing me a typed set of instructions.

"We'll look after him. I promise."

"Don't let Whit speed. He thinks he's still a pilot. Well, I'll have the place to myself." A note of forced enthusiasm rose at the end of her sentence.

"Okay," I said. We hugged again. My father called to her from the upstairs bedroom.

"What's he lost now?" she said, and went to go see. I walked outside and got in the car with Whit.

"Now, I'll take the first shift. I'm good for six hours straight, no stops. More than six and I get a little antsy. You bring a thermos?" he said.

"No," I said.

"Usually on these things every man brings his own thermos."

"Whit, it's not a hunting expedition. We're driving on four-lane freeways to San Francisco. If I get thirsty I'll stop at a gas station."

"All the same. The done thing is to have your own thermos."

He was writing the speedometer reading in a little spiral notebook.

"In a past life you and my father were married," I said.

"No, no. In a past life I was a Tibetan monk. I see prayer flags and I go wonky. I got a reading once from a gypsy woman in Toledo with great legs."

My father emerged from the house and climbed into the backseat. Whit honked the horn three times and we pulled out of the driveway while my mother reluctantly waved from the kitchen doorway.

THAT FIRST DAY WHIT DROVE like a man skipping bail, refusing bathroom breaks unless my father insisted. He commandeered the radio—classic rock and talkback—and

led us out of Middle America bellowing she-bops and rejoinders to inane listeners. We passed seasonal road stands
of folk art and fireworks run by teenage girls. We passed
families in U-hauls, plodding west for the redemptive
powers of California. We stopped for lunch in a small town
with a municipal park and a bandstand. My father napped
in back, reclined without a seat belt. There was a part of
me that wanted to take issue with that choice, point out the
greater tragedy of a man with a terminal brain tumor dying
in a car crash, but I let it lie. Beardless, gauzy-fleshed, he
was a boy we were taking on a road trip, napping under a
plaid picnic blanket. We streamed along the freeway, past a
bedlam of impoverished farms, animals caked in mud, radio
towers rising out of stripped pastures, out of a jigsaw of
Jersey cows. Late in the day, we stopped in Sioux Falls,
South Dakota, for gas and what Whit insisted on calling
"provisions"—Snickers bars and root beer. He cracked
open the cans with an alcoholic's relish and handed one
back to my father.

Whit let me drive. My father took a stint sitting up front
with me while Whit calculated our gas mileage in back, writing it in the logbook.

"Okay, gentlemen," Whit said. "The fuel-to-human ratio
on this trip is starting to concern me. Warm bodies to octane
is a real puddle on the tarmac."

"What are you talking about?" my father said.

"From now on, no more heat in the mornings or AC in
the middle of the day. And no radio," Whit said. "I want to
make the Golden State on ten tanks of fossil fuels."

"I can die early, if you'd like," my father said.

"Not funny," Whit warned.

"The radio doesn't use fuel," I offered.

"Then you better tell us some stories if there's no radio.

I'm bored up here. My neurotransmitters are on strike," my father said.

"It's the first day, gents. Pull yourselves together," Whit said.

"Stories," my father demanded.

"But no space stories," I said, gliding my hands across the wheel.

"No intergalactic masturbation stories either," my father said. He was grinning. We were light, car-fevered.

Whit said, "You guys are really burning a hole in my ass."

"Tell us some things. Go ahead," my father said.

Whit gathered himself, looked off at the horizon. "Did I ever tell you about me and Nancy's honeymoon?"

"Negative," my father said.

"We went to Arizona, a road trip, just like this one. We had an Airstream trailer with a cabin—Christ that thing could drink gasoline—and we pulled through the country-side. Little Indian cities and pueblos made of stone. She bought some of that Navajo jewelry, the kind Cynthia likes, from a guy with no teeth. We made love in a state park. I washed her hair in a claw-foot tub somewhere in New Mexico. I was a fucking king." Something about a road trip, about our errand, allowed Whit to swear and blaspheme un-abashedly.

"Postnuptial wow-time," my father supplied.

"We stopped off at the Grand Canyon and got out of the car and stood there for five minutes. Space ruined me. I looked at it and you know what I saw?"

"Tell us," I said.

"A movie backdrop. Flat, one-dimensional. Some don-keys down in the hole, that's what I saw. In the morning, at sunrise, we made love in the hotel that overlooked the canyon. I promise you, the bed floated nine hundred feet from the bottom, and I could look out the window and see the cactus coming alight from the sun as our hips joined. Then we drove to Tucson to the plane boneyard—"

"The what?" I asked.

"Air force facility. Retirement home for the big birds," Whit said.

"You honeymooned at a graveyard for airplanes?" I asked.

"Old fighters, bombers, DC-10s, B-52s, foreign airlines, Qantas and Thai Air, you name it." Whit's voice pitched higher, took on the bravado of conquest. "I get us a tour and we drive around in an air force–issue jeep, flanked by long rows of gleaming metal birds. Turbines, wingspans, the black-snubbed noses of the bombers. The tour guide tells us how they wrap the planes to preserve them and how the desert knows no rust and I'm getting, well, excited, holding Nancy's hand. I can tell she's bored but trying, you know, for me, for the week-old marriage. Anyway, we come past a big old commercial-looking thing, 740-something, painted with the presidential seal and the guide says that it's Nixon's old Air Force One. But it's only called that when the president is on board. Anyway, I about lose it right there, and all I can think about is getting a peek inside that plane. The guide knows I'm from the service, that I've served the country up there, so he lets us in."

"Into the presidential plane?" my father asked.

"Yes," Whit said. "So we walk around in there. Of course I go straight to the cockpit and I sit in the seat, touching the joystick and staring at the needles and dials and for some reason I'm pitching a tent—"

"A funny time to camp," my father said.

"Dad, he means he had a hard-on, an erection."

"I see, yes, from the context . . . "

"All that fuselage and desert air, Indian villages, I'm hard as concrete all the time. The whole trip. It's like the more we have sex the more I imagine roadsides and ditches, you know, doing it rugged."

"I understand now," my father said.

"The tour guide is out in the jeep smoking a cigarette and I go back to find Nancy. It's still got the Berber carpet, the presidential seal woven in. It's still got the mahogany armrests and the swivel chairs as wide as a bed. It's still got the area for the cabinet members and for the chief executive himself. And I find Nancy sitting in the chair."

"The chair?" I asked.

"The chair!" Whit boomed.

"Nixon's," my father confirmed.

"Her hair is dead straight from all the heat and dry air and she's swiveling, you know, like a prom queen at a malt shop, and I come up beside her and she has no idea whose chair it is. I mean, you can tell it's the throne, bigger than the rest, a red telephone right by the side. I turn to my new wife and I say, 'Nancy, you're the sexiest thing in this boneyard,' and she about slaps me. I have this crazy idea. I can't stop myself. I stand in front of her, my hands on my hips, the position of hope—"

"What we're saying is—" my father started.

"He wanted oral sex, Dad."

Whit said, "Now, we're still in the early days, the marital probation period, and I can't just out and ask, so I stand there, looking out the windows at the sand and the DC-10s all chromed up, and I'm thinking happy thoughts the way they teach you in case you get depressed in orbit, about great meals and first cars and home-team football victories, and it feels like I'm waiting for a goddamn eternity. *Unzip that fly,*

*Nancy, for the love of Christ. I need this.* And finally she speaks."

"What does she say?" I asked.

"She says, 'The day Nixon was impeached I fell down some stairs at work and broke my ankle. Whit, honey, isn't that strange? Isn't that a coincidence?' I wanted to cry. I heard the jeep engine start up and gestured for Nancy to go outside. I stayed there for a moment and sat in the liar's seat myself. I pictured him flying around, crossing the international date line, smug little bastard. I took a little swivel. That was the moment I knew she'd leave me one day. That was the moment I knew the ditches and roadsides would never happen. We were . . . *married*." I watched Whit in the rearview mirror. He looked out his window. Nebraska grain fields streamed by, swatches of mown wheat.

After that story there were hours without conversation. The familiar trees—the birches and pines and buckeyes—gave way to open, weathered fields, some worn to sod. Whit's story was the flagship for silence.

MY FATHER CHOSE A HOTEL for us the first night that featured deck furniture submerged in the swimming pool, slouching balconies, and stained brown carpet. Our room smelled of damp towels. Before bed, I made a neon line out of my father's medication—lithium blue, hot pink, safety yellow. He took them without water, between bites of pizza. I memorized the Gideon Bible while I waited for sleep to come. My father and I shared a bed. He lay on his back, barely moving. I was aware of his breathing, the slight rasp that hooked into his out-breaths, the tension he carried in his bones. I was aware of time, not physicist's cosmic time, not the bending kind that can be slowed or hurried, but the time of days and hours, the kind that knows the exact number of total heartbeats each of us will emit in our lifetimes. Now and then, Whit's breathing climbed into fitful snoring. My father, his eyes closed, suddenly spoke.

"Did you know the answer?"

"When?" I asked.

"Seventh grade. The question about Einstein."

I realized he was talking about the science fair; he made it sound as if it were something that happened earlier that same day. My hands felt cold.

"I knew the answer," I said.

"I always knew that. Was it to get back at me?"

"Not really."

"What, then?"

"That was part of it. But mostly I didn't want to hang out with you in the kitchen and graph sine curves. I'm sorry. I wanted you to be proud of me but I didn't want the pressure. I figured you knew all along."

"But the mind . . . it wants to be tamed," he said, with sudden evangelism.

"Dad, you're not normal. You should know that. Even now, I'm not a genius. I'm a guy who remembers things because he got whacked in the head and he sees and tastes words."

"You've always showed promise."

"I'm as smart as I'm ever going to be."

He sighed and rearranged his pillow. "Genius can arrive from across the void. Einstein's ideas existed in the unified field before he ever thought them. Nothing is created from scratch. We're conduits for the universe's desire to think about itself." He rested his head against the doubled-over pillow.

"I'm being realistic about myself. If you thought with my brain for a day you'd realize."

"If you thought with *my* brain for a day you'd realize. Your memory is a portal. Tap it, tame it, use it, for Chrissake."

I didn't respond. Eventually, his breathing settled and he fell asleep.

ON THE OTHER SIDE OF Denver, my father said, "At nineteen thousand meters the surrounding air pressure is such that the blood and fluids in an unprotected human body will boil." Whit and I nodded in silence. Increasingly, his jibes and observations were beyond our reach. Whit was reduced to a man carrying out a penance; his puns sounded empty and forced. My father found it increasingly difficult to sleep and he developed a headache that lasted an entire day. Nevada was a seamless, tin-colored stretch of sky, an expanse of olive scrub. The image of my father dying in the backseat came to me. We had to get him to Stanford as soon as possible. We drove all night into California and stayed near the Stanford campus.

The next morning we drove along the 280 freeway and the accelerator appeared below an overpass—two miles of tunnel, divided into sections that resembled freight-train boxcars. A steady stream of commuter cars rushed just feet above the accelerator tunnel. They were like colossal versions of the particles pulsing below—waves of electrons captured in the morning pall. We pulled onto the shoulder and Whit and my father stared out the window. Whit, who had never been here before, stared at the gray expanse, slack-jawed. It ended at the base of the Santa Cruz Mountains. Whit said, "Apart from the sight of Earth from an orbiting spacecraft, that is the loveliest thing I have ever seen."

We drove along Sand Hill Road to the main gatehouse and were checked in by a security guard after he confirmed my father's name on a list. We were given visitor badges and drove to a parking lot where a few station wagons and mini-vans of families were unloading for a tour of the facility. A slight man with black-rimmed glasses stood waiting for them to gather. Whit parked and we walked over to the central lab building. Dr. Benson, the man I'd met on my tenth birthday, still with enormous sideburns and an outsize red tie, came striding through the glass doors. "Dr. Nelson, it's good to have you back," he said. "I always enjoy your articles on the charm quark. Charm is still your specialty, correct?"

"Depends who you ask," Whit said.

My father shrugged. Benson laughed, smoothing his waxen hair with the palm of one hand. He appeared per-fectly at ease with my father's appearance; perhaps he didn't remember the beard. He said, "Let's drive down to the main control center." We followed him to a white Department of Energy car and got in.

My father said, "Can we see the tunnel first? Whit hasn't seen it before."

"Of course," said Dr. Benson.

We drove a short distance, passed through another gate-house, and pulled alongside the tunnel.

My father said, "Nathan, since you were here they've upgraded the beam switchyard." He turned to his colleague. "And the linac itself. What are we at now? Fifty giga–electron volts."

Benson said, "Correct. I remember you came here with your son many years ago."

"Yes, in the late seventies for his birthday. Not long after they discovered the bottom quark at Fermilab," my father said. His voice was nostalgic.

"Seems like prehistory. We were much less advanced." Dr. Benson looked at me in the rearview mirror. His shirt collar was frayed at the edges. "You were here in the dinosaur era, young man."

I nodded. In my mind those physicists were members of a strange Greek chorus, an amorphous collection of short-sleeved, hairy-armed men who'd spent their lives in labs and underground bunkers.

"Many changes have occurred." It was unclear to whom Dr. Benson was talking. I suspected the resident scientists took turns showing mortals through their billion-dollar particle amusement park. "We added a storage ring. New dipole magnets. A new electron gun at the western end of the tunnel."

My father said, "Klystron upgrades, no doubt." They could have been talking about custom-built automobiles—their voices had the lilt and veer of an enthusiast's obsession.

Dr. Benson stopped the car and invited us inside the visitor's alcove. We entered through a metal doorway and were suddenly standing inside the vast, fluorescent-lit tunnel. It housed enormous banks of klystron batteries and the air seemed to vibrate with a mechanical hum. A series of red and green lights flashed from the ceiling. My gaze followed an unbroken yellow line painted on the concrete floor. It extended for a mile, diminishing to a single point.

We all stared down the tunnel in silence. Buried below us was the copper braid that carried the particle assault. Everything that we could see merely powered the collision. Dr. Benson said, "When my thinking gets cloudy I come down here and walk the line." He made it sound like a reasonable thing to do, a stroll in a municipal park. My father touched one of the klystrons and said, "Dr. Benson, I assume I will be able to direct some collisions. I have some data I'd like to pull from the database of the field particle collaboration I worked on before."

"I figured as much," Dr. Benson said. "We're very sorry to hear about the condition." Dr. Benson fidgeted with something in his pockets. "You realize of course how tightly we're booked. We have physicists from sixteen countries here at the moment working on a new project. The team spokesman can give you full control of the beam switchyard for twenty-four hours and a desk. This comes out of the reconfiguration budget. Some lateral accounting. Grand Central Station is the situation at present."

"Thank you," my father said.

"We both know that nothing much can be found in a day. But I understand why you'd want to be back in the thick of things. I go on vacation in the Bahamas and I think about the accelerator." Benson turned and headed for the door.

My father nodded and took one final look down the tunnel before we went outside.

WE SAT IN THE CONTROL room. It was a dimly lit space crowded with monitor screens, instruments, and industrial office furniture. My father sat at a console and stared at event displays from previous experiments. A barrage of scattered lines and angles of deflection. He conferred with the shift supervisor, Larry Dunac, and a postdoc about variables. The accelerator was still "warming up." Whit and I drank coffee and ate donuts over in the corner. I watched my father trace a bony finger over the screen in front of him, his lips moving slightly.

After an hour or so, Larry said that the accelerator was ready and the collisions began. Each event was stored in the computer database with a number, the day, and the shift. There were hundreds of millions of stored events—the accelerator had kept decades of collisions in a carefully arranged order. My father and Whit watched as the first events were pulled onto the screens. The shift supervisor and my father conferred. There was a vaguely military feel to the scene, men exchanging target locations.

For twelve hours my father bombarded electrons with positrons traveling close to the speed of light. He walked the perimeter of the control room, wringing his hands behind his back. He talked about the possibility of a new field particle that could be coaxed from a collision with the right amount of energy. It would challenge the notion that there were only three generations of fundamental particles in the standard model. He changed collision energy levels several times and suggested that the accelerator wasn't working properly. Larry and the postdoc listened patiently, but I suspect they knew they were watching a dying man clutch at straws. To coax a new particle into measurable existence was to win the quantum lottery.

By evening, Larry lost the complicit quality in his voice, the congenial tone of an underling at battle. Dr. Benson dropped by and said he would be leaving shortly. "My wife is throwing a dinner party," he said. The word *throwing* struck me; it was metallic and sharp and seemed incompatible with the frayed edges of his shirt collar.

I'd spent an entire day in the stale-air confines of the control room and my mind was caustic. I had an impulse to call Arlen, the psychic at the institute, and ask him to search for the unknown particle. Could he pick up the particle's psychic location? This kind of thing continued in my head for a while. I sat in the corner watching a muted television. I looked up and saw my father squinting at the screens, tapping his chin. I said, "What if there's nothing left to find out there?" These were the first nonscientific words spoken in hours. Larry and Whit and one of the assistants stopped what they were doing and looked at me. Nobody smiled. My father rubbed his eyes wearily. A full minute passed. I could hear the second hand of a wall clock that I imagined was calibrated with an atomic source in Colorado. One by one they returned to their tasks. The thought was so impossible that it didn't even warrant a reply. Although they thought it was highly unlikely to find a new particle in an afternoon with a series of known variables, they all believed physicists would keep finding more layers to the subatomic fabric. In a hundred years particle physicists would look back and see the 1980s as an era of child's play. I went back to my muted game show.

Hours passed. Larry loosened his collar, my father rolled up his shirtsleeves, and Whit stood barefoot, in his undershirt. Pizza boxes and soda cans, a newspaper folded so many times the pages had become soft, almost elastic. The world had been reduced to the size of a living room. People were cagey; my father avoided eye contact. He was entitled to use the facility until eight the next morning, but decency implied he would cut everybody loose before then.

My father said, "I don't understand. We have a decent statistical probability. We've combed the data, other people's footprints, and still nothing . . . "

Whit sat reclined in a chair, cracking his neck from side to side. He looked at my father and said, "View from the cockpit is that it's time to land."

My father looked away, pretending not to have heard.

An hour later, he called Whit and me over to the screens.

"What is it?" Whit said.

"I like the way the antimatter traces across the screen."

Whit and I looked at each other.

My father said, "As you know, every time matter and antimatter collide they cancel each other out. They create nonexistence. In theory, there should be no concrete matter in the universe because when the Big Bang happened the cosmic checking account should have been balanced."

"But antimatter persists, despite the theory," Whit said.

"Correct. Dirac knew about this in 1928. He also knew that antimatter hides."

"Interesting," I said, hearing the fatigue in his voice.

My father stared back up at the screens. "Someday we'll answer the question of where all the antimatter is hiding in the universe and why it sometimes appears out of nowhere."

"It's getting late," Whit said.

My father folded his arms, resigned. "Death is not the same as antimatter."

"The sun's coming up outside," Whit said.

"They both have a negative charge, but death is far too common," my father said.

"What do you mean?" I asked. I couldn't help it. I knew we needed to get him out of there.

"Life is the anomaly, not death."

Whit said, "We should leave, Samuel. These men need to get some rest."

"Whit, I want to play with this awhile. Go take a nap."

"Okay," Whit said.

Whit and I walked back to our seats and dozed while my father played in his subatomic sandbox.

What I want to write is that at 4:15 a.m. on May 11, 1988, Samuel Nelson discovered a particle hitherto unknown to physics, or that he unraveled the mystery of why antimatter and matter do not cancel each other out in all cases. How a spray of light filtered across his phosphor screen like metal shavings glistening in green sunlight. How he woke Whit and me and announced his variables with the reverie of a man whispering the exact location of the arc of the covenant, or the shroud of Jesus, or any number of lost, sacred objects.

But what really happened was this: he woke us at that hour with something new in his face, a certainty that he would die without a shrine on the altar of science, without naming a child of the atomic nucleus, and that certainty took the form of defeat etched in—his mouth stricken, his eyes dilated and lit with the pale incandescence of the control room.

I didn't need to ask for details. We were driven to the parking lot. The security guard waved as we drove past the main gatehouse. It was dark and moonless. The dogtooth Santa Cruz Mountains were all shadow and silhouette. We stood by the Oldsmobile and my father stared at the ground.

*historic assassinations since 1865 | 1865 apr 14 us pres abraham lincoln shot by john wilkes booth | 1881 mar 13 alexander ii of russia jul 2 us pres james a garfield*

# thirty-two

We returned to the hotel and my father slept off and on until the next morning. When he woke he stared up at the ceiling and called me to his bedside. "I can't see out of my left eye," he said. He held a hand over his right eye. "Nothing." Whit came and stood beside me. "Call your mother and tell her to fly out here," my father said. "There's a good hospital at Stanford and you should drive me there shortly." It was rehearsed. "I've prepared a living will, which says I don't want to be kept alive artificially—no respirators, no heart stimulation. You will find this document in my coat pocket." We helped him out of bed and he bathed in the tub. Whit looked up the hospital in the local phone book and called ahead.

"Ambulance or regular vehicle?" he asked my father.

"Regular."

I called my mother. "You'd better fly out here, Mom."

"Let me speak with him," she said, and I handed the phone to my father.

"Hello and I'm sorry to put you through this," he said. A

pause. "I know. No. I love you, too, Cynthia." He put the phone down.

We walked downstairs and checked out of the hotel. Because he was blind in one eye my father walked a little off balance. We drove to the Stanford University Medical Center, where they had the area's best resident neurosurgeons. My father, it turned out, had researched the place thoroughly. He was admitted to a wing where they kept terminal patients— cancer and emphysema and AIDS—and they performed tests, scans, and X-rays. He asked me to tape a copy of his living will to his headboard, which I did. "They make more money if they pull out all the stops. Death itself is still free, however," he said. He refused to wear a gown. The other terminal patients felt uneasy around my father, I suspected. He'd come here to dispense with this troublesome errand, didn't have time for hospital drills or soft-edged euphemisms. Nobody likes a loose cannon in the death wards.

My mother arrived within six hours. She kissed my father on the forehead and cheek and said, "Did you find it?" He shook his head and she nodded, grimly satisfied but also heartbroken. The doctor appeared—hair a little long and sun-streaked, not more than thirty-five—and told us what the X-rays and scans revealed. He held the brown celluloid of an X-ray up to a lamp and pointed to the thing itself. An amorphous blob that now resembled a fried egg. The doctor said, "The tumor has attacked the optic nerve. This is definitely in the final stages. He's not in pain now because it's also affecting neurotransmission."

"You mean I'm in pain but I don't know it?" my father asked.

"Something like that. The brain itself doesn't feel pain, but you may get side effects as systems begin to fail."

The pewter lifelessness of the word *systems*.

"How long?" my mother asked.

"Days," the doctor said. "Days at the most." He walked out into the white-lit corridor.

WE TOOK TURNS SITTING BY my father. He was relieved that there was no pain because he didn't want to spend his final hours in the undertow of morphine or codeine or whatever. There is only so much diversion one can find in a hospital. When it was my turn to wander I walked the wards, past labor and delivery, where I heard the definitive cry of newborns. I passed through the emergency room, where the wounded and sick slumped in chairs and walked out into the bright California day. It was morning again and I had lost all sense of time. I watched a medical helicopter land on a rooftop and they wheeled a patient on a gurney out to meet it. A woman sat half reclined under a white knitted blanket. They put her inside and closed the hatch and the helicopter lifted into the air. The turbine sounded like a confluence of rivers, eddying off the brickwork of the surrounding buildings. I saw coils of silver and turquoise.

I bummed a cigarette from a guy on crutches and realized I hadn't smoked since Iowa. I sat on a bench and watched people coming and going, speculating about their illnesses, about their lives. Here people had been removed from the tenure of daily existence, brought down by the body's propensity to falter or, if you believed Teresa, by the body's lies and deceits—the unspoken truths, the denied regrets, all of them festering and rupturing beneath the surface. Cancer was an admission of guilt, that was how she saw it. What, then, was my father guilty of? I didn't want to let him leave us without knowing something secret, some admission that might illuminate who he really was. I persisted in the delusion that the dying are more capable of self-knowledge than the living.

I sat outside the hospital, watching cars pass by, seeing sick people picked up and delivered.

*chevy nova cream 9tks273 | ford taurus sapphire 3vsr209 | toyota camry red 7dde846 |*

The guy on crutches ambled over to me and sat. He had the jaundiced and unfazed air of someone who'd been in and out of hospitals his whole life. "See that woman that went up in the chopper?" he said. "She don't look that sick to me. Wide awake, she was, like she was taking a scenic flight over Golden Gate. You ever watch *M\*A\*S\*H,* when the choppers come in to land?" I nodded. Actually, I had memorized several episodes. He gave me another cigarette and he took my acceptance as tacit agreement that the evacuated lady was really a faker. "My favorite thing about hospitals is the elevators, so spacious for the gurneys. I could ride up and down in those things all day." I thanked him for the cigarette and went inside.

Whit prowled the vending machines and the cafeteria. I found him with candy bars lined up on a corridor bench outside my father's room. He drank from a large Styrofoam cup of coffee. He hadn't slept well in days and the sugar and caffeine made his hands tremble. "Never can find a Baby Ruth," he said, staring down at a handful of Snickers. My mother came out and told us that the doctors didn't think my father would last the night. The tumor was pushing against all kinds of arteries and cortexes and something was bound to rupture. Then my mother told us that my father would donate his body to science.

I left Whit and my mother and went to take my shift at his bedside. The room was now alive with LEDs and plastic tubing. He was lying in bed, propped by pillows, his knees drawn up slightly. His face had been remade in the last few hours. Something in his talks with my mother had allowed him to let go of the defeat and now there was a look of quiet indifference, a man with nothing left to lose but his body.

"Will you go to college in the fall?" he asked wearily. "Maybe they'll invite you to MIT."

I nodded. But I didn't know if I would go. There were probably letters from admissions offices waiting for me in Wisconsin.

"Be good at something." He looked at the backs of his hands, and then placed them gently on his lap. Then, "Where did you go?"

"I'm right here," I said, moving toward his good eye.

He shook his head gently from side to side. "No . . . where did you go when Pop died? What did you see?"

It was the first time my father had ever asked me what happened during my clinical death. I didn't know how to answer, because I wanted to give him details that I hadn't experienced: weightlessness, everything illuminated, a light so white and pure.

"I fell straight into the coma. I only have before and after, not much during the actual death. I seem to remember a noise. Like a radio between stations. And I felt like I was getting out of water. But I don't know."

"Figures," he said. "I told your mother about arrangements—remains and suchlike. I'll haunt all of you if you bury me in the ground. A physicist can't abide burial. He wants to be combusted, yielded to gas and lighter molecules."

"We'll do what you want."

"I remember things," he said. "The half-life of plutonium and the names of the noble gases, equations . . . Where does that all go? What use is all that information now?"

I shrugged. He took a pause and caught his breath.

We think the moments of truth we seek in death are

going to be about the departing, and then they pass before us, simply like clouds, and we realize it's about us. We want to know about us before they go.

"Were you ever proud of me?" I asked. The word *me* floated around the room as a graphite strip.

My father blinked several times slowly, considering all his options. He unfastened and removed his wristwatch and placed it on the bedside table. The watchband had left his wrist shades lighter than the rest of his arm. He rubbed the mark a little.

"When you were born I forgot to wear my watch. I didn't notice time or that small time still existed . . . you know, hours and minutes time. I took naps with you and your mother . . . hauled firewood and fixed things around the house. I used to wake up in the night just to watch you." He looked around the room. "You did that to me. Of course I was proud."

I felt the metallic chill of the bedrail.

He said, "I want you to have my watch. You don't have to wear it."

"I'm going to wear it, Dad," I said.

"It runs a little slow . . . but there's a jeweler. A fellow in town . . . Lundberg or Klinberg or something." He pinched his eyes closed. "What the hell is that man's name?"

He opened his eyes and looked out the window. I reached over to the nightstand and put the watch on. The back of the face was still warm from his wrist. Then I heard a slight hook in my father's breathing and everything went still in the room. His face startled, then relaxed.

Here it was, the thing he'd been idling for at some 4,500 heartbeats per hour for forty-eight years. He died on the out-breath, with his eyes fixed on a parking garage, trying to re-member the name of the jeweler in our hometown. The air simply stopped. A flat green line dragged across the heart-monitoring screen. The machines flashed. An alarm sounded. Rubber shoes rushed the linoleum corridor. I leaned over the bed railing and placed my hand against his stilled chest until the nurses entered the room. Then I moved out of the way, in the direction of the window. My father's eyes remained open. From where I stood it seemed he was looking directly at me.

# thirty-three

When did I first realize that time was not just a boundless and abstract invention but also an island prison, a contract between the living and the dead? I can remember, for example, the exact moment consciousness took hold and the exact moment I looked at Samuel and Cynthia Nelson and realized they were my parents. The former took place somewhere between age two and three, as I wobbled in front of a mirror in our hallway. *I exist.* The latter took place on a sunlit day in the spring of 1974 as my parents held my hands while crossing a suburban street. An approximation of my thought was this: *These people own me. They stop me from getting hurt.*

But memory, like light and certain kinds of jazz, also warps time. After my father's death, I replayed life with him as if it had unfolded in a single afternoon. A solar eclipse above the blue-white snowfields of Manitoba, darkened clouds in a cobalt sky; huddling in the warrens of the Stanford Linear Accelerator as physicists scratched their paunches and called collision variables through the phosphor haze; a procession of dazzling defeats and minor triumphs in school gymnasiums, a blur of chemical flasks, captured chess knights, and metallic trays of dry ice. During all these re-called events, I saw my father standing by himself, aloof in mushroom-colored flannels, a slight air of contempt in his wringing of hands and tapping of feet, as if the tedium of the event or spectacle were designed to hinder his personal prog-ress through the world, as if it were a ploy by the ordinary masses to keep a strand of the subatomic dynasty undiscov-ered. Yet, he was always there, at every Bunsen burner trial and junior brain match, stuck among the jostling, zealous parents, the shrill mothers, the fathers who talked strategy as if they'd been given a battlefield commission. He'd been de-termined to wait the thing out. He believed mediocrity, like everything else, had a half-life.

I didn't grieve my father so much as waited for his death to make sense. I replayed our life together, looking for clues. Was there a moment he realized who I was? When was the day he began dying? Did the tumor appear that day as we stood on Canadian winter prairie, skirted in snow, sunlight flickering around the dark disk of the moon, and my epiph-any amounted to hunger, to a wish for a belly full of pan-cakes? He must have known I would never be brilliant. And this gift—dice thrown by a convalescing brain—what did it add up to? Had I been resurrected to recite rainfall measure-ments and disaster statistics? I waited for a sign. I half be-lieved the dead listened, were capable of remorse, and kept a meddling hand in the small affairs of the living. So I kept waiting for him to send me a sign, and eventually he did. But first there was a ghost-life, a period when I was adrift.

WHIT AND MY MOTHER FLEW back to Wisconsin. I inher-ited the Oldsmobile and drove it back to Iowa. I was going to spend a final two weeks at the Brook-Mills Institute so they could complete some range studies and videotape one of my sessions for their archives. There was also going to be an informal awards ceremony. I was excited to see Toby and Teresa again.

I couldn't escape my father on the drive from California to Iowa. The dash and the seats of the Oldsmobile smelled like stale coffee and talcum powder. I thought about road trips and family outings. The history of my family was trapped in the odometer. The car had done 289,777 miles. It had driven to the moon and halfway back. It was twenty years old; the original motor still churned inside the hood, the dash was sun-bleached, the seats were gauzy and threadbare. The horn sounded like an underwater fog-blast.

As I drove through highway towns, I sifted through recent events. Then I would catch the image of the Oldsmobile in a storefront window and see my arm limp against the outmoded chassis, helpless as a confession. I was losing track of time. The Stanford teaching hospital had used and cremated my father's body within a week of his death. I imagined an anatomy class in a bleached room, prone cadavers on stainless steel tables, their bodies partitioned with purple dotted marker lines. My father, now without the beard of a czar, without his speculative air, was simply a specimen for sophomore medical students. Not for the arterial estuaries, not for the alluvial fan of veins in the hand, but for the medical jewel buried inside his braincase.

We had picked up his remains from the Palo Alto crematorium. A box weighing fifteen pounds, eight ounces, most of that in wood. The body reduced, minus the blood and tissue, is really nothing at all. A few pounds of ash that remind you that we are mostly water and mind. Right now my mother and Whit were shuttling across the Midwest, carrying this oak box. Whit all hushed concern and gentlemanliness, opening doors and guiding my mother's elbow through the clamor of the airports. I knew my mother was going to be all right. I coldly thought she was going to make an outstanding widow—as if she were preparing to rise, convert her homespun and exotic ways into a kind of resilience. Would she wear foreign mourning garb, the embroidered black shawls of distant women? When we'd said good-bye in California, there was something palpable about her imminent transformation; she wore it as an undergarment to grief.

Thankfully, there wasn't going to be a memorial or gathering as such. None of us could imagine anything worse than a den full of the physics faculty from my father's college, a room of brightly colored socks and mechanical pencils in plaid shirt pockets. What could have been said? These men worked together in the lab, elbow-to-elbow in the mother ship of science, shared their wives' tuna fish sandwiches and celery sticks like schoolboys, speculated about black holes and the end of time, but never shared a single, frank personal conversation. My father once told me a colleague's wife had died from cancer two years before any of them knew. And my father's brothers would have arrived with their buxom wives, orbiting the food table, wringing napkins and offering trite memories of Sammy back in the copper country of Michigan.

I DROVE THE FINAL MILES to the institute late one night. I crested a slight hill and in the distance the Victorian mansion was lit up, blinking through the prairie dark like an ocean liner. I drove up and parked out by the barn. Inside the house, I went to find Teresa. She'd changed the pictures on her door. Now there were images of radioactive fallout, mushroom clouds, fusion-white explosions, great vistas of disaster-scape. I knocked softly and she appeared in the doorway.

"I wasn't sleeping," she said. She wore an oversize T-shirt and tennis socks.

"I just got in." I wanted to hug her but there was something there, some awkwardness.

"You didn't call me when he died. Gillman told me," she said.

"I know. I'm sorry. Are you all right?" I asked.

"I should be asking you that."

"Still."

"Yeah. Lately, it's been getting to me . . . all these dying people. Do you want to come in?"

I entered her room. It was all candles and incense. Her walls were covered in Hendrix posters and magazine pictures, collages with escape and mortality themes: train leapers, cliff jumpers, a woman being sawn in two, her head and feet peeking out of a wooden box. Teresa's bed lay covered with a patchwork quilt her mother had sent her. We sat on the mattress facing each other.

"He died the way he lived," I said.

"How do you mean?"

"He just slipped away in the middle of a sentence about watch repair." I looked down at his watch on my wrist. "I'm feeling weird," I said.

"That's okay. Normal, really."

She was holding my hands.

I said, "There's nobody watching me anymore."

"He always expected things."

"We gave his body to science. He was cremated. The little box full of ashes, that was the only thing that . . . I don't feel much. I wanted to know him, you know, really know him. At the end there, with the tumor, he was different. Approachable." There was the threat of a tear, but as soon as I was conscious of the sting it went away.

"Dying changes people. Buried under all that fear, they become . . . themselves," she said.

"What was it like inside his head?" I asked. I looked at my hands inside hers. "One time I remember a salesman came to our door to sell my father life insurance. My father was on his best behavior. He invites the man in, gets him some lemonade, even manages a few remarks about the weather. The salesman launches into his routine. He mentions mortality statistics and the uncertainty of life. This goes on for thirty minutes, my father nodding now and then, until finally my father stands up and walks into his study. He's in there for fifteen minutes. The salesman's looking at me, trying to get an in, asking me about school. Finally my father returns to the salesman and says, 'Sir, I'm writing a paper about the halo effect of certain kinds of particulate matter. Also, I should tell you, I *self-insure*.' The man looks white-faced at my father and asks him what he means by the term *self-insure*. My father scratches his beard and says, 'My risks are proportional to my expected outcomes. My wife will have some scones for you in the kitchen.' That's it. He closes the door to his study and leaves the salesman looking around. He didn't realize there were things you weren't supposed to say to people."

"Nice story."

"I need to sleep."

She gestured to her pillows and we put our heads down.

After a moment she said, "Personally, I want a sea burial. Fish food. A platform for kelp. Am I being morbid again?"

"Yeah, but that's okay. I've come to appreciate your attitude toward death."

We lay there for a long time, fully clothed, trying to sleep.

THE NEXT MORNING I PASSED the room Arlen slept in when he came to stay. He appeared in his doorway with the paranoid aspect of a dachshund.

"I dreamed about your old man, Nathan. He was in some kind of a tunnel."

I stopped dead, leaned against the door frame.

"It was a very long tunnel. I don't know where it was, but there were mountains."

He gestured for me to come inside. His room was sparse and he'd placed his mattress on the floor. His face was stubbled, but he'd shaved an irregular path around his mouth that, strangely, reminded me of a crop circle. Of course he was referring to the linear accelerator. If my father had a ghost, that's where it was going to inhabit—early mornings hauling above the electron shoot with Dr. Benson.

"Did he say anything to you?" I asked.

"To me? No. But he was talking to himself, you know, the way homeless people do sometimes. The crazies on the subway."

"Did you hear what he was saying?"

"Warm drink? I was going to heat myself some milk. Dr. Gillman lets me have a little burner in here."

"I'm fine, thanks."

Arlen turned his back to me and walked to the corner of the room. He poured some milk into an aluminum pan. He set the pan on a small range and began stirring it with a wooden spoon.

"I love a good glass of bovine lactation," he said.

"Did my father say anything that you heard?"

"Not really. It was kind of noisy in that tunnel. Would

you like some yogurt? I just bought some at the store. *Aci-
dophilus* is a bitch of a word. What do you reckon about
that word, Nathan? I understand from certain rumors and
whispers that you have a thing for words."

"They stick in my head."

He stirred the milk for another minute before pouring a
dash of whisky into it. He came and sat down beneath a
corkboard where various items were pinned—photos of children, ragged clothing and underwear, plastic figurines. I sat
down in a chair.

"What else, Arlen? Anything you—" My voice broke
off.

"Do you have anything that belonged to him?"

I held up my wrist, indicating the watch.

"Hand me that," he said.

I undid the band and passed it to him. Arlen took it and
put it into the pocket of his bathrobe. He blew across the top
of his milk.

"No, I need that. You can't hold on to it," I said.

"Normally they give me things." He squeezed his eyes
shut, indicating some gross violation of protocol.

"You can't have that," I said.

"I put them under my pillow. People's thoughts get into
things. You'd be surprised."

"I want to keep wearing it. Could you take a look now
and see if there's—"

He reached into his pocket and pulled out a handful of
small objects—a yo-yo, a set of car keys, a large fingernail,
and the watch. He singled out the wristwatch and brought it
to his nose. He closed his eyes.

"Nothing," he said. "He wore Old Spice. That's the rev-
elation."

"Nothing else?"

"In the dream, I also saw a hand writing some kind of letter. Did he write you any letters before he died?"

"No."

Arlen studied the watchband. He retrieved a single hair from the weave of the band. "Is this yours or his?"

It was one of my father's wiry wrist hairs. "I think it's his," I said.

"Can I have this?" he asked.

"What for?"

"It's a piece of his body, isn't it? The human body is a hologram. The entire psychic blueprint is contained in a single cell, a toenail, an eyelash, a milligram of saliva. You give me a man's pinkie finger or a swab of urine, doesn't much matter to me."

"Will you study it?" I asked.

"Problem is I lose shit all the time. Nebraska troopers sent me some dead guy's razor, whiskers and all, even a speck of blood, and I'll be damned if I can find it." He surveyed the room with an odd mixture of pride and remorse.

I said, "You could develop a better system to keep track."

"A better system, you say? System is people die, naturally and otherwise, SOS messages sometimes blown through the air, sometimes I hear and smell and sometimes nothing. System is my life sucks; the dead are the boringest motherfuckers to ever chirp their thoughts. I walk through Walgreens and I go into the aisle with all the nose sprays, the decongestants, the zit creams and the inhalants, the corn and hemorrhoid suppressants, the artificial tears, the potions, and I think, we're leasing these bodies from death. You know what the highlight of my life is, Nathan?"

"No."

"Full-cream yogurt and single-malt whisky."

"I see." I wanted to leave the room.

Arlen nodded extravagantly and dabbed some milk from his top lip with a white handkerchief. "I'll tell you what. I'll attach this wrist hair to some clear tape and put it on my headboard. If that hair starts talking to me I'll let you know." He took a last smell of the watch and handed it back to me. "They say I'm losing my gift. Last few times I've fucked up royally. A refrigerator in a ditch instead of a woman's body. You'd be surprised how similar moldy cheese and a rotting brain can be."

"I need to go." I stood to leave.

"Remember something about the dead: only the troubled ones still bother to reach out. The rest of them are tight-lipped sons of bitches."

"I'll remember that," I said, walking out into the hall-way.

# thirty-four

My mother phoned me that same night to tell me that notices from college admissions offices had arrived. I asked her to open them and read me the results over the phone. I had only been accepted to the University of Wisconsin in Madison. It was less than eighty miles from our house. She said, "My alma mater. You'll love it there." But I could tell she was also surprised and disappointed that none of the other schools had found a place for me. I felt an old, familiar ache in my stomach.

Despondent, I spent my last two weeks at the institute with Teresa and Toby. Teresa and I attempted to rekindle our barn rituals—recline amid the bluish tint of cigarette smoke and the metallic sheen of gin. But we barely kissed. Long silences uncoiled through the barn, making us both nervous. The end of our time together seemed to hang in the air.

"We're not good for each other," she said one night.

Her fingers were jaundiced with nicotine. My hair was unwashed.

"Who is?" I asked.

"Nobody I know. My parents write summaries of their arguments on legal pads and file them by subject."

"No."

"Just about."

"My grandfather used to throw soupspoons at my father," I offered.

"Nice little family you have there." She blew a river of smoke at me.

"He should have thrown silverware at me. I was the fuckup," I said.

"Please. Once I didn't tell my dad he had a slipped disk. He just thought he'd slept badly—he was in agony. What kind of person?"

"A girl who gets bored of seeing everything that's broken," I said.

"I should put that on my headstone." She smiled and took my hand in her lap. "I wish you could come with me." In a few weeks she was leaving the institute to work part-time at a hospital in Connecticut.

"Me, too," I said. But I also knew I had no place in her new life in Connecticut. I was waiting for the next thing to happen and wasn't even sure I would go to Madison in the fall. I felt as if I'd run aground.

"Can we just lie in here for a while?" I asked. "We don't have to talk."

She nodded. "Talking is overrated," she said. She finished her cigarette and we lay back on the bed of straw.

TOBY WAS GOING TO STAY another three months at the institute thanks to some music funding from Sony. He had been accepted into the Juilliard music program for the fall. He and I went driving in the Oldsmobile after midnight. We headed out onto the farmhand roads, the detours and back

roads of Iowa grain farmers, going eighty miles an hour, listening to classical FM radio, Toby nodding and swaying like
a Pentecostal, me with a hand outside the window, trailing it
in the night air.

In my absence he'd had a brief encounter with Susan, an
artist from Maine.

"It is not considered statutory rape if I'm over sixteen,"
he said.

"Did you actually penetrate?" I hoped they hadn't had
sex; losing my virginity seemed like another thing I had failed
at.

"I can't be sure."

I didn't know what to say to that. Little wooden houses,
camped among the trees, streaked past our headlights.

"I think you would know," I said.

"Sex for blind people is blurry around the edges," he
said.

It was raining. We were on a patch of sealed road and
the tires felt adrift, hydroplaned. I started to slow and Toby
reached across and put a hand on the wheel.

"I'll steer and you tell me if I'm crooked," he said.

We'd had a beer each, but neither of us was anything like
drunk. I kept my hands an inch above his at first, waiting to
clutch the wheel. The road changed. We were doing sixty
now, on gravel and washboard.

He licked his top lip. "I can feel the bolts on the wheels
shaking," he said.

"Keep her steady, but not tight. You can probably hear
from the tires if we start to go off to the side."

"Of course it would be too late then," he said.

I lifted my foot slightly off the accelerator.

He said, "Stay at this speed. This is something like fun."

We drove like that for a few minutes, down a stretch of

farm frontage, the engine noise rising over soybean fields, now and then a light appearing from behind a kitchen window. We stopped at a T intersection and Toby grinned.

"Let's go into town," he said. "I'm feeling ballsy, like I could take on the small-town constabulary."

We drove into downtown Selby. At night the row of banks and municipal buildings sat solemnly, stone crypts under yellow cones of streetlight. We rounded the block and now the street was dark except for a desolate all-night Laundromat that was lit like an operating room. As we waited at one of Selby's dozen stoplights, I looked into the whiteness of the Laundromat and saw a middle-aged man standing before a dryer, waiting to retrieve his clothes. Something I hadn't remembered in a long time stormed through my head: a night with my father from when I was about seven.

We were walking home from his college physics lab, where he'd taken me to see a cloud chamber. I'd commented that it looked like a fish tank with rain inside—another failed subatomic exaltation. It was a cold night but we were bundled in coats, shouldering into a headwind and enjoying the walk through the commercial center of my hometown. He was deep into a rant about white-hot stars and evolution. Suddenly he stopped speaking and I turned to see that he was standing in front of the Laundromat window. Inside, a bald-headed man in a mustard-colored bathrobe stood waiting for his clothes to dry. A wall of empty dryers—portholes into a black sea—then this single whirl of flecked cloth, reds and blues and tans chasing one another in endless circles. The door to the Laundromat was ajar and we could hear a metallic click, a brass button or a forgotten stray penny, plinking against the barrel of the dryer. We watched as the man, not much more than a ponderous, shiny head above a tatty robe, placed a palm against the dryer door, feeling its warmth. After a moment the man looked toward the window, then took his hand from the round door and waved it at us. My father reeled, grabbed my shoulder, and backed away from the window. He looked away down the street, wincing, as if he'd witnessed a death-camp scene, something debased and horrifying. He began walking and I followed at his side. Quietly, he said, "If we're not careful life becomes very small." We walked the rest of the way home in silence.

The light changed and I pulled away, still staring at the man in the Laundromat. I rolled the window down farther and touched the side of the car—the metal skin sheathed in moisture.

Toby said, "Why don't you come to New York with me? We could get an apartment together and date twin sisters who work at the Met."

"What would I do out there?"

"What are you going to do anywhere?"

I thought about Whit's emergency kit in the trunk of the Oldsmobile; it was comforting to know it was there—the flares and the space blanket, the fierce halogen flashlight.

Toby said, "You do what you want. But it's an open invitation to come and live in New York. What the hell else are you going to do?"

"Who knows," I said.

"How about night shift in a factory, or sweeping up old men's hair in a barbershop? I have visions of you in an apron."

I played with the radio and found a riff of staticky jazz. "Could the apron be monogrammed? Or is that too flashy?"

"You worry me," he said definitively.

I thought now that my father had probably wanted to scream at people—that moribund man in the Laundromat, Pop Nelson, lonely men he associated with soup cans and newspapers, with artifacts of despair. These were the things he'd craved near the end, but before that, before the deathly bloom of the tumor, he'd wanted to scream, *Come out here, you old farts, and look up at the nebula, study the goddamned stars!* He'd surely wanted to scream at me a dozen times.

*the highest scientifically measured scream was by neil stephenson of newcastle upon tyne england on may 18 1985*

We got on the gravel road that led to the institute. Toby turned the radio off and said, "Actual penetration I can't be positive about. But it felt a lot like I imagine it. Let's just leave it at that."

ON MY LAST DAY AT the institute there was an awards ceremony where Teresa, Toby, Dick, Cal, and I received certificates of achievement. We would be receiving our official high school diplomas in the mail some weeks later. Dick and Cal had sold their ethanol process to the U.S. government and had been offered jobs with an energy research company. My mother arrived that morning with Whit. She announced that she had gotten me a summer job at our hometown library. I would work as a page—someone who shelves books, types catalog index cards, and performs other menial tasks. The library was turn of the century, masonry and blown lights, tall windows, and I pictured myself pushing a laden cart through the stacks, amid the bookcloth greens and worn reds. There was something comforting about the simplicity of this job.

Whit sat beside my mother during the awards ceremony and the picnic out on the lawn. He was still in his chivalrous persona, side-mouthing concerned comments, touching the edges of her primrose cardigan. I couldn't shrug the feeling that something was happening between Whit and my mother.

As I crossed the lawn to receive my certificate I smiled at my mother, who was taking a photo of me. The sixteen-millimeter camera had long since been retired. She looked younger, a scarf around her throat, a hat that was smart and under-stated at the same time, her clothes plain and neat, every-thing tucked and trimmed. She was largely giving up on ethnic apparel. She had the intrepid and kind aspect of a nun who's worked in far-flung orphanages her whole life. I came and sat with her and Whit.

"Congratulations," she said.

"He'd be proud," Whit said.

This caught me a little off guard. "No, he wouldn't be," I said. "He'd be making squiggles on the tops of his shoes and picking his nose when he thought no one was looking."

Whit affected a smile. My mother crossed her arms and looked back toward the stage, where Teresa was walking toward Gillman. Gillman handed her the certificate and she tucked it under her arm. Dick and Cal and a boy I didn't know wowed and whistled. When it was Toby's turn to walk across the stage he sauntered across it, flexing his hands like a boxer. He had obviously walked the stage before, practiced and counted the number of steps, because he strode and stood exactly an arm's length from Gillman's podium. They shook hands and Toby took the award and descended the stairs, smiling wildly.

There was a reception after the ceremony. Picnic tables arranged on the cropped lawn, cut sandwiches and soda and potato chips, checkered tablecloths—it had the air of a family reunion. Gillman sliced and distributed a giant cake. Whit hovered by the food table while my mother took snap-shots of random things—the knife descending into the cake, a stray balloon lifting into the sky—as if she were struck nos-talgic, trying to capture anything that moved for posterity.

Gillman lifted his glass of apple juice and made a toast. "To talent made useful," he said.

I went and stood beside my mother, who was about to take a photo of the empty stage.

"Don't photograph that, please," I said.

"Why not?"

"The idea is to photograph people, not things. It's some wood nailed together."

She nodded, conceded my point, and put the compact camera back in her purse.

"I can't wait to have you home. You can use his study. I've done a little tidying in there."

"Yes, it's going to be nice," I said flatly. "I'm not sure I'll go to college in the fall."

"Well, we can see," she said.

We stared at the stage, waiting for something to happen. Here is grief, then, I thought, the wordless stare, an empty stage, my mother with the countenance of a vacationing nun.

"Does Whit still come around the house?" I asked. My voice cracked on the word *Whit*. His name was Mustang red.

She exhaled, brushed her sleeve. "He comes to dinner several nights a week. He's good company for me." She sounded defensive, slightly annoyed.

Whit stood talking to Cal Saunders over by the ravaged cake. It was possible Whit and my mother were like kindred, grown siblings, platonic and rooted in mutual inclination, sensing the hunger and boredom of the other like bad weather brewing. They were content with the ministrations of a house, the mending and antlike diligence. Whit kept her car running, her house pest-free and in good repair. She needed someone to cook for, and he needed errands and lists of household defects on the refrigerator. They had struck an arrangement.

"I was just asking," I said.

She looked back at the empty stage.

THAT NIGHT TOBY, TERESA, AND I sat in the barn and drank from a Coke bottle refilled with Jack Daniel's. At one point we saw Arlen wander past the open doorway. His face was drawn, his eyes maniacal. Was he talking to my father? Was he in the midst of a waking dream, scanning the sequoia in Arizona for a runaway? He bleared in our direction; the kidnapped and the murdered dogged him like an epic hangover.

"He's stopped being any good," Teresa said quietly.

"What do you mean?" I asked.

She drank from the Coke bottle and passed it to Toby, whose eyes were shut. He said, "I can't feel my body."

Teresa ignored him. "He calls the state troopers and tells them he's found something, a corpse, whatever, and then they make the phone calls and they get the warrants and nothing. An old door or a child's bicycle," she said.

Toby said, "Psychics bleed themselves dry. They're like whores out in the desert."

"I have a job to go to," I said.

Teresa and Toby both looked at me. Toby said, "I'm no psychic but let me guess. You've been given a position with the CIA. They want you to memorize briefings and deliver them to operatives in the field. Or how about the Pentagon, they've got to have a use for your memory."

"I've got a job at the library in my hometown. It's for the summer, but if I decide not to go to college in Madison, then I bet I could stay."

There was a long pause.

Finally Toby said, "You can't do that."

"What's wrong with working in a library?" I asked.

Teresa shrugged, her face somber with alcohol. She looked out through the barn door.

"You cannot work in a library." There was something indignant in Toby's voice. "Go work on the fishing boats of Alaska or make trails in the Adirondacks, but for fuck's sake don't become a librarian. Please, I'm begging you. As a blind man."

"It's easy for you two to say. You have real lives to go to," I said.

"I'm not saying anything," Teresa said.

"You don't have to. I don't want to talk about it," I said, taking the Coke bottle from Teresa.

A while later, Teresa and I went for a walk. Under a full moon, the house seemed very secluded, cut off from neighboring houses by acres of corn and soybeans and pasture. With its Victorian sprawl, the high windows, and lathe-work detail, it seemed out of place with the weatherboard houses of its neighbors, the humble pea-green and yellow boxes of hog and soy farmers. I remembered the day my father and Whit drove me here, before anything had been named or lost, and how the house had seemed like a ship, the steepled roofline like the warrior prow of some great battleship. There were moments, I realized, I simply wanted to bring back. I took Teresa's hand and we crossed the lawn in front of the empty wooden stage. It had been over a month since I'd been inside the workshop and I wanted to see the facades and pillars of Roger's city one more time. As we walked, Teresa looked up at the night sky and said, "I don't know the names of any stars. I know pancreatic acids, but no stars."

I pointed west of the Big Dipper and said, "That's Polaris. Over there is Saturn, low down."

*the milky way moves at 1400000 miles per hour relative to microwave background radiation*

We stopped in front of the workshop. I put my hand under the step, pulled out the flashlight, and we went inside. The smell of sawdust and wood glue, the burnt smell of metal shavings, surely these were comfort smells for Roger, the kind of thing that could trance him toward sleep. In the back room I switched on a spotlight that hung from a metal beam and the city gleamed; it now had the formalized presence of an installation, something in a museum. We stood in silence. The peaked roofs with skylights, the terraced rooftop gardens and water towers were all there. No more buildings had been erected, but he'd added features on the ground: fire hydrants and bus stops and park benches, things that gave it human scale. And there were more models of people, molded from lead and wood, caught up in the city bustle, crossing in front of taxis, window-shopping, eating ice cream cones and hot dogs. Inside the stadium there was a single Yankees player—an outfielder with his mitt raised in the air.

I picked up the baseball player. His features were too vague to know what Roger's intention had been. A smear of black ink for a mouth, dots for eyes; it was the suggestion of a face. I placed him in various locations throughout the city: on a water tower, surrounded by tenement laundry, standing on top of a midtown high-rise. It seemed to be lunchtime; people were entering delis and downing hot dogs in the street, men in suits were walking through the park, a vendor was hauling his quilted metal cart in front of a glass-fronted department store. I placed the man in the park, beside the lunchtime joggers and the dog walkers. He stood atop a grassy knoll with his mitt in the air, as if a ball had been launched out of the stadium, across the domes and turrets and the city grid. Face turned skyward, body poised; the catcher was a monument to waiting.

"Are we going to say good-bye?" Teresa asked.

I looked at her. How her eyes and her wary mouth never betrayed her gift. I switched off the light and kissed her. We moved slowly toward the mullioned windows. My hand edged inside her jeans, the seam tight across the back of my knuckles. For a moment I stood behind her, her hips pressing my hand into the wall, and we both looked out onto the fields, where a neighbor's horses stood grazing. The arc of their long necks, the swanlike dip of their heads into the grass, their bone-white flanks in the moonlight all seemed, in that moment, for our benefit.

"We could do it," I said. "Seems a shame not to."

"Here and now?"

"Here and now."

I could hear the friction of my hand against her denim waistline. I unzipped her jeans and pulled them down to her knees. She drew breath suddenly, surprised, and blew some air against the chill glass. A cloud of moisture bloomed, then receded on the windowpane. I could see the dimple in the small of her back, the rise of her ass below the hem of her sweater. She put one hand against the window, framing the horses between her thumb and index finger. This seemed like the perfect place and time to lose my virginity, wedged between the sculpted city and the sight of horses feeding at midnight. Suddenly, the horses startled and cantered in the opposite direction. They wheeled and turned, spooked by something in the night. The moment vanished. Teresa took my hand.

"Wait," she said.

"I really want to." I kissed the back of her neck.

"I want to, but . . . "

"But what?" I said.

"It needs to feel different than this."

She went quiet. I could feel her stomach rise and fall with each breath. She turned around but found it hard to look at me.

"I'm sorry," I said.

"It's okay. We will sometime soon. We'll visit each other. Do it in our childhood beds." I felt her voice around me, consoling and suffocating.

*the lowest recorded note attained by the human voice was a staccato e in alt altissimo—*

I kissed her gently on the cheek, vaguely humiliated, and I could taste the saline of a tear in my mouth. I wiped her face with my sleeve. We held each other in the half-light of Roger's workshop and there was nothing I wanted to say. I didn't want to see the faded ribbon of my voice.

# thirty-five

Grief—or the numbness that came with it—dulled the colors and shapes that trailed through the air. A white, hollow feeling raked at my thoughts. The citrus bite of certain words turned waxy. Memorizing had once been pleasurable but now it turned into a chore. I had to cajole life and character out of receding words and neutered objects. Without the bright contrail of dashes and lines, I lost the thread of meaning when I read. My brain started to insist that newspaper articles were really columns of hooped and stiff-backed symbols, ideas dotted down to black ink. The letter *T* was no longer a stern man with his arms outstretched.

That summer I stopped memorizing and reciting facts. I walked the streets of my hometown during my lunch break and after finishing work at the library. A haziness clung to me. Sometimes I would end up on Main Street and inside a movie theater without remembering how I got there. I followed strangers, somehow drawn into their wake.

One afternoon I was walking past the college campus, and a man who resembled my father—an outmoded beard, a certain stoop to his walk—crossed the street in front of me. He hurried down the sidewalk, carrying a briefcase and looking at his watch. He led me away from the sandstone arches and porticos of the college, down streets where college professors and dentists and lawyers lived. Third-acre plots with well-kept revival houses. As the man rushed along, his briefcase kept hitting him in the thigh. I stayed on the opposite side of the street. At the end of a block he reached into his trouser pocket and retrieved a single key.

I stood behind a hedgerow and watched. He stepped up to a modest timber house with a sharply lit porch and several curtained windows. He opened the front door and I saw a long hallway, a hat stand with umbrellas and coats. There was no way to know for sure that he lived alone—the house was well tended, there were potted flowers here and there—but I guessed from the hat stand and the austerity of the hallway that he was a bachelor. A middle-aged man of few connections. A life reduced to a single key.

He closed the door and I crossed the street to stand on the pavement outside his front door. There was a light coming from the back of the house and I crept down the side passage. I crouched low and looked through the kitchen window. He did not live alone at all. At a small table in a breakfast nook he sat with an elderly woman and rolled up her sleeve. She was in a nightgown and had the sunken aspect of the slowly dying. He took a small hypodermic needle from the table and injected a clear liquid into her arm. When the liquid was spent, he rubbed her arm a little and rolled down her sleeve. Her face was grateful, calm, somehow absolved. He stood up, loosened his tie, and began to make a salad. I don't know why, but I stood outside their window, mesmerized by the sight of the man breaking lettuce and putting it into a wooden bowl.

• • •

WHEN I GOT HOME I entered through the side door, trying to avoid Whit and my mother. The coffee table in the parlor was covered in books about grief. One of them depicted the seven stages of grief as street-name signs—Shock Street, Denial Avenue, Anger Boulevard. Grief was a city or an orderly suburb where people could drive their Buicks down Denial until they got pissed off and turned onto Anger. My mother, ever the pragmatist, wanted to know which block I was on. When I told her I didn't know and to stop asking me, she took that as the broad, one-way boulevard of Anger.

I could hear her bustling in the kitchen.

"Nathan? Is that you?" she called.

"I think so," I said. "Were you expecting burglars?"

"Come and have dinner. Whit and I are waiting for you."

It couldn't have been later than five. Grief was a sentence of early dinners. I went into the kitchen, where the two of them stood by the refrigerator, a tableau of domesticity, smiling at me for no good reason. I had to endure this hour every evening. We sat at the table. In the three months I'd been home Whit had essentially moved in, sleeping in the guest room, and our evening meals had become an absurdist drama.

My mother served herself some navy beans and passed them to me. "Take some beans, Nathan."

"I saw *Die Hard* again today," I said.

"I'm thinking of building a carport," Whit announced.

"Why? We already have a garage," I said.

He said, "The garage is storage. The carport would be for the cars."

"This lettuce tastes acidic. How's the library?" my mother asked.

"The library is exactly dull. Lettuce is alkaline, mostly

water," I said. I pictured the man breaking his lettuce, making a salad for the dying woman.

"I spoke with a woman in Bahrain this morning . . . she grows grapes out in the desert. They sell oil for water. Her English was exemplary." Whit had taken up ham-radio transmission in the basement.

"I'd like to take a long drive tomorrow," I said. "Minnesota maybe."

"Is that wise?" my mother asked.

"Wear and tear, gas mileage decrease," Whit cautioned over his plate.

"I think your driving is a way of dealing with your father's death. Most grief counselors say it's better to do something physical and vigorous."

I imagined a paperback title: *Hustle Your Way Through Grief!* I said, "I'll drive vigorously."

"What color would we make the carport, Cynthia, if I were to build one?"

"Umber. Something Mediterranean. Some kind of sienna."

This went on for fifty-two minutes. After dessert I was excused from the table and made my way into the parlor. The house now seemed empty and cavernous; my mother had been busy with spring cleaning and a Goodwill drop-off. Darkness gathered in the corners. The Shaker furniture floated in lamplight like little ships of oiled teak and pine. It was an exact replica of the house I'd grown up in, but there was no proof of life—no errant home-brew bottles, no Charles Mingus ruminating and bouncing in from the study. Above the fireplace stood the antique urn containing my father's ashes. It was Italian-looking and florid. Yellow ceramic curls lifting and peeling off a vanilla gloss. I stopped in front of it for a moment. It still seemed strange that it was his unhoused body sitting up there, pewter bone shards in white ash.

I walked past my father's study and looked in. Again, it was like a flawed reproduction; in real life he'd had towers of books in the corners, pyramids of scribbled paper. Now the books were pressed tightly together on the shelves and stray paper was nowhere to be seen. I sat at his desk. The one concession to the actual, lived past was a copy of a book open to the page he'd been reading before he died:

> *It is possible that all four basic forces—strong, weak, electromagnetic, and gravity—are really part of a single unifying force which is the source of all matter and energy. Prior to the creation of the universe, this force existed mainly in potentiality and occupied a total space of less than a pinhead in diameter.*

Beside it he had written, A pinhead seems much too large for all cosmic matter yet here i am sitting on top of the pinhead and death seems real.

I left the book and went upstairs. Like the rest of the house, my room was curated, something behind glass. Everything was exactly as it had been when I was twelve, minus the laundry piles and the stash of *Playboy*s. My mother had long since rooted out all symptoms of my early puberty. Her hunches and suspicions permeated the walls of that house. She had a nervy clairvoyance that told her when things went awry, when an inflorescence of mold appeared in the refrigerator, or when I stood in my bedroom, smitten-faced at the sight of naked breasts.

My bed was made with my childhood Superman sheets tucked with hospital corners. A solar system night-light sat on the side table. Why were so many of my childhood motifs about celestial flight? On the windowsill, blots of compounds were pressed inside microscope plates. A sheep's brain swam inside a pickle jar, the embalming fluid brackish and strewn with particles. I sat on my bed, held the jar in my lap, and watched the brain sway and bob. It looked just like the human brain, the cross sections I remembered from *Gray's Anatomy*. A brain up close looks like nothing so much as a gray undulating landscape, a terrain folded with fissures and ravines. The universe, my father said, evolves like an ever-expanding thought. And our brains were vehicles for this widening thoughtfulness—a membrane that weighs less than a loaf of hearty bread, that feels no pain, that transmits our memories between generations of neurons.

# thirty-six

Dear Dad,

I've been thinking about you lately. Arlen told me that you might have been writing letters before you died. Were they to me?

You probably know this but I have a job at the town library shelving books—no NASA or MIT just yet. I know you thought genius was contagious. It's not. I've decided to stop reciting stuff. The colors and shapes and tastes are fading.

Whit is losing his mind and your wife cooks enough food every night to feed an army. All in all, things are just as you left them.

So, what's the unified field like? I read in your notebook the following: "The real study-object of physics is no longer a material phenomenon, such as a star, planet, liquid, gas, molecule, an atom, or an elementary particle, but the energy-rich 'nothingness' of the vacuum." Can you create a vacuum *out of a human life? A state where everything is possible but nothing very likely? Does something new emerge when there's no more empty space?*

*Love,*
*Nathan*

# thirty-seven

At the library I shelved books and showed public safety and archival films to the public. Mr. Rawlings, the town historian, came in on Wednesdays to see Fourth of July parades and inaugurations involving mayoral ribbons. I worked with the middle-aged wives of college professors. My boss, Birdie Peters, wife to a classics professor, was a fine-boned woman of denim skirts and tennis shoes. She drank instant coffee all day long and soundly scolded fine payers: "Mrs. Jervatis, you seem to be borrowing and returning on the Mayan calendar."

After work I went to movies by myself. Our town had a movie theater that had been built in a time of flashy optimism—a cascade of lights, an Art Deco awning with neon trim, an oversize ticket booth with a chrome guardrail in front of it. Inside it was more of the same. Pendant lights swayed from the ceiling plaster, balconies jutted from the walls. I went to the cheap movies, the long runs and revivals. For a dollar I could watch movies that were edging onto video. Their target audience was unemployed, transient, and retired; men in gravy-colored coats, women who peeled oranges during the show.

I always sat near the back, positioned so I could see the moviegoers as well as the film, and from that vantage point, in a darkness more brown than black, it seemed like we were all underwater—the screen was a rippling surface above us. Movies played themselves out, swam toward me through the grainy air: manhunts and murders, car chases through bawling traffic, illicit sex in Vegas hotel rooms. Violence and sex seemed strange to me now. Their images barreled in from somewhere else, a tawdry outpost where people had lives involving vengeance and lust.

I drove the Oldsmobile Omega into the ground, endless miles of browned-out dairy land, hatched greenfields, unsealed market roads. Movies and taking photos and driving made me feel anonymous. Sometimes I felt old memorized lists forming somewhere in my mind—notable disasters and Miss America winners—but I refused to let them in.

Toby and Teresa wrote to me, frequently at first, then less so. Toby was a rising star at Juilliard, giving recitals to packed auditoriums, going on tour with this composer and that philharmonic. Teresa lived in a bungalow a few blocks from the hospital where she worked in Connecticut. She worked part-time, mornings, and had afternoons to herself. She'd taken up painting. They had given her an office and she saw patients face-to-face. She burned incense and laid out cut marigolds and daylilies; she played ambient music while the sick told her stories about their illnesses, gave her metaphors for what was really the matter. She had developed a bedside manner, taken some of the edge off her diagnostic revelations. She said she was learning empathy and that, for the first time, she felt useful.

· · ·

I FOLLOWED PEOPLE AND TOOK their pictures in secret. I borrowed my mother's old camera and tried to capture the essence of what I saw. A new side of my hometown was revealed to me. There were territories and enclaves I hadn't known: a vacant lot by the old meat works where migrant workers gathered in the dawn kicking the gravel, waiting for farmers to drive up looking for help; a deserted foundry that was now a studio belonging to an exiled painter; a nameless topless bar, set above the drugstore; a patch of dirt and mailboxes and trailers on the east side of town that was called the Oasis. I followed old ladies returning from bingo at the United Methodist, factory workers coming home from double shifts, delivery boys making their rounds, a priest riding his bicycle to the cemetery. I watched a man named Bing Peabody, who owned a shoe store, return home to a disheveled house that was full of the shoes that didn't sell— dusty boxes of oversize and undersize and out-of-style shoes that cluttered his living room and hallway.

I saw Leonard Spatz, the deli owner, sit in his store past midnight, mouthing along with a German dictionary. Then I drove past his house and understood by the car in the drive, by the shadow play from an upstairs window, that his wife was having an affair and that this was what he did on those nights. He muttered syllables—the stop-throat staccato of German—while she undressed for another man. It happened twice a week and he obviously allowed it. I watched college kids replace the hoisted flag outside the campus chapel with a stained sweatshirt. Through a fence, I saw a young boy bury his toys for safekeeping while his parents shouted violently from inside the house. I saw a man chip golf balls into his empty swimming pool. I watched an old man sweep his sidewalk with a stiff wire broom, the scratch like a blade on whetstone.

Every life contained a secret gesture and I tried to capture it on film. It never felt like spying, like prowling, and I never watched women undress or lovers park outside a restaurant at 3:00 a.m. I thought about Arlen and Teresa; they were seers of a kind, watching other people and knowing from a smell or a bloated kidney something that it would take a lifetime to know. They knew suicidal tendencies before the person even knew it, about self-loathing while it was still in the stages of throwing up after meals. I'm not pretending that I had any of that, but I began to see people differently. I was observing from the outside, walking up to the shiny rooms of the living and looking in.

# thirty-eight

Dear Dad,

*The Oldsmobile Omega is holding its own. Did you ever change the oil? Not long after you left I changed the oil and the air filter. Both were ancient.*

*Did you know that Melville Dewey, inventor of the Dewey decimal system, was the Einstein of the library world? Before him they had "fixed location" for books and he made it "relative location"—a little bit like quantum theory. Now books were numbered according to their intellectual content instead of their physical address on the shelf.*

*Love,*
*Nathan*

# thirty-nine

Sometimes, at night, after Whit retired to his radio and my mother called her friends—churchly women who did the potluck-hospice-Levart circuit—I took a nightcap in the parlor. I poured myself a gin and tonic from the antique cabinet and sat down on the couch. My mother oiled the leather upholstery so that it smelled like a saddle. In the dimness the urn caught the light from the stairs, giving it a glowing white sheen. In death my father commanded the house in a way he never had in life. In life he'd been a boarder, a hotel guest showing up for meals before retiring to the galleries and curtained rooms of his own mind. He knew we would forgive his eccentricities, his distraction, if he remained relatively inconspicuous and undemanding. Now my mother had made him a patriarch, an ancestor watching over a shrine.

"I'm getting drunk," I told the urn.

Later, I walked past the guest room, where Whit was getting ready for bed. Before retiring he did a regimen of sit-ups and push-ups in his boxers and undershirt. As I watched him huffing in his underwear, I wondered, yet again, about the nature of his relationship with my mother. I could not have broached any discussion in which my mother had a sexual identity. In my mind, sex between my parents had been reduced to an abstract enterprise, my father more puzzled than aroused, silently theorizing about hip-curve coefficients, and my mother wondering if she'd left the oven on. I wasn't about to ask Whit whether he had designs on my mother.

He stopped, mid-push-up, and stared at me. With his crooked arms and quizzical head, he resembled a praying mantis.

"Want to join me?" he asked. "A little roustabout for the ticker before Z-time."

"Big day tomorrow. Nursing home is coming. There's going to be a run on large-print Danielle Steele."

"Roger that," he said, dipping to the carpet.

I walked up the stairs, trying not to hear his out-breath.

# forty

I chose the most normal-looking family I could: a house with a porch swing and wind chimes, a minivan in the driveway. Normal was something I knew nothing about. I'd grown up with a particle physicist, an astronaut, and a woman who kept house with the pluck and verve of a gymnast. Normal could be studied just like anything else. I was an anthropologist sent among the mortgaged and the salaried, the narrowly happy. The name on the mailbox read "Donovan." Opposite their frame house was a tall elm under whose branches I parked the Oldsmobile. It had turned cold. I idled the motor, vented the heat, and watched the business of the household. There was a wife, a husband, a teenage son and daughter. They all arrived home in time for dinner each night.

On a Tuesday evening I crossed the street to stand on their lawn. Their house was dark except for the kitchen and dining room in the rear. I suspected the father was on a conservation kick because I once heard him yell at the kids, "I still don't own shares in the power company!" There was a brief pause after that, a light switched off, then the sound of a hair dryer from the upstairs.

I walked toward the rear of the house. The dog was inside. They spoiled it rotten, calling it Laddie. The house sat on a pier-and-beam foundation, with a crawl space beneath it. I shimmied my way underneath, inching toward the voices. I could see splinters of light between the floorboards above me. The sound of feet, the metallic clack of the dog's toenails on the hardwood. There was enough room to sit upright. I craned one ear to the joists. I seemed to be directly underneath their dining room table.

"Coach says I need to gain weight," the boy said.

"Gain, lose, nobody is happy with their weight," the father said. "Hey, could you stop eating like a goddamn pig! Shovel, shovel."

"Can we eat dinner in peace for once?" the mother said.

"Is that a question?" the father asked. "Because if it's a question it should be addressed to your son."

"Dad, I'm starving, all right."

"I don't care if you're ready to slaughter your own Holstein heifer. I demand some manners at this table."

A pause.

"We forgot to say grace again." That was the daughter.

"Shit!" the father said.

The mother said, "It's your idea, Max. But you always forget."

"Fine. I'll say the thing. Hey! Matthew, bow your goddamn head and keep your peepers shut." The sound of a throat being cleared. "Heavenly Father, bless this food which we use for work and play and fun. Help those who are needy. Help us if you can."

"Amen," the mother said.

"Amen," Max said.

"Can I eat now?" Matthew asked.

"You may," the father said.

The daughter said, "Do I look fat to you guys?"

"See, here we have it, the weight fixation," Max said.

"She's sensitive, Max," the mother said.

"I think my hips are fat," the daughter offered.

"There is not a goddamn thing wrong with your hips," Max said.

Matthew said, "I could use your fat. Coach says I need fifteen pounds in a hurry."

"Eat your steak and pipe down," Max said. "Whole damn family wants to be something they're not. Fat, thin, smarter, better-looking. See this mug, it's mine. Big nose, jowls, sure. All of it, mine."

The clink of silverware, the dog's paws pattering around the table—was someone feeding it on the sly? There was little conversation. I could make out a TV, low and muffled, from an adjacent room. At one point somebody belched loudly, the daughter giggled, and the mother said, "Matthew!" to which Matthew rejoined, "In China and those poor places burping is considered a great compliment."

Max said, "Great. Now you want to be Chinese."

"Eat your steak," the mother said.

So this was normal. Dinners that consisted not so much of conversation but altercations, speculations about body weight, a mutt of a dog scampering around for scraps, a prayer offered in the same tone as the admonishment of a dinnertime belch. At our dinner table my father floated conversation about whether a vortex had infinite mass. I crawled back toward the lawn, but just as I was about to get out I heard the back screen door open. Max appeared holding a pack of cigarettes. I crouched behind one of the piers. He stepped out onto his lawn and lit a cigarette. While he smoked he padded around the yard, singing "American Pie" in a low-set croon. I watched him until he burned out the cigarette and went back inside.

When I arrived home that night, my mother announced that she had closed the parlor. From the kitchen I could see that a yellow ribbon had been taped across both entrances.

"I'd like to keep the parlor and the study out of bounds," she said.

"Less maintenance," Whit attested.

I said, "But it's part of the house."

"Well, perhaps just for a while. I'm tired of vacuuming in there. And you're wearing the rug out with all that pacing in front of the urn."

I thought about it. Some nights—all right, most nights—I spoke to my father a little before going to bed. What was so strange about that? Whit radioed an albino man in St. Petersburg before hitting the hay.

"We think it best if you stayed out of the study and that room for a while," she said.

"Is this some kind of intervention?" I asked.

"Don't be silly," she said, tightening her apron.

"Because I'm not jogging and whistling? Because I have a job whose main requirement is having a pulse and understanding the alphabet?"

"Stop."

"No. Please, Mom. Let me tell you that there are nuances to the alphabet. The *McC* elements, for example, or having to go back three to four letters. Multiple authors can be a horror. It keeps me on my toes, I can tell you."

"I thought we could go bowling this Saturday night, just you and me," Whit said in a mild swagger.

"I have plans, Whit."

"Excellent. What are they?" my mother asked.

"I'm going to stalk our neighbors."

I left the kitchen. As I walked toward the stairs, I grabbed the yellow ribbon that had been taped to the parlor archway and yanked it free. It was back up the next morning.

A WEEK LATER, I LOADED the metal trunk of family films into the back of the Oldsmobile and drove it to work. By now I had been given a key, and I let myself in an hour before I knew Birdie would arrive for her ritual first cup of Folger's. I hauled the trunk downstairs to the projector room. The film canisters were labeled in my mother's hand: "Chess Competition," "Chemistry Quiz," "Nathan Goes to School." I grabbed one marked "Nathan: Early Days," loaded the film into the projector, ran the motor, and switched off the light.

I had never seen or heard of this one before. Jostled shots of my parents in our house carrying a small bundle in a white blanket. My mother nursing me on the sun-trapped divan, a Mexican shawl across her lap; my mother singing to me in the bright kitchen. At first it seems my father is the sole cameraman, the documenter, but then there is a sequence where he is huddled over a white, plastic baby bath. A spindly arm reaches up from the water and grabs his beard. He grins at the camera, pinned. He breaks free and washes me with a cloth as my mother moves in for a close-up. I am all baby—dimpled and milky-pale, veins spread across my body like inky-blue nets—yet my parents seem to be enraptured. My father's face is brimming and in the grain of film I think I can see a glint in his eye. I pause the film; the motor hums through another gear. It's a tear, trapped by the light. I start the film again. Sequences of my father building things, wielding hammers and wood saws, and in these jittered montages his wrists are bare; he's forgotten to wear his wristwatch. He'd mentioned his watchlessness and the household mending in the hospital, but here it was—proof that my arrival had loosed him from his normal routine.

Just then Birdie Peters and Mr. Rawlings arrived at the projection room door. Birdie opened the door a little dramatically, as if she suspected I might be showing snuff films before regular business hours.

"Oh, you startled me, Nathan," she said.

"Good morning," I said, killing the projector motor.

"Mr. Rawlings is here to watch the July parades from 1975 to 1980. Like we discussed."

"Of course. I have them right here."

Birdie lingered a moment, waiting for a complicit silence. Finally, she said, "Well, I'll leave you to it," and disappeared.

Mr. Rawlings, a heavyset man with a homburg, eased into a chair. "Let's see some fireworks and marching bands. Some bandy-legged girls wielding trumpets," he said. He put one hand on his paunch.

"No problem," I said. "But first I want you to see something, sir, if you don't mind. I'd like to ask your opinion, see whether you can spot a man crying in this film."

Mr. Rawlings took off his homburg and laid it on the table. He was the town historian. He knew the past bit at the heels of the present. I threw the motor into gear and switched off the light. Pales of light threw themselves against the screen; my father trotted across the frame.

"He's not wearing his watch," I said.

"Uh-huh." Mr. Rawlings exhaled heavily. "That your father?" he asked.

"Yes, sir. Now, here's the part where I think he might be—"

"Crying, you said. Let's take a look."

I slowed the motor. My father at the tub, his hands basted in light, as he turns toward the windows. I stopped the frame.

"This is it, do you see?" I asked.

Mr. Rawlings leaned forward, extended his lower jaw. "Could be a tear. Is that you? The fat little baby?"

"Yes. Is that a tear on his face?"

"What year is this? Seventies?"

"Winter. Nineteen seventy. It was about the time that one of the *Apollo* astronauts chipped a golf ball on the lunar surface. There were elections in India." A few historical facts still lingered faintly in my mind.

Mr. Rawlings looked at me a little warily, then his face brightened; we'd established the context.

"Is that a tear on his face? Shining," I said.

He took out a pair of bifocals from his top pocket and perched them on his nose. He peered up at the screen, mouth open. "Plain as day," he said. He took the glasses off and rested his elbows on the table.

"Now I'll load the parade reels," I said. I stopped the motor and put the film reel gently back in its case.

AFTER WORK THAT DAY I went by the Donovan house. Matthew set off to take the dog for a walk so I followed him to the nearby park. I sat on a bench while he tied the dog to a swing set and did some pull-ups on a crossbar. He was probably about sixteen, athletic, good-looking in a bucolic kind of way. After the pull-ups, Matthew moved onto sit-ups and push-ups, then he untied the dog and jogged the perimeter of the park. While he jogged, the dog snapped up at him and each time, Matthew smacked it across the snout. The dog kept jumping, jaws open. I got my camera out of my bag and focused it. I wanted a shot of him, midstep, the dog snapping. Just as I was about to release the shutter, I felt somebody sit down next to me. I turned to my left. A man in his fifties, wearing a Greek fisherman's cap, sat with his eyes trained on the vision of Matthew and the mutt running the park boundary.

"That dog's gonna bite the little SOB one day," he said.

It was Arlen, the psychic from the institute.

"I been following you, Nathan, for a day now. Looks like I'm following the follower."

"What are you doing here?"

"Last week I helped find a ten-year-old girl buried in a field in Ohio with her skin peeled like an onion. They brought me the kid's pajamas. It loosened me up, made the signal clearer. I'm back in the big time."

"Did you hear from my father?"

"Then yesterday I spent twelve goddamn hours on a Greyhound bus, sitting next to Jimmy Shitbags, who's out on parole with his possessions in a paper bag." Arlen looked around the park and pulled his coat collar up. Matthew and the dog began the run home. "Your dad's hair got real chatty. So I thought I would come tell you in person. Plus I like to get out and see the country now and then."

I stood up. "Can we go for a drive? My car is around the corner."

"I've been on a bus for an entire day and you want to drive?"

"I can think straight when I drive."

"Yeah, well I got until midnight, when the Greyhound leaves back for Iowa."

We pulled along the highway. Usually I took back roads and rural routes for the backcountry feel, for the look of suspicion that a farmer gave from his tractor as I slipped by. Tonight I wanted to see the flash of traffic. Arlen slumped in the passenger seat, his hands in his lap.

"I appreciate you coming to find me," I said.

"Yeah, well, I'm the delivery boy. Goddamn psychic UPS is what I am."

I cruised the Olds at seventy. After a moment of silence, Arlen said something.

"What?" I asked.

"Heat," he mumbled.

"What do you mean?"

He pointed to the opposite side of the highway.

"I don't see anything," I said.

"Wait a minute."

I waited, continued looking. After thirty seconds, a state trooper whisked past us.

"Radar heat," Arlen said.

I lowered my speed to fifty-five and looked over at him. His eyes were rimmed red.

"Did you dream about my father?" I asked.

"More or less. It kind of crept up on me. I've been in a slump lately. Toothbrushes, bikinis, nothing gives, everything's been kind of quiet, subdued. I taped that wrist hair of his to my headboard and a couple weeks ago I see his hands."

"What was he doing?" I asked.

"Not *he, they*. We're talking about hands and wrists suspended in midair."

"What did the hands do?"

"They were writing a letter. One with the pen and one holding down the paper. Like I seen before, only more information. The reception came in clearer."

"A letter to me?" I asked.

"Jesus, let the story unfold, man. These things are delicate."

"Okay, I'm sorry. Tell me."

"Happened the night after they sent me the murdered girl's pajamas. I see his hands, the nails all bitten down and white, and the watch, but the watch has stopped ticking."

I looked down at the watch face: 9:35. That seemed right.

"And like I say, he's writing a letter on some blank paper. Now, I can't be one hundred percent on this one. There is always the risk of the wrong image getting in there. Static, pulses, interference. I eat a bad burrito, my circadian rhythm is off, metabolism goes cuckoo, and things can get spliced."

"I understand. Would you just—"

"You're in a bit of a slump yourself. If you don't mind the observation."

I hit the steering wheel. "Arlen, what was my dad writing?"

"Fine. Two weeks before he died, he wrote a letter to Him." Arlen pointed at the roof.

"Him?"

He nodded.

"Who?"

"*God!* He was writing a goddamn letter to God, all right."

I looked out at the sodden fields, glints of water in the furrows. "He didn't believe in God."

"Hey, what the hell do I know? Like I say, I'm the UPS driver."

"To *God?*" My voice was high and scoffing.

"The letter is in a room with lots of books. Inside a book, something to do with zero gravity, whatever the hell that is," Arlen said.

"His study."

"I'll leave the rest to you. Now listen, I got to get a bus and you've been driving like a banshee, so how's about we turn around."

I felt a bite at the base of my neck. Had I taken the brisk turn onto Anger Boulevard that my mother feared? "I can't believe he wrote a letter to God and not to me," I said. I braked hard and turned the car around. Arlen fidgeted with his hands.

"Christ I need to sleep," he said.

"Take a nap."

"Yeah. That does sound kind of good. Wake me at the bus station. And Nathan?"

"What?"

"You're lousy at following people. That family? They feel it. They know somebody's listening. They know they don't have a right to be found interesting. Wake me, all right?"

I rushed the car back up to seventy. My mind was off-kilter. If Arlen was right, why had my father written his dying words to God—a figment he didn't believe in—instead of to me? That would be the ultimate insult: at death's door he found it in him to make peace with the alleged creator but couldn't tell me I'd been the answer to all his prayers. Wasn't that all I'd wanted? The unconditional love of my father. Wasn't that the kind of blatant acceptance everybody wanted? *Some are born with genius; others are born with hope.* Gillman had said something like that once.

I thought about the people I followed, about their little wooden or stucco houses, about a life portrayed by the keys a man carries in his pocket or the dumb shows that betray who a person really is—the solo golf game at three in the morning, the rummage of unsold shoes in a man's living room. If I'd wanted to, I could have named every major natural disaster in recorded history, America's favorite television shows for fifty years, the specializations of the five islands of the human brain, but none of it meant anything to me. What use was information if I didn't believe in anything? There was no invisible kindness favoring us; the unified field wasn't the place where all matter and energy coalesced, it was a ticker-tape parade of random data-bytes.

I could feel my chest tighten. I let the car drift for the shoulder. A row of six beaten mailboxes appeared up ahead, lining the roadside in front of a cluster of houses. Scarred metal tubes on stumps, skewed and tilted, betraying the age and economic standing of the subdivision. HAZEL WOOD, a sign read. The Oldsmobile edged onto gravel; the car had always pulled slightly to the right, so loosening my grip on the wheel felt like releasing an animal from its training, back to brute instinct. A series of clipped, scraping noises. Mail scatters. The ungathered credit-card offers and electric bills. Off-white envelopes wheeling through the night.

The steering wheel shuddered. Arlen jolted upright just as a mailbox, now a projectile, hurtled up the hood, into the windshield, and onto the roof. It rolled across the top of the car and I saw a flash of metal in the rearview mirror as it rolled down the trunk.

"We're dead!" Arlen screamed.

"It's okay," I said. I gently guided the car back toward the right lane.

"I don't die in Wisconsin. I die in Mexico, you little creep. What the hell are you doing?"

"I lost control for a second." Technically that was true. "But it's okay. We'll get you to your bus on time."

From behind us, great knives of red and blue cut through the night. At first I thought it was full-blown synesthesia coming back, words glimmering in the air. Then I heard a siren and looked in my rearview mirror and saw a state trooper's car. By now a half dozen people were standing on their front porches.

Arlen rubbed his face and said, "Nathan, I have some screams in my throat with your name on them."

I slowed and pulled onto the shoulder. The trooper came striding toward us.

"Step out of the car, gentlemen," he said. His face was all in shadow from his hat, but his chin seemed enormous.

"Was I speeding?" I asked.

"It's not your rate of speed that concerns me. Step out." The term *rate of speed* made me sound like a particle pulsing down a chute.

We stood beside my car and placed our hands on the roof.

"Are you going to frisk me?" Arlen asked casually.

"Why, do you have a weapon?"

"Nope," Arlen answered.

"I'm sorry if I was speeding," I said.

He patted the backs of my legs, my stomach, then felt the inside seam of my pants. He repeated this inspection on Arlen.

"You know any Iowa troopers?" Arlen asked.

"Turn around please, sir."

"You know Jimmy Hallbeck?"

"No."

"Commendation. Helped him with a drowned boy."

The trooper asked me for my driver's license and registration. I reached inside the car, opened the glove compartment for the registration, and handed him my driver's license from my wallet. He looked at them and then walked back to his cruiser. We stood waiting beside the car, flooded with the whiteness of his headlights.

"Dumb-ass," Arlen said to me. "This is the Midwest, you don't fuck with people's mail-delivery systems. Mail felony is a federal offense. Write me a letter from the big house. Did you think about that when you decided to career off the goddamn road?"

People watched us as they streaked by on the highway, and I wondered, amid a feeling of mild humiliation, where they were headed: leaving spouses, driving stolen cars to distant states, shuttling toward motel-room sex romps. After a while the cop came back.

"Do you want to explain what happened back there?" he said.

"I lost control of the vehicle," I said.

"Have you been drinking?" he asked.

"No."

"Probable cause says I can search the vehicle," he said. He didn't seem to have a face; it was either all washed out by the light or his chin was so enormous you didn't notice anything else.

"Probable cause," I repeated. Again there was something esoteric about the way it sounded. *The uncertainty principle, the probable cause,* was he talking about the possibility of drugs and stolen goods in my car, or was he referring to the unlikely scenario that the universe conceals meaning?

"Have you been drinking?" he asked again. "Either of you."

"I weren't drivin'," Arlen attested.

"No," I said.

He took out a pen from his pocket and held it in front of my face. He did it with a certain hypnotic flourish. "Just keep your eyes on the pen as I move it and don't look at my face."

"You don't have a face, so that's easy," I said.

"What?" the cop asked.

"My night vision is not so good."

He started to arc the pen in all directions, sometimes moving so far into my peripheral vision that I became aware of the backs of my eyeballs, of the things that kept them in place. When he was done he said, "Reckless driving is a serious matter."

"I see."

"I'd like to search your vehicle. You can refuse, but that will complicate things."

"That would be fine," I said distantly. It was my father's intonation.

"I have to get the midnight bus to Iowa," Arlen said.

The cop shone his flashlight into the interior of the Oldsmobile and probed his hands under the seats. He came upon some fast-food wrappers and a biography of Gandhi.

"He could go six weeks without food," I said.

The policeman nodded and tossed the book aside. He popped the trunk from the driver's seat. As he moved to the back of my car he said, "This thing has over three hundred thousand miles on it. You must do a lot of driving," he said. He opened the trunk.

"I like to drive," I said, though I didn't think he could hear above the swish of traffic.

I was still standing with Arlen beside the hood of the car, my hands touching the chill metallic body. After a moment he told us to come and look at something. We walked around to the back of the car, where he was shining his enormous flashlight at the contents of my trunk. He held up several photographs to his light beam: Megan Trudy kneeling beside her bell-pepper plants, weeping; Jim Trollup chipping golf balls into his empty swimming pool; a college girl in a tank top, reading Jack Kerouac in the shade of an elm tree.

"What are these?" he said.

"Photographs, I guess," I said.

"Happy Halloween," Arlen said, looking down at the scatter of photos.

The cop dipped his hand into the box of pictures and pulled out some more. Then he opened the safety kit that Whit had placed in the trunk, with its road flares and space blanket. For a brief second I saw myself through his eyes: a kid driving nowhere in an ancient Oldsmobile, running into mailboxes, snapshots of strangers in his trunk, a delirious-looking man with crazy eyes, a biography of some Indian mystic in the front seat, army rations in the trunk.

"Do these people know you took their photographs?" he asked.

"Not exactly," I said.

"And what's with the flares?" the cop asked.

"In case of emergency. A friend of my father put that in there. He used to be an astronaut and takes safety very seriously."

"Are you on drugs?"

"No, sir," I said.

"I could do a urine test if I suspected."

"I was sleepy. I fell asleep at the wheel, that's all," I said.

"He just received some psychic data about his dead father," Arlen added.

"Where are you going now?" he asked.

"Home. Not far."

"And you? Do you drive?" the cop asked Arlen.

"I prefer not to."

He looked one last time at the photographs and the tinfoil shimmer of the space blanket. "I need to take you to your local police station, Nathan. At a minimum, you'll pay for those mailboxes, but you could also lose your license. You'll need to come as well, sir."

Arlen looked worried. "I have a Grey pooch to catch, Officer . . . Trailways for a patch there out of Dubuque."

"You're arresting me?" I asked. I found myself nodding, agreeing with this course of action.

"No. I'm not charging you with anything yet. We're going to ride back to your town and they'll call your parents. They'll get your friend on a bus once everything is verified."

"His father is deceased," Arlen said.

"Your mother?" the cop asked.

"At home with the astronaut," I said.

He led us toward the cruiser.

"What about my car? I can't just leave it," I said.

"Come get it in the morning. It'll be fine."

We got in the backseat of the cruiser. It smelled like a new pair of shoes. I put the seat belt on as he pulled out into the flow of traffic, lights still flashing for a moment. We pushed through the night, passing sedans and sealed convertibles, people's faces turning toward us. I felt momentarily powerful. To them I was a nameless felon, and I enjoyed the fact that they all turned away before I did.

"Do you believe in God?" I asked the cop. "Anything. Some kind of meaning?"

"Don't worry about him," Arlen said.

The cop pretended not to hear.

At the police station the state trooper handed us over to the locals, who said that they wouldn't charge me as long as I paid for replacement mailboxes. If I committed any more driving violations in the next five years I would lose my license. Arlen missed his bus. They called my mother and made us wait in a conference room—the interrogation room, the windowless, brick cube where alibis were vetted or discarded. Whit and my mother appeared sometime after midnight and my mother refused to speak, as if the station, with its smell of fast food and envelope glue, with its metal desks and Styrofoam cups, was beneath her dignity. Whit didn't look at me; he'd been coached.

"This is Arlen," I said. "A psychic from the institute. He came to visit."

Whit nodded hello. My mother led us to the car in silence.

When we arrived home, Whit called the bus station and found out Arlen could leave at five in the morning. We sat at the kitchen table and my mother made us some tea. Life may come undone, sons may fall to petty crime, but the small details of civilization, the necessity of stern talks over hot steeped beverages had to continue.

"I'd prefer milk," Arlen said. "Full cream, if you have it."

She fetched him some, then came and sat. "Where did you go?" she asked, stirring her cup.

"Went for a drive," I said.

"Do you know what time it is?" she asked.

"Z-time," I said, trying to get a smile from Whit.

My mother said, "Birdie Peters called me tonight. She said you've been coming to work late and shelving books in the wrong place. She's been finding religion and philosophy on the mathematics shelf."

"Oh, really," I said.

"Yes, that's right."

"His mind's on the fritz," Arlen said.

"Do you know the future?" Whit asked Arlen.

My mother shot Whit a stare. "People are concerned," she said.

"People?" I asked. "My father died. It's okay if I'm not adjusting right away. Should I be out jogging and singing in the streets? Who are these *people*, anyway?"

Arlen said, "I'm pretty good with the future . . . it's the present that gives me trouble."

My mother said, "People in general. We'll talk more tomorrow, but this has gone far enough."

Something in my mother's tone. I said, "Mom, don't worry about me. I'll be fine. Worry about yourself. You're shacked up with Dad's only friend and he hasn't even been dead for a year."

Arlen stared at the refrigerator. Whit lowered his eyes, scanned options—a man trained to think during times of conflict. I saw her hand move and felt myself lean into it. She slapped my face so hard it made my teeth grind. I saw faint specks of yellow and gold from the stinging sound. It was the first real sensation I'd felt since my father's hospital room. Whit looked away out of respect. Arlen looked down at his hands. My mother's bottom lip trembled as she rushed from the kitchen.

After a long silence, Whit said, "Arlen, let me get you bunked down and I'll get you up for the bus in the morning."

Whit led Arlen down the hallway. My cheek was burning and I put my hand on it. I was too tired to look for my father's letter. Upstairs I heard my mother open and close a series of doors.

THE NEXT MORNING, AFTER ARLEN left, Whit and my mother acted as if nothing had happened. They wanted to go for a drive, to talk things through, and I agreed. It was a Saturday morning and I planned to see a De Niro double feature later that day. We drove through downtown in Whit's Ford Escort. He drove like an undertaker, a disgrace to NASA.

"How often you change the oil in this thing, Whit?" I asked.

"Every three thousand, like clockwork."

"Figures."

We made a left by the library and headed into the small commercial zone. Our town was a maze of banks, diners, shoe stores, and dental offices. People were shod, they ate, they borrowed money, they had their teeth capped and straightened; this was called existence. Whit stopped the car in front of a small sandstone building with large, shuttered windows.

"What are we stopping for?" I asked.

"I've got to drop something off," my mother said. "But why don't we all go. Maybe we can get a malted at the drugstore."

"It's nine in the morning. Since when is that an hour for malteds?" I asked.

"Come on. Be adventurous," she said. The tone in her voice was so hollow, so foreign to her true demeanor.

We all got out of the car and walked toward the sandstone building. My mother went inside and Whit and I followed, down a hallway and into a reception area that was filled with flowering plants and provincial landscapes on the walls. Did this office belong to an orthodontist? There was no receptionist; it was a Saturday, yet the door had been left open. I looked at a small business-card holder on the reception desk. In elegant, embossed letters stood the name DR. CLYDE KAPLANSKY. My mother had brought me to see Darius Kaplansky's father, the town shrink, the father of the boy who beat me in the seventh-grade science fair and whose image—myopic, slope-shouldered—had lived in my mind ever since as the patron saint of miserable genius.

"What the hell is this?" I said.

"Just talk to him. He's very experienced in grief counseling," my mother said.

"Grief counseling?" I scoffed.

Whit stood like a jailer at the front door. I wanted to punch him in the stomach.

Clyde Kaplansky appeared at the end of the hallway in cuffed pants and boating shoes, a practiced and amiable version of concern in his face. "Hello, Nathan," he said.

"I'd really prefer not to discuss things right now."

My mother said, "We'll come back in an hour and take you out to lunch."

"Let's just have a chat," Clyde said. He extended an arm and gestured toward the hallway. He kept his fingers relaxed and un-pointed, the way you hold your hand out for a dog to smell.

Clyde's office was full of Swedish designer furniture— swayback leather seats and a moleskin daybed.

"Have a seat," he said. His eyebrows were a tangle of gray.

I sat in one of the chairs and leaned back.

He said, "Do you want to tell me some things?"

I crossed my legs and folded my arms.

"Do you want to talk about your father?" He put his hands behind his head, a gesture meant to telegraph ease. "So, what have you been doing with yourself? Last I knew you'd had a terrible car accident."

"For a while I was memorizing the world, one fact at a time. But I think my memory is fading. Sometimes I don't re-member what day it is."

"Memory can be the way back or the way forward."

"Poetic. Could be a bumper sticker for amnesiacs. How's Darius?" I asked.

"Fine, thank you."

"Do you remember the seventh-grade science quiz? You realize that I knew the final answer, right? For the record. I knew it."

"I didn't agree to talk to you because I wanted to revisit the seventh-grade science fair. Your mother thinks you need to get something off your chest."

"But you knew that I knew, right?" I asked.

"We all knew you knew," he said.

"So, I could have beat Darius."

"On that particular day, yes. Why don't you tell me what you're angry about?"

"What do you want to hear? Do people sit here and spill their guts about being angry at God and their parents? No. I'm not angry. Not anymore. I'm waiting."

"For what?"

"A sign of real life," I said.

"Don't you think you make real life happen?"

"No. I think it happens to you."

"That could lead to passivity."

"I've got plenty of time."

"You follow people?"

"Sometimes."

"Why?"

"Espionage. I'm trying to find out what makes them tick."

"What makes you tick?" he asked.

"They teach you that in shrink school? Ask the patient what makes them tick?"

He leaned back, disengaging. "See, now, that's aggression. Are you angry because your father abandoned you?"

He had a little bonsai tree on his desk. I pictured him pruning it with nail scissors. "Whatever you say."

"You never measured up to his standard. Just when you had a chance to be special, he left. I'm filling in the blanks from what your mother has told me."

"You're right. I am angry. I'm angry because people like you chart the stages of grief and think it's reality. Has it ever occurred to you that there might be no plan for things?"

"It's occurred to me. Certain philosophers think the universe is random."

"It's not. It's worse than random. The universe is out to get us."

"Do you really believe that?"

"I said it, didn't I?"

"Tell me what you feel when you think about your father."

"I'm about done talking now. I know you mean well, but everything is under control. Tell my mother that I'm fine and I'll be more discreet."

"Come back and talk to me. It would make your mother happy."

"Is Darius in med school?"

"Not exactly."

"Harvard?"

Clyde looked at his hands through the glass desktop. "Darius lives outside of town. He teaches people yoga and how to meditate. I don't see him much."

"What?"

"He decided not to go to college," he said quietly.

"Wow." I blew some air between my lips.

"Unexpectedly," he added.

"I'd like to see him," I said.

"Come and see me. We'll talk."

I got up to leave.

"Nathan?"

"Yeah."

"It's possible you've had some kind of nervous break-down. This might be beyond the normal range for grief."

His voice had no color.

"So long," I said.

Outside, Whit and my mother were parked, waiting. I got in the backseat and they feigned casualness.

"You're back so soon. How did that go?" my mother asked.

"I'm cured. Thanks for asking."

She sighed and Whit threw the car into reverse.

# forty-one

Dear Dad,

I ran into Clyde Kaplansky today. He said maybe I'd had a nervous breakdown after your death. Emerson said discontent is the infirmity of will. Where would evolution be without discontent—would anything change if we were happy all the time? Darius, the boy genius, decided not to go to college. I don't know why that's such a relief.

Love,
Nathan

P.S. Arlen told me that you wrote a letter to God before you died. If that's true, I'm afraid to read it.

# forty-two

I tracked Darius down through the phone book. He lived in a derelict farmhouse outside of town. It was a kind of commune, full of outcasts from Madison, hippie girls, vegans and fruitarians, people who grew vegetables and made clothes from hemp. I drove out there Sunday morning. A line of children were picking blackberries in the road-ditch brambles as I pulled up. The farmhouse listed to one side and stood wrapped by a rotting wooden porch. As I walked up to the front stoop it smelled of mildew, like sea moss. A woman my age, wearing a sarong and a head wrap, came to the door.

"Hello, stranger," she said.

"Is Darius here?"

"Who?"

"Darius Kaplansky."

"You mean Taro?"

"Do I?" I asked.

"Come inside." She held open the screen door.

I entered the kitchen, which was littered with the remnants of a feast. Large ceramic bowls, clay goblets, and hand-painted serving trays were strewn everywhere.

"We had a full-moon gathering last night," she said.

"It was a full moon? I knew I was having a weird day."

She laughed politely. "I'll go get Taro. Have a seat."

I moved toward an old potbelly stove and sat down in a wicker chair. I didn't know exactly why I was here. Part of it was the shock of Darius ending up as a commune brother, but part of it was something I didn't quite understand. I'd been led back to him.

"Can I help you?"

He stood in the kitchen in mechanic's overalls. He had a thoughtful goatee and shoulder-length hair. I hadn't seen him since shortly after the seventh-grade science fair, when he'd left for an East Coast prep school. He now bore no resemblance to the spindle-necked nerd of grade school. His eyes seemed unnaturally clear and he no longer wore glasses.

"Jesus, is that you, Darius?" I asked.

"Taro. Who are you?"

"It's me. Nathan Nelson."

Darius raised his eyebrows and came forward. "Well, hello. What brings you out this way?"

"I don't know. I wanted to look you up. You look . . . different. I saw your dad yesterday."

He came toward the table.

"Sweet. How is he? Was this, like, in a professional capacity?"

"Long story," I said.

"Hey, about your dad . . . sorry to hear about that." He kept his arms by his side.

"Yeah, thanks."

"Come on up to my room. I'll make us some tea," he said.

Tea? He'd become my mother—Darjeeling and lemon-grass—this couldn't be good.

I followed Darius through a living room where a silk parachute was suspended from the ceiling and Turkish floor cushions were spread in all directions. We climbed a rickety staircase and entered a room at the end of the hallway. A small futon and something resembling a large plastic coffin dominated the room.

"What is that?" I asked. On closer inspection I saw that it was a giant plastic egg.

"Sensory-deprivation tank. I spend an hour a day in there." He placed one hand on top of it gently.

"Doing what?"

"Floating."

"Why?"

"You float in skin-temperature water, loaded with Epsom salts, and it's completely dark. It's just you and your thoughts. It's like swimming in your own consciousness."

"Scary."

He moved to the corner of the room. "How do you take your tea?"

"What kind is it?"

"Licorice and burdock root."

"I'll skip it."

"It's great for the liver."

"So is gin," I said.

"Never touch the stuff." There was no judgment in this comment. He gestured to the futon and we sat. There was a long, awkward silence as we both contemplated the nature of my visit. We sat on his narrow futon and I glanced at the few books on the shelves—*Walden, I Ching, The Bhagavad Gita*. After a few moments, the egg-shaped tank opened and a young woman stepped out and stood naked, dripping onto the jute rug. She was nineteen or twenty, with a face that was pale and freckled.

"Not today," she said, slicking some water off with a towel.

"What's wrong?" Darius asked, a little disappointed on her behalf.

"Too much *me* in the way," she said. She smiled at me, oblivious to her condition. I looked at her bare stomach and breasts.

"This is an old friend from grade school," Darius said.

I stood to shake her hand but she ignored the introduction. Formalities seemed irrelevant in this household. Outside of pornography, I had never seen a fully naked woman before; the closest I'd come was a topless Teresa beside the faux basilica. I watched helplessly as the girl slipped out of the room.

"So what do you do for a living? Your dad said you teach meditation and yoga," I said.

"Pretty much."

"What happened to college? You were so smart."

"I have a high IQ. The score that is designated *smart*. My dad thinks I should be a doctor. It's all so mediocre."

"What do you want to do?"

"Live, man. Just live."

"I'm skipping college for now as well. I shelve books at the town library. Someday they're going to make me a check-out person. I'll carry a little rubber date stamp in a leather pouch on my belt."

He laughed. "What you *do* isn't who you *are*."

I looked around the room some more. A framed picture of an Indian guru drenched in garlands and serenity adorned one wall.

"My teacher," Darius said.

"Your dad's not a very good shrink."

"He means well, but he's too attached to people's suffering."

"What do you mean?"

"They come to him and tell him stories about their suffering. It's not real. Our birthright is twenty-four-seven bliss. Suffering is ignorance. Psychotherapy is like rearranging the furniture in a burning house. You've got to get to the source of the problem."

"The source," I repeated.

"Forgetting what we already know. That's the source of the problem." He massaged the arch of one foot with both hands.

"I know lots of things. Not many of them matter," I said.

"What matters is the knower. The witness of the knowledge. That's why IQ is so bogus. The real *you* is the silent witness of all that crap."

"Where'd you learn this?"

"Here and there."

"So, what, you've discovered God or something?"

"God is just a level of consciousness. I'm looking for unity. Where individual identity stops." His face was so earnest that I had to look out the window.

"I better be going. I don't know why I came. It was kind of ridiculous."

"Why don't you stay awhile? We're having a gathering this afternoon."

"A gathering?"

Out in the hallway the freckle-faced woman sang on her way to the shower. Her voice had a childlike quality to it, a high and clear resonance.

"Yeah. I'd like that."

People drove up from Madison in an old school bus, a mural of peasant liberation painted on the side. A drumming circle started up behind the house after lunch; a girl with dreadlocks shimmied in the middle of it, the air shattered by African rhythms, 5/8 beats, strange algorithms of primal music. Bearded men sat in a hot tub with topless women; a bonfire blazed under an old oak. I moved through the crowd, trying to find safety. Part of me wanted to leave, but I also felt the pull of the night's excess. As the air was mauled by the sweet-fungal smell of cannabis, and a hookah pipe the size of a house cat fumed from the front porch, I felt a real desire to look into people's faces, to make contact.

I tried to move inconspicuously, to appear relaxed and hip. I settled between the teepee and the hot tub, under a planting of birch trees. I watched Darius, now Taro, move through the crowd: what had started as needle-voiced intelligence and lifeless gestures in grade school had developed into a kind of charisma in early adulthood—the dead-rock gait of the unhurried. At nineteen, he was exactly where he wanted to be in life.

After several hours, the drumbeat had become a kind of pedantic refrain, slurring its way across the blackberry rambles. A dozen people lay passed out on the grass and in rocking chairs on the front porch. A man and a woman were having slow, meditative sex under a tree. I heard the woman let out a low moan, like she was easing herself into a hot bath. Sex remained a mystery—there were still forces in the universe waiting to gather me up. Darius didn't drink or smoke. He held court with a clutch of serious-looking Marxists from Madison, including a guy with a Chairman Mao cap. I made my way to the porch to say good-bye. The freckle-faced girl appeared beside me, swaying to the listless beat.

"You're not leaving, are you?" she said, touching my arm.

"Afraid so."

"Have a hit before you leave."

I looked at the hookah pipe—a brass dragon spewing smoke.

"It might kill me," I said.

"It might save you."

She smiled from the corner of her mouth—not so much a smile but the consideration of one. It reminded me of Teresa.

"What do I do?" I asked.

She led me to the pipe, where the stalwart smokers stood bleary-eyed and limp. She took the end of the hose and placed the small wooden tip to her lips. One of the pipe attendants—it was like an amusement-park ride—lit the bowl and she sucked. Smoke streamed up into her eyes. She held the smoke in her lungs, then came and blew it into my mouth. I inhaled and tried not to cough. As I exhaled I noticed Darius looking over at me. There was a hint of disapproval in his face. I shrugged and took a hit on my own.

"Do you want to eat some pumpkin seeds?" she asked.

I contemplated that for a moment, trying to gauge its full meaning.

"Yes!" I said.

We walked out onto the lawn and lay on the grass under a willow tree. On our backs, we stared skyward through the boughs and overhangs. It was going on dusk and we watched the darkness come in measures. *Now and . . . now . . . and now . . .* I tried to count the increments of night. She told me her name was Amber. She kept reaching over to put pumpkin seeds inside my mouth.

"I knew Darius when he was a boy genius, when his name was still Darius," I said.

"Taro still is a genius. He's so sage, you know."

"Why didn't you call him Sage?"

"I guess we didn't think of it in time."

"Is Amber your real name?"

"No. Katie Keegan." I wanted her real name to be Amber.

"Something's happening to my head, Katie Keegan," I said.

"Good."

She put another pumpkin seed into my mouth. I could feel my teeth vibrate as she grazed them with her fingers.

I said, "Did you know they sell more toothpaste the day after the Miss America pageant than any other day?"

"That's way fucked up," she said absently, her eyes scanning the heavens.

"And the galaxies at the end of the universe are moving so fast that their light is never going to reach us. We'll never see them."

"You know a lot of different things."

"The game of bridge used to be called whist."

She laughed through a sigh.

I leaned over and kissed her. Her breath was smoky, her mouth half open.

When it was done, she said, "That was a nice surprise."

Clearly that was the end of it; her voice carried finality, a declaration.

We lay there for some time, watching the night harden against the sky. I told her about my life, about my brief death, about my father. At one point she said, "Resurrection—that is the sweetest thing I ever heard." Then she fell into a deep, unrelenting sleep, a child's sleep, and in some strange way I liked her for that. I put a stray blanket over her and left her dozing beneath the willow.

I went to find Darius, but he'd left the porch. I walked through the house, now lit by candlelight. People slept huddled on the Turkish cushions. Two men were arguing about whether one of them had, in fact, touched the electric cooling fan with his tongue. "Licked the fan, man," he said. "The tip of my tongue is broken." I climbed the stairs and found Darius's clothes sitting beside the flotation tank. I knelt beside the plastic tank and tapped gently. There was no response.

"Darius, are you in there?"

A muffled scratching, then the lid started to move and opened a crack.

He said, "Hey, are you taking off?"

His voice was disembodied, floating somewhere inside.

"I'd like to try that," I said.

"You would?"

"Can I try it?"

"Sure, buddy. How's your headspace? I try to avoid the substances."

"Fine." I knocked on my temple for good measure.

Darius opened the lid and got out. I'd seen more nakedness in that evening than in my entire life—I'd grown up convinced that my mother wore a swimsuit in the shower. "Get your clothes off and climb in. Now just relax. It can be a little claustrophobic at first. And it's absolutely black. Let your body float."

I stood beside the tank and stripped down. He helped me get in. The water felt warm and thick. It had the temperature and viscosity of blood. Darius waited for me to tell him to close the lid.

"Darius?" I called.

"Taro."

"Let me call you Darius, all right?"

"Okay."

"I could have won that seventh-grade science fair."

"Sure, you could have. But you knew what was waiting if you won."

"But I thought you were going to be something big. A rocket scientist."

"I'm me. Isn't that big enough?"

"Close the lid, Guru Kaplansky."

He lowered the hatch. He was right; it was so black inside that not a single photon could get through. The slosh and seep of the heated, Epsom-salted water and my body floating, that was all there was. For the first few minutes I touched the sides, just to make sure I was connected to something. A brief moment of panic came over me; I was convinced that he'd left the room and I would be trapped in there overnight. I pushed and kicked against the sides. I could hear my breathing amplified and echoed, as if through a cave. The marijuana had worn itself down to a humming sensation at the base of my spine.

I relaxed and let my body go loose. I blinked into the darkness, black on black. In a sudden wave, I felt the senseless darkness of the coma and my miniature death all around me. Had they ever left? I reached for the events of that day in 1987. I remembered the sound of Hank Williams inside Pop Nelson's truck cabin, only now I recalled it as sunlike, pales of spackled yellow light shining from the radio. The hills of the copper country were a dusty green. And Pop's silhouette, as he plowed through the windshield, was quaking and silver. I remembered a sound—a dull *thuck*—that ended with a heavy, leaden feeling. Then a lick of static that now, through the perfect blackness, undulated as a steel-blue sine curve. Somehow, these memories were synesthetic. As if my brain had gone back and color-coded each moment. But was the static the sound track to my small death or the sound of coming back to life, of reentering the fray? Somehow, I had squandered my resurrection. I trawled through mental lists—car-repair procedures, tidal charts, historic trade routes, baseball scores, Nobel Prize winners, historic assassinations, scientific inventions and discoveries—and tried to speak them out loud. Many of the words and colors were still there. I lay there for a while, weightless and drenched in salt, watching words like *zeppelin* and *Bengal* flash, then fade into the darkness. I could have watched them all night. But then I heard a knock on the plastic tank and the outside world streamed in.

# forty-three

Later that night I drove home slowly in a light rain. The night felt cracked open, alive with possibility. Whit and my mother were nowhere to be seen, so I sat nursing a drink in the parlor, watching the glint of my father's urn. I drank two glasses of gin and sat, aware of my limbs on the leather couch, the pulse in my hands, a little drunk. Things were moving again. I heard voices from the upstairs hallway. I got up and slipped halfway up the stairs. At the end of the hallway, my mother and Whit stood outside her bedroom door. I leaned against the wall and crouched low, peering over the top step. My mother stood picking lint off the wallpaper while Whit yammered something about unappreciative college students. I could tell from their stances that they were saying good night. My mother was holding one of her favorite blouses.

"I forgot to put this into the clothes hamper," she said.

"I'll run it down for you," Whit said.

"Would you?"

"Of course."

"You are very sweet to me, you know," she said. There was nothing maternal in her voice. She leaned forward and hugged him, her face against his cheek. It was the longest hug I'd ever seen her give. I saw Whit hold his hands two inches away from the curve of her back, afraid to touch her. Then she was gone. Whit stood at her door and brought the favored blouse up to his face and touched his lips to it, the way a priest might bless a vestment.

I went back down the stairs and into the parlor. I stood before the urn. A man who didn't believe in containers and vessels, who told us that our minds were constellations of light, energy, and information, didn't belong in an urn. It was like we'd put a mystic in a jam jar. I took the urn off the mantel and took it into his study. I placed it over by his record player and his jazz albums. Then I began flipping through his books and papers. *Zero gravity* was included in the title of at least a dozen books. The margin notes of the books said things like, *logically impossible* or *not quite Accurate. zero Gravity relies on two input variables: Spin and Electricity.* Other margin notes read like notes-to-self from a dementia patient— *anniversary on june XII, buy present and flowers; nathan's birthday; think of science tie-in; check faculty mailbox each morning and respond*—and all of them written in my father's loping scrawl and with his idiosyncratic punctuation and capitalization. Had he possessed some grand system for his own life? An appointment diary consisting of a thousand dog-eared pages of physics books.

I picked up a book entitled *Zero Gravity and the Promise of Unfueled Flight*. I flipped the pages, past diagrams of metal octagons rising through the stratosphere. Folded in the middle was a handwritten letter. I opened the letter slowly. It was a page of hotel stationery, divided into perfect quadrants.

*samuel nelson*
*tumor patient*
*Planet Earth*

*to whom it may concern:*

*this letter concerns the possibility that you exist. i can't take this very seriously. but it's late. my Wife and Son are asleep. they think i'm doing trigonometry. what's the triangulation effect of our nearest star, the earth, and your left hand? that's a joke. i know for a fact you have a sense of humor. Boy do you ever!*

*i have felt for some time that there are anomalies of science that can only be explained by the presence of a meta-intelligence . . . YOU are the designation that we call "IT."*

*list of anomalies physics cannot explain (no particular order):*

*i. gravity. we still don't know what it really is, how to measure it fully, where it comes from.*

*ii. the transition from the Big Bang to the first Life-Form—how did hydrogen become an amoeba?*

*iii. why antimatter is possible. how can the opposite of existence exist?*

*iv. whether black holes are portals.*

*v. why I've never been very good at being a husband and a father.*

*if you exist then we need to discuss certain things. if we assume for a moment you are who you claim to be, then empirical evidence suggests you operate on some kind of divine plane. well then didn't you make me this way? why have i my whole life wanted to explain everything be told nothing*

*and be free to get up from a table of people and just be with*
*my thoughts? you did that to me. i see myself sometimes but*
*i don't stop myself. i feel . . . Entitled.*

    *look at me. i swore i would never—*
*who cares?*
*Light Waves, Centrifugal Force, these i understand.*
*Motion reduced to Potential. i understand. but why you*
*made me a man who was destined to die before i knew what*
*it all amounted to, that is one thing i will never understand,*
*you Bastard.*

    *forgive me. i'm a little bitter. i've worked my whole life,*
*chasing something that might be nothing more than a piece of*
*dust falling off your cloak. watch out for my Family, please.*
*don't let them bury me. scatter my ashes at the Accelerator—*
*the one place in my life where i felt like i understood why*
*people went to church to call out your name.*

                              *sincerely: samuel nelson*

I QUIETLY CLOSED THE DOOR to the study. I took a Thelonious Monk album from the shelf and put it on the turnta-
ble. When I set the needle it released a bright, golden surge of
piano playing. Not a single chord sounded predictable—a
bread-crumb trail of notes that never felt fully resolved. It
was music that was open-ended, subject to the uncertainty
principle. My father told me that a critic had once said that
listening to Monk's skewed but brilliant sense of timing was
like missing a step in the dark. That was exactly how it felt.

I looked around the study and suddenly wanted to
commit to memory everything in the room, a hundred thousand pages of formal logic and speculation. I was sitting
inside a room of his mind. These books were his trapped

thoughts. Monk ravaged the keyboard and I allowed my sobs to come out whole. It felt inevitable, unstoppable, water through limestone, the last cry of my childhood. My tears spilled everywhere, spidering the ink on the letter, dropping onto his scientific papers that were now neatly stacked. Here, science, a human tear. A drop of brine that under laboratory conditions behaves exactly like seawater, with one notable exception: it has a lower boiling point.

I SAT THERE FOR A long time thinking about our future, how we'd given my dead father the key to our lives. I left the study and collected the bottle of gin. I went down to the basement, where Whit had his transmission room. Whit was sitting at a small table—a grown man in monogrammed fleece pajamas. The overhead light was covered in wire mesh and it sent little shadow lines across the room. The radio appeared to be made of sculpted chrome, like old appliances and automobiles, the toasters and fridges and Cadillacs of the fifties.

"Hello, Whit," I said.

"Howdy."

"Quite an operation you've got here."

"Does the job," he said, glancing around.

Whit moved a dial and flicked some switches, and before long I could hear garbled voices. There were waves of static, then the muffled intonation of a foreign language. Voices came at us as if through a tunnel. All around me the walls were alive with bolts and awls, tempered steel, hand tools, bottles of my father's home-brewed amber ale.

"You mind if I have a turn?" I asked.

"Go right ahead," he said. He moved the microphone and I sat down to it.

"Dad, I don't know where you are, but I read the letter

you wrote to God. I hope you don't mind. I'll make sure we scatter your ashes." I took a swallow of gin, relishing the coated sound of my words. "Whit, have yourself a drink."

"I could use a shot of hooch," he said. He took a swig from the bottle.

"Do you want to say something to my father?" I asked.

Whit ran his fingers against the bottle. "Do you think he's listening?"

"Sure he is. Say something."

"I don't know," he said. The sound of liquor on a nervous throat.

"Let's hear it," I said.

I moved the microphone in front of him. He took another sip of gin. "KC2DJL to Samuel Nelson, do you copy?" Silence. Radio waves sighing toward the vault of heaven, toward the pinhead source of everything. Whit put his mouth so that it was almost touching the metal lip of the microphone. "Hope you're doing well out there. Give my regards to the space plankton." Whit paused, grinned nervously, looked up at the wall, trying to make something more profound out of his words.

"Tell him you're looking after my mother," I said.

"How's that?"

"You heard me."

He swallowed. "Everything is fine here. I'm looking after the house, making sure it doesn't fall to the ground."

"Good," I said. "Now you can say good-bye if you want."

"Adios, then, Samuel," Whit said. He fell into an astronaut's posture—straight-backed, equally braced for mystery or calamity.

A squall of white noise came through the speaker. I looked over at Whit. He was stone-faced, adjusting the reception. I took the microphone. "Also, I suspect that Whit and Mom are in love."

Whit gripped the bottle.

I spoke close into the microphone. "Dad, this house is cursed with your memory. Don't take that the wrong way. I think you're indifferent to what we do. It's us who are holding back. I've been so afraid of letting you down. The thing is, it's even possible to fail at doing nothing."

I moved the microphone to the edge of the table, halfway between us. "It appears you're in love with my mother," I said.

His mouth puckered in the after-bite of the gin and he raised his eyebrows. He held up his hands, as if at gunpoint. "Affirmative," he said.

"We just told my father about it."

"I see," he said.

"I found a letter in his study. He wanted his ashes scattered. She won't love you as long as he's in this house. The urn . . . "

Whit adjusted a slipper. "Where would we take them?" he said, whispering against his own will.

"The accelerator at Stanford," I said. "Up in the mountains behind the tunnel."

Whit looked at me, his face contemplative. "Your mother will need some convincing."

"Leave that to me," I said. A burst of human speech came from the radio, and in my state I considered that it was my father calling out to us from the other side. It was hard to make out. We both leaned closer. It was a police radio, and the dispatcher was assuring the listener, an officer in the field, of armed backup. There was a pause and then a man said, "I'm not going to wait here any longer." It had the veracity of overheard conversation, the undeniable sheen of accidental truth.

# forty-four

The next evening I invited my mother out for dinner. She suspected bad news and dressed somberly—a gray skirt, a mauve scarf, her hair up in a French twist. We sat in a booth. She scrutinized the menu as if it were a real estate contract she was about to sign. Everything was brushed metal and mosaic tiles, Mediterranean colors. I'd chosen this restaurant to set her at ease, to evoke the terra-cotta charm of Italy, a country she'd always felt an affinity for, but everything annoyed her: the temperature of the meal, the island-like grease stain on the waiter's apron, the prices. I rested my elbows on the table and leaned my chin into my hands, looking at her.

"What is it?" she said, mildly irritated.

"This is painful for you. Eating out."

"There's always something they do wrong." She looked down at her pasta primavera.

I sipped my wine. I had ordered a glass of house red and she gave me the look of the Mormons. She smeared a dab of butter onto her bread roll.

"I'd like to scatter his ashes at the Stanford accelerator," I said.

She held a piece of pasta an inch from her plate. In that moment the known universe was contained in the gap between morsel and mouth; I inched forward in my seat. "Why on earth would you do a thing like that?" she said.

"He wanted that."

She folded and unfolded her napkin. "He didn't know what he wanted."

"He didn't want his ashes kept around. I don't think he believed in holding on to the past," I said.

She was chewing now, timing a response so she could think. "Who says it's up to him?"

A silence fell over us for a moment.

She continued, "Those ashes are for me, not him." It was said simply, with no hint of apology. A widow's entitlement.

"I found a letter he left." I slid it across the table, deft as a ransom note.

She held the letter between her fingertips, opened it. Her tight, proud chin quivered slightly as she read. "Where did you find this?" she asked, not looking up.

"In his study."

Her eyes moved across each sentence several times, taking it in.

"Why didn't he leave it with his papers?" she asked.

"He was embarrassed. He always said he didn't believe in God and here he is pouring his guts out to Him. We need to stop having him watch from up on the mantel. He didn't care what happened in that house when he was alive and he certainly doesn't care now."

The words came out harsher than I had expected. She leaned back in her seat, composed. The waiter came and refilled our water glasses.

I said, "We need a fresh start."

"No," she said, placing her napkin on the table. "That is not true. I've moved on with my life."

"Mom, you sealed the parlor with yellow accident scene tape."

"You're the one that's not adjusting," she said.

I turned my water glass in circles. She smoothed the hem of the tablecloth. I mentally counted to ten.

"Whit loves you," I said.

She set her jaw at an angle and looked at me squarely. "Nonsense."

"He always has. I see that now, the way he used to hang around when I was a kid. It wasn't just for dad, it was for you. Why don't you ask him?"

"He's a friend. He helps me around the house. Someone to cook for . . . a mutual arrangement. I'd say that we've struck a very amicable arrangement."

"The man is pining."

She gave a terse head shake. "This is silly."

"He's in that basement talking in code to Russians and Filipinos on the radio. He's doing push-ups before bed. His whole life is one long cold shower."

"Now *that* is enough."

"You don't want to believe it." I looked at her hand, the thin gold band on her wedding ring finger. "You're married to a ghost. Most of the time he was a ghost, even when he lived with us. But he tried in his own way, as best he could."

She put her plate to one side, indicating the end of the discussion, and gestured for the bill. She wrote a check, tore it off neatly, and wrote the amount in her pocket ledger—the little balance sheet that ensured she would never be caught short.

# forty-five

We planned a date for the ash scattering. I invited Toby and Teresa and they were going to meet us in California. Whit paid for their airfares, as a gift to our family. He called ahead to make the arrangements at the accelerator and made a pine box with dovetail joints for the transport of my father's remains. I transferred the contents of the Italian urn to the box and covered it with bubble wrap. As we shuttled toward San Francisco, my mother held the plastic-encased box on her lap, refusing offers of peanuts and soda from the hostesses. I looked at her, thinking here is my mother, holding his body, and surely now he has material presence, can be captured and held the way he never could in life. No wonder she was reluctant.

"We're doing the right thing," I said. "He wanted this."

She nodded, unconvinced.

I stared out the window. Clouds broke apart to reveal suburbs, then wheat-colored fields dotted with stray farmhouses. I could see depth and contour. Chalky river bluffs and canyons, features etched into copper.

Toby and Teresa arrived at the San Francisco airport within

an hour of each other. We found Toby by the baggage claim area. He was dressed like an opera singer or a gangster—a camel-hair coat, collar up, cinched waist, bounding around with his cane. He wore glasses now. Not sunglasses in the fashion of Stevie Wonder, but reading spectacles—they may have even been bifocals—and it was meant to be funny, a kind of antistatement.

"Toby?"

He turned his head slightly and carefully, like a man with a neck injury.

"I thought I heard your shuffle on the approach," he said.

He held his arms wide and we embraced. He smelled of expensive cologne.

"You remember Whit and my mother?" I said.

"Sure," Toby said. "Whit's a fellow disciple of the darkness."

"Glad you could make it," Whit said.

"Yes, it means a lot to Nathan to have you here," my mother said.

While we waited for Teresa by the gate, Toby told me about his life in New York. Several times he'd gone on tour and was recording an album. Recitals in Amsterdam and Prague, standing ovations and flowers and interviews on the radio—these were the brash, spilled details of his new life. He spoke about playing pianos in the cathedrals of Europe, playing requiems and concertos, feeling the air vibrate because the marble and slate floors absorbed nothing. I sat there, nodding, remaining on the surface of his exploits.

"What about you?" he asked.

"The library."

He lowered his voice. "You getting laid?" he asked.

"No."

Teresa arrived late. She had carry-on luggage only and

wore a black miniskirt with knee-high boots. We all stood near the ticket counter.

"I need a cigarette," Teresa said, kissing me on the cheek.

"Hello," I said.

"Hello. Nice to see you again," my mother said, extending her hand to Teresa.

"Hi," Teresa said.

"It's our favorite miracle worker," Toby said.

Teresa kissed Toby on the cheek and told him to be quiet.

"How are the sick and the ill?" Whit asked Teresa.

"They send their wishes," she said.

We walked outside and stood in front of the curbside check-in. "It's good to see you guys," she said, smiling at Toby and me. She lit a cigarette. My mother locked a stare on her for a second, performing some kind of private, maternal calculus.

"I've never been to an ash scattering," Toby said.

"Hope the weather will be nice," Whit said, craning up at the sun.

Teresa blew some smoke downwind.

"I understand you've been working in a hospital?" my mother asked Teresa. There was the slightly formal tone of an interview in my mother's delivery.

"Yes," Teresa said.

"What do you do?" my mother asked.

"I tell the dying how to stop lying to themselves."

My mother adjusted the zipper on her handbag without making eye contact. "Oh," she said.

I stared at Teresa. A year with the sick and dying had given her authority and poise. She now had one of those enigmatic faces you glimpse in the street—the Raphaelite child in the rear window of a car, the seer bum on the curbstone, the wistful and elegant old man smiling at you in the grocery store; a flashbulb of sage, the suggestion of a secret the rest of us will come to learn too late.

WE ARRIVED AT THE STANFORD Linear Accelerator just before dusk. The security guard at the main gatehouse checked us in and issued us visitor badges. He noted on his clipboard "family memorial" as the reason for our visit. My mother looked around the accelerator campus, nonplussed. A metallic freight train, an ugly terminal building with drab bricks and no windows. I could tell she was wondering what all the fuss was about, why my father had made pilgrimages to a place that resembled a series of Leninist public buildings. Whit refrained from mentioning the key facts about this place, that a string of Nobel Prizes had been won within the same three buildings.

We drove out toward the western terminus, toward the Santa Cruz Mountains. In the darkening afternoon the mountains stood serrated against the western sky. We drove beside the tunnel and passed beneath the 280 overpass, a steady stream of headlights passing above us. People were returning home from work, carrying groceries and listening to talkback radio, oblivious to the subatomic war that raged below. We passed the spot where the electron gun lay buried. It was capable of firing electrons at the speed of light, sending pulses of Armageddon down a braided copper wire. This was his resting ground.

Dr. Benson, the director of the accelerator, had informed Whit that there was a picnic spot that overlooked Jasper Ridge, a Stanford-owned ecology preserve where nature had been undisturbed for generations. He suggested it was a good spot for "small-particle dispersal." We pulled up a hill and parked amid a series of picnic tables. A wire fence separated the nature preserve from the accelerator campus. The wind blew out of the southwest and would carry my father's ashes down over the tunnel and partially onto Jasper Ridge.

Whit retrieved the pine box from the car and we all gravitated toward the fence. Everybody stood and waited for me to begin things. I hadn't really planned any kind of ceremony.

"So I thought we should get rid of these," I said. "He brought me here when I was a kid. For my birthday. I thought he was going to take me to Disneyland when I realized the plane was going to California."

"For him it was like the Sixteen Chapel," Whit ventured.

Toby winced and said, "Sistine."

"Anyway, this seems like the place for him," I said.

I opened the box and dipped a hand inside. The ash was the texture of silt, the color of pumice. Shards of bone flaked and studded the mixture. A steady breeze came up, off the mountains that stood behind us. I threw a handful of ash into the air and it shot off the side of the hill. The heavier specks made a brief silhouette against the darkening blue of the sky.

Toby said, "Somebody give me the visuals." Teresa leaned close to him and narrated.

I did this for some time, casting handfuls of my father into the air. I asked my mother if she wanted a turn. She stepped forward and dipped her hand into the box, at first reluctantly. She sprinkled it delicately into the breeze, as if it were oregano going into a simmering broth. Then she began throwing it like confetti, whisking it toward Jasper Ridge. Nobody cried and nobody made any speeches. There was something secretive about it, the way we stood gathered, watching the dregs of a human life pass into the twilight. I imagined my father floating and melding with ozone and oxygen, becoming the air itself.

# forty-six

Toby and Teresa came back with us to Wisconsin for a few days. Toby was on vacation and wanted to visit a fellow Juilliard student in Madison. Teresa said she was curious to see where I'd been "incubated." The five of us flew to Madison on a late-night flight. My mother didn't say much as we performed the errands of travel, passed through metal detectors, had the contents of our carry-on bags reduced to skeletal images on small television screens. Teresa touched my arm and gestured to the screens as we passed by. "Look," she said, "the X-ray channel." We arrived home after midnight to the empty, dark house. My mother turned on a few lights. The mantel stood unadorned. She moved about the house, adjusting the thermostat and drawing curtains, reclaiming her dominion.

My mother's eyes were sunken, her face pale. "Good night, all," she said wearily. She had no patience for houseguests right now. Toby, also tired out, stood in the hallway, tapping a finger at the edge of a picture frame. *"Buona sera,"* he said.

"You, Whit, and I are in the guest room. Straight down the hallway, to the end. Teresa will sleep in my room," I said.

"You mean we bunk down with Buck Rogers?"

"Of course. And you might just be in time for his evening calisthenics."

"Jolly." Toby reached a hand up to his mouth, kissed his fingers, and waved at us. He tapped his cane along the floorboards of the hallway.

Teresa and I went and sat in the kitchen. I made us both some hot chocolate.

"Nobody has ever cooked in this kitchen," Teresa said.

"She waxes the oven knobs," I said.

"People do not live in this house," she said.

"It's embarrassing."

"You've been through a lot, I can tell." She tugged a piece of her hair into place. "Why did you stop writing me?"

"I didn't have anything to say."

"I never cared about what you did with your life."

"I know," I said. "Nobody did except the guy who died."

I poured some hot chocolate into two cups and handed her one.

"How are your patients treating you?" I asked.

"Liars and cheats mostly." She stared into her cup.

"I'm glad you've stayed cynical."

"I stole pills from the hospital for a while, but I just hoarded them at home. Little neon piles waiting for a rainy day."

"Were you depressed?" I asked.

"Not exactly. Those people can get to me. I know you were angry with me for seeing the tumor. It's only natural. I'm the most hated person in the state of Connecticut."

"I wanted to blame someone."

She held her cup between two hands. "Do I make your mother uncomfortable?" she asked.

"She's not used to women in the house. Girls didn't exist in here."

"What did you have instead?"

"Cloud chambers and travel enthusiasts and barbecues with astronauts. I never had girlfriends."

"That's right. I was your first. I forget that sometimes."

"Numero uno."

She considered the kitchen and looked out the breakfast window, where, in the midground, the orchard stood in half-bloom.

We finished our drinks and climbed the stairs to my bedroom. She looked around the room at the chemistry set and the star constellations on the ceiling.

"This is about what I expected," she said.

"We've kept the house like a museum from 1980."

"Your mother could charge admission. People could lie on your bed and stare up at the Milky Way."

She peeled back the bedspread to reveal Superman in various poses: outrunning a locomotive, leaping a building, flying with one arm outstretched.

"Sexy," she said.

"Well, I'll see you in the morning. If you want to make a voltaic cell in the middle of the night, all the ingredients are right here. Good night." I turned for the hallway.

"Nathan?"

"Yeah?"

"Is there—have you been with other people?"

I stood helplessly in the doorway.

*1 in 600,000 that you get struck by lighting during your life*

"No. I mean, one kiss," I said. I studied the wallpaper. "What about you?"

"No one special."

I watched her sprawl across my bed, exhausted, face in pillow, arms flung wide like an adolescent girl captured mid-pout. There was still something there: the thought of her sleeping in my bed made my blood jump. I hadn't felt a clear emotion in some time. Arousal came in over the wire of leveled expectations and I could imagine kissing her again. Time was loosening. Outside, apples were programmed to peak and fall from their stems on a certain day; hyacinths were growing through my father's composted beard, already mulched down to the proteins and enzymes. Nature had been telling us to move on all along.

"It's good to see you again," I said. She got under the covers and I switched out the light.

"You, too," she said.

THE NEXT DAY TOBY, TERESA, and I took a drive in the Oldsmobile. Like me, Toby loved to be in a car, clipping along at seventy, eighty, air siphoning through the windows. In Iowa we'd taken drives, me narrating the scenery, describing the dozen versions of the same farmhouse as they streaked past our windows, the people riding horses and plowing their fields. Teresa was oblivious to car travel. She read a magazine and napped. As usual, I took the rural roads and we found ourselves in a sorry back pocket of dairy land. Muddy cows pulled at round bales of hay at the edge of gravel beds; low-yield fields lay greened out, spent.

As we drove I glanced at Teresa in the rearview mirror while she slept. On the outskirts of Madison we hit traffic. We drove past farms that had now thinned to five-acre plots, pottery sheds with homemade signs, people selling yard shadows from trailers, a string of self-storage businesses, an attack-dog training academy. Soon we came to a standstill. The traffic was gridlocked and the shriek of an ambulance came from up ahead. Drivers all around us began muttering to themselves and obsessing with their dash controls.

After several minutes of idling, I switched off the engine. The traffic moved forward again and I turned the key. The ignition was dead. I tried to turn the engine over again. Nothing.

"That didn't sound very good," Toby said.

A lane of cars was trapped behind us. Somebody sounded their horn. A chorus of honking erupted. Teresa woke in the back and stuck her head out the window. Within seconds the two-lane freeway came alive: cars and pickups calling to one another like territorial birds, accusing one another, because nobody could remember who was the cause anymore. I saw a flurry of colored arrows and darts take to the air. I tried to start the engine several times but it didn't even click over. I put the hazards on, popped the hood, and stepped outside. The horns were belligerent, a distant then a close bawl. Toby and Teresa stood beside me as I opened the hood. The engine was neglected but intact: starbursts of corrosion in the welded joints, grease stains, but nothing like dismembered hoses or a shredded fan belt. The noise by now was deafening and Toby clicked his tongue several times in disgust.

"Fucking cheese farmers," he said.

"There's a problem here," Teresa said, staring into the engine, "a system problem."

"It's not an organism," I said.

"The problem is people are barbarians. Listen to them. Like hyenas out on the savanna." Toby put his fingers in his ears and winced. "I came to the country to get away from this mob mentality. Close it up," he said. He placed his cane on top of the roof.

I let the hood fall. He grabbed my shoulder and lifted himself unsteadily to stand on the front fender.

"Um, what are you doing?" Teresa said.

He moved across the hood, toward the windshield, and stepped up onto the roof of the car. He retrieved his cane. The metal sank and popped under his weight.

"Enjoying the moment," he said.

The car horns rose still louder, but now some of them

joined in with appreciation for the sight of a man standing on the roof of his car. The white cane angled from his body, attached at the belt. Toby closed his eyes and tensed his shoulders like an Olympic weight lifter, somebody about to clean-and-jerk twice his body weight. Then he raised his arms slowly into the air and began conducting the cacophony. It was possible that every single motorist on the freeway sounded their horn, some in anger, some in a kind of stilted elation. People pointed and applauded; a man in a pickup pumped his horn and rambled to himself, already hearing the story he would tell his workmates the next morning. The sight of a blind man suspended above a fleet of cars, conducting the symphony of pissed and waiting motorists.

Toby swayed and grinned wildly; one arm was up high, guiding the altos and the sopranos, while the other, down low, captained the basses, the bassoonlike blares, the foghorn semis. He did this for what seemed like a long time but was probably only thirty seconds. Teresa and I watched, stunned and exhilarated. The cars behind us began to merge with the traffic to our right. Some people called out as they moved slowly by. Toby bent at the waist in a samurai bow. A man called out from his truck, "Hey buddy, thanks for the show. That car is a freakin' pile of junk." To which Toby pointed in my general direction and said, "It's his name on the title."

I helped Toby step down off the car. "Nice performance," I said.

"I thought the tenors were a little shabby."

A moving van stopped and two guys in coveralls came trudging toward us. The side of the van read WHITE GLOVE MOVING—THE TOUCH OF SOPHISTICATION.

"You need some help moving this clunker?" one of them called, a cigarette hanging from his mouth.

Now was not the time to defend the Oldsmobile and all it

had endured. I quietly nodded. I got inside the car and pushed
down on the clutch. Toby and Teresa stood by as the two men
pushed on the trunk and I steered onto the shoulder.

"You want me to radio for a tow truck?" one of the men
asked me.

"Unless you have a blowtorch in your van," Toby said.

"Please," I said. "That would be great."

The men hauled back to their van and drove past us
without so much as a second look. The death of a twenty-
year-old car wasn't even a blip on their morning radar; they
were on their way to move antique vases or Queen Anne furniture while they wore white cotton gloves at the end of their
hairy, tattooed arms.

"This feels terminal," Teresa said.

"Dead. Kaput. No more," Toby offered.

"This car will outlive us all," I said.

We all got back into the Oldsmobile and waited for the
tow truck.

WHEN WE ARRIVED HOME TERESA and I left Toby to the
sound of Whit's calisthenics, the huff of his fight against
mortality, and took the stairs to my bedroom. Upstairs, I felt
a sudden pitch of nostalgia for the contents of my room, precisely because I knew that tomorrow I would clean it all out,
box the chemical glassware, the beakers and the flasks, pack
the science books and the microscope, and trundle it all
down to Goodwill, where a family whose idea of fun was
effervescence and magnification would pick it up for a song.

"Tomorrow I'm going to clean this room out. Give it all
away," I said.

"I can help you."

"It's a deal."

Teresa slumped on the bed.

"I know a woman who cured her cancer by cleaning out her garage."

I went and sat at the small desk that supported my junior microscope. The magnification was slight; with an instrument like this, cells and crystals sometimes appeared as amorphous brown planets.

"What are you doing?" Teresa said. She came and stood beside me.

I fingered through the collection of glass slides, the trapped compounds and minerals. I found a slide that contained a drop of purified water. My father used to tell me to find the hydrogen molecules in the water. He told me that little slivers of time were lurking in there, that hydrogen had set the universe ablaze, even though we both knew that the junior microscope's magnification was not strong enough to see molecules. But for years I squinted into the eyepiece anyway, scanning for the origins of the universe. Now I slid the plate into position and looked at the water drop. It was dotted with tiny specks and whorls, an island-studded ocean seen from above. I could hear Teresa breathing behind me.

"What are you looking at?"

"My father thought that chemicals and elements had memories, that the history of the universe was trapped inside their structure."

"Let me take a look."

Teresa leaned forward and put her eye over the microscope.

"What do we have here?"

"A drop of water. Nothing special."

"Those dots look like tiny gallstones."

Her hair hung close to my face.

"Hold still," I said, pulling a single strand of hair from her head. "Let's do some hair analysis." I put the hair into a fresh glass slide and put it under the lens.

"Hair has memories, too," she said.

"I see a lot of drug use."

"Let me see." She leaned forward again, squinting at her own hair. "That's the most disgusting thing I've ever seen. Rope with little furry things attached."

She went and slumped on the bed. I leaned into the eyepiece.

After a long silence she said, "Do you ever think about kissing me anymore?"

I felt my pulse in my ears. I looked up from the microscope and saw that her eyes were on the ceiling. I got up and went to lie on the bed beside her. We both looked up at the Milky Way before she finally took my hand and kissed the back of my knuckles.

"Superman could orbit our bodies," she said.

"My mother has a set of Inspector Gadget sheets tucked away in a closet somewhere."

We got under the covers and the house slipped away. Everything went quiet. A slow procession of kisses under a tent of superhero bedsheets. The unpeeling of clothing. The breathiness of our words, the little ironies of insight and humor, the comments designed to assuage the initial awkwardness of our two bodies enfolded. I was nervous about having sex for the first time and could tell, by the way she touched me, that she had done this before. I was praying that the sealed packet of condoms in my dresser had not expired. I closed my eyes and tried to relax. Then Teresa whispered my name and it appeared before me, perfectly rendered and, strangely, in my father's loose handwriting: *nathan* It was the same unremarkable scrawl he used for a Greek-lettered equation, a letter to God, or the margin note in a book about gravity. He didn't bother to capitalize or punctuate most of the time; if the outward pull of the universe warped time, then what business did we have capitalizing our names or using commas to give us pause? But here was the mirrored symmetry between the *na* and the *an*, holding my name together like bookends, and the subtle peak of the *th*; and all of the letters appeared loosely strung together and winking like delicate beads of glass.

# forty-seven

It is four in the morning and I sit by the kitchen window, watching the hour of bakers in the streets below. A single guest-room light is on at the budget motel across the street. It is, in fact, the darkest and coldest hour before dawn, and as I look below I see only a few cars. A newspaper delivery van and a police patrol car prowl the emptiness. I am aware of the apartment. Like my mother, I can expand my awareness to take in all the rooms of a house at once. There are times, especially sitting by the window in the embryo of day, when I imagine I can hear the appliances—the toaster, the alarm clock—drawing current down from the walls.

Each morning I sit and rehearse my lines. This has been my practice now for several years. I transit from sleep and dreams directly to the role at hand, to the conjured life. Today I am speaking the words of Hamlet by rote. It's a role I have wanted to play for some time. What has kept me back until now is the feeling that the role was somehow too personal: a son who loses his father, a ghost on a rampart, grief tinctured with madness. My method is simple: I memorize the play, not just my lines but everybody's, from the soliloquy of the king to the stray lines of the messengers. I internalize the information, make it my own. Hamlet's words, as I say them, are a series of sensory experiences. His character is the sum total of all these blobs, textures, and tastes; the word *rank,* addressed to Gertude, actually makes my mouth go bitter. It tastes like an old house key, and when I say it I feel a surge of remorse. Most of the time the sensory experience of the words and the right emotion can be matched in this way. But I also invent words for him, to better understand his mind. Sometimes I walk the streets and try to find Hamlet's words for ordering bagels or coffee. I imagine the way he would leave a message on an answering machine.

Without knowing it, I spent years preparing to be an actor. The summer I spent watching people in my hometown, reducing their lives to a single gesture. The nights at the institute I spent mimicking the drawl and slant of TV actors' words. Watching people and finding their lives more interesting than my own. Feeling empathy to the point of identity loss. But it wasn't until I came to control my gift that I found a use for it. My synesthesia returned to its fullness—but in a more manageable form—once I got out from under the weight of my father's death. I learned to modulate the world as it sung its hymns of information at me. The world did not need a mind stuffed with trivia. But there is always a place for story, the reflective surfaces of woven lives, the illusion that time is suspended and I am not *me* up there. There is something like quantum physics going on here. At some level, when I walk around up there onstage, I merely allow the information to pass through.

Later today, Whit and my mother will arrive for a two-day visit. They will be, unequivocally, themselves; Whit alive with chatter (he's discovered renaissance fairs), mother cooking nonstop and hauling in flowers—daisies and daffodils, the plain and optimistic flowers of the fields. They will sleep in the same room but out of respect, or imagined respect, for the memory of my father, they will not be seen touching each other. We carry things; it's as simple as that.

SINCE MY FATHER'S PASSING, PHYSICISTS have learned more about the neutrino, the subatomic particle that makes the quark look like old news, like Newton's apples rotting in the quantum orchard. The neutrino is a particle that has mass but is also pure energy. The vast emptiness of space, the blackness, they think, is made mostly of neutrinos. This particle can pass through a trillion miles of lead and leave no trace. It is both object and nonobject, contained in every cell of our bodies. It seems we are made of pure energy and light, and it just happens that the aggregate has mass. We move among the constellation of everyday things, little pockets of nonmatter who are insistent that our borders are fixed. These are the thoughts you get at the hour when dough rises and cops on the overnight shift refill their coffee cups.

I won't be so terribly disappointed if they discover that the universe is not unified. My father looked for elegancies of form and structure, the way a neuron might be a hologram for the entire universe, as if creation were an errand for an inspired bureaucrat with a rubber stamp, forever replicating at various levels of scale the cosmic ink stain. But he never could properly explain the anomalies. The psychic who dreams a missing child back into the fold, the musical prodigy who hears concertos in city traffic, the medical intuitive who sees the fabric of human illness and demise. Are these elements of the whole or elements of the uncategorized, members of the miscellaneous? Not just appealing mysteries, either. The fatal plane crashes, the atomic babies with mutilated organs, the fact that every one of us knows good people who meet with cruel and unusual punishment at the hands of the clock of fate. Surely, there is randomness. And information cascades with a life of its own; it's not out there waiting for the grand interpretation, it's weaving stories, showing up to the party of the living like a man with scraps of paper in his pockets.

But what can be learned from trivia? A history of inventions reveals we made the gun silencer (1908) before air-conditioning (1911), the kaleidoscope (1817) before Braille printing (1829), cocaine (1860) before penicillin (1929). It's a story about pleasure before usefulness, about ingenuity in killing before improving our everyday lives.

IN MY EARLY THIRTIES I am prone to nostalgia. I keep in touch with Toby by phone and exchange cryptic e-mails with Darius Kaplansky every once in a while. These connections seem important. Teresa and I write letters. For a year we shared a Madison apartment, tried to be adults in love. Then the present began to reveal itself and she chose a date to return to the East Coast. Now, years later, she's pregnant by a cardiologist in Pittsburgh and she sends me photos of her growing stomach. She knows it's a girl and that it's healthy. She knows this the way she knows the terrain of human enclosure, only now it's her insides she daydreams about. Strobe-lit images of the unborn child, swimming in the amniotic ocean. She is fearless, confident as a bronze bell. She does yoga and takes walks before noon.

Her pregnancy has made me think of my own beginnings. Not long ago my mother brought me the metal trunk containing the family film archive and the old sixteen-millimeter projector. My parents exposed a mile of celluloid that first winter of my life—as the South Vietnamese pushed toward Laos, as elections began in India, as astronauts played an impromptu game of golf on the moon. There are a dozen canisters and reels, coiled bromides of domestic fantasy. My parents playing house, living in lamplight and soup steam, scooped inside their wintry nest; my father, occasionally bare-wristed, watchless, attempting minor household repairs and the bathing of his new son; my mother breast-feeding me by uncurtained windows, watching trapezoids of sunlight move across the lawn. There are aimless sequences, my father at the camera helm: blurred textures, looming brass door handles, then a stream of sky, shots of snow, the blue glimmer of a winter's night.

But somehow I am drawn to that single reel of them before I came along. There's something closed-circuit about it, as if this were surveillance footage, a private investigator out to nail the case for suburban monotony. Quiet break-fasts, fires in the hearth, my father reading at the kitchen table, my mother kneading bread. My mother chitchats, my father mutters, they share odd little moments—laughter at a misplaced set of keys—and most of the time the camera is on a tripod, clicking away, spooling tedium from the fathoms of time. But at the end of this reel there's a montage that stuns me. My parents stand on a windy hillside beside the sea. It's some kind of vacation, possibly Maine. My mother is pregnant and stands with one hand on her stomach. There's a lighthouse and fishing trawlers, the sky is dark and brooding, and a bell is sounding somewhere in the distance. People are hurrying to their cars, the boats are coming ashore, sails are being furled; it may be some kind of provincial storm warning. My parents appear unfazed, as if the commotion is un-warranted. My father looks around him, nonplussed, like he's witnessing a commotion of the devout, a call to vespers. My parents stand their ground, watching lobster fishermen and vacationers haul across the hill. The last image of that film, just before the camera is switched off, is my father and mother waving at the camera. At first it's a bemused gesture—tourists pulling a prank—but then their faces grow earnest. It's the poignant, solemn wave given from the decks of departing warships. For once my father looks dead into the eye of the camera, his gaze unwavering, the wind playing havoc with his beard. Strangely, it seems he's waving at me—at the unborn, at the person he hopes and imagines I will become.

# acknowledgments

Iam deeply thankful to the Michener Center for Writers at the University of Texas at Austin for moral and financial support during the early phases of this novel.

Special thanks to Darold A. Treffert, MD, who consulted on the film *Rain Man,* for sharing his expertise on savant syndrome and prodigious memory. Also, in that regard, I benefited from A. R. Luria's classic memory study *The Mind of a Mnemonist: A Little Book About a Vast Memory.* In particular, the synesthetic examples and clinical test results pertaining to Luria's subject S inspired some of my own fictional details. Any distortions based on these sources are due to my error, not theirs.

Neil Calder, Director of Communications at the Stanford Linear Accelerator Center, was extremely helpful in answering my questions and refining my fledgling knowledge of particle physics. Thank you.

My sincere and heartfelt gratitude to Thom Knoles for offering up his childhood story of having an astronaut come over for family barbecues. Likewise, thanks to Jeff Waite for inadvertently giving me the idea for the novel's title.

Thanks to James Magnuson, Elizabeth Harris, Vivé Griffith, Steve Gehrke, and Darin Ciccotelli. They each read early drafts of the manuscript and shared their insights. A final and special thank-you to my daughters, Mikaila and Gemma, and to my parents and three sisters for their long-term encouragement and love.

# the beautiful miscellaneous

## Dominic Smith

*A Readers Club Guide*

# Introduction

At seventeen, Nathan Nelson is the mildly gifted son of a genius. His father, Dr. Samuel Nelson, is a particle physicist whose three passions in life are quarks, jazz, and uncovering Nathan's prodigious talents. Consequently, Nathan has spent his formative years in whiz-kid summer camps, taking trips to particle accelerators, and plotting simultaneous equations to the off-kilter riffs of Thelonious Monk. An only child, Nathan is painfully aware that he "swims like a tadpole in the deepest place of the bell curve" and slouches through puberty looking for an escape from his parents' lofty dream.

Everything changes when Nathan is involved in a terrible accident. After a brief clinical death and a two-week coma, he awakens to find that his perceptions of sight, sound, and memory have been irrevocably changed. The doctors and his parents fear permanent brain damage, but the truth of his condition is much more unexpected and leads to a renewed chance for Nathan to find his place in the world.

Nathan's father arranges for him to attend the Brook-Mills Institute—a Midwestern research center where savants, prodigies, and neurological misfits are studied and their "talents" applied. Immersed in this strange atmosphere—where an autistic boy can tell you what day Christmas falls on in 3026 but can't tie his shoelaces, where a medical intuitive can diagnose cancer during a long-distance phone call with a patient—Nathan begins to unravel the mysteries of his new mind and tries to make peace with the crushing weight of his father's expectations.

# QUESTIONS AND TOPICS FOR DISCUSSION

1. Nathan's parents seem to live apart from both outsiders and each other. Discuss Nathan's relationship to his parents. How are they connected to and disconnected from one another? Why do you think they keep a distance between themselves and people outside the family?

2. After the accident Nathan's father says, "This was not supposed to happen." (p. 65) What role does fate play in this novel? Was the accident "supposed" to happen?

3. Nathan's father says that Nathan's grandfather "thinks God's an old guy with a beard and an ulcer and a scoreboard." (p. 71) Nathan's father believes in a "unified field." (p. 70) What are Nathan's beliefs about God? Do his convictions change through the course of the book? How?

4. Synesthesia, Nathan's condition, is described as a blending of the senses. How does the author use sensory details in his writing to convey this condition?

5. Mozart, perhaps the most famous historical child prodigy, is mentioned early in the book as part of an experiment on rats. (p. 44) Identify and discuss the skills of the other prodigies at the Brooks-Mills Institute. Who is the most talented? Who is the most driven to use his or her talents? Why?

6. Toby asks Nathan what he is "in for," (p. 112) referring to the Brooks-Mills Institute as if it were a jail. Is the Institute a kind of prison? If so, for which students? What benefits do they get from being at the Institute?

7. Nathan refers to silence as the "sound of not remembering." (p. 131) What does he mean by this? Soon after, Dr. Gillman says, "Forgetting is when things slip [out]. Not remembering is when you filter things out." (p. 132) Do you think he is right? Why or why not?

8. Dr. Gillman says to Nathan that knowledge is pointless unless you do something with it. Nathan asks in return, "Why does information have to be useful? Does music need to be useful?" (p. 133) Discuss their arguments. Who do you agree with?

9. Generally, Whit is interested in the world on a planetary scale while Nathan's father focuses on particle and sub-atomic science. Where do Nathan's interests fall in the scope of the universe?

10. Collision, whether it be particles, cars, or people arguing, plays a large role in the book. Which of the many sudden impacts, either physical or emotional, are the most important in the novel?

11. Toward the end of the story the author includes letters from Nathan to his father. Why? What do these letters reveal about Nathan that the author might not have been able to convey in another style of writing? How do these letters connect, compare, and contrast to Samuel's letter to God?

12. At many times in the book Nathan is clearly the central character. His father, however, casts a long shadow over Nathan's life and the course of the novel. Who is the most powerful driving force of the action in the book?

13. What is the significance of Samuel's watch? What role does time play in the story?

14. Clyde Kaplansky says, "Memory can be the way back or the way forward." What does he mean by this? Do you think he is right? Why or why not?

15. What does Nathan learn after seeing Darius/Taro?

16. What is the meaning of the title *The Beautiful Miscellaneous*? Discuss the arc of the storyline. What is the central conflict? What is the rising action? What is the climax? Does it have one?

## TIPS TO ENHANCE YOUR READING GROUP

1.  The Stanford Linear Accelerator is one of the world's leading research laboratories. Established in 1962 at Stanford University in Menlo Park, California, its mission is to design, construct and operate state-of-the-art electron accelerators and related experimental facilities for use in high-energy physics and synchrotron radiation research. Learn more about the center at: http://www.slac.stanford.edu

2.  The Davidson Institute at the University of Nevada (http://www.ditd.org/) is an example of a nonprofit school for America's gifted children. To learn more about how education for the gifted functions on a state by state basis visit: http://www.gt-cybersource.org/StatePolicy.aspx?NavID=4_0

3.  Each year the USA Memory Championships are held. To learn more about the event or how to participate visit: http://usamemorychampionship.com

# A CONVERSATION WITH DOMINIC SMITH

1. **What was your inspiration for writing a book about a prodigy? Do you know any prodigies? Do you have any extraordinary talents yourself?**

*The book came to me in pieces. A friend told me a story about her college roommate whose father had won the Nobel Prize in chemistry. The daughter of this man was a complete mess and could barely function in life. It was as if she felt there was no point in trying to excel at anything. That got me thinking about growing up in the shadow of genius. Later, I heard a story about a ten-year-old boy who developed a prodigious memory after being hit in the head with a baseball. He became an "accidental prodigy." The novel in some ways fuses these two ideas. I wondered what would happen if the ordinary offspring of a genius was, somehow, given a second chance.*

*In the course of researching this book I spoke to a number of prodigies—people with encyclopedic memories or rare musical talents or gifts for dozens of languages. They spoke of the triumphs and struggles of having a profound gift in one area.*

*I can't say that I have any extraordinary gifts. Before the age of twelve I experienced a number of serious accidents—a near-drowning, a knife in my eye, a house fire starting beneath my bedroom—so I consider making it to my thirties to be a paranormal feat.*

2. **Authors often remark that they put a little bit of themselves into their characters. Do you identify with any of your characters?**

*I agree that we subconsciously filter our personalities into the characters we create. I think I identify with many of the characters in the novel—with Samuel's desire to drift and live in his head, with the way Cynthia romanticizes the past, with Nathan's search for identity, and even with Whit's well-intentioned but sometimes corny cheerfulness.*

3. **Why did you set the book in the time period and place that you did?**

*I grew up in the 1970s and '80s, so it seemed natural to tell this coming-of-age story from within those decades. Also, there was a certain amount of quantum physics that needed to be in place for the story to make sense. As for the Midwest, I went to college in Michigan and Iowa and this is a landscape I'm compelled by.*

4. **What research did you have to do on memory, particle science, and astronauts to write this novel?**

*There was a lot of research that went into this book, particularly on particle physics and memory. I benefited a great deal from the classic memory study* The Mind of a Mnemonist *by A. R. Luria, and also from the work of Dr. Darold Treffert, who is a leading authority on savant syndrome and consulted on the film* Rain Man. *I needed to understand what kinds of brain injuries can result in a prodigious memory and how that memory might function. I also soaked in a lot of particle physics by reading people like Paul Davies and Stephen Hawking, and by thinking about the implications of unified field theory. The dilemma was always how to make the science dramatically interesting. I lucked out on astro-*

nauts—*a friend of mine is the son of a former U.S. Air Force general and he told me stories about having an early astronaut over to the house for dinner. I went and read a few books on the space programs of the '70s for the rest.*

5. **At the end of the book Nathan uses his talents to become an actor. As a writer, what role do you think artists play in society?**

*I like to think artists play a very active role in society. Good art raises important questions about our place in the world. It lifts us out of our workaday lives and makes us consider new ideas. Although artists pursue their own "selfish" creative agendas, we sometimes benefit from their labors. If they can give us something important and universal, then they have given us a great gift.*

6. **Does memory play a particularly special role in your own life? What is your fondest memory?**

*I have always been attracted to memory and its limits. When my mother was in her late thirties she had a stroke and lost a significant part of her short-term memory. I was about eleven at the time. It had never occurred to me that memory could be lost. The fleetingness of memory and the nature of nostalgia are things that I'm interested in as a writer.*

*My fondest memories are from my childhood in Australia. I'm not sure there is one that stands out above all others. Until I was nine we lived in the Blue Mountains, outside of Sydney. Our house was surrounded by acres of bush and I spent my afternoons building forts and chasing after lizards and frogs. Later, we moved to Sydney and I discovered the ocean for the first time. Summers were spent on Bondi Beach. The air smelled of melting gelato and coconut tanning oil.*

7. **Nathan's father is a big jazz fan; are you as well? If so, what is your favorite album?**

*I was late to discover jazz but I find myself listening to it more and more. My favorite album is probably the Dave Brubeck classic* Time Out.

8. **The subject matter of the book is refreshingly original. To what other writers would you compare your writing style? Who do you enjoy to read? What books influenced you to become a writer?**

*I really admire the writing of James Salter, Don DeLillo, Salman Rushdie, Peter Carey, J. D. Salinger, Joy Williams, and Denis Johnson, to name a few (or seven). I find myself coming back to their work again and again. I also love to read Woolf, Dickens, and Nabokov. Reading DeLillo's* White Noise *and Salinger's* Nine Stories *really opened up my idea of writing. I was in awe of James Salter's language in* Light Years.*

*I don't know that I am capable of comparing my writing style to other writers. I would be flattered if I'd picked up anything from the names mentioned above. But I think the "anxiety of influence" works in a very subconscious way. In some ways we bring everything we've read to the table when we write. Somehow certain traits from our reading life make it onto the page and not others.*

9. **How was writing your second novel a different experience from writing your first? What was harder about the process? What was easier?**

*They were both difficult to write. I felt a little bit more like I knew what I was doing with the second novel. I managed the research more efficiently and knew when to dive into the writing. But I found it harder to grasp the characters and the storyline. It fell into place slowly.*

*Moving from one novel to the next can feel like you're setting out with no experience under your belt. It's a whole new roadmap.*

10. **Do you have plans for your next book?**

*I am working on a third novel but at the moment it's a string of muddled ideas floating around in my head. I'll do us both a favor by not trying to describe it coherently.*